Kat Martin is the *New York Times* bestselling author of more than fifty historical and contemporary romance novels. To date she has over fifteen million copies of her books in print in seventeen countries, including Sweden, France, Russia, Spain, Japan, Argentina, Poland and Greece. Kat and her husband, author L. J. Martin, live on their ranch outside Missoula, Montana, and spend winters at their beach house in California. Kat invites you to visit her website at www.katmartin.com.

Brenda Jackson is a *New York Times* bestselling author of more than one hundred romance titles. Brenda lives in Jacksonville, Florida, and divides her time between family, writing and traveling. Email Brenda at authorbrendajackson@gmail.com or visit her on her website at brendajackson.net.

New York Times **Bestselling Author**

KAT MARTIN

AGAINST THE NIGHT

⬙ HARLEQUIN® BESTSELLING AUTHOR COLLECTION

ISBN-13: 978-1-335-97272-9

Against the Night

Copyright © 2018 by Harlequin Books S.A.

The publisher acknowledges the copyright holders of the individual works as follows:

Against the Night
Copyright © 2012 by Kat Martin

The Object of His Protection
Copyright © 2008 by Brenda Streater Jackson

Recycling programs for this product may not exist in your area.

HARLEQUIN®
™ www.Harlequin.com

Printed in U.S.A.

CONTENTS

Visit the Author Profile page
at Harlequin.com for more titles.

AGAINST THE NIGHT

Kat Martin

To all my Rock Creek pals. You guys are the best!
Thanks for the fun times!

Chapter 1

Johnnie Riggs was a night owl. Tonight he sat at a table at the Kitty Cat Club on Sunset Boulevard, watching a little blonde pole dancer with the hottest body he'd ever seen and trying like hell not to get an erection.

He reached for the Bud Light sitting in front of him, took a swallow and set the barely touched bottle back down on the table. He wasn't there to get drunk. He wasn't there to get turned on by some sexy little piece of fluff.

He was there to make a collar and a nice chunk of change.

A former Army Ranger with a P.I.'s license, Johnnie spent most of his time in the bars and clubs of Los Angeles, digging up information for clients who could afford his fees. And the occasional recovery job, if the money was high enough.

He glanced around the club, one of the better run strip joints in the area, a place an out-of-town businessman could go for a little harmless fun and not feel like he was about to get mugged when he walked outside to catch a cab.

Johnnie knew the owner, a guy named Tate Watters, a reasonable sort who ran a clean operation. Tate knew Johnnie was there to collect a skip, but Tate was a stand-up guy who did his best to stay on the right side of the law, and having a pervert around—Johnnie's target—wasn't good for business.

It was dark inside the club except for the neon beer signs behind the bar and the soft glow of lights over gilt-framed photos of nineteen-fifties strippers that hung on the walls. A row of colored spotlights lit the woman performing onstage.

The place smelled like stale beer and cheap perfume, and rock music hid the sound of clinking bar glasses and the heavy breathing of the men. Customers sat in the darkness at small round tables sipping whiskey or beer, staring toward the entertainment with big smiles on their faces.

Johnnie didn't blame them. He'd be wearing a big smile, too, along with a raging hard-on if he wasn't there on business.

He watched the woman on the stage. She was twenty-five or -six, a pretty little exotic dancer wearing nothing but red sequined pasties and a matching G-string. She wasn't just petite, she was dainty, little more than five feet tall, with the shiniest, straightest, long blond hair he'd ever seen. Short bangs fluttered across her forehead above a pair of blue eyes that made him shift in his seat against his growing arousal, and muttering a curse between his teeth.

The music played, the beat steady, loud and erotic. She raised a red spike heel, wrapped her calf around the pole and slid up, then sank back down, rubbing the pole between her pale, perfectly proportioned legs. He felt a tug in his gut so strong he had to shove back his chair and get up from the table. Grabbing his beer bottle, he walked to the back of the club where he could survey the room and put a little more distance between him and the scrumptious piece of ass on the stage.

He scanned the patrons, keeping a careful watch for his target.

Earlier in the week, he'd gotten a call from his Ranger buddy in Houston. Trace Rawlins owned a security firm with branches in Houston and Dallas. In the years since they'd left the army, they had worked together a dozen times, most recently on an abduction case that had led them into Mexico.

According to Trace, a guy named Ray Carroll had jumped bail and was on the run. Rumor was he had friends in L.A. and odds were good that was where he had gone to ground. Good ol' Ray had been arrested for possession and trafficking in child pornography—the lowest of the low as far as Johnnie was concerned. He would have taken the guy down for free if he'd had to, which fortunately he didn't.

The case was interesting because Ray was the grandson of the late Texas oil billionaire, C. P. Carroll. C.P.'s widow was filthy rich and she doted on her grandson, which, with that kind of money at his disposal, made Ray a flight risk. His bail had been set at a half-million dollars, which his grandmother had posted.

But Ray had taken off for parts unknown, leaving grandma on the hook for a boatload of money if her boy wasn't caught and brought back to appear in court. For ten percent of the bail fee, a cool fifty thou less a referral fee to Trace, Johnnie had agreed to find him. Surprisingly, once he'd started digging, narrowing his search hadn't been all that hard.

Since leopards didn't change their spots and jackals like Ray were fairly predictable, it didn't take long to find out that Carroll hung out in the local strip clubs.

The Kitty Cat was his favorite. According to the bartender who ID'd the photo Johnnie had shown him, a guy calling himself Ray Conners had been in the club both Wednesday and Thursday nights. Johnnie had come in on Friday and again tonight but so far hadn't seen any sign of him. Not until now.

The black padded vinyl front door swung open, letting a thin slice of street noise into the club. Recalling the photo, Johnnie recognized Ray Carroll as he ambled over to the bar. He was an average-looking forty-year-old, with thinning brown hair and the kind of greasy smile you'd expect to see on a creep like him. He sat down on one of the black vinyl bar stools, and the bartender, a tall, spare, good-looking Hispanic guy named Dante, flashed Johnnie a heads-up glance before taking Ray's drink order, a double Grey Goose martini on the rocks.

A cocktail waitress walked past. The girls who performed also served drinks, though for that they wore a few more clothes. This one, a brunette, was tall and svelte, dressed in a little blue satin two-piece number, the bottom cut high on the sides, a built-in push-up bra shoving her heavy cleavage nearly over the top. Not indecent, but definitely less than the old bunny outfits they wore at the Playboy Club.

Johnnie sipped his beer, his attention fixed on Ray, who stared with fascination toward the stage. The dancer, Angel Fontaine, being not much bigger than a kid, was Ray's favorite according to Dante. He watched as she dipped and swayed to the music, the red sequins on her nipples flashing in the spotlight, the light changing color to the rhythm of the music.

Johnnie tried to look away, but found himself as mesmerized as the drunks at the tables. Like the rest of her body, her breasts were perfectly formed, not too large, not too small and tilted provocatively upward.

Her face wasn't perfect, he had finally gotten around to noticing. Her mouth was a little too wide, making her pouty lips a little too pronounced. Her cheeks were as flawless as rose petals but her chin was a little too pointy.

She was the sexiest woman Johnnie had ever seen.

She turned, thrust her pale, luscious ass into the air and wiggled it suggestively, and his groin tightened. If he didn't make his move soon, he wouldn't be able to walk, let alone make a collar.

Ray came off his stool just then and started toward the stage. Johnnie noticed the folded dollar bills in one hand as he approached the little blonde.

Another man beat Ray to her, leaning over and stuffing a ten-dollar bill into Angel's sequined G-string, the scrap of red barely covering the spot every guy in the place dreamed of touching. Angel whirled away from him and smiled, mouthing a thank-you. When she turned her back, raised her arms above her head and began swaying to the hard rock beat, another man stuffed a bill into the glittering strip of red around her waist above that sweet little ass.

Ray moved closer, hovering as Angel approached the edge of the stage. He leaned toward her, stuffed the money into her G-string. He was grinning when he turned away, his mind on pussy instead of escape.

Johnnie made his move, slamming into Carroll, knocking him over an empty table, both of them crashing to the floor. Ray struggled as Johnnie caught his arm, cranked it behind his back, lifted and hauled him to his feet. Johnnie caught sight of the club's big Asian bouncer moving toward them, but he didn't seem to be in much of a hurry. Guess he'd got word about the pervert, too.

Carroll squirmed in his grasp. "What the fuck? Who the hell are you?"

"I'm your worst nightmare," Johnnie said, cranking the arm a little higher, eliciting a satisfying grunt of pain. "I'm the guy who's gonna make sure you get back to Houston safe and sound." Ray stumbled a couple of times as Johnnie's heavy frame propelled him forward, slamming him into the wall beside the door. "I'm the guy who's gonna put your sorry, sick ass back in jail."

The moment the song ended and she stepped down from the stage, Amy started to tremble. *Angel,* she reminded herself. *Angel, not Amy.*

"You okay?" Her roommate walked toward her, Babs McClure, Sugar Babs, she used as her stage name. She was five foot seven with a curvy figure and chin-length dark brown hair she sometimes covered with a hot-pink wig.

Amy managed to nod. "I will be in a minute." It was

one thing to be out there beneath the spotlights, dancing almost naked as Angel Fontaine, another entirely to be just a normal woman again. Onstage, she could fool herself into thinking she *was* Angel, a woman who enjoyed every catcall, every wolf whistle from the men she danced in front of without her clothes. An illusion she worked tirelessly to achieve.

But it didn't last long once she stepped out of the spotlight.

"That was quite a scene." Babs cocked her head toward the side door where the brawny, dark-haired man had just hauled a scummy-looking customer out of the club.

Amy followed Babs's gaze. As if she hadn't noticed the brawl just a few feet in front of the stage.

"Dante says the creep that guy busted is into kiddie porn."

Amy shuddered. "He certainly looks the part." She crossed the backstage area and started up the stairs leading to the studio apartment she and Babs shared above the club. "So I guess the other guy is a cop or something."

"Or something." Babs fell into step beside her, pulled off her pink wig and ranked a hand through her dark hair. "He was in here last night, too."

"I saw him."

Babs grinned. "Hard to miss a guy who looks like that."

Amy grinned back. "No kidding." Six feet of solid muscle, barrel-chested with a thick neck and shoulders. As he'd walked—more like swaggered—toward the stage, she'd noticed a tattoo of an eagle on his very impressive biceps. Every move he made spoke of power and strength, and in a rugged, masculine way, he was handsome.

"I asked Tate about him," Babs said. "Says his name is John Riggs. He's an ex-Army Ranger. Does P.I. work and pretty much anything else he can make a buck at." Babs rolled her eyes. "What a hunk."

Just hearing the words brought his image to mind: dark brown hair and eyes such a deep brown they looked black, strong jaw roughened by the shadow of a beard. He was the kind of guy who should have *Dangerous* stamped on his forehead.

Amy's mind slipped back to her performance on-stage and the way he had looked at her, his eyes following her every move. She had never felt a gaze so intense.

It was late, nearly closing. Amy blew out a breath, suddenly exhausted.

"You look like you could use a cup of coffee," Babs said as they reached the small apartment they shared and Amy unlocked the door. There were other small apartments down the hall, cheap places for the girls to live. "I put on a fresh pot before I went downstairs."

"Sounds good." The rich aroma filled the room as she stepped inside. She and Babs hadn't known each other long yet Babs watched out for her. She was Amy's only confidante, the only person who knew the truth, knew she wasn't really an exotic dancer, had never done anything in her entire life remotely as wild as what she was doing now.

She wasn't a stripper, a pole dancer, a lap dancer or anything the least bit similar. She was a schoolteacher from Michigan, a woman who had absolutely no business being naked up onstage.

They crossed the studio apartment: two single beds, a kitchenette, and a small living area with a sofa and chair. Babs went to the kitchen counter and took down two mugs, pouring coffee into each one. Amy grabbed her robe from the hook beside the door, slipped it on and breathed a sigh of relief once she was more decently covered. Babs was still wearing her dark blue satin cocktail waitress costume, sexy but no worse than the bikinis women wore on the beach.

She took the mug Babs held out to her and they carried them over to the tiny round table in the corner.

"So what about the hunk?" Babs asked, watching her over the rim of her cup.

Amy's blond brows went up. "What about him?"

"He was certainly giving you the eye."

Amy just shrugged. "When you're up there naked, they all give you the eye."

"This was different—and don't tell me you didn't notice."

Oh, she'd noticed all right. She could feel the heat in those dark eyes all the way across the room. It was what that hot look did to her that was startling. The Kitty Cat Club was filled with men every night. None of them made her stomach flip the way a single look from John Riggs had. Two nights in a row, he'd sat in the shadows watching, his fierce gaze singularly focused on her. At the same time he seemed aware of every other person in the room.

"He got his man tonight." Amy sighed. "We won't be seeing him again."

Babs sipped her coffee. "Wanna bet?"

Amy glanced up. "You don't think he'll come back because of me?"

"I've been doing this for almost three years, hon. One thing you learn to recognize is when a man is interested. And let me tell you, honey, John Riggs has a major interest in you."

Her stomach contracted. If she closed her eyes, she could almost feel the heat in those dark eyes burning into her. "You're crazy. He was here on business, that's all."

"Five bucks?"

Amy laughed. "You're on."

Chapter 2

The club was closed on Sunday, and John Riggs wasn't there the next night. As Amy finished her first dance set Tuesday evening, she felt oddly disappointed. She told herself it was just that she had been thinking she might ask him for help. He was a private investigator, after all—or something close to that—and he had been an Army Ranger. They were tough guys, she knew, and even if she hadn't read about them, one look at that hard jaw and powerful body would have made that clear.

But he didn't come back and the truth was she didn't have enough money to hire him if he had. She loved teaching, but it didn't pay that much to start with and she wasn't a very good saver. Seemed like there was always something she needed for the kids in her class, and everything else went to rent and bills.

Amy thought of the weeks before her arrival in L.A.

Back home in Michigan, the children at Grand Rapids
Elementary School had been ready for summer vacation. Amy was packed to leave the afternoon of the
last day of school. As soon as she had seen the final
child safely out of her kindergarten classroom, she had
headed for the airport to catch her flight to L.A. From
the airport, she had come directly to the Kitty Cat Club.

It was the place where her sister, Rachael, was working when she had disappeared.

The music stopped. Her set was over. Pulling dollar bills out of her tiny costume as she left the stage,
she hurried upstairs to change into her cocktail waitress outfit. Thoughts of her sister crept in, along with a
sharp pang of loss. Rachael had gone missing more than
six weeks ago. The last place she had been seen was the
Kitty Cat Club where she worked as an exotic dancer.

Babs had been Rachael's roommate and one of her
closest friends, the person who had reported her missing when she failed to return to the apartment in time
for her performance the following night.

"At first I just thought she was screwing off," Babs
had told Amy on the phone, the first of many conversations that followed. "Maybe she got drunk or something, you know? Not that she usually did that kind of
thing. But she'd been acting strange for more than a
month, being secretive, staying out all night. She was
seeing a couple of different guys, but she didn't talk
much about them."

More and more worried, Babs had called the police, who had taken a statement and started an investigation into Rachael's disappearance. It was Babs who
had first contacted Amy. Several times a week after
Rachael's disappearance had been reported, Amy had

phoned the police from Michigan, pushing them, trying to make sure they were doing everything in their
power to find her. So far the police had come up with
nothing—though Babs didn't believe they had tried
very hard to find a missing dancer who worked at a
place like the Kitty Cat Club.

Babs had also kept calling, figuring two people
pressing the police would get more results than one.
Babs had also done some digging on her own. She
had talked to everyone who worked at the club—the
bartenders and waitresses, the guys and gals on every
shift. She hadn't expected any of them to be involved
in Rachael's disappearance and that was the conclusion
she had come to in the end.

If something terrible had happened, Amy sensed it
had to have involved one of the club's customers, or
someone Rachael was seeing.

From the start, Babs and Amy had connected. Both
of them cared about Rachael and both were beginning
to suspect the worst—Rachael had either been kidnapped or killed. As the weeks slipped past with no
word from her, the devastating scenario seemed more
and more likely.

Amy's chest tightened. Though she and Rachael
hadn't been close for years, they were still sisters, best
friends once. Amy had decided to come to L.A. to find
out what had happened. Since there was no way she
could just walk up to a customer, tell them she was
Amy Brewer and ask them if they had murdered her
sister, she and Babs had come up with a plan. Amy
would go undercover, take the job Rachael's disappearance had left vacant, and start digging. Amy would find
out what happened to Rachael—no matter what it took.

Amy raced up the stairs to the apartment to get ready for her waitressing shift, hoping that maybe tonight she would turn up something useful. Her costume, a two-piece dark blue satin number just like Babs's, lay on the bed, ready for her to put on.

Before Amy got to L.A., Babs had spoken to the club owner, Tate Watters, and told him she had a friend who was looking for a job. Watters had hired her sight-unseen, even though she had "limited experience." Fortunately, Amy and her sister had both been blessed with good figures, and faces that weren't too bad, either, so he didn't seem to regret giving her the job.

Babs had promised to show her the ropes, and after her first self-conscious, clumsy efforts, she had been able to get through an entire performance onstage. A couple of summers ago, she had learned a self-hypnosis technique at a teaching seminar in Detroit. The trick was good for controlling anxiety and aiding in memory work. Amy had used the technique to help her get over her stage fright and embarrassment.

She had always been a pretty good dancer, not the exotic sort, of course, and she had been on the cheering squad in high school. Her movements were fluid, and if she could forget she was almost naked and gave into the suggestions she put into her head, if she could manage to let herself go, she wasn't half bad.

Which surprised the heck out of her. She guessed a person never really knew themselves completely.

A last glance in the makeup mirror above the dresser, a few quick strokes of the brush through her long blond hair, a dab of blush and a fresh application of lipstick and she was ready to go.

Her stomach tightened. By some ironic twist, being

onstage as Angel Fontaine was the easy part. Mingling with customers, putting up with the risqué remarks while quietly digging for information that might lead to finding her sister—that was the tough part.

And no amount of self-hypnosis had helped. She was nervous and edgy the entire time she worked the floor, always trying to stay just out of a customer's reach, trying to keep a smile on her face as the men flirted and propositioned her.

Not that they were usually that bad. Tate wouldn't put up with harassment. And there was a house rule that the girls couldn't date the customers, which all of the regulars knew. And after a warning or two, if any of the men got too far out of line, big Bo Jing, the bald-headed, oversize Asian bouncer who stood at the door with his legs splayed and his arms folded over his massive chest, looking like a half-ton Mr. Clean, made sure they left the club and never came back.

The club allowed lap dancing, both in the bar and in private VIP rooms, which was a good way to make a little extra money, but so far she had never done one, and it wasn't something any of the girls had to do if they didn't want to. Tate was clear on that.

Making her way over to the bar, Amy picked up a tray and headed for the table of new arrivals in her assigned section. One of the other dancers, a redhead who called herself Honeybee, kept their attention fixed on the stage until Amy could get their drink orders.

She plastered on a smile. "Hello, gentlemen, what can I get for you?"

An overweight businessman in a wrinkled three-piece suit was the first to reply. "A big taste of you, sweetheart, would suit me just fine."

The other men laughed.

Amy ignored a wave of nerves and turned her attention to the customer beside him, gray-haired and a little too bright-eyed. "For you, sir?"

"Bombay martini," he said, his gaze still fixed on the stage. "Very dry, and I want it up."

"Hell, Sam, a martini won't help you get it up!"

The men roared with laughter. Amy pretended not to have heard the remark, smiled and took the rest of their orders, grateful she had already learned the majority of the drinks people wanted and relieved there were no more comments. At the bar, Dante filled the orders and she returned to the table to deliver the drinks, setting the right order in front of the right customer, which wasn't as easy as she would have guessed.

Waitresses earned their money, she had learned in a very short time, more so when they were only half dressed.

Babs walked past just then, wearing a pale blue wig tonight. "Far left corner. Kyle Bennett just walked in."

Amy's gaze swung in that direction. She was getting used to the dimness, getting to know her way around the tables and chairs, better able to work in the low light than she had been when she had first started.

She spotted Kyle Bennett, a regular customer and one of the men her sister had been dating in the weeks before her disappearance. He was sandy-haired, lean and elegant, almost effeminate. She might have thought he was gay except for the lascivious look in his eyes when he watched the girls onstage.

"Thanks," she said to Babs. Babs had tried talking to Bennett after Rachael first disappeared, but as soon as he found out she was Rachael's roommate he'd clammed up tight. Amy knew she couldn't tell him her real name, or her connection to Rachael.

She took a breath to steady herself and started in Kyle Bennett's direction. There was no one else at the table, which would make things a little easier.

"Hello, Mr. Bennett, what can I get you this evening?"

He looked up at her and smiled. "Tanqueray and tonic, doll, and a little conversation." He wasn't handsome but he was attractive, and so far whenever she'd talked to him, he'd been polite.

Entertaining the customers was part of the job, and it gave her the chance she needed to dig for information. "Let me get that for you and I'll be right back."

She hurried to the bar, waited for Dante to fill the order, then walked back to the table. "Here you go."

Kyle stirred the drink with the plastic swizzle stick, tipped his head back to look up at her. "You know, Angel, with a face and figure like yours, you could be a whole lot more than just a dancer."

She managed to look surprised. "You really think so?"

"Sure I do. Hollywood is always looking for the next big name. Angel Fontaine could be it."

Amy figured that was probably the line he had used on Rachael, who had come to Hollywood with dreams of becoming a star. He was rumored to be a movie producer but no one really knew if it was true.

Fortunately, she and Rachael looked nothing alike, Rachael being several inches taller, with softly curling dark brown hair and green eyes. Amy took after her mother's side of the family, Norwegians who had immigrated to Michigan during the past century to work in the logging industry.

She gave him a bright, interested smile. "I've always dreamed of being famous. Do you really think I might have a chance?"

"You'd have to do a screen test first, but I could arrange that for you. In fact I'm working on a film right now that might have just the right part for you. What do you say?"

She knew where this was leading and her nerves kicked up. "What...what would I have to do?"

"When's your next day off?"

She moistened her suddenly dry lips. "Thursday."

"All right, then. We'll do it Thursday. You just come to my house and I'll have everything set."

She swallowed, knowing she had to say yes. Then she thought of how Rachael had just disappeared as if she had never existed, how there was a chance this man might have had something to do with it, and a chill slipped down her spine. "I need to check with Tate...see if that will work in my schedule. If I had your number, I could give you a call and confirm."

"Sure, sweet thing." He took out his wallet and handed her a business card. It was too dark to read what it said, but she had what she needed to find him.

"Just remember," he said, "opportunities like this don't come along very often."

She nodded, smiled. "I'm really grateful, Mr. Bennett, truly, I am."

His lips curved. "Keep my tab open, will you? I may stay for a while." His gaze ran over her, ended up on the cleavage pushed up in her blue satin top.

Amy kept her smile in place. "No problem." She

started walking, grateful to escape. She would call Kyle Bennett and set up the screen test, but she wasn't a fool. If she went to his house, she wanted to be sure Babs knew the address and time she was going to be there.

She had almost reached the next table when she caught sight of a dark-haired man sitting in the shadows a few feet away. He was staring at her with intense brown eyes and she felt the impact in every pore in her body.

Babs breezed past her just then. "You owe me five bucks." Babs grinned as she hurried off with a tray of drinks propped on her shoulder.

For several seconds, Amy just stood there, her gaze locked with his. Even in the dim neon light, she could see the outline of his muscular body, see the faint glint of the eagle tattoo on his biceps just below the sleeve of the tight black T-shirt he wore with a pair of black jeans.

"Hello, Angel."

His voice was rough and sexy and just hearing it made her stomach quiver. He was even better looking than she had thought.

She managed to smile. "Hello. May I get you a drink?"

One of his dark eyebrows went up. She had slipped and used proper grammar, *may* instead of *can,* the way everyone else did.

"I suppose you can. How about a Bud Light?"

Most of the guys drank microbrews, which were the vogue these days. No one drank light beer—not in here. Except for John Riggs. She wondered if he was working.

"Certainly. I mean…no problem. I'll be right back."

He unsettled her, this man. Just looking at him made her heart pound and her mouth go dry. And when his eyes moved over her the way they were now, she could barely breathe.

She headed for the bar and gave Dante the order. The handsome Latino tipped his head toward the man in the shadowy darkness.

"That guy over there…his name's Johnnie Riggs. You be careful, *querida.* That one is out of your league." Dante didn't know she wasn't really Angel, but he had been in the business long enough to recognize a novice.

"I will. Thank you, Dante."

He just nodded. She returned to the table with the beer, wondering if the bartender could tell how attracted she was to Johnnie Riggs.

Crazy as it was.

She was a schoolteacher, for heaven's sake! Riggs was an ex-soldier, a hard, dangerous man who clearly thought she was something she wasn't, interested in her for only one reason.

On the other hand, she was attracted to him for the same exact reason. She hadn't been to bed with a man in years, and never a man like John Riggs. Her last boyfriend, Tom Coleman, was a history teacher. And their affair, bland as it was, had been over for nearly two years.

She set Johnnie's bottle of beer down in front of him and he caught hold of her wrist. "Why don't you join me? You look like you need a break."

She eased her hand from his. She didn't need a break. She wasn't tired; she was nervous. More so when she was talking to him.

"What happened to that guy you arrested?" she asked, just to have something to say.

"I didn't exactly arrest him. He jumped bail. I was hired to take him back to Houston so he could appear in court."

"I see."

"Probably not. It's kind of complicated."

"I imagine it is."

"When do you get off?"

"What?"

"I asked when you get off work."

She gave him a wary glance. "Why?"

"Because I want to take you out for a drink or a cup of coffee or something."

Her chin firmed. "That isn't what you want and we both know it."

"I want you. Every man in the place wants you. But you don't look at the rest of them the way you look at me."

She blushed clear to the toes of her high-heeled shoes. It was true. From the moment he first walked through the door last week, she could barely keep her eyes off him. Still, she couldn't believe he had come right out and said it.

"Even if I wanted to, I couldn't go out with you. There's a rule against employees dating customers."

"Which nobody pays any attention to. Besides, I don't give a damn about the rules."

"Look. I need this job, okay? Please don't make it hard for me."

He chuckled. "Why not? You're making it plenty hard for me." Hot color washed into her cheeks. She turned to walk away, but Riggs caught her arm, his hold gentler than she expected.

"Sorry. I was out of line. I won't do it again." He meant it. She could see it in his face. Why it pleased her, she refused to say.

"I appreciate that."

He let her go and she hurried over to the next table. In a different way, she was even more relieved to escape John Riggs than she had been Kyle Bennett.

What was there about him? Was she really that sexually deprived? A last glance in his direction and her stomach lifted. Apparently, she was.

Johnnie watched the little dancer walk away. There was something off about Angel Fontaine, something he had picked up on when she took his drink order. Onstage, she was confident, just another exotic dancer doing her job. But once she was out of the lights, she became a different person, shy and uncertain, barely able to make conversation with a man.

All evening, he had watched her. That she was new to the job was clear, but it was more than that. Some bone-deep difference that intrigued him. He liked solving puzzles. He wanted to solve the puzzle of Angel Fontaine.

On top of that, she was beautiful, and he had a weakness for sexy blondes. He wanted her. There was no denying it. But he also wanted to know her story, her secret. Find out what that subtle incongruity was that drew him like a moth to a lightbulb.

And he thought that she wanted him, too, though it was an attraction she clearly didn't want to feel.

He chuckled and took a sip of his beer. Well, that

was just too bad. He wasn't about to let her off the hook so easy. He was going to find out Angel's secret. He had a hunch once he knew what it was, she would trust him enough to let their mutual attraction progress to its logical end.

He wasn't in any hurry. If the stakes were high enough, Johnnie could be a very patient man.

"You can't be serious. You don't really plan to go to Kyle Bennett's house?" Babs pulled on a knee-length T-shirt with a teddy bear on the front in preparation for bed.

"I have to," Amy argued as she slipped into a pair of soft flannel pajamas. It was two-thirty in the morning. The club was closed and both of them were dead on their feet. "Maybe I'll have a chance to look around, find some kind of clue. You said he and Rachael dated for a while. Kyle probably made her all sorts of promises, lured her into going out with him by saying the kind of things he said to me. Rachael wanted to be a star. She might have trusted that he could help her get the break she needed."

"I don't like it. It's too dangerous. What if Kyle killed her? Maybe he'll make you disappear, too."

Amy ignored the little shiver that crawled down her spine. "That's not going to happen because you aren't going to let it. I'll call him tomorrow, get his address and set up a time on Thursday to go to his house. If I'm not back in a couple of hours, you'll call the police."

"How's that gonna help if you're already dead?"

Amy ignored that bit of wisdom and the little shiver it sent down her spine.

Babs slipped between the sheets on her twin bed and

pulled the covers up over her. "How are you gonna get there? You don't even have a car."

Amy brightened. "No, but you do." She gave her friend a sugary smile. "And I know you're going to let me borrow it."

Babs scoffed. "Traffic's a lot different in L.A. than driving in Grand Rapids."

Amy sat down on the edge of the bed. "You said you'd help me."

"I know, I know. It isn't the car. It's just that I'm afraid something will happen to you."

"We don't even know if Kyle's involved."

"Even if he isn't, he might try something and then where will you be?"

Amy didn't want to think about that. Getting attacked by some Hollywood weirdo was a terrifying thought. "Okay, so you'll loan me your car *and* your pepper spray."

Babs laughed. "I knew I liked you the first time I talked to you on the phone. Okay, we'll figure something out." She yawned behind her hand. "Listen, what about getting the Ranger guy to help you? He's supposed to be an expert on that kind of thing."

Amy drew back the covers and slipped beneath the sheets. "I thought about it. But I can't afford him."

"I saw you two talking tonight. Maybe he'll work for something besides money." Babs wiggled her eyebrows. "I wouldn't suggest it except that you're thinking about doing it anyway."

"I am *not* thinking about doing it." Oh, she so was. She had always walked the straight and narrow, always been the good little girl. But since she had come to L.A. and started dancing half naked, she felt free for the first time in her life. She knew that if she got the chance, she was going to have sex with Johnnie Riggs. "Besides, he might not show up in here again."

"He'll show up."

Babs was probably right. Just thinking of the determined way he had looked at her tonight made her stomach contract. "Maybe I'll talk to him a little, see what he has to say."

"Good idea." Babs yawned again. "In the meantime, turn out the light. We both need to get some sleep."

Amy thought of the conversion she needed to have with Johnnie Riggs. She closed her eyes, but she couldn't fall asleep.

Chapter 3

Johnnie arrived at Cisco's Cantina a little after eleven the following night. The bar, decorated in a south of the border style with cactus painted on the walls and leather-covered tables and chairs, was crowded. The clientele was mostly white-collar, lawyers and secretaries, corporate types and office assistants, a lot of men in designer jeans. The drinks were only moderately expensive and at this time of night, the lights were turned low.

Johnnie was there to meet DEA special agent Kent Wheeler, who had been working for years to build a case against a high-level drug dealer named Carlos Ortega, one of the major players in the San Dimas cartel. Over the years, Johnnie and Wheeler had helped each other a number of times and tonight was no exception.

"I appreciate your call," Wheeler said, joining him at the bar, a lean, athletically built man with slightly receding brown hair and a pale complexion. Johnnie had left a message on the agent's cell phone that he had information Wheeler might need. "What have you got?"

"Might be nothing, but my guy's pretty reliable. I had Ty Brodie helping me with surveillance on a guy whose wife wanted to find out if he was cheating. According to Ty, turns out the husband wasn't screwing around. He's into some major shit with the San Dimas cartel."

Wheeler whistled softly. "Got a name?"

"Joseph Pandaro. Ty picked up on some of the guy's conversation with a couple of lowlifes down at The Cave. Heard them talking about a big load of coke coming into the San Pedro docks the end of the month."

Wheeler was nodding. "We've been hearing rumors, nothing specific."

"He didn't get a date, but it's sometime in the next few weeks."

"Anything else?"

Johnnie shook his head. "I pulled the kid off the case. He's ex-military, tough as nails, but he doesn't have the street savvy to deal with thugs like those."

Wheeler took a sip of his drink, nearly as untouched as Johnnie's beer. "Thanks, I really appreciate the info."

"Just remember where you got it. I may need a favor sometime."

It was quid pro quo, and both of them knew it. As a GS-13, the highest rank in the DEA, Wheeler was a powerhouse and dedicated to the service. At the moment, Johnnie didn't need anything from him, but there would likely be a time when he would.

From Cisco's, Johnnie climbed into his black Ford Mustang G.T. and fired up the powerful V-8 engine. He'd just bought the car, his pride and joy, a couple of months ago, black leather interior, 412 horsepower, 5.0 engine. Plus, he'd had a mechanic friend of his soup it up even more. The beast could really move. The car and his Harley Sportster helped him do his job and have a little fun while he was at it.

He eased the car into the traffic moving down Sunset, taking in the crowds prowling the sidewalks and the laughter and music spilling out of the clubs crowded together on each block. He wasn't ready to go back to his apartment up the hill. Not yet.

His destination lay ahead. Just past La Cienega, he turned into the parking lot next to the Kitty Cat Club and slipped the car in one of the empty spaces. There was something he needed inside and it wasn't a bottle of beer. Though he'd probably have to settle for that again tonight.

He climbed out of the Mustang, locked the car and sauntered toward the door leading into the club. The music was blasting, a steady hard-rock beat. The redhead he had seen the other night was dancing onstage. He glanced around, spotted his quarry even before he reached what was lately becoming his regular table at the back of the room.

Angel's gaze collided with his and she nearly dropped her tray. Damn, she was cute. Johnnie winked at her and smiled, sat down at the table, leaned back and waited.

Amy forced her legs to keep moving. She felt like an idiot. One glance at the man in the snug black T-shirt and she turned into a bumbling fool. As she walked past Babs, her friend raised a hand and wiggled the tips of her fingers.

"Still owe me that five bucks, kiddo. Tonight, I intend to collect."

"Okay, I owe you, but that doesn't mean he's here tonight for me."

Babs just rolled her eyes and kept walking. Riggs was sitting in Amy's section. There was no way to avoid him. She took a calming breath, forced a note of cool into her demeanor and started toward his table in the back.

She pasted on a smile. "Welcome back to the Kitty Cat Club, Mr. Riggs. What would you like to drink?"

A corner of his mouth edged up. He had the sexiest mouth. "You know my name. That means you asked. That's good. It's even better if you call me Johnnie."

Her mouth went dry. "Johnnie. All right, what can I get for you... Johnnie?"

"Bud Light." His gaze slowly took in every inch of her body. Her stomach swirled as she turned and walked toward the bar to get his beer. She delivered drinks to a table on her way to his, then set the Bud Light bottle down in front of him.

"Thanks." He tipped his head toward a girl named Ruby, who gyrated in a G-string, performing a lap dance for a customer sitting at a table not far away from his. "You do lap dances?"

Amy's hand trembled and she had to take a better grip on her tray. "No... I'm, uh, I'm kind of new at this." Tate had suggested she wait until she was more comfortable with the customers. Her plan was not to do them at all.

"That so…? How about doing one for me?" He was leaning back in his chair, those powerful arms crossed over his massive chest. He could have been wearing sunglasses for all she could read in those dark, dark eyes.

"They…umm…cost fifty dollars," she said, hoping the price would dissuade him.

"Private costs seventy-five. That's what I want."

Her breath stalled. "That's a lot of money." The dancer got a percentage, a way to make extra cash.

"Think you're worth it?"

"I don't…don't know…"

His smile came slow and easy and it made her skin feel hot. "Oh, yeah," he said. "I think you'd be worth every dime."

Her legs were shaking. "Even…even if I said I would, you know you can't touch me." There were rules about what she could and couldn't do, how far she was allowed to go. What the customer could and couldn't do. She wasn't a prostitute, after all, she was a dancer.

Well, actually, she was a kindergarten teacher, but he didn't know that.

"I'll talk to Tate, arrange for a private room." He slid back his chair and stood up. Even in six-inch heels, she had to look up at him.

When he started to leave, she grabbed his arm. "Wait a minute. I—I didn't say I'd do it."

His mouth edged up. "What's the matter? You aren't afraid, are you?"

She stiffened. Of course she was afraid. She was

terrified. But she wasn't about to let him know. "No, of course not."

"Good." He turned and started walking. As he sauntered off toward the owner, Amy stared after him.

Oh, my God! She was going to do a lap dance for Johnnie Riggs! And the weirdest part was, deep down in her womanly core, she *wanted* to do it.

Johnnie took a seat in one of the comfortable rooms the club provided for private dances. For seventy-five bucks, he got three songs. He wasn't sure he could handle one.

The truth was, he had never bought a lap dance in his life. Watching a naked woman parade around in front of him just didn't cut it, not unless he was taking her to bed.

But there was something about this particular woman. He wanted her. More than he could remember wanting a woman in a very long time. Maybe ever. He had a feeling it wasn't going to happen—not without a great deal of trouble.

He was pushing her buttons, he knew. She wasn't comfortable dancing for him. Hell, she wasn't comfortable just being in the room with him, and yet he had a hunch the only way to reach her was to push her hard enough to cave.

So he walked into the small, dimly lit room he had paid for and sat down in the only piece of furniture inside, an overstuffed mauve velour chair. He took a long swallow on the fresh beer he'd picked up at the bar then set the bottle down on the table built into the arm. Leaning back, he made himself comfortable and prepared to watch the show.

* * *

"You're kidding, right?" Babs stood with Amy outside the door to one of the private lap dance rooms. She had changed back into her red sequined G-string and the red sequined pasties that covered her nipples, proper attire for the show.

"It's just a dance," she said, trying to sound more confident than she felt. "We need this man's help. I'm going to dance for him and then I'm going to see if I can hire him to help us."

Babs stood there in her shiny blue wig, the fake hair thick, straight, blunt-cut and just a little longer than her own dark hair. She planted her hands on her hips, a thoughtful look in her eyes.

"Actually, it's not a bad idea. Nothing's going to happen. Tate's got cameras in there. He gets out of line, you just yell, Bo Jing comes in and it's over."

"I don't think he'll get out of line." She wasn't sure why she felt that way, she just did.

"He's a pretty cool customer, all right. I can't see him turning into a lust-crazed maniac. On the other hand, sometimes the quiet ones are the ones you have to watch."

"I'll keep that in mind." But as she walked into the room and spotted John Riggs in the chair positioned in front of the fake parquet dance floor, her mind went completely blank and she couldn't think of anything at all.

One of his big hands curled around the beer bottle sitting on the built-in table. He watched every move she made as she approached, but he didn't get up from his chair.

"Just so you know, this is a first for me, too."

That surprised her. "Really?"

"Really."

"Why me?"

He took a sip of his beer. "You intrigue me. I want to take you out. I'm hoping once you realize how harmless I am, you'll agree."

He didn't look harmless. He looked like a big, lazy cat ready to pounce at any moment. She thought of the help she needed to find her sister. In the time she had been in the club, she hadn't accomplished much. Getting an appointment with that cheese-ball Kyle Bennett was the only real progress she had made.

The music started just then, saving her from having to make some sort of comment. She took a few steps away from him, turned her back and tried to fill her head with the heavy beat of the music, the thud of the bass, the rhythm of the drum, tried to relax.

It was a lot harder to perform in here than onstage, a lot more difficult to block out the image of John Riggs watching her every move when she knew exactly what he was thinking. Knew he was here because he wanted her in his bed.

The music swelled. She let her head fall back, felt her long straight hair brush against her bottom. Instead of blocking him out of her mind, she decided to go with it, set her sexuality free, dance for Johnnie Riggs, a man who attracted her physically as no one ever had.

She slid her hands into her hair and lifted it away from the back of her neck, turned toward him, let the hair slide down around her shoulders. His face was partially hidden in shadow, but she could see his eyes, read his hunger.

She moved toward him, stopped just inches away.

Her breath rushed in and out, hot and sharp. She closed her eyes, let the music take over, arched her back, thrust out her breasts, and began to sway. Even with her eyes closed, she could feel him, feel the powerful lust he barely contained. Her body heated, softened, silently responded.

Dear God, she had never felt anything like it. She undulated, lifted her hair, turned and let it glide down her back, then spun away.

A few beats later, she sat down on his lap facing him, reached up and ran her hands down the sides of his face. She could feel the late night stubble along his jaw and it drove her crazy. He was hard beneath her, iron hard inside his jeans, and throbbing. For an instant, she couldn't breathe.

She forced herself up, forced her body to move away, to fall back into the dance. She spun and shimmied, then returned to his chair. She sat down facing him again, her legs splayed over his. Something shifted inside her, loosened, expanded, and desire took over. When she draped her arms around his neck, the last of her inhibitions slipped away. Amy leaned forward and kissed him, just a soft melding of lips. It was against the rules to kiss a client during a lap dance and yet she did it again, another soft brush of lips that only made her want more.

Every muscle in his body felt rigid beneath her and yet the only thing that moved was the hot mouth gliding over hers, the lips that began to take instead of leisurely accept. She opened her mouth and his tongue slid inside, and the next thing she knew, his arms were around her, crushing her against him, the kiss blazing hot, deep and erotic.

His hand found her breast and the heat of his palm engulfed the fullness. She couldn't think, couldn't breathe. A little whimpering sound came from her throat, and in some deep part of her mind, sanity began to return. Johnnie kissed her again, long and hard, and fear hit her. God in heaven, what was she doing?

Trembling all over, Amy broke the kiss. Her heart was pounding with a combination of desire and embarrassment. She had never behaved so insanely. And she had never wanted anything more than Johnnie Riggs.

For an instant their eyes locked, his hot and dark, hers wild and frightened. Then the oddest thing happened. Johnnie came out of the chair with her still in his arms and set her back on her feet.

At the same instant, the music ended, the silence in the room a second splash of cold water hitting her squarely in the face.

"Oh, my God," she said, backing away from him. "Oh, my God." She turned, started to run for the door. Johnnie caught her wrist, turning her toward him before she could escape.

"Easy, honey. Just take it easy."

"I'm sorry," she said. "I don't... I don't know what happened."

"It's all right," he soothed as if she were a frightened child. "I'm not going to hurt you."

"I'm sorry," she said again because she had broken the rules and she didn't understand how it had happened. He led her back over to the chair he had been sitting in only moments before and urged her down in the seat.

"We need to talk," he said, "but this isn't the place. What time do you get off work?"

She started shaking her head.

"Listen to me, Angel. We'll go out and have some coffee. I promise we won't do more than talk, all right?"

Her nerves settled a little. *This is the opportunity you've been wanting,* she reminded herself. The chance to tell him about her sister and see if he would be willing to work out some sort of arrangement to help her. "I have to go back to work," she said lamely.

"When does your shift end?"

"I'm… I'm on the early shift tonight. I get off at eleven."

He nodded. "Good. That's good. I'll be waiting in the parking lot when you come outside."

She just stared at him. Johnnie caught her chin and tipped it up, forcing her to look at him. She felt like crying and didn't know why.

"Just coffee. I give you my word."

Her throat ached. She had no idea why she believed him, but she did. He was a Ranger, wasn't he? Surely Rangers didn't lie. "All right."

He bent and kissed her cheek. "I'll see you at eleven." He didn't say more, just left her there and quietly slipped outside the room.

Babs hurried in after him. Amy was still sitting in the chair. "Jesus, what happened? You look shell-shocked."

Amy blinked to keep from crying. "I don't know what happened. I completely lost control."

"He didn't… Riggs didn't…"

"He was a gentleman. I was the one. I still can't believe it. God, I'm so embarrassed."

Babs started to smile. "Sounds like it went exactly the way we planned. When are you seeing him again?"

Amy glanced up. "What?"

"You're seeing him again, right?"

Amy nodded numbly. "Tonight. After my shift. We're going for coffee. He gave me his word we'd just talk."

Babs seemed to approve. "Smooth, not too pushy. I think I like this guy."

"I don't know what it is, Babs, but there's something about him."

Her friend just smiled. "Honey, you can say that again."

Johnnie slid behind the wheel of the Mustang, tipped his head back against the headrest and just sat there.

"Jesus." He couldn't quite catch his breath. He was still so hard he hurt and at the same time he felt completely drained. Watching Angel Fontaine was like waging a war with himself, a war he'd barely won.

He'd almost lost it tonight, but as hot as he'd been and still was, as hot as Angel had been—and man, the lady was on fire—something just wasn't right. He had to know what it was and he was determined to find out.

He believed she would show up tonight. Angel was even more baffled about what had happened in there than he was. Whoever she was—and he was sure Angel wasn't her name—she wasn't used to the kind of desire that had hit them both tonight.

The kind that struck like lightning, turned into a blazing inferno and flat-out sucked you dry. In another minute, he'd have had her on the floor and been inside her. He still didn't know how he had managed to hang on to that last shred of control.

Maybe it was his Ranger training. Maybe it was

seeing the fear in her pretty blue eyes when she had realized how close they both were to losing complete control.

He raked a hand through his short, dark hair. He couldn't figure her out and that was part of the attraction.

Later tonight, he was going to find out what was going on with Angel Fontaine.

Chapter 4

At the end of her shift, Amy changed into a pair of skinny jeans, tucked in a red print shirt, fastened a silver belt around her waist and slid her feet into a pair of red, open-toed high heels. At five foot one, she was shorter than nearly everyone. High heels gave her a psychological boost as well as a physical one and she almost always wore them.

She glanced in the mirror. She had washed her face and removed her stage makeup. She ran a brush through her hair and fluffed her bangs, fastened a small gold hoop in each ear, then applied a little blush, mascara and pale pink lipstick. Nothing too heavy. She wasn't Angel now and she didn't want to be.

Amy thought of her performance in the private lap dance room and felt a rush of embarrassment. What in the world had possessed her? During her few relationships, she had never been the aggressor during sex and basically preferred it that way. But tonight… Tonight something insane had come over her. She'd felt bold, empowered. She had practically attacked John Riggs right there in his chair.

Closing her eyes to block out the image, she reached for her small red leather purse and slung the strap over her shoulder. She couldn't imagine what Riggs must think of her or how she could possibly explain. At the apartment door, she paused. Maybe she should wait, talk to him after a cooling-off period. It would certainly be easier to face him.

On the other hand, maybe this was the perfect opportunity. With a sigh, she pulled open the door. The man was taking her out for coffee, nothing more. He had given her his word and she believed him. This was the chance she needed.

Maybe.

She hadn't thought past the part about trying to hire him. She would just have to play it by ear.

Babs met her as she crossed the backstage area toward the door leading out to the parking lot.

Babs propped a hand on her hip. "I talked to Tate. He says Riggs is an okay guy."

Amy just nodded, trying to forget the feel of those hot, possessive lips moving over hers.

"I pressed the boss a little to see what I could find out and Tate told me Riggs is a good investigator but he doesn't work cheap."

"I had a feeling."

"It never hurts to ask, right? You never know till you try."

Amy drew in a breath. "I don't know quite what I'm going to say, but I guess I'll think of something."

"Are you kidding? After that little performance you gave him, the guy is going to be toast."

Amy thought of her behavior during the dance and closed her eyes against a blush. "I guess we'll see." She waved over her shoulder as she pushed open the door.

"I won't wait up," Babs teased with a grin, and Amy's stomach knotted.

What would Riggs expect?

What would she be willing to do?

With a breath for courage, she stepped out into the parking lot and spotted him behind the wheel of a black Mustang. The car fit him perfectly, dark and powerful, dangerous and predatory. Her insides tightened.

Dear God, how far would she be willing to go to get John Riggs to help her?

Leaning back in the seat, Johnnie spotted Angel the minute she walked out into the night. He knew the instant she saw him. She froze like a deer in the headlights, and Johnnie didn't hesitate, just shoved open the car door and came out of his seat, started striding toward her.

"I'm glad you came," he said with a smile meant to put her at ease. "I know a little café just a couple of blocks away. We can get some coffee there."

She nodded. He could feel the tension thrumming through her, figured if he didn't get her out of there now, she was going to turn and run.

"It isn't that far," he said, setting a hand at her waist and urging her back to his car, not giving her time to change her mind. He led her around to the passenger door and helped her climb in, reached over and pulled the seat belt across her lap and fastened the buckle.

"Thank you."

Always so polite. Almost prim. Angel Fontaine was about as far from his idea of a stripper as a woman could get. And yet he had seen her up onstage and she was hot.

Maybe that was the appeal. Sweet and hot at the same time—sort of like cinnamon candy.

He chuckled to himself as he slid behind the wheel. If Angel was a piece of candy, he'd be the man to eat her up.

Looking uncomfortable, she shifted in her seat. "About what happened tonight… I want to apologize. I've never—"

"It was only a kiss, Angel. Nothing to get upset about."

She fell silent as he shoved the key into the ignition and the engine roared to life, then started to purr. He drove toward the café, pulled into the lot, which was full, but his luck was holding and a gray-haired couple in an old brown Buick was backing out. He parked in the space left behind, guided Angel inside, and they slid into an empty booth.

The Eatery had a kind of retro decor with pink-and-white vinyl booths and a long lunch counter with a row of round stools. The café had been there for years, had once been called Norm's but that was a long time ago.

A waitress in a black skirt and white blouse showed up to take their order. Sheila, he recalled, frizzy blond hair and big boobs. He was kind of a regular, though he rotated his meal stops to keep his information channels open. In his line of work, you never knew what rumors might come in handy.

Sheila pulled a pencil from behind her ear. "Hey, handsome, what can I get you?"

He looked across at Angel. Damn she was pretty. More so, he thought, without all that makeup. He tried not to look at her mouth, since now he knew exactly how good she tasted. "What would you like?"

"Just coffee," she said. "Cream, if it isn't too much trouble."

"Two coffees," he said. "One with cream. Thanks, Sheila."

They made small talk for the short time it took for the coffee to arrive. Angel poured cream into her cup and daintily stirred.

She looked up at him and smiled, but it looked a little forced. "I'm…aahh…glad you asked me to come here."

"Oh, yeah?" *Here we go,* he thought. He'd known something was off. He had a hunch he was about to find out what it was.

"The thing is, I heard you were a private investigator."

"Of sorts." He took a drink from the heavy white china mug in front of him, set it back down on the Formica-topped table. "That why you agreed to the dance? You wanted to talk to me about business?"

Soft color washed into her cheeks. "That was part of it. I really don't…don't know exactly what happened in there. I just… I guess I got carried away."

Amen to that. "So what did you want to talk to me about?"

"I…umm…want to hire you."

"You in some kind of trouble?"

Her eyes rounded. "Me? No! Of course not."

"Of course not," he said with a hint of sarcasm she seemed to miss.

"It's my sister. Her name is Rachael."

"Then it's Rachael who's in trouble."

"I don't know. A little over six weeks ago, Rachael disappeared. I talked to the police, of course. Babs says they haven't tried very hard…you know…because she's an exotic dancer."

He leaned back in his chair, trying not to be disappointed that her real interest came in wanting something from him. "So you want to hire me to find her. Is that it?"

"Not exactly. I want to hire you to help *me* find her. I could do some of the work, and that way it wouldn't cost as much."

"Okay, I get it. You want to hire me but you don't have any money."

She sat up straighter in her seat. "Well, I have a little. Some savings from my job back home, but I've gone through a lot of it for my plane ticket and phone calls. I could borrow some, maybe a couple thousand. I get the feeling you don't come cheap."

She was right. He charged up to a grand a day, plus expenses. She looked across the booth at him, bit her plump bottom lip, and heat throbbed low in his groin.

Her fingers tightened around the handle of her coffee mug and the skin over her knuckles turned bone-white. "I thought…you seem to be attracted to me. I thought maybe we could…" She swallowed. "Maybe we could…you know…work something out."

A jolt of anger slipped through him. It began to fade when he noticed her face had turned as pale as the hand that gripped the mug. He hadn't pegged her for a prostitute. He looked at her and he didn't buy it now.

Still, he could be wrong.

He stood up from the pink vinyl bench across from her. She had barely touched her coffee. He tossed down a five and a couple of ones, more than enough for the coffee and a tip, and hauled her to her feet.

"Let's get out of here." Angel didn't protest when he caught her hand and led her toward the door, didn't say a word as he guided her out of the coffee shop back to his car. But as she slid into the seat and fumbled to fasten her seat belt, he saw that she was trembling.

Johnnie fired up the powerful engine, slipped the car into gear and pulled out onto the busy street. It didn't take long to drive the winding road up the hill above Sunset to the guesthouse on the estate that was his home. He used the remote to open the gate then turned into the long narrow driveway, pulled into the guesthouse garage and parked next to his Harley. Up the drive a little farther, the main house, a big white modern structure, edged out over the hill.

Angel flashed a look at the motorcycle as he helped her out, but she made no comment, just let him guide her up on the porch, waited while he unlocked the door, then walked past him into the entry. The lights of Los Angeles glittered in front of them through the wall of windows in the living room, a view that never failed to impress.

She stared in that direction. "It's beautiful."

He tossed his keys into the glass dish on the table in the entry. "I got lucky. I did some work for the lady who owns the estate. She's older, feels safer having someone living in the guesthouse." Eleanor Stiles was not only his landlady but also a very close friend. She was seventy and smart as a whip.

"Someone who was once an Army Ranger?"

He shrugged. "I suppose. My office is downstairs. I do most of my work out of the house."

She looked calmer now, and yet he could feel her underlying tension.

"How about a drink?" he asked. "Maybe a glass of wine or something?"

He sensed her relief. "Wine sounds good."

"White or red?"

"White...if you happen to have it open."

The most polite hooker he'd ever met.

He opened the little fridge underneath the counter of the wet bar, took out an open bottle of chardonnay and poured her a glass, pulled out a Bud for himself and twisted off the cap. He carried the wine back to Angel, who stood in front of the window, staring out at the city lights.

"It's amazing, isn't it? The lights go on forever."

"I take it you aren't from L.A."

She shook her head. "Michigan."

"Detroit?"

She steadied the glass, took a sip of wine. "Grand Rapids."

Too old to be a runaway, but she was obviously new to the city. "So you came here to find your sister."

She looked up at him with those big blue eyes. "Yes."

Johnnie forced himself to concentrate. "Have you reported her disappearance to the cops?"

"I didn't, but Rachael's friend Barbara McClure called the police the day after she disappeared. They haven't found her or even a clue as to what happened to her. I'm not sure they're even still looking."

He took a drink of his beer, set it down on a nearby table. Angel took a large, nervous swallow of her wine as he moved closer. Reaching out, he took the glass from her hand and set it down on the table next to his beer.

"So now you want to hire me to help you find her."

"Y-yes…"

"And in exchange you're willing to make a trade."

She swallowed, nodded.

"I like this idea, Angel. I like it a helluva lot." Then he hauled her into his arms, bent his head and very thoroughly kissed her.

Amy gripped Johnnie's powerful shoulders and just hung on, reeling at the powerful jolt of desire that shook her. Hot lips, softer than they looked, moved over hers, nibbled the corners of her mouth. He deepened the kiss, coaxed her lips apart and his tongue slid inside.

Heat engulfed her; need curled in her belly. She wanted to have his hands on her, wanted him to touch her. She wanted him to make love to her. She had never felt this way before, never experienced this intense, mindless hunger. She wanted to give in to it, let him have what he wanted.

What she also wanted.

She pressed herself more firmly against him, felt the heavy weight of his erection. He was going to help her. In return, she was paying him with her body. It didn't matter that she was selling herself like…like a prostitute, behaving like…like a whore.

Her throat closed up. A little sob got caught there.

She felt his mouth against the side of her neck, trailing scorching kisses along her throat, and her eyes stung. His fingers worked the buttons on her blouse and tears welled.

She wasn't a whore. She didn't sell herself to strangers.

What about Rachael? What if she isn't dead? The awful thought both she and Babs secretly believed. *What if she's in terrible trouble and there is no one to help her?*

He kissed her again, long and deep, but the desire was fading, replaced by a sick feeling in the pit of her stomach. The tears in her eyes slipped onto her cheeks.

Johnnie must have felt the wetness because he broke off the kiss and jerked away. "All right, that's it!"

Hard fingers dug into her shoulders. Her head came up as he backed her against the wall and she stared into his dark, angry face.

"Who the hell are you?" he demanded. "And don't even think of telling me your name is Angel Fontaine."

She shook her head, misery sweeping over her. She had failed Rachael, failed herself.

"I'm so s-sorry. I thought…thought I could do it. I didn't mean to lead you on, I just…" Fresh tears welled and the sob locked in her throat finally escaped.

Johnnie blew out a breath and eased her back into his arms. "It's all right. I had a feeling this wasn't going to work." He held her a moment, giving her time to compose herself, then moved away.

"I was going to tell you my name," she said, brushing away a drop of wetness with the tip of her finger. "I didn't mean to deceive you. I just…"

"You just what?"

"There's something about you… I don't know, I just… When I get around you, I can't seem to think straight."

A corner of his mouth edged up and some of his anger faded. "Go on, let's hear it."

She swallowed. "My name is Amy Brewer. I'm not… not a stripper. I'm… I'm a kindergarten teacher."

Johnnie groaned.

"The part about my sister is true. After Rachael disappeared, I flew out here from Grand Rapids. Babs—that's my roommate, Barbara McClure—she and Rachael worked together at the Kitty Cat Club. They were friends. Babs got me the job at the club. She helped me deal with my…my inhibitions and learn to dance—which wasn't all that easy. Eventually, I got the hang of it. And then I saw you and I found out you were an investigator and we sort of came up with this plan."

"This plan being for you to sell yourself to me in exchange for my services."

Fresh tears welled. She wiped them away. "I guess so. It sounded like a good idea at the time, considering…"

"Considering what?"

She looked him in the face. "Considering what happened in that room."

Johnnie's eyes seemed to darken. There was no mistaking what she meant. She was attracted to him or she wouldn't be sitting in his living room.

"Anything else?"

"There's more, but it isn't important now."

"Why don't you let me decide that?" He led her over to the sofa, as modern as the rest of the apartment, which had high, open ceilings, a sleek dark brown sofa and chairs, and everything perfectly in place. He was, after all, an ex-soldier.

He picked up her wineglass and handed it back to her, grabbed his beer, and sat down beside her on the sofa.

"Okay, tell me the rest."

Amy took a fortifying sip. "Once I started my sister's old job, I began to dig around. That's the reason I came to L.A., to try to come up with information that might help me find her. There's a man my sister dated before she disappeared. His name is Kyle Bennett. He's supposed to be a movie producer. Tomorrow afternoon, I'm going over to his house for—"

"No way. I know Kyle Bennett and the guy is a scumbag. He's about as much a movie producer as I am."

"I kind of figured that, but it isn't the point. The point is, my sister came to Los Angeles to try to get into the movie business."

"Gee, there's a good idea."

"I know, but that's what she wanted to do. So she might have believed Kyle Bennett could help her. If she was involved with him, maybe he had some part in her disappearance."

"Fine, I'll talk to him."

"He isn't going to tell you anything. He'll be a lot more likely to open up to me than he will be to you."

"You're a schoolteacher, remember? Not a cop. There is no way you should involve yourself in something like this."

"It isn't as bad as it sounds. Babs knows Kyle's address and what time I should be back. If I don't get home when I'm supposed to, she's going to call the police."

He just shook his head. "No way, no how."

She set the wineglass very carefully down on the coffee table and stood up.

"You've been very nice, Johnnie. Especially considering the way I've behaved. Now I'd appreciate it if you would take me back to the club."

"Shit."

"I'm doing this. I'm going to find out what happened to my sister."

He set down his beer and slowly stood up from the sofa. He was a big man, powerfully built, intimidating just standing there in front of her. She forced herself not to back away.

Johnnie looked down at her and his breath whispered out on a sigh. "All right. I'll help you."

Amy opened her mouth to tell him she had changed her mind about paying him with sex, but he cut her off.

"No strings," he added. "I'll do some digging, see what I can come up with. I'll do what I can to find out what happened to your sister."

She started shaking her head.

"What now?"

"I need to be involved in this. I owe it to Rachael. I can't just sit back and do nothing."

"Were you listening to what I said? You aren't a cop. You aren't trained for this kind of work."

"I'm keeping my appointment tomorrow with Kyle Bennett. I might find out something important."

His jaw clenched and unclenched. He must have noticed the mutinous set of her chin because he simply nodded. "Fine. You're probably right about getting him to talk. But if I'm going to help you, we do things my way. Is that understood?"

He was an investigator. He knew what he was doing. She gave him the first sincere smile she had felt all evening. "Understood."

"One last thing."

"What's that?"

"Sooner or later, I'm taking you to bed, but it won't be because you owe me. It'll be because the time is right and you want me as much as I want you."

Her stomach contracted. Just looking at him made her want him but she knew he was right. Her mind wasn't ready even if her body was more than willing. She didn't reply. God only knew what she might say if she did.

"We'll talk more tomorrow," he said. "Right now, it's time for me to take you home. I think we both know what will happen if we stay here much longer."

Ignoring a rush of embarrassment, Amy nodded and let him guide her out the door. Of all the endings she could have imagined for the evening, this wasn't one of them.

She wasn't sure if she was relieved or disappointed.

Chapter 5

Johnnie backed the Mustang out of the garage and headed down the hill. A freakin' schoolteacher. Jesus, just his luck.

At least his instincts hadn't been wrong.

He shifted in the seat, trying to get comfortable. He'd had a hard-on nonstop since the first time he had seen Angel at the club.

Not Angel, he corrected himself. *Amy.* Amy Brewer. Kindergarten teacher.

Christ, how much worse could it get?

"Nice car," she said, drawing his attention back to the moment.

"Four-hundred-twelve horses under the hood of this little beauty."

As they passed beneath a streetlight, he caught her soft smile. "When I was in high school, my dad had a

Stingray. It was old, but it was hot. He was a mechanic, great with cars. Once in a while, he'd let me drive it."

"You like cars?"

"I do...yes. I love speed. I like to go fast—when it's safe. I like the sound a car makes when you step on the gas. I guess I picked it up from my dad."

His lips faintly curved. The lady was just full of surprises. "So, your dad still around?" If he was, the guy had to be crazy to let his daughter get involved in something as dangerous as this.

"He died three years ago. He was cutting firewood. Tree split wrong. He was killed instantly."

He could read the sorrow in her face. "That's too bad."

"My mom's back in Grand Rapids. She didn't want me to come out here."

Imagine that.

"She's afraid something will happen. She said losing one daughter was enough."

He tossed a glance her way as he made the turn off Laurel Canyon onto Sunset and merged with the traffic. "Your mother's right. Snooping around the way you've been doing...that's dangerous business, honey."

"Maybe, but so far I haven't found out much of anything. I'm hoping tomorrow will be different."

"What time's your appointment?"

"Two o'clock at Kyle's house. He lives in Bel Air so it isn't that far a drive."

"Bel Air, huh? Pretty ritzy for a scumbag. You got a car?"

"Babs is lending me hers."

"I need your cell number. Write it down on a piece of paper."

She pulled a pen out of her purse and scribbled the

number on the back of a Kitty Cat Club napkin she dug out of the bottom.

Johnnie pulled into the parking lot and stopped beside the rear entrance. "If Tate gives you any trouble about being out with a customer, tell him I'm helping you with a personal problem. He knows what I do for a living. That should be enough to keep him off your back."

"All right." Amy handed him the napkin, opened the car door and got out. He rolled down his window as she walked around to his side of the car.

"I'll call you late morning," he said, handing her a business card. "We need to work out the details before you go in. And I need to talk to your sister's friend Barbara. Can you make that happen?"

"Babs usually sleeps till noon, but I can get her up a little early."

"I'll call, set up a place for us to meet."

She just nodded. "Thank you, Johnnie. I really appreciate this."

"Yeah, well, I'll see you tomorrow." He watched her walk into the club and realized it bothered him to think of her working in there. She was a schoolteacher, for chrissake. She shouldn't be dancing naked in a goddamned tittie bar.

He sighed as he turned the car around and drove away. There wasn't a damn thing he could do about it. Except find her sister. Then he could send her sweet little schoolteacher ass back to Michigan where it belonged.

Amy usually slept late on her day off, but her nerves were strung too tight. Instead, as the sun came up, she

Against the Night

dressed in a pair of white stretch Levi's and a pink T-shirt, left Babs asleep in the apartment, and walked a block down the street to a little espresso bar called The Caboose.

"I'll have a skinny double-shot latte," she said to the barista, a dark-haired girl with braces who didn't look old enough to be out of high school. With a chocolate biscotti in one hand and the coffee in the other, Amy sat down at one of the small square tables.

She reached over to the table next to hers and picked up an *L.A. Times* someone had left behind. She did a quick perusal, checked the local news, which was nothing but murder and mayhem, the weather, which never changed in sunny California, and the comics, which at least made her smile.

When she finished her coffee, she headed back to the apartment and found Babs up and dressed in jeans and an orange tank top. Babs was extremely big busted so no matter what she wore, she looked top heavy, as if she would topple onto the floor if she leaned too far over.

"Oh, good, you're awake," Amy said.

"My cell phone rang and woke me up," Babs grumbled. "Wrong number, can you believe?"

"Why didn't you just go back to sleep?"

"You said the Ranger wanted to talk to me. I figured I might as well get up and get ready."

Last night, Babs had still been awake when Amy got home. Her friend had been worried, she knew, though Babs would never admit it. Amy had told her all the gory details, how she had made a fool of herself by reneging on her sex-for-work proposal and how John Riggs had again behaved as a gentleman.

"Johnnie was really great last night," Amy said. "I

was starting to freak and he knew it. He didn't push me. He agreed to help anyway."

Babs scoffed. "Don't expect the same treatment from Kyle Bennett. Your sister said he was a real horse's ass."

Amy grinned, having no difficulty imagining her outspoken sister saying something like that. The grin slid away. "I'm not looking forward to meeting him, especially not at his house. I feel a lot better knowing Johnnie is going to be helping us."

"You can say that again."

Amy paced over to the window. The room they shared wasn't glamorous, their only view the parking lot below. Still, she felt safe here, with Bo Jing and Tate to look after them, Dante and the rest of the crew. In the beginning, she had worried that someone Rachael had worked with might have been responsible for her disappearance, but Tate screened his employees well and after she got to know the men she worked with, she didn't believe they'd had anything to do with it.

Along with that, no men were allowed upstairs, which was one of the reasons the girls liked living there. They could work, pay cheap rent and save their money, and not be hassled by drunken Kitty Cat patrons.

Amy walked over to the kitchen counter, where Babs was making coffee. "Do you think he'll be able to find out what happened to her?"

Babs pressed the start button on the coffeemaker. She knew what Amy was asking. "In a city this size, women disappear all the time. Some of them are never seen again."

A cold chill slipped through her. "You mean their bodies are never found."

"I'm sorry, honey, but yeah. That's what I mean."

"We pretend she's still out there, but I'm not sure either of us really believes it."

"Oh, she's out there. We just don't know if she's alive or not. Until we're sure one way or another, we'll do whatever it takes to find out."

Amy felt better just hearing the words. They wouldn't give up—not until they knew what had happened. She could handle Kyle Bennett. He was just a man and their plan was a good one. At least it was a place to start.

And now she had John Riggs to help her.

Johnnie climbed the short flight of steps and shoved through the front door of the redbrick building on North Wilcox Avenue. The Hollywood Community Police Station handled La Brea, Sunset, Hollywood and a half dozen surrounding communities.

First thing this morning, he had run a check on Amy Brewer. Looked like she was exactly what she said—a kindergarten teacher from Grand Rapids. He groaned. Last night's hot kiss popped into his head and he thought how much he still wanted her, bit down on a curse and forced his mind back to business.

He'd also run Rachael Brewer's name, and read the few newspaper articles about her disappearance he'd found on the Net and anything else he could find about her. It was a start, but not much help.

Making his way over to the counter in the police station, he recognized Officer Gwen Michaels working behind the front desk.

"Hey, Gwen."

She looked up at him and a smile broke over her

face. "Johnnie! You devil, where you been? And don't tell me you've been staying out of trouble, 'cause that just ain't happenin', honey."

Johnnie grinned. "Trouble's my middle name, Gwen. You know that."

"Sure do. So what can I do for you, J-man?" Officer Michaels was in her twenties, black and gorgeous. And a damn fine officer on top of it.

"Is Detective Vega around? I need to pick his brain a little."

"I think he left a while ago, but let me check for you." She rotated her stool toward the computer on the desk in front of her, checked the monitor. "He's out on a call, not due back until the end of the day."

"Leave him a message, will you? Ask him to give me a call when he gets in?"

"No problem."

"Thanks, Gwen."

"Take care, J-man."

He chuckled. She always called him that. He wondered why he'd never asked her out. Probably because she was a cop. When he got off work, police business was the last thing he wanted to think about.

He headed for the door, wishing Vega had been in but figuring he could count on the detective's help. He didn't get much resistance from the LAPD. In fact, he could usually depend on their cooperation with just about anything. His younger sister, Kate, had been an LAPD patrolman. Four years ago, Katie had died in the line of duty during a bank robbery. At the time, Johnnie had been in Mexico on some shit boat-recovery job for J. D. Wendel, one of the dot-com billionaires. The eighty-foot, million-plus Lazzara was chump change for Wendel, but the man wasn't about to let one of his employees get away with stealing it from him.

As Johnnie walked back to his car, he remembered returning to the States to find out he'd lost the sister he adored and his chest tightened. Katie was the only real family he'd had. He sure didn't count the deadbeat dad who'd raised them in a crappy apartment off Los Feliz Boulevard.

Max Riggs only worked hard enough to keep the power turned on and put a little food on the table. The rest of the time he was hustling some sucker out of his paycheck, or drinking and gambling with his buddies down at Pete's bar. With their mother long gone and never to be heard from again, Johnnie and Katie were left to fend for themselves.

He'd finally gotten over his mother's abandonment, though as a kid, he'd often wondered what he and Katie had done to drive her away.

As he grew older, he liked to think he'd had some part in how well his kid sister had turned out. He had worked two jobs to buy her the clothes she needed for school. After he joined the army, he'd sent money for city college, where she took classes in police science and finally landed the spot she so badly wanted on the force. Katie had been well respected in the department, intelligent and competent, a young woman dedicated to her job.

Officer Kate Riggs had been part of the police family, and with her death in the line of duty, forever would be.

Which made him family, too.

Sort of.

His Mustang sat at the curb. Johnnie slid behind the

wheel and fired up the engine. Sooner or later, he'd talk to Vega, who wasn't just a good cop but also a friend. In the meantime, he'd see what information he could pry out of Rachael's sister and her friend.

Amy's pretty face popped into his head, only she wasn't Amy, she was Angel, flaunting her beautiful, mostly naked body up onstage. He could remember every delicious curve, every swing of her perfect little ass.

Johnnie closed his eyes, forcing the image away. It wasn't Angel he was helping. It was Amy, a freakin' kindergarten teacher.

Johnnie cursed.

Chapter 6

Amy's cell phone rang. She ran over to the kitchen table, dug it out of her purse and pressed it against her ear. "Hello?"

"I'm on my way to the Sunset Deli. You know where it is?" Johnnie's husky voice made her stomach flutter.

"I know it. We eat there sometimes." It was on the opposite side of the street just half a block from the club.

"I'll meet you there in ten minutes. Bring your room-mate along and bring me a picture of your sister."

"Okay, we'll see you there." Amy ended the call and turned to Babs, who was finishing the last of her coffee.

"I take it that was Mr. Hot," Babs said.

Amy nodded. "He wants us to meet him at the Sunset Deli." Amy picked up her sister's acting portfolio, a book of photos Rachael used to take to auditions. "Let's go."

Babs took a last swallow of coffee, set her empty mug down on the kitchen counter and grabbed her purse. Amy slung the strap of her white leather bag over her shoulder and they headed for the door. She still had on the white jeans she'd worn that morning, but had changed out of her sneakers into strappy high-heeled sandals, and a pink silk blouse that tied up in front, showing her midriff. Kyle would be expecting an exotic dancer. She had to look at least a little like one.

It didn't take long to reach the deli, a place they occasionally went for lunch. As they made their way between the tables, Johnnie stood waiting at the back of the room. She could feel his eyes on her, dark and intense, taking in every curve, and her stomach did that same nervous flutter. He pulled out a couple of chairs around the wooden table and she sat down, setting the portfolio in front of her.

Amy tried for a smile, thought about what had happened between them last night, and her face heated up. She fixed her attention on Babs. "This is my friend Barbara McClure. As I said, Babs was Rachael's friend and roommate."

"Hello, Johnnie." Babs flashed him a bright white smile.

Johnnie just nodded. "Babs." Pulling out another chair, he sat down himself. "If we're going to do this, I'm going to need as much information as I can get. You ready for that?"

Both of them nodded.

"Good, then we might as well get started."

Like a lot of places on Sunset, the deli had been there for years. The wooden floors were old and warped, the tables battered and scarred. Cured salami and loaves of

crusty bread hung on the walls, and the smell of roast-
ing meat and baking bread filled the air.

As Johnnie reached over and pulled the photo album
toward him, a waitress in a dark green apron with Sunset Deli stamped on the front appeared to take their
orders: a bagel and cream cheese for Babs, pastrami
and rye for Johnnie. Amy ordered coffee with cream.
No way could she possibly eat with John Riggs sitting
across from her with his biceps bulging, a tight black
T-shirt stretched over his massive chest, reminding her
what she had missed out on last night.

"You're not hungry?" he asked.

Amy shook her head. "I had a little something earlier."

He cast her a glance that said he wasn't convinced.
"Let's start at the beginning." His intense gaze held
hers. "First off, as long as you're in this, you're Angel.
Amy Brewer is still in Michigan as far as this investigation goes. You want answers, you've got a helluva
better chance of getting them if you're Angel Fontaine,
not Rachael's sister. Just an acquaintance. The thing is,
I don't want anyone finding out you're playing detective. All you'll do is piss someone off, and if it happens
to be the guy who…had something to do with her disappearance, you could be next. You got it?"

"All right."

"I'll need one of these photos."

"Take whatever you need," she said as he opened
the portfolio. "I had some extras made."

He slid a four-by-six glossy out of the plastic sleeve,
the photo of a beautiful girl with shoulder-length mink-
brown hair and pale green eyes. The angle of her head
gave her smile a hint of mischief.

"Pretty girl," Johnnie said, examining the picture.

Amy felt a tightening in her chest. "Rachael's beautiful. She was homecoming queen in high school. She always had her pick of the boys."

Johnnie studied the photo as if he were trying to see deeper than the pretty smile and glossy dark hair. "How long since you last saw her?"

"Not since my dad's funeral. About three years. Rachael's twenty-eight. She left Grand Rapids when she turned twenty-one, right after she finished city college. She came back to visit a couple of times, but it always ended in a fight with Mom. Rachael was smart. My parents wanted her to finish her education, but all Rachael wanted was to be onstage. She got the lead in a couple of high school plays, then did some local theater, and that was it. She believed she had found her calling. She was determined to become an actress."

"Well, she was onstage," Babs drawled, "but the Kitty Cat Club isn't exactly what your sister had in mind."

Johnnie's mouth edged up, then he returned his attention to Amy. "How about phone calls, email, that kind of thing?"

"We talked on the phone a few times a year, but it was mostly about superficial stuff. I didn't know she was working as a...a dancer until I talked to Babs. There's a computer in the office downstairs. The girls use it for email. She said she had a job as a cocktail waitress. I guess that was kind of the truth."

"What about boyfriends?"

"She never mentioned anyone special. She never talked to me about her boyfriends or anything like that and I never talked to her about mine."

Johnnie sliced her a glance. "You got a guy back home?"

There was more to the question than it seemed; she could see it in his eyes. Amy shook her head. "We broke up a couple of years ago. I'm not seeing anyone now."

Johnnie seemed to relax. "Any other family members out here?"

"No, just me, and I've only been here the past couple of weeks."

"How about friends of hers from the past? People she knew back home?"

Amy shook her head.

"Anything about her you can think of that might help me find her?"

"I don't know...we drifted so far apart over the years." Amy smiled sadly. "Rachael could really sing... A voice like a songbird, you know? Only she wasn't interested in a singing career. She wanted to be a serious actress."

Johnnie was making mental notes, she could tell. "Anything else?" he asked.

"Only that she wasn't the type to just go away and not tell anyone."

"I'm sure you believe that, honey, but as you said, you don't really know your sister that well—not anymore."

It was true. Sadly. She should have come out to California sooner, tried to rebuild the close relationship they had once shared.

The waitress arrived with their food, her coffee and two glasses of iced tea. Johnnie stuck the photo into his back pocket, picked up his pastrami sandwich and dug in. Babs slathered her toasted bagel with cream cheese

and jelly, tore off a bite and began to nibble. Amy added
a little cream to her coffee and managed to take a sip.

"Who've you been talking to in the department?"
Johnnie asked around a mouthful of pastrami and rye.

"A woman detective, Lieutenant Carla Meeks. I talk
to her pretty much every day. She says they haven't
come up with anything new."

"Sometimes making a pest of yourself works. Sometimes it's just a distraction."

She glanced down at the table. "I know."

Johnnie turned to Babs. "What did Rachael do before she started working at the Kitty Cat Club?"

"She was a waitress down at Milt's Coffee Shop. But
working at the club paid a lot better, and she wanted to
save some money."

"What for?"

"I think she was hoping she'd get an acting job and
if she did, she wanted to have enough put away to get
a place of her own. I know she did casting calls whenever she got the chance. As far as I know, not much
ever came of it."

"She dating anyone you know of—besides Kyle Bennett, I mean?"

"I knew about Bennett, but she was only seeing him
because she thought he might help her get a break. I
know she and her mother never got along. I think she
wanted to prove something to her."

That was probably true, Amy thought with a pang.
Rachael had desperately wanted her parents' approval,
but it never came. After their dad's funeral, the split
with her mother had only gotten worse.

"What about Bennett?" Johnnie asked.

"I told her he wasn't for real," Babs said, "but Rachael had a lot of ambition. She did what she thought she needed to do."

"So she was sleeping with him."

"I'm not really sure. I think she might have been playing him the same way he was trying to play her. The month before she disappeared, she kind of clammed up, you know? I figured she was seeing someone else, but she wouldn't talk about it. She only went out with Kyle a handful of times. She rarely mentioned where she was going or who she was going out with."

"Any problems with any of the customers? Anyone she blew off who might have had a grudge?"

Babs shook her head, her dark, chin-length hair sliding around her cheeks. "Rachael kind of kept to herself. She and I were pretty good friends, but she didn't tell me everything. She was popular with the customers. Her stage name was Silky Summers. Everyone called her Silk."

Babs had told Amy that. Still, hearing it now made her see her sister in a way she hadn't before, as a woman who did exotic dances for a living, someone who could be made to disappear without much trouble and never be seen again. A trickle of unease slipped through her, reminding her that she was doing the very same thing.

Johnnie finished his sandwich, devouring it with manly enthusiasm and finishing the last of his fries. He waited impatiently while Babs finished her bagel, then shoved back his chair and came to his feet.

"We need to get going. Time's slipping away and Amy and I have a few things to work out before she meets Bennett."

Her stomach sharply contracted. She glanced down at the pink-and-silver watch on her wrist. It was only costume jewelry but it was pretty, a birthday gift from Rachael last year. "I'm ready whenever you are."

The women stood up from the table while Johnnie took care of the bill, then he walked them out the door. As they stood on the sidewalk, Babs dug her car keys out of her purse. A little metal palm tree dangled from the end.

She handed the keys to Amy. "Be careful. I don't have any insurance."

"Jesus." Johnnie shook his head and raked a hand through his short, dark hair.

Amy's fingers tightened around the keys. She drove a little Honda back home and it was insured. Hopefully, that would cover any problems but she wasn't really sure. "I'll be careful."

Babs waved and started walking back to the club, and Johnnie led Amy toward his car, parked in the lot next to the deli. He pressed his key to unlock the Mustang then opened the door. "Get in."

Amy slipped into the passenger seat and Johnnie rounded the car and slid in on the driver's side. Reaching across her, he opened the glove box and pulled out a padded envelope. He tipped it over and a silver, heart-shaped locket fell into his big hand.

"I want you to wear this. There's a microphone inside. I'll be able to hear everything you say and whatever's going on inside the house. If you get in trouble, just sing out."

Amy glanced up. "You're going to Bennett's house with me?"

One of his dark eyebrows went up. "You thought I was going to let you go into that creep's place on your own? I told you that wasn't going to happen last night."

"Yes, but—"

"I drove by there this morning. Expensive area, plenty of parking on the street. I won't be far away if you get into trouble."

The nerves returned. "Surely you don't think…think he'd…he'd do anything to hurt me?"

"You never know with a weasel like that. Just remember I'll be close enough to hear what's going on." Johnnie swung the locket over her head and fastened the catch on the silver chain. Just the brush of his fingers against the back of her neck sent goose bumps over her skin.

She glanced in the mirror. "My earrings are gold. They don't match."

"Take them off," he said.

Amy unfastened the small gold hoops and stuck them into her purse. She reached up and fingered the locket. "You have no idea how grateful I am for this."

The edge of his mouth faintly curved. "Don't worry, when the time comes, you can show me just how grateful you are."

A little curl of heat settled low in her stomach. He hadn't forgotten about last night.

Amy tried not to be glad.

Chapter 7

She had driven Babs's beat-up blue Chevy a few times before, just little jaunts to the store or the drive-through for some snack they wanted. Driving the car to Kyle Bennett's house was a far different thing.

Amy took a deep breath and stuck the key into the ignition, the metal palm tree key chain clanking against the dash. She put the car in gear, pulled onto Sunset and drove west toward Bel Air.

During their brief phone conversation yesterday, Kyle had given her directions to his house. Following Sunset, a tight four-lane with everyone going too fast, she eventually reached Stone Canyon Road, turned right, then made a left onto Bellagio and continued up the winding streets until she came to the address he had given her. Every once in a while, she caught a glimpse of Johnnie's black Mustang in her rearview mirror, and knowing he was back there kept her from turning the Chevy around and speeding back down the hill.

She wouldn't, she knew. Though her nerves were tingling and her stomach felt like a ball of snakes. She was committed to finding Rachael, no matter what it took.

Amy slowed, checked the address stenciled on the curb in front of the house and pulled the car over. The residence, a single-story Spanish-style home, was nice but not pretentious, the kind of house she might have expected his parents to live in instead of Kyle.

Turning off the engine, she sat for a moment collecting herself, then grabbed her bag, opened the door and climbed out of the car. The place was well kept, the plants and shrubs along the brick walkway leading up to the house neatly pruned and watered.

She took a quick glance behind her but saw no sign of Johnnie. He would be parked around the corner out of sight, she figured. At least he was out there somewhere.

"I'm walking toward the front steps," she said into the mic hidden inside the locket, figuring she was still far enough from the windows no one would see her talking to herself. She steadied her nerves as she pushed the doorbell and heard it chime somewhere inside.

It didn't take long for the door to swing open. A smiling Kyle Bennett stood in the doorway.

"Come on in." He was dressed in designer jeans, loafers and a yellow Izod knit shirt, his sandy hair neatly combed. He was casually GQ, exactly what she had expected.

Amy walked into the Spanish tiled entry noticing a heavy wooden chandelier overhead, and Kyle closed the arched front door.

He surveyed her head to foot. "You look just as good in clothes as you do out of them. That's definitely a plus."

She swallowed, not happy with the reminder he had seen her all but naked. "Is…is everything ready for the screen test?"

"My camera guy is running a little late, but he'll be here soon. Why don't we go into the studio and I'll fix us something to drink?"

She let him guide her through the house into what looked like his study, done in dark wood paneling with a wide, ornately carved oak desk, and a dark brown leather sofa and chair. A camera on a tripod pointed toward the sofa, apparently where Bennett planned to film the audition.

"Have a seat," he said.

She sat down on the couch, nervously smoothed her palms over her white jeans.

"What would you like to drink? Glass of white wine, maybe, or something stronger? How 'bout I make you a cosmo?"

Amy shook her head. "A Diet Coke would be good… if it isn't too much trouble."

"No trouble. I just figured you might want something to help you relax in front of the camera."

"I think…think I'd do better if I wasn't drinking anything alcoholic."

His smile looked more feral than friendly. "How about some orange juice? It's pretty much all I've got."

"That would be great."

He walked over to the bar in the corner and began fixing their drinks. A blender sat on the back bar next to a row of mixes, and a pink silk geranium in a small woven basket. A couple of padded leather stools sat in front of the bar.

Kyle returned with their drinks, handed her the orange juice and sat down on the sofa beside her. He lifted his glass. "Here's to a great test today."

Amy lifted her glass and he clinked his against hers. She took a swallow and then another, hoping it would help calm her nerves. "You know, a friend of mine came here for a screen test," she said, easing into the subject of her sister.

One of his sandy eyebrows went up. "That right?"

"Silky Summers. She worked at the club before I started."

"Oh, sure, I knew Silk. I tried to help her." He shook his head. "It was sad, really. Silk had big dreams, but I'm afraid she didn't have much talent."

"Is that right?" Amy thought that was probably a lie. Rachael was good at most everything. "She always wanted to be an actress."

"They all do, sweetheart. But most of them just can't cut it." He smiled. "Not like you. I've got a good feeling about you, Angel. I've got a hunch you're going to show real promise."

She took another sip of juice, buying herself some time. "I wonder what happened to her? Silky, I mean. You haven't heard from her, have you?" She yawned behind her hand, feeling a little tired, and wished she had slept better. "I mean, she thought you could get her into show business. I figured she would try to stay in touch with you."

He shrugged his shoulders, which were slim and made her think of Johnnie's thick shouldered, muscular build.

"Haven't heard a word," he said. "The police asked me about her, you know. I told them I hadn't seen her for a couple of weeks before she disappeared."

"She didn't say anything, then…? About where she was going?" She felt like yawning again, but managed to resist.

Kyle leaned in closely. "What's your interest in Silk?"

Amy tried to shrug, but her shoulders barely moved. "She owed me some money. I'd like to…get it back."

He relaxed at that. "Stick with me, kiddo, you'll make plenty of money."

She looked up at him and tried to smile, but her eyelids felt heavy.

"Now that I think of it," Kyle said, "she did go out with a guy I knew. Kenny Reason. He's a DJ down at The Rembrandt Club. I introduced them. Maybe Kenny'll know where you can find her."

Amy blinked up at him owlishly. "Thanks." The more she stared, the fuzzier his features became. She started frowning. "I don't know what's…what's the matter with me but… I'm starting…starting to feel really funny."

Kyle smiled kindly. "You're probably just nervous. Why don't you lie down for a few minutes? I'll wake you up when my camera guy gets here."

She didn't want to lie down, but her mouth wouldn't move to form a protest. Instead, she let him help her to her feet and the next thing she knew, she was leaning against him, letting him guide her down the hall. She caught a glimpse of a big king-size bed, realized in her foggy brain that something was terribly wrong.

"Johnnie…" she whispered, and prayed he could hear her as the world went suddenly black.

"Son of a bitch!" Johnnie was out of the car and charging down the sidewalk. He raced across Bennett's front yard, darted around the corner into the side yard, ran toward the rear of the house and up the back porch steps where he could break in without being seen.

The door was an older style with a curtained window. He pulled his Beretta from where he'd stuffed it into the back of his jeans, used the barrel to break the glass pane and reached inside to turn the lock. No alarm went off as he opened the door. He kicked his way through the shattered glass on the Spanish tile floor and rushed toward the bedroom, figuring that was the mostly likely place Bennett would have taken her.

The minute Amy had begun to slur her words, he knew what was happening, knew the weasely little bastard had loaded her drink.

The door at the end of the hall was closed. He paused when he reached it. Hearing Bennett's voice in a one-sided conversation, he clamped down on the rage swelling inside him, turned the knob but found it locked. He raised his heavy boot and kicked the door open.

He aimed the pistol at Bennett. "Move, you little prick, and I swear I'll blow your head off."

Leaning over the bed, Kyle froze. Johnnie's gaze shifted to Amy, who lay on her back on top of the mattress, completely unconscious. Bennett had unbuttoned her pink blouse, giving him a view of the plump cleavage above her push-up bra. He'd unzipped her white jeans, but that was as far as he'd gotten.

"Move away from her. Now."

Bennett held up his hands as if they could stop a bullet and backed away from the bed. Just beyond it, the closet doors were folded open, revealing a wall filled with kinky sex toys: padded handcuffs, a leather headdress, a roll of duct tape, and every shape and size of dildo imaginable.

The rage returned, so thick and hot he could barely see. His finger itched where it curled against the trigger.

"Who are you?" Bennett demanded, but his voice shook. "What are you doing in my house?"

Johnnie lowered the pistol, shoved it into his pants behind his back. He moved into the room, over toward the bed. "Rape's against the law, buddy, or hadn't you heard?"

Bennett kept his hands in the air, trying to ward off the anger rippling toward him in waves.

"Take it easy, okay? This isn't what it looks like. Angel came over here on her own. We were just having a little fun."

"That so?" He looked down at Amy and felt a pinch in his chest. Now that she was there, he couldn't call the police. For chrissake, the lady was a goddamn kindergarten teacher. The last thing she needed was a sex scandal. Whatever kind of roofie Bennett had given her would knock her out for eight to twelve hours. He needed to get her out of there.

His gaze shifted back to Bennett and his rage boiled back to the surface. If Amy had come on her own, Bennett would have raped her. It took every ounce of his will to not beat the guy into a bloody pulp. Instead, he strode to where Bennett cowered against the wall, grabbed his shirt and started dragging him toward the closet.

"What are you doing?" Bennett's weak struggles were almost funny. "Get away from me. Leave me alone!"

"I'll leave you alone, you freak." Johnnie reached for the padded handcuffs hanging on a peg on the back wall of the closet, clamped them onto Bennett's slim wrists, then lifted him up and draped the chain linking the cuffs together over a peg on the wall.

Bennett hung like a landed fish. "You can't do this!"

"Yeah?" Reaching into his boot, Johnnie pulled out his Ranger knife and flipped it open. Bennett's eyes turned into watery, frightened orbs as Johnnie held up the gleaming six-inch, serrated blade.

"Oh, God. Don't hurt me! Let me go!"

"Not likely."

Bennett closed his eyes as Johnnie started cutting off his clothes. It took only minutes to have the bastard naked except for his socks and shoes. Johnnie reached up for one of the dildos. He knew where he'd like to shove it, but then again, Bennett might like it.

Instead, he stuck it into the man's mouth, tore off a strip of duct tape and slapped it over the end to hold it in place. Satisfied Bennett wouldn't choke to death or have trouble breathing, he grinned.

"The cops are gonna have a real laugh when they come to your rescue, buddy."

Turning toward the bed, he reached down and fastened the buttons on Amy's blouse, zipped her jeans and lifted her into his arms.

"Come on, baby. Let's get you out of here."

He flashed a last ruthless smile toward Kyle Bennett. "Have fun—*kiddo*."

Closing the door behind him, Amy snuggled against

his chest, Johnnie carried her down the hall. Knowing a woman's most valuable possession was her purse, he ducked into Kyle's office, grabbed her small white bag, and left the house.

He was taking the little dancer home with him where once again, he wouldn't be able to touch her.

God had an amazing sense of humor.

Johnnie glanced at his heavy chrome wristwatch for the twentieth time. Ten hours. Amy had been out like a light for ten freakin' hours. He wanted to go back and tear Kyle Bennett's head off. The guy deserved a far worse punishment than he'd gotten. Johnnie would have been happy to rip him apart limb by limb if the little pervert hadn't been so puny.

Instead, after he had brought Amy back to his house, he had used one of the disposable phones he kept on hand to call the police. He had given them Bennett's address and told them a man was in trouble and needed their help. He couldn't help grinning when he thought of the look on the officers' faces when they found Bennett naked and trussed up like a pig with his own kinky toys.

He'd been tempted to call Vega, let him in on the fun, but he had more important work for his friend. He needed to talk to Rick in person. He wanted answers to his questions about Rachael and he had a better shot at getting them face-to-face.

In the meantime, he was keeping close tabs on Amy, regularly checking her pulse and breathing, making sure there weren't any unforeseen complications aside from the powerful hangover she was going to have when she woke up.

He opened the bedroom door and looked down at her lying on his bed. He had imagined her there a dozen times but not like this. Johnnie sighed. He hadn't taken off her clothes. Though she'd been dancing nearly naked in front of a roomful of men, he had a hunch she would prefer to keep her clothes on, no matter how uncomfortable they might be. She was still sleeping soundly, he saw, her long blond hair spread around his pillow like a sleek gold curtain. He had taken off her high heels and tossed a blanket over her bare feet.

He started to close the door and return to the living room when he saw her stir.

Slowly, Amy opened her eyes. It seemed to take Herculean effort. When she moved, her body ached all over. She felt groggy and disoriented, her brain mushy and her stomach queasy. She must have been sleeping the sleep of the dead. Her gaze surveyed the bedroom: white walls, black bedside tables with silver lamps on top. A black dresser with silver handles. There were photos of motorcycles and fast cars on the walls. None of it looked familiar.

With a panicky gasp, Amy jerked back the blanket that covered her, her last memory one of Kyle Bennett leading her down the hall to his bedroom.

"Easy, baby. You're safe. Everything's all right." Johnnie's deep voice washed over her from a few feet away and her fear began to recede. She saw him, then, big, dark and menacing, standing at the side of the bed.

"Where am I?"

"My house. I brought you here after Bennett drugged you."

"Oh, my God!" She shoved herself to an upright position and pain slammed into her head.

"Take it easy." Johnnie reached out and eased her back down on the mattress. "You've been out for nearly ten hours. You need to take it slow."

"What…what happened?" She looked down, saw she was wearing her clothes. "He didn't…didn't…?"

"He didn't have time to do much of anything. I was there, remember? Bennett put a roofie—that's a date-rape drug—in your drink. I came in just a few minutes after he took you into his bedroom."

She closed her eyes, trying to replay the scene, but her memory was completely blank. Still, Johnnie had been there, so nothing terrible had happened. She felt a sweep of relief.

"What happened to Kyle? Did you call the police? Oh, my God, I could lose my teaching job."

"You could lose your job if someone back home finds out you've been working at the Kitty Cat Club. But you don't have to worry. I handled Bennett myself and no one knows you were ever there."

She glanced at the biceps bulging beneath his T-shirt, thought of what might have happened if one of those powerful arms had connected with Bennett's face, and her eyes widened. "What…what did you do to him?"

Johnnie grunted. "Nothing permanent—unfortunately. But the police found him naked and handcuffed in a bedroom full of kinky sex toys, so I don't think you'll be seeing him at the club for a while."

Kinky sex toys? Her stomach rolled. If Johnnie hadn't gone with her, Kyle would have been using them on her while she had been unconscious.

"I need to get up," she said, feeling suddenly sick. "I have to use the bathroom."

Johnnie reached down and took her arm, helped her sit up and swing her legs to the side of the bed, but the minute she tried to stand, nausea hit her.

"Oh, God." Clamping a hand over her mouth, she bolted for the bathroom, bent over and threw up what little there was in her stomach. Her hands were shaking as she flushed the toilet. She washed her hands, then cupped water in her palm and rinsed her mouth. In the mirror above the sink, she saw Johnnie standing behind her in the open doorway. He pulled a washcloth off the towel rack and handed it over.

"Wash your face. You'll feel better."

Amy took the cloth from his hand, waited until he stepped back, and then closed the door. The last thing she wanted was for John Riggs to see her being sick.

Fortunately, the cool cloth helped. By the time she came out of the bathroom, she felt a little better. Johnnie was waiting, one thick shoulder propped against the wall a few feet away.

He shoved off and came toward her. "You're getting a little color back in your face. Feeling any better?"

She nodded, but sank back down on the edge of the bed. "If you hadn't been with me, Kyle would have raped me." She looked up as another thought struck. "Do you think he did that to Rachael?"

"Babs said Rachael dated him a few times. Your sister had been working at the club for a couple of years. She was probably too savvy to fall for Bennett's tricks."

"Unlike me," Amy said glumly.

"You're a schoolteacher, honey. You've never been around guys like that. At least you found out what you're up against. You can let me handle things from here and—"

"Wait a minute!" She shot up off the bed, felt a jolt of pain in her head and sank back down. "You don't think this changes anything? I'm finding my sister, Johnnie. I'm not letting some weirdo like Kyle Bennett keep that from happening."

"Listen to me, Amy. You're in way over your head with this. What happened today should have shown you that."

She bit her lip. "Maybe Bennett killed her. Maybe he drugged her and something went wrong. Maybe she died and he had to get rid of her body." Imagining her sister dead, she felt a sweep of pain mixed with anger. Amy steeled herself against it. "It's possible, isn't it?"

"Anything's possible. Look, I've got a friend in the homicide department, Detective Vega. I'm hoping he'll let me take a look at your sister's missing persons file. I'll find out what the police know about Bennett's involvement with Rachael, and find out who else they might be looking at in regard to her disappearance."

She nodded, careful not to move too fast. "All right, that sounds like a good idea."

"I probably shouldn't encourage you, but if it makes you feel better, you got a name from Bennett before you passed out."

"I did?"

"Kenny Reason. He's a disc jockey over at Rembrandt's."

"Rembrandt's? I don't think I've heard of it."

"It's a nightclub, not a strip joint, fairly upscale clientele. Bennett said your sister dated Kenny for a while."

Against the Night

"She must not have mentioned it to Babs. Maybe Mr. Reason will know something that will help."

"Maybe." Johnnie glanced down at his watch. "It's getting late. If you're feeling well enough, I'll take you home. If you'd rather, you can spend the night in my guest room."

Amy shook her head. "I need to go home."

Johnnie didn't argue. This was one time sex didn't seem to be on either of their minds. Spotting her purse on the dresser, she rose carefully from the bed, walked over and picked it up. "Whenever you're ready." She slung the purse strap over her shoulder. "I really appreciate what you did today. There's no way I can ever thank you enough."

A hot gleam appeared in his eyes. "Our business isn't finished. The next time you're in my bed, honey, I promise you won't be sleeping."

Chapter 8

Johnnie called Rick Vega first thing Friday morning and the detective agreed to meet him at the station. As she had the day before, Gwen Michaels sat behind the front desk. When she spotted Johnnie walking toward her, she smiled.

"Vega is expecting you," Gwen said. "You know where to find him."

"Thanks, Gwen." Heading down the hall, he waved to a couple of beat cops he knew, turned the corner and pushed through the doors of the detective bureau. The place was well lit, lined with rows of desks, each with its own computer, and always humming with activity as cops came and went. Rick motioned him over and Johnnie sauntered in his friend's direction, then sat down in the chair beside the desk.

"Heard you were in here looking for me yesterday.

I meant to call, but things got crazy." Vega was handsome as sin, about the same height as Johnnie, with gleaming black hair slicked back from his face and smooth dark skin, a bachelor who spent too much of his paycheck on the perfectly tailored suits he liked to wear.

"Not a problem."

"Must be important if you're back again today."

"I need a favor, Rick."

Vega scoffed. "So what's new?"

Before he'd been promoted to detective in the homicide division, Rick had been his sister Katie's partner, which was how he and Rick had become such good friends.

"I need to take a look at a file. Girl reported missing a little over six weeks ago. Name's Rachael Brewer. She worked over at the Kitty Cat Club."

Vega frowned. "Brewer... Brewer...that name sounds familiar."

"At the club, she used the name Silky Summers," Johnnie added.

Rick shoved up from his chair and walked over to speak to Mitch, a balding older guy, who after a departmental shake-up had just been reassigned as Vega's new partner. Mitch said something and Rick headed back to his desk, his strides long and confident, not a wrinkle in his perfectly pressed navy blue suit.

Though her death was not his fault, Vega had never forgiven himself for Katie getting killed that day in front of the bank. It was part of the reason the detective usually agreed to help him. Since Johnnie helped the police in return as much as he could, he didn't feel a damn bit bad about benefiting from Vega's guilt.

Rick sat back down and started typing on his keyboard, pulled up Rachael's missing persons file and pushed the print button.

"I could catch holy hell for this."

"They say anything, tell 'em I'm working on a lead. I'll let them know if it comes to anything."

"It's still against the rules." But Rick handed Johnnie the pages spitting out of the printer. There weren't all that many.

He studied the pages. "Brewer, Rachael Carolyn. Age twenty-eight. Five foot seven, one hundred-twenty pounds. Brown hair, green eyes. Employed two years as a dancer at the Kitty Cat Club, before that, a waitress at Milt's Coffee Shop. Reported missing May first of this year." Most of which he already knew. He skimmed down the page, shuffled through the next and the next. "Looks like the suits questioned Kyle Bennett."

Rick made a rude sound in his throat. "There's a real scumbag. She was scraping the bottom of the barrel if she was running with him." Rick started grinning. "Matter of fact, we got a call on Bennett yesterday. Uniforms found him naked in some kinky sex deal."

Johnnie grinned. "That so?"

Rick eyed him with suspicion. "You wouldn't know anything about that, would you?"

Johnnie's shoulders went up in an innocent shrug. "Who me?"

Rick shook his head. "I don't want to know."

Johnnie returned his attention to the pages in Rachael's file. "According to this, Bennett said he hadn't seen Rachael for at least two weeks before she disappeared. Says the info checked out."

The police had also interviewed the employees Rachael worked with at the club but had come up empty.

"Mentions a Realtor named Peter Brand. Doesn't say much, though, just that Brand knows Rachael through some charity he's involved with."

"Interesting."

"Looks like he has an alibi for the night she disappeared."

"Anything else?" Vega asked.

"Says here she and Honeybee didn't get along."

"Honeybee?"

"Redhead named Vicky Thomas, dancer at the club." Johnnie remembered talking to her when he was hunting Ray Carroll, the skip he'd returned to Texas. "I'll take another look at her." He studied the words on the page. "Rachael's car is also missing. Blue, 1998 Toyota Corolla. Haven't found a trace of it."

"Maybe she took off with a boyfriend."

"Maybe, but they didn't find her cell phone, and according to this, no calls were made from her number after she went missing. No new credit card charges, either."

"Not good. If she'd just left town, she'd have taken her phone and cards and probably still be using them."

Johnnie glanced down. "Had eighteen hundred dollars in her savings account. None of it's been withdrawn. Nothing useful on the email she posted from the office where she works."

"Listen, you need to talk to Carla Meeks," Rick said. "She's the detective assigned to Rachael's case. Maybe she can think of something that isn't in the file."

Amy had mentioned her. Johnnie knew her a little too well. He had broken his long-standing, no-cop-dating rule and hooked up with the good-looking lieutenant a couple of times, but they hadn't clicked as far as he was concerned. Unfortunately Carla hadn't felt the same way and she was beyond pissed when he stopped calling.

"I plan to," was all he said. He also wanted to talk to Kenny Reason, the DJ down at Rembrandt's. But it wasn't worth the department's time if it turned out to be nothing. "You run across anything, let me know, will you?"

Rick nodded. "Same goes."

Johnnie shuffled the file pages back together and stood up from his chair. "Keep an eye on Bennett. The guy's giving roofies to the girls he brings to his house."

"Shit."

Johnnie held up the pages as he started for the door. "Thanks, Rick."

"Good luck with it."

Johnnie left the department and headed to the downtown station on First Street that housed the missing persons unit, though he wasn't looking forward to his encounter with Carla Meeks, and he wasn't counting on getting much help from her, either.

Amy sat stiffly in the beauty chair at the Studio Salon, her head stuck under a dryer, hot air burning her scalp. After yesterday, she still felt a little out of sorts, but the last remnants of the roofie Bennett had given her had finally worn off and she was ready for her shift this afternoon.

She touched one of the curlers beneath the hood. When her hair finally dried, she'd have a head full of ringlets—bouncy little curls the beautician said would look "just darling." The curls wouldn't be permanent, thank God.

But she hadn't wanted her natural blond hair dyed and she didn't need it cut. Getting it curled was all she could think of as an excuse to talk to Sherry Mullins, Rachael's former beautician.

It wasn't until yesterday that she'd come up with the idea of questioning her sister's hairdresser, not until yesterday's fiasco with the pseudo movie producer. When that near-disaster had provided a clue—a lead, the police called it—she started trying to think outside the box, think who might have information about Rachael aside from the people who worked with her or were patrons of the club.

The timer went off, ringing a little bell. The dryer shut down and Sherry came over to get her. "Come on, let's see how you look."

Like an idiot, she was sure, but a good shampoo would solve the problem and put her hair back to normal. She followed Sherry across the salon and climbed up in the chair in front of the mirror. The shop wasn't fancy, the contemporary furniture a little worn, the photos of male and female models showing different hairstyles slightly dated. The pink silk flowers on the table were a little faded. The place wasn't fancy but the prices weren't fancy, either, which was the reason so many of the girls from the club came to the shop.

"So where were we?" Amy asked, hoping to return the conversation to the topic they had been discussing before she went under the dryer, which, of course, was her sister. She wished she could just tell Sherry who she really was, but she'd promised Johnnie. Sherry did the hair of half the girls from the club—news of Amy's true identity would be out within the hour.

The beautician just laughed. "Are you kidding?

These days, I can barely remember where I parked my car." She was only in her forties, but she was a smoker and she looked much older. Tiny wrinkles puckered around her mouth and the corners of her eyes, and her skin was rougher than it should have been.

"Oh, I remember," Amy said as if the memory had just returned. "We were talking about Rachael Brewer." Sherry, who had been doing Rachael's hair for years, knew her real name as well as the one she used onstage. "My roommate says Rachael's been missing for weeks. You don't think… You don't think someone might have *killed* her, do you?" She widened her eyes and put as much drama behind the words as she could manage.

She wasn't an actress; she left that to her sister. But she wanted the woman to be intrigued enough to keep talking. Maybe some new information would surface.

Sherry started pulling out curlers. Her shoulder-length hair was dyed a little too black and her eyebrows were plucked a little too thin, but she was friendly and well liked by her customers, and she had been nice to Amy.

"You never know anymore what can happen," Sherry said. "I know she was seeing a couple of different guys. Could be one of them got jealous."

Amy's stomach squeezed. She had posed a similar theory about Kyle Bennett.

"Did she happen to mention their names?" When Sherry began to look at her curiously, she added, "I wouldn't want to meet up with any of them at the club. I wouldn't feel safe."

Sherry dragged out a couple more curlers, tossed them into the sink. "She talked about someone named Danny. And a guy named Ken."

"Kenny Reason?"

"She didn't say. Rachael wasn't much of a gossip."
She took the last curler out of Amy's hair and ran her
hands through the now *curly* blond mass. "Maybe one
of them was giving her trouble so she just left town. I
sure hope nothin' real bad happened to her."

Amy made no reply. She was praying Sherry was
right and Rachael had simply left town. Maybe she'd
gotten into some kind of trouble and had to get away
before it got worse. Maybe she went into hiding somewhere until it was safe to return.

But Amy couldn't make herself believe it.

Johnnie called Lieutenant Meeks from his cell
phone. "I'm working on a case," he said, careful to
keep the conversation brief. "If you've got the time,
I'd like to talk to you about it."

"All right." Her reply was perfectly professional, but
he could hear the venom in her voice.

"I'm on my way." He ended the call, and half an hour
later, the lieutenant led him into one of the conference
rooms in the downtown police station and he sat down
at the table across from her. The multi-story building
on First Street was new, all sleek steel and glass, with
the most modern equipment.

Lieutenant Meeks, a member of the missing persons unit, part of the vice squad, sat down at the table
across from him.

"So what can I do for you, John?" She always called
him that, always kept a distance between them, even
when they'd been in bed.

"I'm looking into the Brewer case. I'm working for
her sister."

She scoffed. "Good luck with that." She was average height, with short brown, naturally wavy hair. She was a year older than he was, good-looking in a stiff, uptight kind of way, and she had curves in all the right places. "The woman's a real pain in the neck," Carla said.

He thought of the sexy little blond pain-in-the-neck he was helping and smiled slightly. "No doubt about it. She's determined to find Rachael. I'm trying to give her something new, something hopeful."

Carla looked him over, gave him a catty smile. "Pretty girl. I imagine you'll be able to give her what she needs."

He ignored the innuendo. "So what have you got I might be able to use?"

Carla sighed, her mind back on business. "Not much. The night Rachael Brewer disappeared, no one saw her leave the club. Her roommate figured she was spending the night with one of the guys she was dating, maybe got to drinking, didn't want to drive. But she'd been keeping to herself the past few weeks and the names we checked all had alibis."

"Kyle Bennett?"

"That's right. And a real estate agent named Peter Brand. He was attending a company function the night she disappeared."

"Nothing on her cell?" he asked, just to see what she'd say.

"Never found it or her car. No calls made from her number after she went missing."

"Anything else?"

"No, but there's something you can do for me. The sister gave us an address in Culver City. Turns out, it belongs to an actress friend of Rachael's but the sister isn't staying there. Her cell number's all we've got. Where is she?"

It wasn't exactly a secret. And Carla was a good cop. She'd understand the situation. "Amy took her sister's old job at the club. She's using the name Angel Fontaine. They don't know who she is and it would be better for her if it stayed that way."

Carla frowned. "She'd better be careful. If her sister was into something kinky, it might come down on her."

"That's what I've been telling her. Eventually, I'm hoping she'll quit. In the meantime, I'm keeping an eye on her."

Carla gave him a knowing half smile. "I'll just bet you are."

Chapter 9

On the way back to the club, Amy wandered along Sunset into a couple of trendy dress shops. The boutiques were designed for young women, the prices on the top edge of affordable. The clothes—lots of black leather and lace, short skirts and plenty of bare skin— were hardly her style, but it was fun to look.

A hot little number caught her eye. At home, she would have been embarrassed for anyone to catch her admiring it, but this was California. She was a different person here, freer, more open to new ideas. Eventually, she would go back to being the simple, conservative young woman she was before, but for now, for this one brief moment in time, she was Angel Fontaine and she could do anything she pleased.

She went home with the sexy black outfit tucked

in a Mitzy's Boutique shopping bag, wondering if she would ever wear it.

As she walked back into the club, she spotted Johnnie sitting at the bar, his intense gaze finding her all the way across the room. He looked dark and rugged and amazingly handsome, and her stomach lifted alarmingly.

This early in the afternoon, the club was mostly empty. It got busier as the sun went down. The Sunset Strip came alive at night.

Johnnie stood up as she approached and she felt a little dizzy at the sight of all that masculinity so nicely packaged in black jeans and a T-shirt.

Johnnie grinned. "Hey, Goldilocks."

She had almost forgotten her hair, forgotten that too much gel had turned her long, sleek strands into a riot of curls. She reached up and touched it, made a face at the springy texture.

"It'll wash out," she said glumly.

"I thought maybe you were going to change your act, bring in a couple of guys in bear suits."

"Very funny." She managed to climb up on a bar stool, though being so short, it wasn't easy. Johnny sat back down on the stool next to hers.

"How you feeling?"

"Normal again. Better than I should be feeling…considering." She looked across at Dante, who mopped the top of the bar in front of her with a clean white towel. "I could really use a Diet Coke…if you wouldn't mind."

"You got it, Angel." The handsome Latino grinned, then turned to Johnnie. "You wanna beer or something?"

"No thanks, I'm working."

Amy sighed. "So was I. That's what happened to my hair."

Johnnie reached out and slid a hand into her bouncy blond locks. "This, I gotta hear."

But Amy didn't reply. Transfixed by the feel of his fingers slipping through the heavy curls, she just sat there like a cat being stroked and wanting to purr. She felt his eyes on her, intense now, sensing her interest, the heat beginning to build between them. She wanted this man. Maybe it was time to do something about it. Maybe she should—

Dante set an icy glass of diet soda in front of her and walked away, and Johnnie's hand slid free of her hair.

Amy swallowed. "I…ummm…went to see Rachael's hairdresser. I wanted to see if maybe she'd heard some gossip or something that might help us. Getting my hair done was the only excuse I could think of to talk to her. The curls were her idea."

Johnnie chuckled. "Do any good?"

"Sherry—that's the stylist—said that Rachael was seeing a couple of different guys. One of them was named Ken. I figured Kenny Reason. The other man's name was Danny."

"*Danny.* No reference to a Danny in the police reports."

"You saw them?"

He nodded. "My sister, Katie, was a cop before she died. Her former partner is a friend of mine."

"You have…had a sister?"

He nodded. "She was killed during a bank robbery. She was a really great kid."

She reached over and caught his hand. "Oh, Johnnie, I'm so sorry." He ran his thumb over the back of her hand and a little tremor went through her.

"Katie always wanted to be a cop," he said. "She was doing the job she loved, but she was way too young to die. She deserved to have more time."

She let go of his hand, though she didn't really want to. "Your sister is gone and now so is mine. It isn't fair."

"There's still hope we'll find Rachael."

She took heart at that, managed to smile. "Yes, there is."

"Because of what happened to Katie, I get to call in a favor now and then. I got a look at Rachael's file and I talked to Lieutenant Meeks. She pretty much hates you, by the way."

Amy laughed. "I know I've been a nuisance. I figured the squeaky wheel and all that."

"Doesn't always work."

She took a sip of Diet Coke. "So what did Lieutenant Meeks tell you?"

"Not much. Mentioned a real estate agent named Peter Brand, but according to the report, he came up clean."

"Nothing else?"

He shook his head. "Unfortunately, I'm not exactly on the lieutenant's favorite persons list, either." At her inquisitive look, he held up a hand. "Don't ask."

Amy smiled. "You mean she didn't fall prey to all that Johnnie Riggs charm?"

He flashed a crooked grin. "You think I'm charming?"

"Maybe. I think you can be very sweet at times, even if you won't admit it."

"Sweet! You think I'm sweet?"

She laughed. "You were sweet last night. You came to my rescue. You took care of me when I was sick. If it hadn't been for you, I would have been in serious trouble."

"I'm not sweet. How do you know I didn't ravish you when you were at my mercy?"

Her smile returned. "I don't think that's your style."

Johnnie reached out and touched her cheek, just a featherlight brush of his fingers, yet goose bumps rose beneath her skin.

"You're right," he said. "I want you wide-awake when I take you. I want you to know exactly what I'm doing to you."

Amy couldn't breathe.

He reached up and playfully tugged on one of her curls. "In the meantime, no more detective work, okay?"

The curls bobbed as she firmly shook her head. "I'm not quitting. No way, no how."

Hearing his own words played back to him, Johnnie smiled.

"In the past two days," Amy continued, "I've found out more than I have in the past two weeks. I need to talk to Kenny Reason, and I need to find out who this Danny person is."

"I'll talk to Reason, see what he has to say."

"I want to go with you. He might say something that clicks with me, or I might think of something to ask him you wouldn't."

When he started shaking his head, she caught his arm. "You said Rembrandt's was a nightclub, an upscale place. If I'm with you, I won't be in any danger."

"I don't like it, Am—Angel."

"You said you'd help me."

"I'm doing my damnedest, honey."

"Please, Johnnie. I've got to do this. I owe it to Rachael." She looked up at him, trying to work her womanly wiles the way the other girls did. "Please..."

He sat there for several long moments, then gave up a sigh of defeat. "All right, damn it, you can go. But we need to keep moving on this. Can you get off early tonight?"

One of the girls had called in sick, so she was working a split shift. "I'm off at ten." She had to be back by midnight, but she didn't want him to have an excuse not to take her.

"All right, I'll pick you up and we'll go to Rembrandt's. Until then, try to stay out of trouble."

The afternoon was slipping away. Johnnie had a half dozen calls to make on cases he'd been working and paperwork to do back at his home office. Instead he sat next to Amy at the Kitty Cat bar.

"Listen, I need to talk to Honeybee. You know where I can find her?" He told himself he was still working, even if he wasn't getting paid for it.

The music shifted. The stage had been dark but now the lights came on for the next performance. The spotlight shined on a black-haired dancer named Ruby. Then a blonde the announcer introduced as Brittany, a new addition to the show, strutted onto the stage. The entertainment continued from opening to closing, but during the day, performances were farther apart.

"I'm not sure where Bee is," Amy said.

Babs walked up next to them just then, a tray balanced on her shoulder. "Bee's on a break. She's in the employees' lounge." She tipped her head toward Amy. "You can take him back. It's okay for a guy to go in there as long as he's with one of the girls."

Onstage, the music swelled and the show began. Johnnie barely noticed. He didn't give a whit about the naked women gyrating beneath the spotlights. He didn't get the clenching low in his groin that he felt when he watched Amy dancing as Angel.

That he felt just sitting beside her.

"Why do you need to see Bee?" Babs asked.

The question dragged his thoughts back to the moment. "She and Rachael had a fight. I want to know what about."

Amy looked up at Babs. "Did you know about that?"

Babs nodded.

"Why didn't you tell me?"

"I like Bee. She and Rachael didn't get along very well, but I don't believe Bee had anything to do with her disappearance and I didn't want to cause her any trouble."

"So you aren't the one who told the police about the fight," Johnnie said.

"No. Maybe Tate mentioned it."

"What was the fight about?" he asked.

Babs hesitated, then sighed. "Bee's got a kid, all right? Rachael thought she should see her little boy more often, but Bee's just not the kid type, you know? It's not her fault. It's just the way she is."

Amy's smile looked wistful. "My sister was always softhearted. When we were little, she brought home a constant stream of stray dogs, cats and injured birds. Kids and animals. Rachael loved them. We both did.

I always thought she would make a great mother. We both wanted that someday."

Johnnie glanced down at Amy. She was a teacher. Of course, she loved kids. She didn't belong in a place like the Kitty Cat Club.

"Take me back to the lounge," he said to her, torn between wishing he could find her sister and send her back home, and wishing he could just take her to bed.

Slipping down from the bar stool, she left her half-finished Diet Coke and led him toward the back of the club. He followed her into the employee lounge, which had a kitchenette along one wall, a coffeemaker on the counter and a couple of Formica-topped tables. Plastic chairs clustered around each one, and a dark blue, vinyl sofa with light gray throw pillows, the color scheme of the club, rested against the wall.

Honeybee sat at one of the tables, sipping thick black coffee out of a Styrofoam cup, the only person in the lounge.

He walked in her direction, paused a few feet away. "I'm John Riggs," he said. "We met last week. You helped me locate a guy named Ray Carroll."

The redhead gave him a slow, sexy smile, her green eyes lingering a little too long on the bulge beneath the zipper of his jeans.

"I remember you, honey. What can I do for you this time?"

Clearly she was offering more than information and Amy's pretty lips thinned, a good sign, he thought.

"What were you and Rachael Brewer fighting about?"

Bee didn't bother to deny it, just shrugged her shoulders. Dressed in the two-piece, blue satin costume the girls wore to serve drinks, she was at least five foot ten, with a mane of fiery-red hair that tumbled in wild disarray around her shoulders. She was a pretty woman, though the years she had spent in the business were beginning to show.

"Silk didn't approve of the way I was raising my kid," Bee said.

"That right?"

"Yeah, that's right. I don't have an old man, so Jimmy don't have a father. Silk thought I ought to do both jobs."

"How old is he?"

"Jimmy's almost four."

"So you fought with her over the boy? Did it come to physical blows?"

Bee just laughed. "Are you kidding? Silk tried to convince me I should see the kid more often. I told her if she thought he was so neglected, she could take my place and visit him herself."

"Which I'm betting she did," Amy added. "If Rachael thought someone needed mothering, she wouldn't have been able to resist."

"Yeah, she went to see him," Bee said. "Jimmy was crazy about her. He hasn't been the same since she left."

"Is that what you think happened?" Johnnie asked. "Rachael packed up and left?"

Bee fiddled with her cup, pressed a long red nail into the soft foam rim. "I don't think Silk would have left Jimmy without saying goodbye. She had all the motherly instincts I never had. I think something happened to her. Silk and me, we were never friends. We were just too different. But she was good to Jimmy and I wouldn't have wished anything bad on her."

The Styrofoam squeaked as Bee set the cup down on the table and stood up. "Look, I've got to go. I need to change and be onstage in fifteen minutes."

"Thanks, Bee," Johnnie said.

"Anytime, hon." Bee flicked Amy a dismissive glance, then strode out of the lounge.

Johnnie set a hand at Amy's waist, urging her to follow.

"She and I aren't best of friends, either," Amy said as they stood outside the door, "but I believe her. I don't think Bee had any part in my sister's disappearance."

"Rachael was concerned about Bee's son," Johnnie said. "Whatever she says, she's still a mother. I think she was grateful for Rachael's help. She had no reason to hurt her."

Amy's gaze went toward the stairs. "My shift starts in twenty minutes. I've got to wash my hair and get ready." Even in the low light backstage, he could see those big blue eyes looking up at him, and heat settled low in his groin.

Johnnie thought of her gorgeous little body in that tiny red G-string, dancing in front of a bar full of leering men, and his stomach knotted. He wanted to haul her out of there, demand she quit, tell her she didn't belong in a place like this. But he had no say over her.

Hell, he hadn't even taken her to bed. Instead, he was living in a constant state of arousal. It had to end and soon. Christ, he needed a woman. Unfortunately, now that he'd met Amy, no other woman would do.

He cleared his throat but his words still came out husky. "I'll see you at ten." Turning, he forced himself to walk away, trying not to wonder when he finally made love to her, how much of Amy would turn out to be Angel Fontaine.

Chapter 10

Going to Rembrandt's was bound to be interesting. Amy was glad she had purchased the sexy black dress from Mitzy's. The material was a soft knit with a lace midriff and a short, gently gathered skirt that clung to her curves. The lace top was cut low enough to show a little cleavage.

It was odd. She'd been dancing practically naked, but she felt sexier tonight in her short black dress and black spike heels.

Amy left the apartment and headed downstairs. Waiting at the bottom, Johnnie followed her descent, his intense brown eyes raking her from head to foot. "Nice dress."

Her cheeks warmed. It was amazing how he could do that. She looked down, smoothed the skirt a little. "Thanks."

He was wearing his usual black jeans, but he had thrown a cream-colored sport coat over his black T-shirt and exchanged his high-top boots for a pair of black loafers, John Riggs's idea of dressing up. He looked good. Really good.

He led her out of the club and over to his Mustang, helped her inside and closed the door. Sliding into the driver's seat, he fastened his seat belt, waited until she fastened hers, then cranked the powerful engine and eased the car out of the lot onto the street.

Sunset Boulevard was lined with cars. There was never a time it wasn't. Johnnie expertly wove the Mustang in and out of traffic, driving west down the Strip and beyond, through an area of elegant mansions that lined both sides of the road. It didn't take long to reach Rembrandt's, which was upstairs over a restaurant on Canton in Beverly Hills.

Johnnie pulled the car up to the valet parking attendant, handed the keys to a young man in a short white jacket, and a few minutes later, they were climbing the stairs to the club. They paused on the landing outside the door where a lean, good-looking African-American man collected the ten-dollar-per-person cover charge.

"Hey, man, good to see you," the bouncer said to Johnnie, reaching out to shake his hand.

"Good seeing you, too. What's up, T.J.?"

"Not much, man. Business is a little slow."

"Probably just the economy," Johnnie said. T.J. looked at Amy, then back at Johnnie, waiting for an introduction but it never came.

"I guess things are slow everywhere," T.J. said, accepting a twenty from a couple who walked up behind them, the man in a pair of skinny designer jeans, the girl in tight black pants and a leopard print top. They disappeared inside the club and T.J. returned his attention to Johnnie, who held up the photo of Rachael that Amy had given him.

"You ever see this girl?"

She was grinning, striking a cocky pose for the camera. Just seeing it made Amy's heart pinch.

T.J. nodded. "I seen her. She used to come in once in a while with a hot-looking brunette."

"Babs would have mentioned it," Amy said. "So it was probably Mary Lou Kammer. She's an actress friend of Rachael's."

Johnnie cast her a glance. "That the address you gave the police?"

"Yes, how did you know?"

He rolled his eyes, but didn't bother to answer. He was a private investigator, for heaven's sake. And he was no fool.

"The girl in the photo is Rachael Brewer," Johnnie said to T.J. "She went missing a few weeks back. She dated Kenny Reason for a while. What can you tell me about him?"

"Ken's all right. Not a big brain, but a straight shooter. I heard he was gay, but I don't really think so. I didn't know about him and the girl."

Johnnie pressed a folded up twenty into T.J.'s palm and handed him another for their admission. "Thanks, man."

Amy took Johnnie's arm as they walked into the club. "I'll pay you back," she said. "You're already working for free. I don't expect you to pay for information."

He flicked her a glance so sensual her toes curled

inside her spike heels. "I'm running a tab, baby. I plan to take it out in other ways."

Her breath caught. Amazing how that kind of payback could actually sound so good. And the more she was coming to know him, the more she understood that money had nothing to do with him helping her— or how much he wanted her.

The club throbbed with a deep, rhythmic beat. The interior was done in shades of burnt-orange and midnight-blue and the bar was long and curved and ultramodern.

Johnnie led her over to a quieter place in the shadows at the edge of the crowd where they could survey the room and get a good view of the glassed-in area where the DJ sat. Wearing headphones with a mic, he worked behind a bank of dials and levers, controlling the tunes he played and the volume, adjusting the blaze of lights that roamed over the dance floor.

"That's him," Johnnie said, tipping his head toward the man behind the glass. "That's Reason. He's got a website with his picture."

"He dresses nicely." Dark suit and burgundy shirt open at the throat. "But he isn't very good-looking. Then again, I guess you can't tell much about a person by the way he looks."

Johnnie's dark eyes took in the short skirt that showed off her legs and came to rest on the shadow between her breasts. "Not much. Take you, for example. You don't look much like a schoolteacher in that dress."

She toyed with the hem of her skirt, pleating the fabric between her fingers. "I won't be taking it with me when I go home, that's for sure. But here, things are different."

He grunted. "That's right, Dorothy—you ain't in Michigan anymore."

Amy laughed. "The thing is, since I came here, I've been finding out a lot about myself, things I didn't know."

"Such as?"

"Such as… I like it when men look at me the way you're looking at me now. I've never had that before."

His eyebrows went up. "You're kidding, right?"

"I'm afraid not. I was always so conservative. The clothes I wore, the way I wore my hair. The guys I dated saw me as a schoolteacher, first and last. I never really explored my sexuality."

"What else?" he softly urged.

"The thing is, when I'm onstage, I feel womanly. Powerful. Until I came to L.A., I never thought that much about sex. I never would have believed exotic dancing could make me feel so sensual, so—"

She gasped as Johnnie backed her up against the wall and took her mouth in a hot, demanding kiss. For an instant, she forgot to breathe. She could feel his erection pressing into her, thick and hot with need. The music throbbed and so did he. Amy wrapped her arms around his neck and kissed him back as hotly as he was kissing her.

Dear God, the way his lips moved over hers, taking what he wanted, letting her know that he could give her exactly what she needed. Her body tingled and her skin felt tight. His tongue slid into her mouth while his big hands moved down to cup her bottom and draw her more firmly against him.

Desire curled in her stomach. She was hot and wet.

If he hadn't stopped right then, she would have melted into a puddle at his feet.

"Easy," he whispered when he felt her trembling. Leaning down, he kissed the side of her neck, nipped an earlobe. "We're leaving," he said. "Now."

As he started tugging her to the door, it dawned on her they had been carrying on in a room full of people.

He led her a couple more steps before she pulled away. "Wait! Wait a minute, we can't just leave!"

He was breathing hard, staring at her with those hot brown eyes. "Why not?"

"We...we have to talk to Kenny. We have to find Rachael."

Muscle bunched in a jaw roughened by the shadow of a beard. He ran a hand over his face and took a deep breath. "I need a drink."

"You're working."

"That's why I need a drink." He led her up to the bar and ordered a cosmo for her, Jack on the rocks for himself. When the bartender delivered their drinks, he lifted the glass and downed the whiskey in a single gulp.

"Jesus, I want you," he said.

Amy trembled, her heart still thundering. Her mind remained foggy as she relived that incredible kiss. She forced the words past her tingling lips. "Rachael has to...has to come first."

With a thud, Johnnie set his empty shot glass down on the bar. The bartender cast him a glance, silently asking if he wanted another. Johnnie just shook his head.

"You're right," he said. "We'll finish this later."

Later? She inwardly groaned. Later she had to go

back to work. She had purposely not told him because she was afraid he wouldn't let her come along. Johnnie was going to kill her.

She remembered the way the muscles tightened on his chest, his heavy erection pressing against her, thought how much she wanted him to make love to her. *Maybe I'll just kill myself.*

Taking her hand, he led her around the edge of the dance floor toward the man in the booth. Walking up beside him, Johnnie pulled out his wallet and slid out a business card.

It read simply John Riggs. Private Investigation. The only other information was his cell phone number. Johnnie handed it over. Kenny Reason read the card, started another song, set the lighting to match the beat of the music, took off his headphones and stood up. The music was too loud for them to be able to hear so he led them a little ways away where they could talk over the noise.

"What can I do for you?" the DJ asked.

"We're looking for a girl named Rachael Brewer. You might know her as Silky Summers."

"I know Silk. She and her friend used to come in here together."

"You take her out?"

"A couple of times. It was no big deal, just coffee after closing."

"When was the last time you saw her?"

"I don't know. Been quite a while, well over a month."

"Silk went missing six weeks ago. You know about that?"

"I heard."

"You wouldn't know anything that might help us find her?"

"The police asked me about her, but no, I can't think of anything. We were just friends, you know? She wanted to get into show business. Her girlfriend worked fairly often, bit parts and commercials, nothing permanent. Sometimes some of the movie crowd comes into the club. I know a few people. I tried to help Silk but nothing ever came of it. I saw her dancing in here a couple of times after the last time we went for coffee, but I don't know who she was with."

The song was coming to a close, the hip hop dancers revved up and ready for the next tune. "Listen, I gotta go. I hope you find Silk. I liked her."

Amy felt a tug at her heart. Everyone liked Rachael. She thought of Bee, who had made her feelings clear. And of course there were a couple of girls back in high school who were jealous of Rachael's good looks. And Mick Swenson, the boy she jilted when she was a senior. Well, almost everyone.

One of Johnnie's big hands wrapped around her arm and he started for the door. "Come on, baby, time to go home."

She looked up at him. There was no mistaking which home he was talking about and what he meant to do when they got there.

She moistened her lips. "I can't go home with you, Johnnie. One of the girls called in sick and I have to work the second half of her shift."

He stopped and turned, his gaze dark and turbulent. "Let's get something straight. I told you from the start, I didn't expect any kind of payment, okay? If this thing between us isn't what I think it is—"

"No! That isn't it. I swear it!" To prove she wasn't just using him or being a tease, she went up on her toes and pressed her mouth against his. Neither of them moved. In an instant, the kiss turned hot then went to searing. Her tongue was in his mouth and his was in hers and she thought she was going to have an orgasm right there in the back of the nightclub.

Johnnie broke the kiss. "Jesus!" Breathing hard, he raked a hand through his hair. "If you had any idea how much I want you—" He took her hand, pressed it against the fly of his jeans. Amy's eyes widened. He was as hard as granite. "Honey, I don't know how much more of this I can take."

Grabbing her wrist, he tugged her toward the door, led her outside and down the stairs. At the curb, they waited until the valet brought up his car. The young man helped her inside while Johnnie tipped him, rounded the car, climbed in and slammed his door. He didn't say a word as the car roared through traffic, punching in and out with a skill she couldn't help but admire.

He was in a foul mood and she didn't blame him. Not only had they gotten no new information, he was going home alone.

Or maybe he wasn't. Her stomach tightened. A virile man like Johnnie Riggs didn't go long without a woman. She wondered if he would find someone else. She didn't want that, but as much as she wanted him to make love to her, she was afraid of what would happen once he did.

She knew the kind of guy he was, knew he wasn't a reliable, one-woman sort of man. While she was definitely a reliable, one-man sort of woman.

She rode in silence the rest of the way back to the club and Johnnie walked her to the back door. The beat of the music throbbed inside and his features darkened. He looked as if he wanted to say something, but in the end just shook his head.

"I'll call you tomorrow."

Amy nodded. Tomorrow she was going to see the woman who took care of Bee's little boy—assuming Babs would let her borrow the car. Rachael had been to see little Jimmy a number of times. Maybe the sitter had information they could use.

Her gaze swung to the brawny man crossing the parking lot. Just the way he moved turned her on, the confident strides, the way the muscles in his legs lengthened and tightened as he strode toward his car. She was wildly attracted to him. She had never desired a man the way she did John Riggs. Never even known she was capable of feeling such burning lust for a man.

She was going to have sex with him—wild, passionate, uninhibited sex as she had never experienced before.

She just had to figure out when.

Chapter 11

At ten o'clock the following morning, Amy pulled Babs's rusty, dented blue heap of a Chevy up in front of the Culver City address Bee had given to Babs. Being a practical sort, before she'd left the apartment, she had phoned Alliance Insurance back in Grand Rapids and asked if she was covered driving someone else's un-insured car. They had assured her she was. At least if she wrecked it, she'd be able to get it fixed.

She reread the tarnished brass numbers on the front of the house and turned off the motor, hoping it would start again. This morning, the engine hadn't wanted to turn over, but she had used a metal brush on the battery cables to remove the corrosion as her dad had taught her, cranked the engine and it had fired right up. So far it seemed to be running all right. Thank God it was

American-made instead of some foreign job, which would be totally Greek to her.

Unfastening her seat belt, she reached for the door handle just as her cell started ringing. She dug it out of her purse, checked the caller ID and recognized her mother's number.

Amy pressed the phone against her ear. "Hey, Mom."

"Hi, honey. I just wanted to check on you. When you didn't phone yesterday I got worried."

They talked every few days. Though her mom knew she was in L.A. looking for Rachael, she had no idea Amy had taken Rachael's exotic dancing job.

"Everything's fine, Mom. I've got someone helping me now, a private investigator. We've already got a few leads."

"I didn't think you could afford to hire someone."

"We've…ummm…kind of gotten to be friends." That was a big fat lie. The heat burning between them had nothing to do with friendship. "Anyway, he's working for free." Kind of. He'd said he was running a tab, which could mean any number of things. One possibility made her stomach flutter.

"So you haven't heard any news?" her mother always asked, though the answer was always the same.

"No, Mom, not yet. Listen, I've got to run. I'm talking to a woman who takes care of a little boy Rachael used to visit. Maybe she'll have some news."

"Your sister always loved children. Just like you. Call me if you find out anything."

"You know I will."

"I wish you'd just come home and let the police handle this. I couldn't stand it if something happened to you, too."

"I'm being careful, Mom. I promise."

"I love you, honey."

"Love you, too, Mom."

Amy hung up and leaned her head back against the headrest. Talking to her mother was always draining. She didn't want to lie but she couldn't possibly tell her the truth. And neither was she ready to give up and go home.

With a sigh, she reached for the door handle, then jumped and shrieked as the door jerked open and she nearly fell out of the car.

"What the hell are you doing here?" Johnnie stared down at her, his features dark and grim.

"I could ask the same question of you."

His scowl deepened. "I'm doing the job you aren't paying me to do."

"I just want to talk to her, okay? I phoned earlier. Mrs. Zimmer said I could come over."

"Fine. Let's go." He caught her arm and started hauling her out of the car. Amy grabbed her purse and the bag she'd brought along and started walking in front of him toward the pale yellow, single-story, wood-frame house. She crossed the porch and knocked on the door, and a few minutes later, a tall, thin woman with iron-gray hair pulled it open.

"Mrs. Zimmer?"

"That's right." The lady smiled. "You must be Angel."

She hadn't told the sitter she was Rachael's sister. She was still playing a part and the fewer people who knew the truth the better. She glanced at Johnnie and saw a dark look of warning. She was Angel until all of this was over.

"That's right, and this is John Riggs, another friend of Rachael's."

He flicked Amy a sideways glance and pasted on a smile that fortunately looked sincere. "Thank you for seeing us, Mrs. Zimmer."

"Please come in." The woman stepped back out of the way and they walked into the living room. It had olive-green shag carpet, and a brown-and-olive-plaid, overstuffed sofa and chair, old but serviceable.

"I'm sorry about your friend," Mrs. Zimmer said. "I liked Rachael very much and Jimmy adored her. I hope you find her and everything turns out all right."

"That's what we're all hoping," Amy said.

"Would either of you like a cup of tea?" the older woman asked, giving Johnnie a quick once-over. The olive drab T-shirt he wore had U.S. Army Rangers stamped on the front. It nearly matched the carpet. Though he had shaved, a faint shadow already darkened his jaw.

Amy smiled. "It's nice of you to ask, but no thank you."

The woman turned to Johnnie, who looked like the ex-soldier he was, until he smiled at her sweetly and shook his head. "We're fine."

A noise came from the hallway. An instant later, the sound of a little boy zooming his miniature Tonka truck into the living room drew their attention. He raced it right up to Mrs. Zimmer's sturdy brown leather shoes.

"Jimmy, these are friends of Rachael's," the woman said, stepping a little away. "Mr. Riggs and Ms. Fontaine."

Jimmy's features turned solemn. He had his mother's red hair and pale, lightly freckled skin. At not quite four years old he was tall for his age. He slowly came to his feet. "Is Rachael coming back?"

Amy knelt in front of him, putting herself at eye level. "I don't know, sweetheart. Maybe she will."

"Why did she go away? I really miss her."

"I miss her, too," Amy said, a lump forming in her throat. "I think maybe Rachael had to leave on some really important business. Otherwise she would still be coming to see you."

"She didn't even say goodbye."

"I know. I'm sure she misses you, though, just like you miss her." She pulled the little stuffed bear she had bought at a souvenir shop out of the bag and held it out to him.

Jimmy took the bear from her hand and grinned.

"What do you say, Jimmy?" Mrs. Zimmer prodded.

"Thank you."

"You're welcome." Amy leaned over and hugged him, then came to her feet. Mrs. Zimmer reached down and picked Jimmy up, propped him on her hip.

"Say goodbye, sweetie. It's time for your nap."

"Will you come back and see me?" Jimmy asked.

"I'll come back," Amy said, her eyes a little misty. Rachael must have loved the adorable little boy. "I promise."

"Bye." Jimmy waved as Mrs. Zimmer carried him out of the living room and disappeared down the hall. A few minutes later, the woman walked back into the living room.

"He's a darling little boy," Amy said.

"Yes, he is. I feel like he's my own. Still, he misses his mom. She doesn't come by very often."

"So Jimmy stays with you full-time?" Johnnie asked.

"That's right."

"I guess that's how Rachael got involved," Amy added. "She was kind of playing stand-in for Jimmy's mom. She's always loved children."

Mrs. Zimmer smiled. "That was clear the first time I saw the two of them together."

"Did Rachael ever bring anyone with her when she stopped by?" Johnnie asked.

"No. She always just came by herself."

"Did she mention any future plans she might have had?" Amy asked. "Anyplace she might have been going?"

"You know, now that I think of it Rachael said something about taking a vacation. Said she had met someone special and he was taking her on a trip to the Caribbean."

Amy's pulse kicked up. "Did she mention his name?"

"I'm afraid not. But I really don't think she ever went."

"Why is that?" Johnnie asked.

"Because at first, she seemed really excited about going. Then she kind of stopped talking about it. She didn't mention it at all the last time she came over. A few days later, Vicky said she had disappeared, said the police were worried something had happened to her."

Vicky. That was Honeybee's real name.

"Anything else you can think of?" Johnnie asked.

"I'm afraid not." The woman smiled sadly. "I like to think she ran off to some romantic island with her *someone special* and they were so happy they didn't come back."

Amy's throat closed up.

"Thank you, Mrs. Zimmer," Johnnie said.

Amy felt his hand settle gently at her waist as he guided her toward the door. "I'll stop by again, if that's okay," she said as they stepped out on the porch, and then Johnnie was leading her down the steps to Babs's car and urging her in behind the wheel.

She didn't realize she was crying until he pulled a folded white handkerchief out of his back pocket and handed it over.

Amy wiped her eyes. "I just… I wish it were true. I wish she had fallen in love with some wonderful man and they had run off to some romantic island."

Johnnie's big hand came to rest on her shoulder. "Maybe she did. We'll follow the lead, see if the information turns up anything new."

"How?"

"Find out if her name pops up on any airline passenger lists. If it does, we'll see who was traveling with her. These days, you have to use your real name when you fly."

She frowned. "Can you do that? Surely you can't just Google up passenger lists on the internet. How can you—"

"Believe me, you don't want to know."

Before she could make another comment, Johnnie closed the car door. "I'll call you if I come up with anything," he said through the closed window.

She had no choice but to nod. He waited until she started the car, then walked back and climbed into his Mustang. Maybe they'd found another piece of the puzzle. It was hard to know for sure, but she had a feeling the information Mrs. Zimmer had supplied was part of the overall picture.

It sounded as if Rachael had fallen in love.

But if she had, clearly she hadn't told anyone who she was in love with.

The question was, why not?

As Johnnie drove up the winding canyon road to the guesthouse, he tried not to think of Amy, of how sweet she had looked kneeling in front of the little boy. In that moment, there was no sign of Angel Fontaine, just Amy Brewer, kindergarten teacher.

He could tell she was good with kids. In those brief moments, she had fallen a little in love with Jimmy Thomas. She'd go back, he knew. She wouldn't abandon the little boy the way her sister had.

Not that he believed Rachael had any choice in the matter. The girl had been missing for nearly two months. The odds of her being alive were slim at best. Still, it could happen.

He pulled the Mustang into the garage. On the front porch, he wiped his heavy boots on the mat, opened the door, and started down the hall, heading straight for the stairs leading to his lower-floor office.

It was a walk-out the size of the entire upstairs and, like the living room, had a wall of windows that looked out over the city. At one end of the room, there was a desk that housed his computer, a row of file cabinets and a round chrome table with four black leather chairs. At the opposite end, a first-class home gym.

He liked to stay in shape. And it was handy having the equipment he needed right there in his house. He sat down at the desk and pulled out his cell phone, dialed his ex-Ranger friend in Houston, Trace Rawlins.

"Hey, Ghost, how's married life treating you?" Ghost was Trace's Ranger name for how silently he could move. A longtime bachelor, the Texas cowboy had finally met the woman of his dreams. Maggie O'Connell Rawlins was a well-known photographer. Trace had always had a weak spot for hot-tempered redheads, though over the years they had caused him nothing but trouble.

This time, Johnnie believed, his friend had finally found just the right one.

"Hey, Hambone," Trace replied, the name Johnnie had acquired because he could eat his weight in food and never gain a pound. "Married life is great. You need to find yourself a woman and give it a try."

"I've found myself a woman. Not interested in wedding bells—I'd be happy just to get her in bed."

"That so? Not the kind of problem you usually have."

A muscle tightened in his jaw. "Yeah, well, shit happens."

Trace chuckled. "So what can I do for you?"

"You know that computer whiz kid you got working for you?"

"Sol Greenway? What about him?"

"I need him to do a little digging, see if he can find the name Rachael Carolyn Brewer on a passenger list somewhere. Probably a flight out of L.A., possibly to the Caribbean, around the first of May. If he gets a hit, I need to know who she was traveling with."

"Not a small order, especially with the TSA and security the way it is these days."

"No small order, but he can do it, right? I'm working a missing persons case for the missing girl's younger sister. There's still some hope Rachael might be alive."

"I see. And this sister...she wouldn't be the one you're trying to get in bed?"

Johnnie grunted, trying not to see the image of Angel Fontaine dancing in her miniscule G-string. "That would be the one."

Trace's smile reached him through the phone. "Let me talk to Sol, see what he can do. I'll be in touch."

"Thanks, buddy." Johnnie signed off and went to work on the files on top of his desk, an insurance fraud case and an irate husband. He'd call the husband, see if he could talk some sense into him; and put his part-time employee, Tyler Brodie, on the insurance fraud watching the guy who was supposed to be disabled but was looking a lot like he wasn't.

He made the call to Martin Lewis, the husband. Since he was busy with Amy and hated spying on errant spouses, he told Lewis the truth—he would be better off trusting his wife or divorcing her. Lewis, calmer than when he'd initially called, said he'd give it some thought.

Johnnie ended the call and looked up at the sound of a familiar male voice.

"Hey, Johnnie." Tyler Brodie worked freelance whenever Johnnie needed him. On his last job, he had uncovered a possible drug deal, the info Johnnie had reported to Special Agent Kent Wheeler. He wondered if the deal had ever gone down.

"Hey, Ty, what's up?"

"Hadn't heard from you in a while," Ty said. "Thought I'd drop by, see if you had any work for me." Tall, lean and solidly built, with dark brown hair and hazel eyes, Ty had spent four years in the marines, serving in Iraq. The kid had worked for Trace Rawlins in Texas, wore beat-up cowboy boots and had a slight Texas drawl.

Ty was capable and tough, but young, and he didn't have much street savvy. Still, he was great at surveillance and good at gathering information.

Johnnie leaned back in his chair. "I was just getting ready to call you. Got an insurance fraud case, a fireman who put in a claim for early retirement after a work-related disability. The company thinks he's faking it and they want evidence to prove it." He handed the file to Ty, who opened it and thumbed through the pages.

"Doesn't look too tough."

"If the guy is guilty, it should be a walk in the park."

Ty smiled. "Thanks."

"There's something else you might be able to do."

Ty sank down in the chair beside the desk. "I'm all ears."

"I'm working a missing persons case. Rachael Brewer, a dancer down at the Kitty Cat Club. She disappeared the first of May. She was a regular at Rembrandt's. I'm not sure where else she might have hung out. Maybe you can find out."

Confident as always, Ty nodded. "Hey, no problem."

Johnnie filled him in on what they had so far and gave him one of the photos he'd had made from the one Amy had given him.

"Wow," Ty said, staring down at the picture. "She's a beauty."

Her sister's not bad, either, Johnnie thought but didn't say it.

Ty stood up from the chair. "I'll get on this right away. I'll let you know if I come up with anything on the girl." Ty headed out and Johnnie went back to work, only to have another visitor a few minutes later.

"Johnnie? Johnnie, are you down there?" His land-lady's voice floated down from the top of the stairs. Eleanor Stiles had a key and didn't hesitate to let herself in—as long as she was sure he didn't have an overnight guest. Which was rare, since he didn't like to wake up with a woman in his bed. He didn't like having to worry about what to say the morning after when he was beyond ready for her leave.

"I'm here, Ellie. Come on down."

She descended the stairs and walked toward him, a tall, slim woman with short, wavy silver hair. She was wearing jeans and a lightweight sweatshirt. Sometimes she used his workout equipment, but usually when he wasn't there.

"What's going on?" he asked as she moved gracefully toward him.

"A woman was here to see you. A lady police officer, a lieutenant named Meeks. She said she had information you might be interested in."

If Carla had something for him, he wondered why she hadn't just called. "Thanks, Ellie. I'll call her."

Ellie was giving him her famous cat-licking-cream smile that said she knew more than she should.

"All right, what is it?"

"I don't think giving you information was the only thing the lieutenant wanted. I think she wanted to give you something a little more personal."

One of his eyebrows went up. "Such as?"

"Sex."

He grunted. "And why would you think that?"

"Because she said it was her day off and she asked if she could wait. She wanted to know when you would be home. She had sex on her mind, for sure."

His back teeth ground together. He never should have gone to bed with the woman. Besides Carla being a cop and someone he occasionally had to work with, he'd had a helluva time finding a way to politely end the relationship, which wasn't a relationship at all and nothing more than a two-night stand. Johnnie almost smiled. *Nothing worse than a woman scorned with a Glock 9 mil to back it up.*

Now it looked like his little visit had fired her up again.

Or maybe she had something important to tell him. He could only hope.

"I had a hunch you wouldn't want some police-woman prowling around your house when you weren't home, so I told her you would probably be gone most of the day." She handed him Carla's LAPD card.

"Thanks, Ellie. I'll give her a call." Though, man, he didn't want to. It had been months since they'd last hooked up. He wasn't interested in going down that road again.

"Mind if I use your treadmill?" she asked.

"Help yourself."

She held a paperback book in her hand as she crossed the room toward the machine at the opposite end, looked like a murder mystery, her favorite.

"She was pretty," Ellie called over her shoulder.

He scoffed. "She's also a cop who can cause me a lot of trouble."

Ellie paused when she reached the machine. "So who's the new one?"

Johnnie glanced up from the notes he was going over, stuff that related to the Brewer girl's disappearance. "What new one?"

"The woman who's snared your interest. You've been coming home at night, not early in the morning, so odds are you aren't sleeping with her. At least not yet."

He tossed the papers down on his desk. "I'm working a missing persons case, all right? I've been too busy to think of women." Except for the one who seemed to be on his mind twenty-four hours a day.

"I see.... She didn't jump into bed with you the first time you kissed her, which means she's not like the rest. Maybe this one has a brain."

He slid back his chair. "I'm going out. Enjoy your workout."

Ellie's laughter followed him up the stairs. "I think this is a lady I'd like to meet."

If only she knew, he thought. At least Ellie'd got one thing right. This one was definitely different.

He went out to the garage, walked over to his car and slid behind the wheel, but instead of starting the engine, he pulled out his cell phone, read the number off the card Ellie had given him and phoned Lieutenant Meeks.

"My landlady said you stopped by," he said when she answered. "You got something for me?"

"Maybe. Mary Lou Kammer came into the station. You remember her? Rachael's friend? Her sister used Mary Lou's address as her contact location."

The girl who had gone with Rachael to Rembrandt's. He planned to pay her a visit this afternoon. "What'd she want?"

"Mary Lou found some travel brochures that had slipped down behind the cushions in her sofa. She thinks they may have fallen out of Rachael's purse. Looks like she was planning a trip to Belize."

Belize. Fit into the puzzle he was mentally putting together. "Who was she going with?"

"Mary Lou didn't know. She said Rachael was being really secretive before she disappeared."

That seemed to be the consensus. But if she was planning a trip, she was going with someone. Someone she didn't want anyone to know about. Shouted married man to him.

"Anything else?"

"Actually, I was thinking…maybe we could get together for a beer or something. We could meet somewhere or… I could stop by your place."

Jesus. "Look, Carla. To tell you the truth, I'm kind of involved with someone." It wasn't exactly a lie. He planned to be very involved, as soon as the lady was in his bed. "If I wasn't, I'd jump at the chance to see you. You know that."

Her voice hardened. "Sure I do. Just like the last time." The phone went dead. He was pretty sure that would be the last info he got from Carla Meeks.

He took a deep breath and stuck the key into the ignition.

First Amy, then Ellie, now Carla.

He fired up the powerful engine. He had things to do and thankfully, at least for the moment, none of them involved women.

Chapter 12

Just one more dance set and the club would be closing. Amy glanced at the hands on the clock on the wall
backstage. Two minutes until showtime. Dressed in her
dance costume, she listened for her cue and started up
the stairs to the stage.

The music was loud and she knew the song well. It
took a few seconds to orient herself, to clear her mind
and let her body merge with the sounds. The rhythm
was soft and seductive at first, and she began to sway to
the beat. A few more bars and she forgot that she was a
proper, unassuming schoolteacher, a woman who lived
a conservative life in an unassuming town in Michigan. Little by little Amy Brewer faded and blossomed
into Angel Fontaine.

And Angel was good at this, she had discovered.
The girls on the high school cheering squad weren't

as athletic as the fancy squads today, but she could kick over her head and do the splits and she did them now onstage.

But here she wasn't dancing for the home team or the parents in the stands. She was playing to the eager crowd of males lined up in front of her. When she danced for them, she never felt more sexy, more alluring. These men wanted her. And though she didn't feel that same desire for them, she reveled in the power they gave her when she was onstage.

She shimmied and glided, propped a foot on the pole, caught hold and twirled around it, moved up and down erotically. She felt like a seductress, a tigress. She felt as if she controlled every man in the room.

For a brief few moments, she did.

The music swelled. She arched her back and swung her head from side to side, swirling her long blond hair around her hips. She ran the tip of her tongue over her bottom lip, and closed her eyes, let out a soft low moan.

Then she opened her eyes and summoned a seductive smile, let her gaze wander slowly, teasingly over the men. A movement in the distance caught her attention, a dark, forbidding man sitting at one of the tables. Only his outline was visible and yet she knew with every ounce of her soul who sat in the shadows at the back of the club.

Johnnie was here.

Her breathing quickened. In the space between them, the air seemed to crackle with tension. The atmosphere thickened and heated as she moved, twirled, arched and swayed, dancing now for Johnnie.

The faces of the other men faded and disappeared.

There was only one man now and with every move, she let him know.

The music swelled, reached a crescendo. Angel tipped her head back, rolled her head from side to side, and her hair slipped smoothly around her shoulders. Even from a distance, those fierce brown eyes watched her, the heat there burning with an intensity that made her insides go hot and liquid. Her nipples were hard inside the glittering red pasties that covered the small pink crests. Her body softened, dampened with every throbbing beat.

She watched him rise from his chair and start toward her, kept herself moving, though she couldn't quite breathe. The end of the set was nearing. She could barely remember how to finish, but her timing was good and she struck the final pose at just the right moment.

The men were on their feet, whistling and cheering, throwing dollar bills onto the stage. Her gaze searched for Johnnie but she couldn't find him. She hurried to pick up the money, knowing she had never danced so well, never been so perfectly in tune with her body.

She ran off the stage, taking a last glance around the room, certain he was there somewhere, then turned and walked into the hard wall of his chest.

"Johnnie…" His name came out half sigh, half sob.

"I'm taking you home," he said, his voice deep and rough. "There's no way you're telling me no. Not tonight."

She shook her head. "No. I mean yes, I want you to take me home." She glanced toward the stairs. "I—I need to change."

His gaze ran over her, blazing hot, utterly insistent. "I'll be waiting outside the door."

Her apartment was empty, thank God, Babs was still working last call on the floor. She changed into a pair of red thong panties that didn't cover much more than her G-string and a matching red lace push-up bra. Skinny jeans and a white tank top, a pair of red spike heels. She wasn't Amy tonight. Tonight she was Angel Fontaine.

Hurriedly, she washed off her stage makeup, applied a little fresh lipstick, a dab of blush and some mascara, then stuck the makeup kit into the small travel bag that held her toothbrush, and headed for the back door.

As promised, when she pushed it open, Johnnie stood just outside.

He looked her up and down, taking in the sexy jeans and high spike heels. "Tonight you're Angel, right?"

She knew what he meant. "Yes."

He cast her a wicked glance, bent his head and took her mouth in a ravishing kiss. "Good. That's good." Johnnie caught her hand and they hurried to his car. In minutes the Mustang was winding its way up the hill to his house overlooking the city.

He parked in the garage next to his Harley. As soon as she stepped out of the car, his mouth swooped down over hers in a long deep kiss, a hot, sexy kiss that made her insides liquid. Then he scooped her into his arms and started for the house. Beneath his T-shirt, his heart pounded nearly as hard as her own. He kissed her again as he climbed the few steps to the porch, making her head spin and her body go soft and warm.

She hardly remembered him carrying her inside, closing and relocking the door. She knew they were in the entry and Johnnie was backing her up against the wall and his tongue was in her mouth and hers was in his and she had never felt so hot and wild in her life.

"Johnnie…" Her arms locked around his thick neck. "God, I need you. I need… I need…"

"I know what you need." His heavy erection pressed against her. "Baby, I'm gonna give you exactly what you need."

And then her tank top was gone and her high heels were missing. Her jeans and push-up bra were lying in a puddle on the floor.

He paused a moment to look at her, his gaze dark and hot. His attention fixed on her red thong panties and his expression turned so fierce the muscles across her stomach contracted. There was lust in his eyes and a wildness that any other time would have frightened her.

But tonight she was Angel Fontaine and she could handle a man like Johnnie Riggs.

He kissed her again, deeply and thoroughly, ripped away the tiny thong, lifted her up and wrapped her legs around his waist. She was open, exposed to him as he parted her sex and began to stroke her. Dear God, she was wet, wet and hot, throbbing and burning with desire. She had never felt anything like it.

She whimpered his name.

"It's all right, baby." His skillful hands continued to work their magic. "Just let yourself go."

And she did, giving in to the powerful climax that splintered through her body, pleasure so sweet and intense she cried out his name.

Johnnie kissed her deeply. "We'll explore your sexuality next time," he promised, repeating her earlier words. "I've waited too long to have you." And then he was deep inside her. His hands cupped her bare bottom, holding her in place as he began to move. Her arms went around his neck and she clung to him as he took her with deep, powerful strokes that made her hot and tight all over. She felt a second climax building, felt her muscles clenching around him.

It wasn't until she came again that he followed her to release.

Amy slumped against Johnnie's wide, muscular chest. His T-shirt rubbed against her cheek, and a rush of embarrassment hit her when she realized she was naked while he still wore his clothes.

He set her back on her feet, caught her horrified expression, and a soft chuckle rumbled in his chest. "I figured this would happen. You're Amy again, right?"

She made a little sound in her throat. "You didn't even take off your pants."

"I couldn't wait." Scooping her up in his powerful arms, he strode off down the hall. "I plan to remedy that in about five seconds." The minute she was settled in his king-size bed, he began to strip off his clothes. Any embarrassment she might have felt turned into fascination.

She had never seen a man with a more spectacular body. Wide, thick-muscled shoulders, a deep chest and heavily muscled arms. The tattoo of an eagle, wings spread, covered one bulging bicep.

Johnnie strode to the bed, naked and magnificent, and once more heavily aroused. She tore her gaze away from all that masculinity and looked up into his face.

"I didn't think men could...could do that."

"Do what?" he asked, coming down on the mattress beside her.

"Perform again so soon."

He chuckled. "Not a problem for me." He leaned over to kiss her, but she held him off with a hand on his chest.

"What about protection?"

He grinned. "I'm definitely in bed with Amy. I took care of it. You don't have to worry. We won't have unprotected sex." She spotted the foil wrappers on the bedside table as he started to kiss her, but she held him off once more.

"What if…what if you don't like being in bed with Amy?"

A deep rumble vibrated the muscles across his chest. "Then I'll just turn Amy back into Angel. Here, I'll show you."

This time when he kissed her she didn't try to stop him and in a very few minutes, as she dug her nails into his broad back and begged him for more, she understood exactly what he meant.

A purple haze lightened the sky outside the bedroom window. Johnnie had slept only briefly. He'd been too busy making love to the woman in his bed.

Jesus, she was something. Amy or Angel, it didn't matter. Each was a beautiful, responsive woman and in truth, the two were one and the same. Amy was the only one who didn't get that. She was part lady, part vixen. It was a heady mix for a man like him.

Johnnie watched her sleeping beside him, her long golden hair spread across his pillow as he had imagined a dozen times. She was lying on her side, her back to him, the sheet bunched below her perfect little ass. He silently chuckled. She wanted to explore her sexuality.

During the night, he had given her a few preliminary lessons. But he had let her off easy.

This was new to her, he could see. In time, he would teach her about pleasure. In time—

Frowning, he broke off the thought. Time was something they didn't have. They were working together, involved in a search that would eventually end—one way or another. Amy had a job in Michigan. By the end of the summer, she would be gone. Out of his life for good.

Which really *was* good, he told himself.

Getting involved with a woman—any woman—was the last thing he wanted. He wasn't a settle-down kind of guy. It wasn't that he needed to screw a lot of women to feel like a man, the way some guys did. He just couldn't handle the closeness, the intimacy. Seemed like all his life, whenever he got close to a woman, he wound up getting hurt. First his mother, who had left when he was eight years old, then Katie getting killed, then Lisa.

He'd been crazy about Lisa Desmond, a woman he'd met a few years after he got out of the Rangers. He'd wanted to marry her, but Lisa was more interested in how much money he had in the bank than how much he loved her.

Funny thing was he had a lot more than he let on: his savings while he was in the army, which he had invested and had earned a tidy profit, later high-paying, off-the-record assignments, mercenary work, jobs he'd taken he didn't like to think about but had to be done.

He hadn't told Lisa. He needed to know if her feelings for him were sincere so he hadn't said anything about the money, and when he found a note telling him she'd left town with Aaron Sespe, a real estate broker down in Orange County, he had his answer.

He wasn't good with relationships. He'd figured out long ago it was better to keep his emotions in check, do what he was good at and not get mixed up with a woman who was either bound to die or leave him.

He glanced down at Amy. He wanted her. He was hard again, even after making love to her most of the night. And she always seemed to want him.

Figuring it was time to give her another lesson, he kissed the back of her neck and moved behind her spoon fashion. She moaned as he eased her leg over his thigh and slid his erection inside.

"Johnnie…" She sighed, whispering his name like an answered prayer.

He smiled as he felt her body moisten and stretch around him, felt her skin flush as her arousal strengthened. In minutes she came, and so did he, and afterward she kissed him softly, curled around him and went back to sleep.

Even as he held her, he reminded himself she wasn't for him and never would be.

The reminder kept him from falling asleep.

His cell started playing the National Anthem at nine the next morning. Johnnie grabbed the phone off the nightstand, swung his legs to the side of the bed and walked out of the bedroom into the hall so he wouldn't disturb Amy.

"Hey, Hambone, hope I didn't wake you."

He knew the voice. Dev Raines, one of his best friends. He yawned. Fortunately, he didn't need a lot of sleep, which considering how little he'd gotten last night was good.

"Hey, Daredevil, what's up?" Dev's Ranger name—which he fully deserved. Of course he was married now, living with his wife and adopted daughter in Scottsdale and mostly settled down. Mostly.

"I'm working a case in L.A.," Dev said. "Auto theft ring. Insurance company's getting tired of dishing out money for expensive stolen cars."

"Must be pros if they've figured a way past the security systems. Those high-dollar jobs are really tough to steal."

"Which is why the police so far have zilch. I've got Chaz working on it." Dev had his own computer geek, a guy even better than Trace's whiz kid. "He's come up with a couple of names, people in the area with the technical know-how to pull it off. Delta Insurance is hoping I can figure out who's behind the thefts and find a way to get inside. The thing is I may need some backup."

"Hey, not a problem."

"Clive's in. Molly's not too happy about it, but you know Madman."

Johnnie chuckled. Another friend, Clive Monroe, lived in L.A. but they didn't see each other much now that Clive was married. "Most of the time, he's a cream puff where his lady's concerned, but deep down, he hasn't changed much since he left the Rangers. He likes the action too much to quit completely."

"I promised Molly I'd make sure he didn't get hurt."

"Oh, yeah, that worked great last time." In Mexico on a rescue mission Dev had organized, Clive had taken a bullet in the shoulder. Luckily it wasn't too serious, and Molly had only been mad at Dev for a couple of weeks. "So what's the plan?"

"Not sure yet. Lark's gotta come to L.A. on business." Dev's wife was fairly famous in the fashion industry for her expensive LARK designer bags. "I'm coming with her. We'll set up a meet."

"Sounds good."

"I'll get back to you." Dev hung up and so did Johnnie.

Looked like he had another job lined up. Still, finding Rachael had to come first. He'd given Amy his word and he wasn't about to break it. He'd work around the other.

Walking naked back into the bedroom, he grabbed a T-shirt out of a drawer and pulled it on, then slid on his jeans. Snuggled beneath the covers, Amy stirred and her eyes cracked open. They widened as she glanced around the room and realized where she was.

Resisting an urge to climb back in bed and make love to her again, he pulled open the dresser drawer, drew out a clean white T-shirt, and tossed it on top of the covers where she could reach it.

"I'll make us some coffee," he said. "You look like you could use a cup."

Amy spotted her clothes in a tangled heap on the floor, and her cheeks went pink. Grabbing the T-shirt, she pulled it over her head, glanced wistfully toward the bathroom but made no attempt to leave the protection of the bed. His gaze zeroed in on her long, golden, sleep-tangled hair. She didn't seem to know the bed was the least safe place she could be.

"Coffee first," he said a little gruffly, "then you can hit the shower."

Amy nodded, waited until he turned his back, and climbed down from the bed. Light, feminine footsteps hurried into the bathroom and the door softly closed.

Johnnie smiled. A modest stripper. Now, that was a new one.

A few minutes later, Amy walked into the kitchen, yawning behind her hand. The T-shirt hung like a sack to her knees and she wasn't wearing any makeup. His gaze ran from the peaks of her breasts, down to her tiny feet and red-painted toenails. She looked sleepy and well-tumbled and it turned him on like crazy.

He should be thinking of a strategy to get her out of his house, the way he normally would, but all he wanted to do was take her back to bed.

"You look good enough to eat."

Amy's eyes widened. "Don't even think about giving me another one of your lessons."

Amusement trickled through him. "No?"

"Well, at least not right now."

He laughed. He couldn't help it. "I guess we do have a few things to do besides try different positions."

She blushed, as he knew she would. "We need to find my sister."

"Exactly." He poured her a mug of coffee, added some of the Coffee-Mate he kept for guests, then pressed the cup into her hands. Her palms curled around it and she blew on the surface to cool it, took a tentative sip.

Her eyes closed and she sighed with pleasure. "That tastes wonderful. Thanks." Her gaze slid back toward the bedroom. "I'd better get dressed. You said I could use your shower."

"Sure, go ahead. The towels hanging next to the sink are clean."

Amy turned and headed in that direction. Johnnie didn't mention he planned to join her.

Chapter 13

Freshly showered and desperate for another cup of coffee, Amy walked barefoot back into Johnnie's kitchen. Dressed in the jeans and white tank top she had worn the night before, her damp hair pulled into a rubber band at the nape of her neck, she carried her high spike heels, which seemed absurdly wrong for the morning after.

As she set her purse and makeup kit on the counter, she looked at Johnnie and couldn't stop a blush. She had never had this much sex in her life. The man was insatiable. Worst of all, he made her feel that way, too. Just looking at him leaning against the kitchen counter in his jeans and Ranger T-shirt made her want to jump him again.

It was embarrassing. And ridiculous. After last night and this morning, she didn't have the strength.

"You ready for another cup?" he asked, distracting her, thank God.

"Absolutely."

He poured her a mug and handed it over, opened the oven and took out a tray of perfectly baked cinnamon rolls. The delicious aroma made her mouth water.

"Wow, a man who can cook."

Johnnie chuckled. "They're out of a can but I figured you could use a little nourishment."

Oh, Lord, could she. Every bone and muscle in her body felt limp and sated. Her appetite was fierce, her stomach growling for food. She felt wonderful.

Johnnie frosted the rolls with the orange topping out of the can, took down a couple of plates and filled them, and they sat down at the table. Amy ate two delicious rolls, Johnnie polished off the rest. The man could really eat and yet he certainly didn't have a weight problem. Muscle burned more calories than fat did, she had read. Looking at the impressive muscles beneath his T-shirt, clearly that was the answer.

She tore her gaze away. "So what's our plan for the day?" She licked a dab of frosting off her finger.

"Yesterday I went to see your sister's friend, Mary Lou Kammer. So that's out of the way."

"You talked to Mary Lou? I talked to her when I first got here, but she didn't know anything useful. She was nice, though. I met her through Babs. She knew I was going to take Rachael's old job. Mary Lou said I could use her address so the police wouldn't know I was working as Angel and living at the club."

He took a sip of his coffee. "A couple of days ago, Mary Lou found some travel brochures down behind the cushions in her sofa. She thinks they fell out of your sister's purse."

Amy's interest sharpened. "Where was Rachael going?"

"Looks like Belize."

"*Belize*. That's in the Caribbean. That fits with what Mrs. Zimmer said. Have you heard anything from that friend you called about the passenger lists?"

"Trace Rawlins." He shook his head. "Not yet."

"Has Mary Lou told the police about the brochures?"

"Yeah. She went in to see Lieutenant Meeks, so we're all on the same page. Mary Lou confirmed that she and Rachael went to Rembrandt's more than once. She said your sister occasionally went there alone. She thinks maybe she met a guy, someone she was interested in. She thinks they might have been dating."

"Danny?"

"Maybe."

Amy set her mug down on the table. "Let's go back to Rembrandt's, see if we can find Danny."

"I stopped by last night before I came to the club to see you. I talked to T.J. and Kenny. They said they knew a couple of guys named Danny who came in once in a while, but they didn't have any last names and they never saw either of them with your sister."

Amy chewed her lip. "Maybe if we went back, we could find the Danny that Rachael was seeing or find out if there was somebody else."

"We can try, but she could have met him anywhere."

It was true, but they were running out of leads and she was beginning to panic.

She started to say something, but the doorbell rang

just then. Johnnie set his mug down and walked out of the kitchen to see who it was.

A few minutes later, he strode back in with a handsome, black-haired Latino trailing behind him. In a perfectly fitted chocolate-brown suit and a pair of expensive loafers, the man was downright dapper. She bet women fell all over themselves for this guy.

"Amy, this is Detective Rick Vega. Rick, meet Amy Brewer."

His dark gaze skimmed her, sending a rush of color into her cheeks. From the way he was looking at her, he knew she had been there all night. She should have left earlier. Thank God, she was fully clothed, though the way he was looking at her, she might as well have been naked.

"Nice to meet you," he said with just enough of a Spanish accent to sound sexy.

Still, he wasn't her type. Not that she had a type. At least she hadn't until she'd met Johnnie.

"Back off, Rick." Johnnie eyed him darkly. "This one's off-limits."

The detective actually flushed, faint color staining the bones in his cheeks. "Sorry."

The stiffness in Johnnie's shoulders eased. "Coffee?"

"Sounds good."

Johnnie went over to the counter and poured the detective a cup.

"Thanks." Vega took a sip, sighed with appreciation.

"Late night?" Johnnie asked.

Vega smiled, flicked a glance toward Amy. There was no heat in his gaze this time. Johnnie had made his ownership clear. Amy wasn't sure how she felt about that.

"Probably no later than yours."

Johnnie's gaze slid over her like a warm caress. "Probably not." He took a sip of his coffee. "So what's got you up here on a weekend?"

Vega tipped his head her way. "Maybe we should talk in private."

"This about Amy's sister?"

He nodded.

"She's come a long way to find out what happened to her, taken a few hard knocks trying to dig up information." She knew he was talking about Kyle Bennett and how close she had come to being raped. It made her stomach churn to think of it. "She has a right to know."

"If that's what you want."

"She…she isn't dead?" Amy blurted out, her chest squeezing as the thought struck that he might have come for that reason.

"No, not that we know of." Vega took a drink of his coffee. "The thing is, I've been keeping an eye on Rachael's file. I figured if something new turned up you'd want to know."

"So what turned up?"

"One of the undercover narcs picked up a rumor. Street talk has it Rachael was involved with Manny Ortega."

Johnnie hissed out a breath.

"You can say that again," Vega added.

"Who's Manny Ortega?" Amy asked.

"He's the son of a big-time drug dealer," Johnnie explained. "Carlos Ortega's a high-ranking member of the San Dimas cartel. Their territory runs from here all the way into the Baja Peninsula."

"Carlos Ortega—El Caballo," Vega said. "They call him The Horse. He's into everything from cocaine to human trafficking and anything in between. So far he's been able to skirt the law and get away with it. He's powerful and as mean as they come."

"Carlos lives on a guarded estate in Ensenada but his son lives here in L.A.," Johnnie explained.

The detective took a drink of his coffee. "Manny's tried to keep his nose clean, but Papa wants his little boy to take over the business. Manny's not a guy your sister should have gotten involved with."

Amy's heart was beating a little too fast. "Maybe she wasn't. You said it was only a rumor." She looked over at Johnnie, saw sympathy etched in his face. Her eyes widened. "Oh, my God. It wasn't *Danny,* it's *Manny.*" And she could tell by looking at him, Johnnie had already figured that out.

Vega sipped his coffee. "If the rumor's true, she was playing with fire. If Ortega wanted her to disappear, we might not ever find her."

Amy looked away. Her chest felt tight as she walked to the window above the kitchen sink and stared outside, seeing nothing but sky and the flowers planted along the drive. It was clear today, not smoggy or cloudy, as it was on occasion. The sun was shining, warming the kitchen, but Amy felt cold to the bone.

"Listen, I've got to go." The detective took a last drink of his coffee then set the empty mug on the kitchen counter. "It was nice meeting you, Amy."

She turned. "You, too, Detective. Whatever happens, I really appreciate your help."

He just nodded. Johnnie walked him to the door. Though Vega spoke softly, she could hear enough to know she was the topic of conversation.

"She's a what?" Vega said incredulously.

"Kindergarten teacher."

"I saw her dancing at the club. What the hell is a schoolteacher doing in a place like that?"

She couldn't hear Johnnie's reply but she assumed he was saying she was trying to find her sister.

Vega flicked her a final glance and she thought it held a hint of respect that hadn't been there before. He mentioned something about Rachael, then disappeared out the door.

When Johnnie returned, his features looked grim. "That wasn't good news," he said. "Carlos Ortega's as bad as they come."

Amy bit her lip and turned away. She heard his footfalls coming up behind her, then his arms slid around her waist, easing her back against his chest. His body heat dispelled some of her chill.

"We'll keep looking," he said softly, "if that's what you want. But sooner or later, baby, you'll have to come to grips with the fact your sister might have done something to piss off the wrong people. If she did…"

She turned in his arms and looked up at him. "If she did, she's probably dead."

Johnnie made no reply, which was a reply in itself.

Amy swallowed, blinked back the faint burn of tears. "To tell you the truth, deep down I've been afraid she might…afraid she might be dead from the start. We weren't close anymore, and Rachael and my mother didn't always get along, but she wouldn't have wanted us to worry. She would have reached us by now if she could have."

"I know it isn't what you planned, but maybe you should go home."

Amy slipped out of his arms. "I came to find out what happened to her. That hasn't changed. I'm not leaving. Not until I know the truth."

Johnnie said nothing.

"I don't expect you to keep working for free. You've done more than enough already."

Johnnie bent down and lightly brushed her lips. "I told you I'm running a tab. Last night was just a down payment."

She fought a blush. Looping her arms around his neck, she went up on her toes and very softly kissed him. She knew he didn't expect that kind of payment and never had.

"Thank you," was all she said.

Johnnie was saved by the ringing of his cell. One little kiss and he was getting hard. He couldn't remember a woman who aroused him the way Amy did. Still he had work to do.

Digging his phone out of the pocket of his jeans, he checked the caller ID. Trace Rawlins.

"Hey, Ghost, you got something for me?"

"Yes and no," Trace said. "No sign of Rachael Brewer on any airplane passenger manifests. Doesn't mean she didn't make the trip."

Johnnie frowned. "You're thinking they could have flown private."

"It's possible."

"Probably need a jet to travel that far."

"So who was Rachael seeing with that kind of money?"

Johnnie thought of the news Rick Vega had brought. "Word is she might have been seeing Manny Ortega."

"Carlos Ortega's son?"

"That would be him." On the other end of the line, Johnnie could hear the clatter of computer keys as Trace pounded the keyboard.

"Looks like good ol' Carlos owns a Citation. A Sovereign. That's the big one. Maybe Manny borrowed it to make the trip. Or maybe Daddy took them down."

"Could be they left from right here in L.A."

"Let me talk to Sol, see if he can get the call numbers. For international travel, the pilot would have to file a flight plan."

"If it's Ortega's jet, it probably left from Ensenada. Maybe stopped here, maybe went direct."

"Still goes. Carlos wouldn't want to break any laws...at least not the minor ones. I'll get back to you."

"Thanks, and thank Sol for me. Tell Annie to send me a bill." She was Trace's office manager and she ran the place like a drill sergeant.

Trace just laughed and hung up the phone.

"I guess your friend didn't find Rachael's name on any of the passenger lists."

Johnnie turned at the sound of Amy's voice. "No."

"But you think they could have traveled in a private plane."

"Jet, most likely."

"And Carlos Ortega owns one—that's what you said."

He nodded. "Trace is going to see if a flight plan

was filed for a trip to Belize around the time Rachael disappeared."

Amy wrapped her arms around herself as if she were cold. Johnnie knew she was thinking that if Rachael went to Belize with the son of a drug lord and didn't come back, she was probably dead.

And she was exactly right.

"I…ummm…need to go home. Would you take me back, please?"

His gaze found hers and his jaw clenched. Taking Amy home meant taking her back to the Kitty Cat Club where tonight she would be dancing naked in front of a room full of sex-hungry men. Every one of them would be fantasizing about the things he wanted to do to her in bed.

His stomach burned. For the first time in years, Johnnie had a woman in his house he didn't want to take home.

"You got your stuff?" he asked, reminding himself that taking her back was the only real option he had. Aside from the fantastic sex, getting involved with a woman wasn't something he was willing to do.

Amy picked her purse up off the counter, grabbed the small red canvas pouch beside it, her toothbrush and makeup, he figured and almost smiled. Spending the night with a man she barely knew, Angel would have thrown caution to the wind, but Amy would want to be prepared. He wondered if she'd brought a handful of condoms, just in case.

He corrected himself. Before last night, Amy would have figured one would be enough.

As he walked her to the door, Johnnie grinned.

Chapter 14

The remote clicked and the garage door began to swing open. They had almost reached the car when Amy heard someone behind them.

"Johnnie! Oh, Johnnie!"

She turned to see an older woman, wavy silver hair, trim figure, jogging toward them.

A bemused expression settled on Johnnie's face. "Morning, Ellie."

"I didn't mean to bother you. I just happened to see you walk out of the house and thought I'd say hello."

"Yeah, well, hello."

Dressed in a navy blue jogging suit with a white stripe down the leg, breathing a little faster from her exertion, Ellie gave Amy a very thorough inspection. When Johnnie didn't introduce her, the woman smiled and stuck out her hand.

"Hi, I'm Eleanor Stiles. I live in the big house. And you must be…?"

Uncertain whether to say she was Amy or Angel, she looked up at Johnnie for guidance and he blew out a long, slow breath.

"Ellie, this is Amy Brewer. I'm helping her find her sister."

"Oh, yes, I believe you mentioned you were working on a missing persons case." Ellie turned to Amy. "I'm sorry to hear about your sister, but you've got a good man working for you. He'll do everything he can to find her."

Amy glanced over at Johnnie. "He isn't really working for me. He's helping me. I really appreciate it."

Ellie gave her an even more thorough perusal. "I see."

"Listen, we've got to go," Johnnie said. Setting a hand at Amy's waist, he steered her toward the car.

"It was nice meeting you, Mrs. Stiles," Amy called over her shoulder.

"It's just Ellie," she called back, "and it was nice meeting you, too, dear."

Johnnie said nothing as he backed out of the garage and the car rolled down the driveway.

"She's your landlady, right?"

"That's right. My very nosy landlady."

"She seemed nice."

He smiled. "Ellie's great. Just kind of a busybody. She's been a very good friend."

Amy wondered if he had been living in Ellie's guesthouse when his sister had been killed. "How long have you known her?"

He caught her eye in the mirror. Though he had only just shaved, a faint shadow had begun to darken his jaw.

"After I left the army, I traveled around for a while. I did some private security work out of the country. I moved in a couple of years after I got back to the States."

And they had been friends ever since, the kind of friend who would have helped him through the pain of losing his sister.

As the Mustang continued down the hill, Amy thought of her own sister. Detective Vega believed Rachael had been involved with the son of a notorious drug lord. But there wasn't any proof, and rumor and conjecture didn't make it true.

Both Babs and Mary Lou had told her very firmly that Rachael did not take drugs. She was only working at the club because the pay was better, room rent was cheap and she could save more money. She was determined to become an actress. Drinking, partying and getting involved with drugs would keep her from achieving her dream.

"Maybe the rumors aren't true," Amy said aloud to Johnnie as he turned onto Sunset, heading for the club. "Babs and Mary Lou said Rachael wasn't into drinking and partying. She wanted to be an actress more than anything. She wouldn't throw her dream away on a guy who was mixed up in something like that."

Johnnie flicked her a sideways glance. "Manny's a good-looking guy. He's only a few years older than your sister and he's charming. His father's the gangster, not Manny. It's Carlos who's the problem."

"You're thinking maybe Carlos didn't want his son getting involved with a stripper."

"Yeah, something like that. At least not seriously involved."

"We need to talk to Manny."

"I plan to."

"I'm going with you."

He turned the car into the parking lot next to the club and pulled up near the back door. "Not a chance."

Her chin went up. "You said the father was the criminal, not the son. As long as I'm with you—"

"No." He turned off the engine, cracked the door open, rounded the car and helped her climb out.

"I want to go," she said.

"You're Angel Fontaine, remember? You don't have any reason to be talking to Manny Ortega."

He was right, damn it. She couldn't have it both ways. If she wanted to continue working undercover at the club, she had to be Angel. And a private investigator wouldn't take an exotic dancer with him to talk to a drug lord's son.

"All right, you win." *For now,* she added, her mind spinning ahead to what she might accomplish while he was talking to Ortega. "Tonight we're doing a private function, a bachelor party for one of the guys who works at Brand Realty. Peter Brand is the owner. He's the man you mentioned, the one in the police report."

He nodded. "I've seen his name on for-sale signs on property all over town. He's got a dozen branch offices, makes a boatload of money. The cops say his alibi checks out. He hadn't seen your sister for a couple of weeks before she disappeared and he was working the night she didn't come home."

"Still, if he's here tonight, I'm going to talk to him, see if he might know something useful."

Johnnie's jaw hardened. "We've already been over this. I don't want you playing detective."

Amy jerked to a halt next to the door. "That's why I'm here, Johnnie, working at the club. I appreciate what you're doing—I can't begin to tell you how much. But I intend to do my part. I'm going to do everything I can to find out what happened to my sister."

"Damn it, Amy."

"It's Angel, and I have to go in."

Johnnie took a breath and released it slowly, clearly resigned that she was going to do exactly as she pleased.

"You've got my number in your phone. Call me if you run into a problem." His dark gaze narrowed on her face. "And don't even think about leaving with that guy."

Amy flashed him a smile. "I won't leave with him, I promise. I won't leave with anyone but you."

A hot gleam appeared in his eyes. Apparently mollified, he nodded. "Fine." Turning, he strode back to his car.

Amy watched him drive away and felt a sudden pang. Not only was she wildly attracted to him, but she liked him.

Well, except when he was acting like a domineering, overprotective male.

Liking him should have been good, but wasn't. A man like John Riggs wasn't someone she could afford to get involved with. He was the kind of guy you had fantasy, one-night sex with and never saw again. He wasn't the kind of man a schoolteacher from Michigan took home to meet her mother.

He was the wild, dangerous, reckless kind of guy who ended up breaking your heart.

* * *

Detective Rick Vega returned to his desk in the homicide bureau at the Hollywood Community Police Station. Turning on his computer, he sat back to wait while the machine booted up.

All the way back from Johnnie's place, Rick had thought about Rachael Brewer and her sister, Amy, the schoolteacher who had come to California from Michigan to find her.

Clearly, Johnnie was taken with the little blonde. Rick and Johnnie had been friends since the day Rick had become Kate Riggs's partner. He had dropped in at Johnnie's for a morning visit any number of times and never found a woman in his house. That Amy was still there *the morning after* said a lot.

Johnnie was helping her, which was great, since he was exceptionally good at his job and the police so far had come up with squat. That Amy was working as a dancer in a strip club to dig up information was over-the-top insane. The lady wasn't a cop. She had no experience dealing with the kind of guys who frequented a place like the Kitty Cat Club.

Still, he couldn't help admiring her moxie and her determination. It was obvious she loved her sister. It made him wonder what there was about Rachael Brewer that deserved that kind of loyalty.

As soon as the computer was ready, he clicked on Google and typed in Rachael's name. Half a dozen *Rachael Brewers* popped up. He checked each listing but none of them was the woman he was looking for. No Facebook…no Twitter…no LinkedIn. Nothing on any of the usual social networks.

No web page.

This last seemed a little odd to him. Rachael wanted to be an actress. Most would-be actresses had an internet presence of some sort. He knew working as a dancer didn't pay all that much, but she must have had friends who could have helped her.

He typed in Silky Summers, did the same check on the people who popped up, and still came up with nothing.

He leaned back in his chair, steepled his fingers and studied the screen. Maybe instead of using her real name or her stripper name, she was using something else. On a hunch, he typed in Rachael Summers, a combination of the two, and the usual list of names popped up. She wasn't on any of the social networks, but he struck gold with the website www.rachaelsummers.com.

He recognized her instantly from the photo he had seen in her missing persons file. On the website, she had an entire photo portfolio. It was nicely done, the pictures all professional and tasteful. He jotted down the name of the photographer who had done the work, and there was a biography, as well.

Born in Grand Rapids. Daughter of an auto mechanic dad and a homemaker mom. Graduated high school and city college with a 4.0 grade average, but didn't continue her education and instead moved to Hollywood to pursue an acting career.

The site listed parts in Grand Rapids little theater productions of *South Pacific, Camelot* and *Our Town,* and a couple of TV commercials as credits.

He jotted down a contact number that probably belonged to her missing cell phone, pulled out the copy he had made of her file and saw that he was right, and that the second number listed belonged to her friend Mary Lou Kammer.

He flipped back to the photos, tried to make the woman he had found on the web match the stripper Silky Summers he had once seen onstage. On occasion he used the Kitty Cat Club for a meet with an informant. The owner, Tate Watters, was solidly pro-police, and the place was dark and noisy.

At the time, Rachael hadn't made much of an impression. In fact, he hadn't remembered seeing her until he had pulled her file for Johnnie.

He dug around the web a little more, then went to www.KittyCatClub.com just to see what might show up. A number of videos were posted. He recognized the dark-haired dancer, Silky Summers, among a row of video clips, and clicked on the image.

The video lasted only a minute. Rachael had a beautiful body as well as a gorgeous face, but the thing that struck him was the detachment in her eyes, the distant quality that said she was only doing a job. She had no interest, no personal stake in her performance.

Rachael was dancing, but her soul was somewhere else.

Rick reached for the mouse, ready to end the session, paused for an instant, then flipped back to her web page for one last glance. A line at the bottom of the site caught his attention.

Rachael has been a longtime supporter of the Dennison Children's Shelter. Donations can be made through the following link: www.dennisonchildrensshelter.com.

He clicked on the link, saw that it was a sanctuary for homeless children and jotted down the address.

Rick leaned back in his chair. He was beginning to think there was a lot more to Rachael Brewer than he had believed.

Amy finished her second set for the evening and changed into her cocktail waitress outfit. So far the Realtors who had rented the club for the night had been fairly well behaved, but it wasn't that late yet. The Kitty Cat wasn't the kind of place most of the agents frequented and they were dribbling out of the club a little at a time and heading home.

The bridegroom was younger and he and his friends were beginning to get pretty rowdy. Fortunately, there was a limo waiting for anyone who drank too much and needed a ride back to his house.

When Peter Brand excused himself from the group and started for the door, Amy set her drink tray down on an empty table and hurried to intercept him.

"Excuse me, Mr. Brand. I don't mean to bother you, but I was wondering if you might have a minute to talk before you leave."

He eyed her with speculation. He had thick salt-and-pepper hair, and though he'd had a couple of glasses of beer, he wasn't drunk. He was in his forties, attractive in a pair of stylish, silver-rimmed glasses.

"My name is Angel," she said. "I'm a friend of Silky Summers."

"I'm afraid I don't know anyone by that name."

"I'm sorry. I meant to say Rachael Brewer. We were friends. I heard she went out with you a few times. I was wondering if you knew anything about her disappearance."

He frowned. "The police asked me about Rachael. I told them I hadn't seen her in a couple of weeks."

"I know. I was just hoping that maybe you could think of something. I'm really worried about her."

Brand's blue eyes softened. "Rachael is a really nice girl, but we never dated. I told the police that. We knew each other through the Dennison Children's Shelter. Rachael volunteered there and helped us raise money for the home."

Amy was stunned. And yet it was exactly like her.

"My sis… Rachael worked there?"

He nodded. "Volunteered. Whenever she had the time. She was busy a lot, holding down a job and taking casting calls. I never knew she worked at the club until the police came to see me. As pretty as she was, I was surprised she'd never caught a break."

"Where…where is the shelter?"

Brand gave her the address, which she jotted on a cocktail napkin.

"Rachael loved the children in the shelter and they loved her," Peter said. "I'm sure they miss her."

"We all do. I really appreciate your help, Mr. Brand."

"It's just Peter. And I hope they find her."

Amy watched him walk away, thinking that her sister continued to surprise her. First Jimmy, now the shelter for homeless children. The good news was, in talking to the real estate agent, she had come up with another place to look for information. She couldn't wait to tell Johnnie. She tried not to wonder what he was doing tonight—which made her think of last night, and color washed into her cheeks.

It was supposed to be a single night of wild, fantasy

sex, but here she was, wishing she was with him, wishing he would take her to bed again.

With a sigh, she turned back to the tables surrounded by rowdy men and went to get another round of drinks.

Johnnie shoved through the etched glass doors of the Vieux Carre, a ritzy supper club in downtown L.A. Manny Ortega was the owner of the place, along with a chain of El Pueblo Mexican restaurants that ran along the coast from L.A. to San Diego.

A tuxedo clad maître d' stopped him as he walked through the door. Obviously, the leather jacket he wore over his T-shirt didn't meet the dress code for a swanky place like the Vieux Carre.

"May I help you, sir?" Tall and thin, classy but not effeminate. Manny would have chosen him specifically to work the front of the club.

"I'm looking for Manny Ortega. Word is he's usually here in the evenings."

"Mr. Ortega takes pride in seeing the restaurant is properly run. Unfortunately, he isn't here tonight. In fact, he will be out of town for the rest of the week."

Johnnie glanced around the restaurant, a single large room with an open two-story ceiling surrounded by a dining balcony. It was art deco, with candlelit, linen-draped tables, and an expensive menu that served a combination of French and Cajun food. The internet gave it a five-star rating. Manny had the money to make sure he could offer his customers the best of everything.

The question was where had he gotten it?

"You know where I might be able to find him?" Johnnie held up a hundred dollar bill pinched between his fingers.

The maître d' eyed the money, but didn't take the bait and simply shook his head. "I'm sorry. I really don't know."

Johnnie stuffed the money into the pocket of his jeans and pulled out one of his nondescript business cards. "Give him this. Tell him I'd like to talk to him."

"Certainly, Mr.…." The maître d' looked down at the card. "Riggs." The man stuck the card into the pocket of his tuxedo and turned his attention to the well-dressed couple who had come in behind Johnnie.

Johnnie headed out into the night. As he handed his parking ticket to the valet and waited for the kid to bring up his car, he ignored an itch to head for the Kitty Cat Club. The urge to watch Angel Fontaine erotically dancing onstage was nearly irresistible.

He reminded himself Brand Realty had rented the place for the night and he wouldn't be welcome. His jaw tightened as he tipped the kid a five and slid behind the wheel. Since when had he ever given a fat rat's ass whether he was welcome or not?

Shoving the car into gear, he stepped on the gas, leaving the restaurant rapidly disappearing in his mirror. The urge to see Amy hit him again as he roared up the on-ramp onto the 110 heading north. When he merged onto the Hollywood Freeway and took the exit into Hollywood, it was all he could do not to keep driving until he reached the parking lot of the Kitty Cat Club. Instead, he turned up Laurel Canyon and forced himself to go home.

Little Amy Brewer was getting under his skin and he didn't like it. Not one bit. He was helping her and that was fine, but he needed to put a little distance between them, keep things businesslike.

Still, as he climbed into bed alone, he thought of Amy and her sweet little body and how good it had been to have her there beside him. It was hours before he fell asleep.

Chapter 15

Johnnie didn't show up at the club last night and he hadn't called this morning. Maybe their night together had meant a lot more to her than it did to him. Maybe it had only been the fantasy, one-night sex Amy had imagined.

The thought made her stomach churn.

"So where's lover boy?" Babs asked as Amy was getting dressed to leave the apartment. "I figured he'd show up last night for an encore."

Amy tried for a nonchalant shrug. "I kind of thought so, too."

One of Babs's dark eyebrows went up. "I thought you said the sex was fantastic. Amazing, even."

Amy looked up at her, hoping her disappointment didn't show. "It was. At least for me."

Babs smiled knowingly. "He'll be back. No way is one night going to be enough for a guy like that."

Amy made no reply. She had no idea what John Riggs was thinking. She wasn't that experienced in bed. Maybe she just didn't do it for him.

"Listen, I've got to run," she told Babs. "I've got some things to do before my shift starts." She worked from six until two tonight and it was already after noon.

"You need my car?"

"I appreciate the offer but I've decided to rent one for a couple of days. I printed a coupon off the internet so it isn't that expensive, and I can go wherever I need."

Babs shrugged. "Whatever you think."

"I'll see you later." Amy headed out the door then down the block to the National Car Rental place she had occasionally passed on her way to lunch.

Twenty minutes later, she drove out in a little white subcompact that got more than thirty miles to the gallon, and headed for Culver City.

Earlier, she had called Mrs. Zimmer and the woman had been delighted that Angel was coming over again to see little Jimmy. As Amy stood on the porch and knocked on the door, she heard small feet pounding across the carpet.

Jimmy pulled open the door. "Hello."

"Hi, sweetie." She went down to his eye level, an arm behind her back, hiding his surprise. "Guess what I brought you?"

The little boy's eyes widened. "A present?"

"That's right." She handed him the box. "It's a puzzle. I thought maybe you'd let me help you put it together."

Jimmy studied the box. The picture on the front

showed cartoon animals in a jungle setting. Jimmy looked excited and at the same time uncertain.

"Here, let me show you." Amy took the box from his small hands and pulled off the wrapper. From the corner of her eye, she saw Mrs. Zimmer standing a few feet away, a big smile on her face. "Can we use the coffee table?" Amy asked her.

"Sure. Would you like a cup of tea while you're putting the puzzle together?"

"I'd love one."

Mrs. Zimmer disappeared into the kitchen and Jimmy knelt on the carpet next to her as she dumped the puzzle pieces out on top of the table.

"All we have to do is put the puzzle together and we'll be able to see the picture." Jimmy watched as Amy stuck a couple of puzzle pieces together. "See how it works?"

She could feel his excitement as he found a piece that locked into another piece. "Look! I did it!"

"Yes, you did." She had chosen a puzzle that fit Jimmy's age so it didn't take him long to see how putting the pieces together worked. Mrs. Zimmer set a steaming mug of tea next to her and she took a warming sip.

"Chamomile… It's wonderful. Thank you."

The older woman smiled. "Thank you for coming. Jimmy's really been looking forward to your visit."

"So have I," Amy said, which was true. She loved kids, always had. It was the reason she had decided to become a teacher. She returned her attention to the puzzle. It didn't take long to put the picture together. Jimmy looked so proud of himself when they finished that Amy reached over and hugged him.

"That was really fun, Miss… Fountain. Can we do it again?"

Fountain? Amy bit back a smile. "Why don't you just call me… Angel? And yes, we can do it again."

They played with the puzzle for an hour. Putting it together, taking it apart then rebuilding it. She made a mental note to buy him some Lincoln Logs. She used to love playing with them when she was a kid.

Then it was time to leave. While Amy was saying her farewells to Mrs. Zimmer, Jimmy raced back to his bedroom.

"I've really got to go," Amy said, checking her watch.

"Jimmy! Come say goodbye to Angel."

A couple more minutes passed.

"Jimmy!"

The little boy raced out of the bedroom, waving a piece of yellow drawing paper in his hand. "I made a present for you."

Amy took the paper and unfolded it. There was a stick drawing of a woman holding a little boy's hand. Both of them were smiling. It was signed with a row of *x*'s and an oddly printed version of his name.

"Those are kisses," Mrs. Zimmer explained. "His mother taught him that and how to print his name."

So Bee wasn't as immune to her son as she wanted people to believe. Interesting.

Amy leaned down and hugged the boy. "Thank you, sweetie. Have fun with the puzzle."

Jimmy looked up at her, his expression somber. "Are you coming back?"

Amy smiled. "Of course I am. We're friends, aren't we?"

Jimmy grinned and wildly nodded.

"All right then." Feeling a lump in her throat, Amy hugged him one last time then waved to Mrs. Zimmer and headed for the door.

Johnnie's cell phone rang. He recognized the caller ID as belonging to Dev Raines.

"What's up, Dare?"

"Chaz came up with the info we needed to narrow down the search. We've set a time for the meet if it works for you. Tomorrow night at Lark's condo." The place they stayed when Dev's wife was working in L.A.

"I'll be there with bells on."

"Since Lark's here with me, Clive's bringing Molly. I figured the ladies could talk while we make some plans. You can bring someone if you want."

Did he want to bring Amy? It would be like taking a woman to meet his family. He shouldn't do it, he knew, and yet he wanted to. He blew out a breath. Hell, it was just a group of friends. It didn't mean anything.

"Yeah, all right."

"All right? That means you're bringing a date?"

"If she can get off work."

A long pause on the phone. "Great, we'll see you tomorrow night." He needed to call Amy. He didn't know her schedule. Maybe she'd have to work. Hell, maybe she wouldn't want to go.

He brought up her cell number and pressed the button. "Hey, baby, it's me."

"Johnnie?"

"Yeah."

"I'm in the car. Let me pull over." She came back on the line a few seconds later. "Hi."

The warmth in her voice made his chest feel tight.

"I'm glad you called," she said. "I talked to Peter Brand last night and guess what he told me?"

"What'd he tell you?" He didn't like her playing detective—especially when it involved some hotshot real estate broker. He'd been down that road once before.

"He said he and Rachael never dated. He said they worked together to raise money for the Dennison Children's Shelter. I'm headed there now."

The name rang a bell. He remembered seeing it in the police file, but since Brand's alibi checked out, he hadn't pursued it. Maybe it was time. "What's the address?"

She gave him a number on Franklin.

"All right, I'll meet you there." He ended the call before she could argue. This case was getting more and more interesting. A kindergarten teacher/exotic dancer searching for an exotic dancer/social worker. He told himself the case was the reason he was meeting Amy, that he was just doing the job he'd volunteered for.

He stepped on the gas pedal, weaving the car in and out of traffic, driving a little faster than he should have been.

It was just the job, he told himself.

And knew it was a big-ass lie.

Amy pulled back into traffic, heading her little rented subcompact toward the address for the Dennison Children's Shelter she had written on a cocktail napkin last night.

Her heart was pounding, reminding her that Johnnie would be meeting her there. She told herself he was just following the lead she had picked up last night.

That his meeting her there didn't mean anything. She needed to stay focused on finding Rachael and let the man do his job.

It didn't take too long to reach the shelter, which was in an actual house, she saw as she pulled up in front of the two-story, Spanish-style building with a red tile roof, the walls painted a soft shade of pink. The yard was neatly trimmed and there was a big leafy tree in front that shaded the porch.

As she headed up the walk, she heard children's laughter coming from inside. She had almost reached the front steps when the screen door opened and a man walked out. Dressed in an expensive navy blue suit, he was extremely handsome. Johnnie's detective friend, Rick Vega.

"Detective Vega," she exclaimed, halting him directly in front of her. Clearly his mind had been on something else and for an instant, he didn't know who she was.

"Amy Brewer," she reminded him. "Rachael's sister."

"Yes, of course. Hello, Amy." He flicked a glance toward the house. "What are you doing here?"

"Last night I spoke to a friend of Rachael's…a real estate agent named Peter Brand. Peter told me she volunteered here at the shelter."

"Yes, so I discovered."

"So you talked to them here? I assumed the police would have spoken to them already."

Vega made no comment, and she realized he was thinking the same thing, but being a policeman himself, couldn't afford to agree.

"Did you find out anything?" Amy pressed.

"I talked to one of the counselors. Apparently Rachael came here often. Looks like whenever she wasn't working or trying to get an acting job, she was here. The kids adored her."

Amy felt a pang in her heart.

Heavy footsteps sounded behind her coming up the walk. Amy turned to see Johnnie striding toward her and her stomach floated up beneath her ribs.

His gaze skimmed over her, went to the detective. "You here about Rachael? I didn't think you were working that case."

"I'm not. I just ran across a connection between her and the shelter and thought I'd follow up."

"I really appreciate what you're doing," Amy said to him.

Vega just nodded. "I've got to go. Good luck in there. Maybe you'll get something I missed." Vega strode off down the walkway, and Johnnie turned to Amy.

He didn't say a word, just slid his hands into her hair, cupped the back of her head, bent and very thoroughly kissed her. She was trembling, her lips tingling, when Johnnie let her go.

He tipped his head toward the house. "We're here," he said a little gruffly. "We might as well go in."

The door stood open to let in the warm June air. Just a screen blocked the entrance. Johnnie rapped on the door frame and a young woman with short blond hair appeared on the opposite side of the screen.

"Hello. May I help you?"

"My name is… Amy Brewer. Rachael Brewer was my sister." Rachael wasn't Silky here at the shelter so Amy didn't need to be Angel. "Peter Brand told me she volunteered here on occasion."

"Why, yes, she did."

"I'm John Riggs. I'm a private investigator. I'm helping Amy locate her sister."

"Please come in." She opened the screen door and stepped back out of the way. Amy walked in ahead of Johnnie into the foyer. In the living room off to one side, a group of children of various ages huddled around the coffee table playing a game of Candy Land. Amy smiled. She and Rachael used to play that game as kids.

"My name is Eileen Caulfield," the woman said. She was wearing jeans and a Dennison Shelter T-shirt that read Where There's Love There's Hope. "I liked Rachael very much. We all did. Why don't we go someplace we can talk?"

Eileen led them into the dining room and indicated they should sit down at a long oak table that seated at least twelve people.

"Detective Vega was just here," Eileen explained. "He spoke to Melinda Richards—she's the director of the shelter. I'm afraid she's gone to lunch but maybe I can help."

"Thank you," Amy said.

"Peter told us Rachael was missing. We're all praying for her."

Amy's heart squeezed.

"When was the last time Rachael was here?" Johnnie asked.

"Just before the first of May. She couldn't stay long. She said she had some errands to run. I thought maybe she was trying out for a part or something. She wanted so much to be an actress."

"She say anything about going on a trip?" Johnnie asked.

"Not then, but earlier. A couple of weeks before that she mentioned she was going to the Caribbean. She seemed really excited about it."

Johnnie flicked a glance at Amy. Another confirmation that Rachael was planning a trip.

"Did she say exactly where she was going?" Amy asked.

"She might have. If she did, I don't remember."

"Could it have been Belize?" Johnnie asked.

The woman frowned, then shook her head. "I don't know. She did say that she and a friend would be staying in some fancy villa. But that was a week or so earlier. She didn't mention it after that."

Amy's heart was pounding.

"She happen to say who she was going with?" Johnnie asked.

"No, but I think she was dating someone she really liked. She seemed happy, you know? I thought maybe she had met someone really special. Rachael deserved a man like that."

But she had never told anyone his name. If she was seeing Manny Ortega, a drug dealer's son, she might not want anyone to know.

"Anything else you can tell us?" Johnnie asked.

"I wish I could. Like I said, she didn't mention the trip after the first time."

"We appreciate your help, Eileen."

They left the house a few minutes later and headed down the concrete path to the street.

"I rented a car," Amy said. "That little white one over there."

Johnnie walked her over, waited until she unlocked the car and opened the door.

"Did you talk to Manny Ortega?" she asked.

"I went to his place last night, a restaurant called the Vieux Carre. Manny wasn't there. He left town yesterday. He'll be gone for the rest of the week."

Disappointment slipped through her. "Oh."

"I'll talk to him as soon as he gets back. Sooner if I can find him."

Amy just nodded.

"Listen… I was thinking…wondering…" He cleared his throat. "I've got some friends coming to town. I'm going over for dinner tomorrow night, do a little business. I was wondering if you would maybe…ah, like to come with me. I mean, if you can get off work."

He seemed nervous. She couldn't believe it. He was always so firmly in control.

She beamed him a smile. "Tuesday's one of my nights off this week, so yes, I'd love to meet your friends."

Johnnie looked down at his feet. "It won't be anything fancy, you know, so you don't have to dress up or anything."

"Okay, what time?"

"I'll pick you up at six. That'll give us time to get downtown."

"All right." She glanced at her watch. She needed to get back to work, but she didn't really want to leave. "I'd better go."

"Yeah."

She started to get into the car but Johnnie turned her into his arms and kissed her, a hot, deep kiss that should have embarrassed her since they were standing right there on the street. Instead, she slid her arms around his neck and kissed him back.

Johnnie broke away. The hot gleam in his eyes said he wanted a lot more than kisses.

"I'll see you tomorrow night," he said gruffly, then stood back as she got into the car. Her hands were trembling so badly she could barely stick the key into the ignition. She finally got the engine running.

When she looked back out the window, Johnnie was gone.

Chapter 16

Rick Vega pulled off Melrose down a lane lined with box hedges and palm trees and stopped at the gatehouse at the entrance to Paramount Studios. The place was impressive. Rick knew a little of the history—everyone did who lived in L.A. Paramount was the oldest running studio, started way back in 1912. Every major actor from Rudolph Valentino and Mae West, Gary Cooper and Elvis, to Mel Gibson and Sean Connery had made movies there.

The guard leaned through the window and Rick flipped open his badge. "I need to talk to Marvin Bixler. He's the director on the *LAPD Blue* series."

Information he had received from Melinda Richards at the children's shelter. According to Melinda, Rachael had interviewed for a part in a new TV series, a take-

off on the old *NYPD Blue* show. She had been waiting to hear from the studio when she had disappeared.

He hadn't thought to give the information to Johnnie, figured his friend would get the news when he
talked to the people at the shelter. And Rick wanted to
check it out himself.

"They're shooting in studio twelve," the guard said,
after a quick look at his notes. "It's around the corner
near the back of the lot." He handed Rick a clipboard.
"You'll need to sign in."

He printed his name on the appropriate line, noted
the date and time and signed his name, then handed the
board back to the guard.

"Go on in."

Rick drove his brown, unmarked Chevy police car
toward the back of the lot, parked and went into the
big steel building, number twelve, the guard had indicated. It was huge. He figured somewhere around
fifteen-thousand square feet of soundstage, with every
conceivable sort of staging equipment.

He snagged a guy in the lighting crew, young with
short brown hair combed skyward, as the man walked
past. Rick held up his badge.

"LAPD. I'm looking for Marvin Bixler."

"You one of the technical advisors? Marv's over
there—" He pointed across the set. "The bald guy with
the mustache."

"Thanks." No point in correcting him. Rick wasn't
there to give advice. He just wanted information.

"Mr. Bixler?"

"Yes?"

"LAPD. I need a few minutes of your time."

"Look, we won't be needing you for at least a few hours. Why don't you wait over—"

"I'm not here as an advisor. I'm hoping you'll be able to help me with a missing persons case."

The director's gaze sharpened. "All right, sure, go ahead."

"I was told a woman named Rachael Brewer tried out for a part in your series. A few days later, she disappeared and no one has seen her since."

"I heard about that. She was using the name Rachael Summers so I didn't put it together till I saw her photo in the newspaper. Rachael was a really talented young actress. She was perfect for the role of Heather Stone, one of the female officers in the show, tough but a heart of gold. I felt like I'd made a real find."

"So Rachael got the part?"

"Would have. No one ever reached her to tell her the news. Then we heard she'd disappeared. Damn shame."

"Did you interview Rachael yourself?"

He nodded. "She talked to the producer and ran some lines with a couple of the lead actors in the show, as well. We all agreed she was perfect for Heather."

"You ever meet any of her friends, a man, maybe, or a girlfriend?"

"She interviewed more than once but she always came by herself. She was beautiful. Attracted plenty of male attention, I can tell you." He shook his head. "Hard lady to replace but we had no choice. We were scheduled to start shooting a few weeks after she disappeared."

Rick pulled out an LAPD business card and handed it over. "If you think of anything that might help us find her, I'd appreciate a call."

Bixler read the card then stuffed it into his shirt pocket. "Happy to help if I can." When someone yelled his name, he started toward a group of actors dressed in blue uniforms standing on the stage.

Rick turned and headed for the door. Beautiful and talented. Generous and caring. This was not the woman in the department's missing persons file. Those documents portrayed Rachael as a woman on the lowest rung of society, with few friends, most of whom were other exotic dancers. A stripper without much of a future, maybe even a prostitute. Then the whispers began linking her with Manny Ortega and the possibility she had been involved with drugs.

It didn't make sense.

The next time he saw Johnnie he'd relay the conversation he'd had with Bixler. He figured in some small way Amy would be pleased to know her sister had finally gotten the break she had been working so hard to get.

He'd do that much, but this wasn't his case and he was spending department time on a matter that shouldn't have involved him. He was supposed to be investigating a homicide down on Sunset that appeared to be gang-related.

But there was something about this case that bothered him, something that niggled the back of his mind but stayed just out of reach. He told himself to mind his own business, that he needed to refocus, stay away from the Brewer case.

Rick was determined to convince himself.

Johnnie stood at the far end of the bar talking to Tate Watters. A man in his late forties, when his hair had begun to thin, Tate had had a transplant, which had only half-ass worked. Now his head was covered with little spikes of hair in what looked like corn rows. Aside from that, with his slender build and blue eyes, he wasn't bad-looking, and amazingly enough, he was happily married to a lady named Linda who kept his account books.

"I hear you're helping Amy look into what happened to her sister," Tate said.

Hearing Amy's real name jerked Johnnie's attention away from where Angel danced, moving as if she owned the stage and every man in the room.

His head whipped toward Watters. "What'd you just say?"

One of Tate's dark eyebrows went up. "You didn't think I knew her real name? I know everything that happens in this place. I knew as soon as I met her. She looks nothing like Rachael, but they both have a way about them. The way they move, the way they walk. And Angel was way too interested in what had happened to Silky Summers. It wasn't hard to find out who she really was."

Johnnie looked hard at Tate. "The fewer people who know the better. We still don't know what happened to Rachael. Angel asks too many questions and somebody might decide to shut her up."

Tate's blue eyes shifted toward the stage. "I'm with you there. I've tried to keep an eye on her. I put her on the early shift as much as I can, but I don't want the other girls to think I'm playing favorites."

"Which you are."

"A little. These women expect me to protect them. Somehow I let Rachael down."

"There've been rumors she was seeing Manny Ortega. You know who he is?"

"The drug lord's son? Haven't seen him in here. Guy does his best to protect his reputation. Since he can't escape the connection to his family, it hasn't done him much good."

"So he didn't come in to see Rachael."

"No. She didn't date much. At least not that I know of. Rachael wanted to be a star and she had the talent and brains to make it happen."

Johnnie looked back at the stage. Amy hadn't spotted him, which gave him a chance to watch her without completely losing it. She was a really good dancer, lithe, graceful, sensuous. Every movement spoke of pure, unadulterated sex and every man in the place wanted to carry her off over his shoulder.

Johnnie was one of them.

Worse yet, he didn't want her dancing for anyone but him. He didn't want the other men to lust after her the way he did. He tried to separate the nearly naked woman onstage from the sweet little schoolteacher who had shared his bed, but it wasn't working.

He ground his jaw, told himself he had no say over her. Still...

"Looks like trouble's brewing," Tate said, his gaze sweeping over the crowd of men to a group in the middle of the room who were starting to shove back their chairs. Tate started walking. "If I hear anything useful, I'll let you know."

Johnnie watched the club owner make his way toward the men pushing and shoving, yelling obscenities near the front of the stage. Across the room, the big Asian bouncer, Bo Jing, was also walking toward the men.

The show came to a close and Angel disappeared offstage, heading upstairs to change.

Johnnie watched the scuffle that broke into a full-blown Donnybrook and smiled, glad for once he wasn't in the middle of it.

Bo Jing gripped one guy by the back of the neck, grabbed another the same way and started hauling them toward the door, one in each massive hand. Tate was reading another guy the riot act. From the corner of his eye, Johnnie saw Babs rushing toward him and he didn't like the look on her face.

"Johnnie! Some guy's got Angel—"

Johnnie was on his feet and running. Babs pointed toward the backstage area where girls started and ended their shows; he ran past her, and Babs fell in right behind him.

"I think he might have forced her into the equipment room!" Babs shouted as he charged in that direction.

There was a sign printed on the door in big black letters Employees Only. When he shoved the door open, he saw Angel struggling beneath the weight of the slick-looking muscle jock Johnnie had seen sitting alone at one of the tables. He had her on her back, sprawled over a workbench, and was fumbling with his zipper. Johnnie's vision turned red.

"You lowlife prick! Get away from her!" Before he realized he had moved, he was dragging the man off Amy, slamming a fist into his face. He brought his knee up hard into the guy's privates, and the jerk let out a shriek of pain. Johnnie didn't stop. He hit him and hit him and hit him. When the man crashed into a heap on the floor, Johnnie grabbed him by the hair, dragged his head up and hit him again. He wanted to hurt him, wanted to beat him to a bloody pulp. He wanted to kill him.

"Johnnie! Johnnie, please stop!" Amy's voice, high-pitched and nearly hysterical, finally cut through his rage. When he glanced over to where she stood, he saw that she was trembling, the little red pasties missing from her nipples, her arms hugging her chest in a futile attempt to cover herself.

Johnnie stepped over the unconscious man on the floor, reached for her and folded her into his arms.

He forced himself to breathe. "It's all right, baby, I've got you. You're okay. You're safe."

"Johnnie…" She melted against him and just hung on. She was crying and shaking and he wanted to destroy the man who had tried to hurt her.

"It's all right," he whispered into her ear. "It's all right."

Babs rushed in, carrying a red silk dressing robe and wrapped it around Amy.

"Honey, are you okay?" Babs asked. "He didn't… he didn't hurt you, did he?"

Amy shook her head. Her eyes filled. "Johnnie got here in time." She swallowed and glanced away, tears rolling down her cheeks.

Johnnie eased her back into his arms. "You don't have to cry. You're safe. You're with me."

Amy swallowed. Still shaking, she hung on for a couple of seconds longer, took a deep breath and straightened away from him, pulling the sash on her robe a little tighter.

"I'm… I'm okay."

"Should we call the police?" Babs asked. "The boss won't like it. Tate has his own way of handling guys like these. Usually saves the cops a lot of trouble."

Tate Watters stormed into the tiny room, which was getting more and more crowded. He took in the scene in an instant. Then Bo Jing appeared in the doorway, filling it completely.

"You all right?" Tate asked Amy.

She wet her trembling lips. "Johnnie came just in time."

Tate looked down at the man on the floor. "This the scum who assaulted you?"

Amy nodded. "I saw him out in the audience. I didn't see him disappear but he was waiting backstage when I came off. Bo Jing is usually there but he was helping you with the fight out front."

Tate turned to the massive Asian standing a few feet away. "Get this piece of shit out of here. Make sure he never comes back."

"You got it, boss."

Johnnie didn't have to ask how the massive man was going to manage that. He was pretty sure he knew.

Bo lifted the guy as if he were a kitten, tossed him over his shoulder and did a fireman's carry out the door.

Tate turned to Amy. "Tomorrow's your day off. Why don't you take an extra day? You'll feel better after a little time away from this place."

"Good idea," Johnnie agreed, thinking if he had his way, the extra day off was going to escalate into a week, then the rest of the summer.

He wanted Angel Fontaine's dancing career to end.

Maybe after what had almost happened, Amy would

realize he was right and give up trying to help him find her sister.

He grunted. Good luck with that.

Chapter 17

For the second time, she had nearly been raped. Her run-in with Kyle Bennett had been frightening, but tonight had been a real eye-opener. Even in the club, with men like Tate and Bo Jing to watch out for the girls, she wasn't really safe.

She looked over at Johnnie, who stared straight ahead as he drove his Mustang up the hill to the guesthouse. After demanding she go with him and refusing to take no for an answer, he hadn't said three words since they'd left the parking lot.

She knew he was angry. What had happened, he believed, was partly her fault.

"You shouldn't have been there in the first place," he growled into the silence between them, proving she was right. "You can't get a roomful of men all hot and bothered and not expect sooner or later some jackass will act on his urges."

"It's my job. Lots of women do it."

"Women with a lot more street savvy than you have. If that bastard had gone after Babs, his balls would be aching a lot more than they are right now. Christ, you don't even know how to defend yourself."

She looked up at him. "That's not true. I've had self-defense classes."

He scoffed. "Yeah? Well, why didn't you try to defend yourself tonight?"

She glanced away. Why hadn't she? "For one thing, it's been a long time since I took the course. And Bo is usually there to watch out for us when we come off stage. Tonight he was busy, and the guy took me by surprise."

"So if you'd realized the bastard was going to attack you, you would have been prepared."

"Yes. Plus I would have been a lot more prepared if I had been wearing clothes."

His dark eyes ran over her and made her think of sex, which after what had happened, should have been the last thing on her mind.

He pulled into his garage and they got out of the car and walked into the house. She had changed into jeans and a T-shirt before they left the club and brought a small overnight bag he had insisted she pack to get her through the next two days.

She wasn't sure what Johnnie expected from her tonight.

She wasn't sure what she wanted from him.

Instead of going into the living room, he carried

her bag down the hall and dropped it off in the master bedroom.

"Come on," he said, urging her toward the stairs leading to the level below. She followed him down, waited while he turned on the lights. Taking her hand, he led her across the room, which was the size of the entire upstairs, over to where he had set up a home gym.

There was all kinds of workout equipment—a treadmill and weights, a padded mat stretched out on the floor in front of the big picture windows that looked out over the city.

Johnnie led her up onto the mat, then turned to face her. "Okay, I'm going to attack you. You've got fair warning—let's see what you can do."

"Are you crazy?"

Apparently he was because he dove for her, took her down easily on the thick foam pad.

"I thought you said you knew self-defense."

Amy gritted her teeth as she pushed to her feet. "I said I'd had classes. I also said I was out of practice."

"Let's try it again."

He came in the same way he had before. Amy grunted as he took her easily down to the mat. But her limited training was beginning to come back to her. Mr. Stevens, the gym teacher who taught the class, was very determined that each of his female students learn to protect herself.

"That's okay," Johnnie said. "Tomorrow I'll show you some moves."

Amy accepted the hand he offered and let him pull her to her feet. "Try it again," she said.

A little tilt of amusement curved his lips. "You sure?"

"Come on. Do it again."

She splayed her legs, readied herself. She wouldn't have this much time to prepare for a real attack, but still...

Johnnie rushed her and she braced herself. At the last second, she sidestepped, letting his momentum carry him toward the mat, whirled and kicked him in the stomach as he went down.

An *ooof* of surprise escaped.

"Oh, my God, I didn't hurt you, did I?"

Johnnie just grinned. "Okay, that was better. Here, let's try this." He turned her around. "Pretend I'm coming at you from behind."

Amy braced herself, felt the heavy movement of his feet on the mat. He came up fast and she almost missed her chance, but her hours in class were finally coming back to her. A last-minute duck and twist, and she pitched him over her shoulder.

Johnnie sprawled on the mat looking stunned. "I can't believe it."

With a triumphant smile, Amy clamped her hands on her hips. "I told you I had classes."

Johnnie bounced effortlessly to his feet. "So you did." He looked her over, head to foot. "You're so damned little you're gonna have to be ruthless if you want to stay safe. Pretend I'm coming at you head-on."

She knew what to do. "No way. I'm supposed to gouge out your eyes or slap my hands over your ears to break your eardrums. Sorry, but I'm not going to do that."

He came in anyway, caught her around the waist and dragged her hard against him. "Try it."

"No!" What she really wanted to do was kiss him, not hurt him.

"Do it, damn it!"

He made her just mad enough. She went for his ears but he blocked the blow. She went for his eyes, but he knocked her hands away.

"Good girl. With a little more practice you might just have a chance." That said, he knocked her legs out from under her, dropping her down on the mat and came down on top of her, careful to keep most of his weight on his elbows so he wouldn't hurt her.

"Like I said, you need practice, but I have to give you credit, you know a lot more than most women."

Amy barely heard the words. With his powerful body pressing her down on the mat, all she could think of was how it had felt when both of them were naked. She moistened her lips and his gaze fixed on her mouth. His eyes glinted, darkened. His breathing quickened and she realized he was aroused.

Amy reached up and slid her arms around his neck, pulled his head down for a kiss, and Johnnie kissed her back. He tasted yeasty from the beer he'd drunk, and smelled like soap and man. Her insides went hot. She could feel the bulge of his erection behind the fly of his jeans, remembered how good it had felt when he was inside her.

"Are you sure about this?" he asked between soft, nibbling kisses. "After what happened, I wasn't sure you'd want—"

She cut off his words with another burning kiss. It was like a nuclear explosion, a scorching heat that swept them both away. Amy slid her fingers into his thick dark hair and arched upward, wishing their clothes were off and she could feel all those beautiful muscles against her bare skin.

Johnnie groaned. "God, I want you so much."

She wanted him, too. She reached for the hem of his T-shirt, pulled it free of his jeans and off over his head. Johnnie did the same to hers. She wasn't wearing a bra—not much point tonight and she was beginning to get used to going around half naked.

"So pretty," he said, bending his head to take a nipple between his teeth. The bud was stiff and aching. Oh, dear God, it felt good. Johnnie suckled and tasted, laved and pulled the fullness of her breast deep into his mouth.

Amy whimpered.

The snap popped open on her jeans and then he was tossing her high heels away and dragging her pants down over her hips. Her little white bikini panties went next, he parted her legs a little wider, kissed his way up her thighs, then his mouth settled over her sex.

Oh, oh, oh! She couldn't catch her breath. She had never let a man do this. Actually, none had tried, but no way was Johnnie backing off and so she let him have his way.

She felt his tongue sliding over her most sensitive places and heat erupted inside her. Her skin prickled and her stomach quivered. Her body drew taut as a bow string and her eyes rolled back and then she flew over the edge.

"Johnnie!" she cried out, her climax so sharp and sweet it was almost painful. She barely noticed when he left her. Then he was back, beautifully naked, settling himself between her legs. He came up over her, claimed her mouth in a hot, wet kiss, and drove himself deeply inside.

For a moment, he stilled. The tension in his shoulders eased as if he were finally where he wanted to be. Needed to be.

"Johnnie," she whispered, feeling the ridiculous sting of tears. Reaching up to touch his face, she swallowed against the lump that formed in her throat. When he started to move in a slow, easy rhythm, she melted from the inside out. Johnnie kissed her and kissed her, kissed her until she was squirming beneath him, digging her nails into the heavy muscles across his shoulders, urging him faster, deeper, harder, arching upward, demanding more.

Johnnie gave it to her. Drove into her as if he claimed her in some way. Then she was there…soaring, soaring, so sweet, so impossibly delicious. She felt his big hard body stiffen, felt the powerful surges of his climax deep in her womb. Seconds seemed like hours, her mind spinning, filled with thoughts of him.

Then they were drifting back down, finding their way back to earth. She registered the burn of his late-night beard against the side of her neck and the dampness of her skin as he moved off her, settled himself at her side.

Amy's eyes widened. For the first time she realized they had just made love on the floor in his gym.

Johnnie's cell phone started playing. He grabbed it off the nightstand, got out of bed so he wouldn't wake Amy, then realized she wasn't there.

The rich smell of coffee hit him and he smiled as he pressed the phone against his ear. "Riggs."

"It's Trace. Sol found your flight plan. Ortega's jet. The tail numbers were blocked but…" The rest went unsaid. The kid was good. One of the best. "At any rate, the flight was scheduled to leave from Ensenada at 8:00 a.m. May 2, stopover in L.A. to pick up passengers, then arrive in Belize City late in the afternoon."

"She'd been missing a couple of days by then."

"If they took her by force, they could have stashed her somewhere then loaded her on the plane."

"Or she went without being coerced."

"Could be."

"Did you find the return?"

"Yeah, a week later, May 9, and here's the interestin' part. The pilot and four passengers left LAX on the second. The pilot and three passengers returned direct to Ensenada."

"Not good news."

"No." A pause on the other end of the line. "You still seein' the little sister?"

Johnnie flicked a glance toward the door, heard Amy in the kitchen talking on her cell phone. "I guess you could say that. We're having supper with Dev and Clive and their wives."

"That so…?" Trace's tone held a note of interest, since it was way out of character for Johnnie to take a woman to meet the men he considered family.

"Don't get your hopes up," he said. "Amy's a great lady but I'd make a lousy husband. Plus she's leaving the end of the summer, sooner if we find out what happened to her sister."

"Too bad. Say hello to the guys and gals."

"Will do."

"If you need anything more, Cantrell's back from

Mexico. He's running things here while Maggie and I are in Australia."

"Finally taking that honeymoon you've been planning."

"Well-deserved honeymoon."

Johnnie smiled. "Have a good time. Try to see something besides the inside of a hotel room."

Trace laughed and ended the call. Padding across the room, Johnnie grabbed his jeans off the back of a chair where he'd tossed them last night, dragged them on and headed for the kitchen.

Amy was still on the phone. As he walked into the room, she looked up at him and smiled, and that simple gesture made his chest clamp down. This wasn't good.

She returned her attention to the phone in her hand. "I'm doing fine, Mom, really." She rolled her pretty blue eyes. "We know a lot more now than we did a few weeks ago."

Her mother said something on the other end of the line.

"I'm not giving up, Mom. Not yet."

Amy started nodding. "I'll be careful, Mom, I promise." She signed off and cast him a glance. She looked sleep-rumpled and as satisfied as a lazy cat, and thinking about the times he'd made love to her last night made him want her all over again.

Barefoot and shirtless, he padded toward her. "Your mom, I take it."

She sighed. "We always have the same conversation. She presses me to come home and I tell her I'm staying."

"Maybe she's right."

Her chin shot up. "Not you, too."

Making his way over to the counter, he poured himself a cup of coffee, tasted it and grimaced. "Next time, maybe you could put a little coffee in the coffee."

Her eyebrows went up and he realized he'd said "next time," as if there was going to be one. Something he had refused to contemplate until now.

"Okay, I'll make it stronger…next time."

He didn't reply. Just having a woman in his kitchen the morning after was a novelty. He wished it didn't feel so good having her there.

"Are we still going to dinner tonight?" she asked.

"Game plan's on as far as I know."

"So what do we do today? We've followed every lead and we still don't know much more than when we started. Did you hear from your friend about the flight plan?"

He'd almost been hoping this wouldn't come up. He had even thought about lying. "Trace called this morning. His whiz kid found the flight plan. Ortega's jet flew out of Ensenada, made a stop in L.A. to pick up passengers, then headed for Belize."

"Oh, my God. When?"

"A couple of days after your sister disappeared."

"Do you think…do you think she was on that plane?"

His gut tightened. "I think she could have been." Which meant he had to go to Belize.

And Amy wasn't going with him.

But he wasn't ready to tell her that. "The bad news is, the jet flew south with four people and returned with only three." That was the part he'd been dreading.

Amy's face went pale. She sank down on one of the kitchen chairs. "I have to go down there."

Here we go. "If she left on Ortega's jet, then somebody's got to go down there, but first we need to dig a little deeper, try to find something that will confirm she was on the plane or locate someone in Belize who saw her once she got there. Hell, she may have been one of the ones who came back. We need more information."

But if he didn't get it soon, he'd go anyway. That he didn't say.

"I'll get on it," he continued. "I know some people who might be able to help us." Like DEA agent Kent Wheeler. Wheeler had been after Ortega for years. He knew as much about the drug lord's movements as any man on earth. He might be able to find out who was on that plane.

And which of them didn't return.

"In the meantime, tonight we're having dinner with friends." He'd promised to help Dev, promised to help Amy. He was still working other cases. He felt like a juggler trying to keep all his plates in the air.

"Would you like me to fix you some breakfast?" Amy asked. "I looked in the fridge. You've got bacon and eggs. I'm a pretty decent cook."

His interest stirred and his stomach rumbled. "You can cook?"

"Hey, I'm from the Midwest. Of course I can cook."

He hesitated, thinking of all the work he had to do downstairs. It must have shown in his face.

"It'll take me a while," Amy said. "Go do whatever it is you need to do. I'll call you when it's ready."

He nodded, flashed her a grateful smile. "Sounds good." As he took off down the hall, the thought occurred, *I could get used to having a woman around.*

Which wiped the smile right off his face.

No way was that happening. Not now, not anytime

in the future. He was just doing the lady a favor. And enjoying great sex with a knockout babe. That was all there was to it.

Johnnie headed for his lower floor office, forcing his mind to focus on work. He needed to find out if Rachael Brewer was on that jet. He needed to find out whether or not she was still alive.

But deep in his gut, he was afraid he already knew the answer.

Chapter 18

When supper was over, Johnnie and the other men—Clive Monroe and Dev Raines—went to the living room of the ultramodern, downtown condo that was Dev and Lark's home when she was in L.A. for work. Clive was big, buff and sandy-haired. Dev was lean and hard, blue-eyed and movie-star handsome, one of the best-looking men Amy had ever seen. He should have looked almost pretty, but instead he just looked tough and masculine and as dangerous as Johnnie.

The men talked business while Amy, Lark and Molly sat at a stainless steel table in the state-of-the-art kitchen drinking wine.

The entire apartment was high-tech and beautifully furnished, though not at all what Amy would choose for herself. She didn't have Lark's flash, or her amazing confidence.

At least when she wasn't onstage.

Amy hid a smile. Johnnie had introduced her to his friends as *a friend,* a schoolteacher from Michigan who had come to California to search for her missing sister. It was the truth—clearly he would never lie to these people. He just hadn't mentioned the part about her dancing, which he knew would have embarrassed her.

After introductions had been made and each had been poured a glass of wine, they sat down for dinner in the dining room and enjoyed a delicious catered Italian meal: focaccia bread, linguini, ravioli in cream sauce, misto salad and tiramisu for dessert.

Amy was nervous at first, since it was clear these people were more than just Johnnie's friends. They were his family and they loved him. But Molly, a petite, curvy redhead who was very pregnant, had put Amy at ease from the moment they had met.

"You two make a great-looking couple," she said. "Johnnie must think a lot of you. He's never brought a woman to meet his friends before."

Amy wondered about that, but made no comment.

Tall and gorgeous, with a stunning figure and crimson streaked, short dark hair, Lark was a little more standoffish. She was reserving her judgment, it was clear, making sure Amy was good enough for Johnnie. Obviously, Lark loved him like a brother and would go to any lengths to protect him.

"Sooo, how long have you two been seeing each other?" Lark asked.

"Not long," Amy said. "We met sort of accidentally. I found out he was a private investigator, but I didn't have enough money to hire him. But Johnnie agreed to help me anyway. He's really been sweet."

A look passed between the women.

Maybe sweet wasn't how they saw Johnnie but deep down, Amy knew he really was. And Amy didn't think Lark needed to worry. Whatever Johnnie felt for her had more to do with sex than any sort of long-term commitment. Amy refused to think about what she felt for him.

"So when is your baby due?" she asked Molly.

"It's a boy and he's due next month. With a husband like Clive, it didn't take me long to get pregnant. I mean, he was a Ranger, right?" She grinned. "We all know what that means."

"What?" Amy blurted out before she could stop herself.

Molly grinned. "It means they're all oversexed and highly potent."

Lark laughed and Amy blushed.

They talked about Lark's little girl, Chrissy, who had stayed in Phoenix with her nanny so she wouldn't miss a special friend's birthday party. Somehow the conversation came round to how Dev had helped Lark find the child after the little girl's adoptive parents were killed. Johnnie and Clive had been involved in her rescue, which explained the strong bond the couples felt for each other.

As the evening progressed, Amy began to relax.

"Johnnie must think you're pretty special," Lark said, looking pointedly in Amy's direction. "He's usually kind of a loner, keeps his personal life separate even from his friends."

Amy tried for a nonchalant shrug. "We're...having fun. I have to go back to Michigan the end of the summer, so it isn't going to be a long-term relationship."

There must have been something telling in her face because Lark looked at her with a trace of sympathy. "Sometimes things change," she said softly.

Amy took a sip of her white wine. "Not for Johnnie. Even if things were different, he isn't ready to settle down. I don't think he ever will be."

The other two women exchanged glances. Then both of them smiled knowingly.

Amy had no idea what that meant.

Johnnie settled back against the white sofa, after the guys tossed a mountain of colored throw pillows into a pile on the floor to make room for them to sit. He took a sip of his beer. "So that's all we've got to go on?"

"So far," Dev said. "Chaz came up with three names, guys reported to be in the L.A. area and have the expertise to disable the alarms and steal the cars." Chaz could find out almost anything—as long as you didn't ask him how he did it.

"Stealing luxury cars is a real bitch today," Clive said. "With the GPS systems they've got now the engine can be turned off remotely. Even if the thief gets inside, he can wind up in a car going nowhere."

"True," Johnnie said, "but the satellite folks won't turn off the engine unless they can stop the vehicle without causing an accident."

"So the OnStar people wait till it's safe," Clive argued. "By then, the cops are on the way. Thief still can't get away clean."

"That's the rub," Johnnie said. "They can't steal the car and get away with it unless they disable the GPS without setting off any alarms. And the system's buried so deep in the wiring the thief can't tear it out."

"Which means the only way for them to get the car is to block the signal," Dev said.

"Take some brains for that," Clive said.

Dev took a drink of his wine. "Which brings us back to the three names Chaz came up with—Jack Romano, Reggie Silvers and Sergio Delinsky. Romano worked for General Motors in the auto design division. He was highly thought of—till he decided he could make more money selling GM secrets to their competitors. Reggie Silvers was jailed for hacking into the DMV. Cops never found out what he planned to do with the info."

"And Delinsky?" Johnnie asked.

"Worked for the Russian mob. Busted for manipulating the betting at the Santa Anita Race Track. All of them have the know-how to pull off something like this and all of them are currently out of jail."

"So how do we figure which one?" Clive asked.

Dev set his wineglass on the glass coffee table. "Lark's got to get home to Chrissy, but I'll be staying in town awhile, doing my best to dig up the info we need and find out where the cars are being rebuilt. I just wanted to bring you guys up to speed and make sure you'll be able to come in if this gets hairy."

"I'm in," Clive said.

"Me, too. I may have to make a trip out of the country, but if I go, I won't be gone long."

"Amy's sister, right?" Dev said.

Johnnie nodded. "We got a tip she may have been taken to Belize. You must have talked to Ghost." Trace Rawlins knew what was going on with Rachael. Johnnie had left Dev out of the loop, figuring his friend had enough on his plate with a new wife and kid and his auto theft investigation.

"I talked to him." Dev grinned. "Now that I've met your lady, I can see how you got into this so deep."

"She's not *my lady,* just a real nice girl who needed help." Johnnie tried not to think of Angel onstage or Amy in his bed. *Nice* was far too bland a word.

"You said she was a kindergarten teacher?" Clive added, tipping back his beer. "Not exactly your usual style."

No, but then you haven't seen her dance. "I'm just trying to do her a favor."

"Oh, yeah," Dev said, "I could see that when you looked at her like she was little red riding hood and you were the big bad wolf."

Clive grinned. "Yeah, like you were about to self-combust."

Johnnie grunted. "Very funny."

He was grateful when Dev took a breath and brought the conversation back to business. "So we're all on the same page. I'll be working on this, and you guys provide backup if I need it."

"I've got a man who can do some checking," Johnnie said. "Name's Tyler Brodie. Former marine. Not long on experience at this kind of thing, but useful. Kid has a way of coming up with information. I'll have him give you a call."

"Sounds good."

"We're set then," Clive said, coming to his feet.

"If I decide to leave town I'll let you know," Johnnie added, figuring he'd be back from Belize by the time Dev's info had all come together.

Now that their business was finished, Johnnie followed the men back into the kitchen. Dev's brilliant blue eyes went straight to Lark, ran over her as if he couldn't wait for the rest of them to leave so he could haul her off to bed. Clive smiled at his pregnant little Molly with the sappiest, proudest expression Johnnie had ever seen.

Johnnie told himself the only thing his eyes revealed when he looked at Amy was a strong dose of lust.

And prayed to God it was the truth.

Darkness hovered above the bright glow of lights along the Sunset Strip. Johnnie sat in a rawhide chair in the bar at Cisco's Cantina, listening to the sound of trumpets blasting out a spicy Mexican tune.

At this late hour, the crowd had faded to a few remaining tables. He ordered a beer and quietly waited for Special Agent Kent Wheeler. He was hoping to get something, some crumb of information that might confirm or deny Carlos or Manny Ortega's involvement with Rachael Brewer.

All day, he'd been working one case or another. Ty had found the info they needed to close the insurance fraud case, a fireman who was golfing and playing football with his buddies while he collected disability payments, supposedly in far too much pain to work. But Ty hadn't found anything more on Rachael's movements around the city.

Instead, Johnnie put him to work trying to come up with a location for the chop shop Dev was searching for that was rebuilding expensive stolen cars.

"If you find them," Johnnie had said to Ty, "whatever you do don't try to get inside. Just give me the info and back off. We've got a team put together to deal with it once we have what we need."

"Okay, but I want in," Ty said. "I know how to follow orders, and I'm good."

The kid still had the marine gung ho gleam in his eyes. Might be interesting to give him a try.

"I'll think about it," Johnnie said. "You just find out where they're working on those cars."

After his meeting with Ty, he'd called Wheeler and told him he was looking for information on the Ortegas. Wheeler had called back to set up a meet. During the day, Johnnie had been in and out of his home office at least three times. He didn't like to think how hard it was to stay away from Amy, who was watching TV right upstairs, force himself to think about work and not spend the day in bed with her.

Since it was her last day off, she had used the exercise equipment in his gym—warming up, she said, for the round of self-defense techniques he planned to show her. Then she'd made coffee for Ellie, who had blatantly shown up at his door, probably to give Amy another once-over. He had a bad feeling about that. The women would likely get along a little too well, which could lead to serious trouble for him.

At least Amy wasn't down at the club being Angel, asking dangerous questions, strutting around without her clothes and flaunting her luscious little body.

And she would be waiting for him when he got home from his meeting with Wheeler—something he shouldn't be grinning about, but stupidly was.

The music in the cantina changed tempo, increased to a hot salsa beat, drawing him back to the moment. Across the room, he spotted Kent Wheeler's slim frame walking toward him.

Wheeler sat down across from him, the silver in his

thinning brown hair glinting in the light of the candle on the table. "I've got something for you. Not much. I figure I owe you after the tip you gave me on that shipment into San Pedro."

"How'd that pan out? Didn't see anything about a bust in the papers."

"We were there. The shipment came in just like your guy said, but there was nothing in the containers. They knew we were coming."

"You got a leak then?"

"Looks that way. Could have been some other problem."

A cocktail waitress appeared. Johnnie's Bud was nearly full. Wheeler passed, and the waitress disappeared.

"What about Pandaro?" Johnnie asked. He was the errant husband Ty had been following who turned out to be involved with the San Dimas cartel.

"He's disappeared off the map."

"Not good."

"No, it isn't."

"So what about Ortega's connection to Rachael Brewer?" The question he was meeting Wheeler to ask.

"I've heard the same rumors you have. Manny was supposed to be seeing her, but there isn't any proof. He denies it, and he has a solid alibi for the night the girl disappeared."

"Doing what?"

"Working at the Vieux Carre. A dozen people saw him that night."

"Or he paid a dozen people to say they saw him."

"Either way..."

"Where is he now?"

"No one seems to know. He isn't in town, though. His condo's empty. Supposed to be back the end of the week."

Nothing new there.

Johnnie took a swig of his beer. "I've been following a lead that puts Rachael on Ortega's jet to Belize two days after her disappearance from the Kitty Cat Club. Nothing solid yet. You keep pretty close tabs on Ortega. Got anything that might confirm it?"

"According to our sources, the jet made a trip to Belize on May 2. Ortega's got a villa in the southern part of the country, big, well guarded. We know a woman was on the plane. We know the jet arrived in Belize City. No idea of the identity of the female passenger or where the passengers went after the jet landed."

Johnnie raked his hands through his hair. He thought of Amy and her missing sister and a knot tightened in his belly. "What about the return? Did the woman come back on the plane?"

"According to the flight plan, the jet returned from Belize nonstop to Ensenada. Reported three passengers aboard. We don't know who they were."

"So they could have left her in Belize."

"If they did, she's in more trouble than Pandaro."

"If she's still alive."

"Yeah."

Johnnie blew out a breath. "Looks like I'm going to Belize."

"I can put you in touch with someone there. A local we work with. Nathan Dietz can get you where you need to go and anything else you need. Best I can do."

"That'd be great."

Wheeler stood up. "Keep us posted, will you?"

"You know it." Johnnie watched him turn and walk away, dreading the confrontation he was about to have with Amy.

She'd want to go with him and he wasn't about to take her. He wished she didn't know he was meeting with Wheeler. He'd rather tell her the bad news after he took her to bed.

Which likely wouldn't happen once she knew she would be staying in L.A.

Chapter 19

Sitting in the living room waiting for Johnnie, mostly staring out at the lights of the city, Amy finally gave up and headed down the hall to his bedroom. She took her time changing out of the tight jeans, crop top and heels she'd put on earlier, wanting to look good for him, and instead slipped into one of his Ranger T-shirts.

It was well past midnight, but as she slipped beneath the covers of his bed, she wasn't the least bit sleepy. Sometime tonight, Johnnie would be talking to a drug enforcement agent and that agent might have news about Rachael. As it got later and Johnnie didn't come home, her nerves grew more and more taut and kept her on edge. She was dying to know what he had found out about Rachael. He might even have learned something that would tell them whether her sister was alive or dead.

But Johnnie was a night person. He worked late hours and had warned her he probably wouldn't be home until the bars closed.

She glanced at the clock. One in the morning. She was beginning to feel a little drowsy. Maybe if she closed her eyes, she would fall asleep. If she did, she knew Johnnie would wake her when he climbed into bed.

The thought made her pulse kick up. All she had to do was think of that strong male body and she was hot for him. It was kind of amazing, considering she had never felt that way about a man before.

She yawned as she reached over to turn off the light on the bedside table, heard the sound of the front door opening, and paused. The thud of heavy boots coming down the hall had her sitting up in bed, swinging her legs to the edge of the mattress.

"Johnnie?" she called, though she was already so aware of him she recognized the cadence of his footsteps.

"It's me," he answered, stepping into the room.

Amy shot out of bed and hurried toward him. "Did you meet with Wheeler? What did he say?"

Johnnie rubbed his forehead. "He didn't have much. He knew about the plane trip to Belize. He said there was a woman aboard."

Amy's stomach knotted. "So Rachael was one of the passengers."

"Could be. Or, could be any other woman in L.A."

"But the timing...everything fits. Did...did he say if the woman returned?"

"Said he didn't know."

Amy gripped his arm. "She could be down there,

Johnnie. My sister could be in Belize. I have to go, see if anyone there has seen her."

Johnnie gently caught her shoulders. "I'll go. I'll get a plane out tomorrow if I can. Wheeler gave me the name of a contact, someone who can help me while I'm there. I'll go down, ask around, see if I can find anything that will prove she was actually in Belize."

Amy felt a rush of relief. "We need to get on the internet, book some airline tickets. I'll pay, of course. The pay at the club isn't much but my tips have been terrific."

His eyes darkened. "I'll bet."

"So we're leaving tomorrow?"

Johnnie shook his head. "You can't go with me, baby. The places I'll be going aren't places you'd want to be. Let me handle this for you."

She studied his ruggedly handsome face. He was planning to leave her home—she couldn't believe it. "I can't stay here and do nothing. Rachael's my sister. I need to be there."

"It's too dangerous. And we don't know for sure your sister was ever there."

Anger began to churn in her stomach. "I'm going. Don't even think you're leaving me here. If Rachael's in Belize, she would have called if she could. That she hasn't means she's in some kind of trouble. Which means if we find her, she's going to need me."

"All right, I'll go down first, find out what I can. If the information looks promising, you can join me."

Her expression went from stubborn to mutinous. "I'm going."

Johnnie's grip on her shoulders tightened. "Damn it, you're staying right here! If Rachael was on that plane, she was somehow involved with Ortega. If that's true, then she was playing with fire. The man is a ruthless, conscienceless animal. I won't let you get into something that might just get you killed!"

Amy worked to rein in her temper. Arguing wasn't going to sway him. She would do what she had to, what she had come to Los Angeles to do.

She was going to Belize—one way or another.

They went to bed angry, lying on the mattress with their backs to each other, the clock ticking off the seconds, both of them wide-awake.

An hour later, Amy rolled onto her back and looked up at the ceiling. "In our family my dad and mom had a rule."

"Yeah, what's that?" Johnnie growled from the other side of the bed.

"They never went to bed angry. They might argue again in the morning, but at night, they were together. It worked great for almost thirty years."

Johnnie rolled over beside her. "Amy, I just don't want you getting hurt."

"I know."

He ran a finger along her cheek. "I missed you tonight."

"I missed you, too." And then he was kissing her and she was kissing him back and her heart felt a whole lot lighter. It didn't take long for her body to soften and warm, responding to him the way it always did, and then they were making love.

Amy smiled into the darkness. At least for tonight, everything was going to be all right.

Her smile slipped a little. In the morning, that was probably going to change.

Johnnie yawned as he eased out of bed late the next morning. While Amy was still asleep, he went downstairs to his office and sat in front of his computer. Once the machine had booted up, he went on the Net and booked an open-ended flight to Belize.

He thought of last night and smiled. Amy's parents must have been pretty smart people. He liked their rule, liked the idea of never going to bed angry. He liked making love to her after they had made up.

The attraction between them was as strong as ever. The problem was, his attraction to her went deeper than just sex and that was not good. He was letting down his guard, getting in too deep. He needed to pull back a little, keep his emotions in check.

He told himself it was better that Amy was staying here in L.A., going back to the club this afternoon, that he didn't mind her working tonight, dancing onstage for the men.

What a fucking lie. He hated just thinking about it.

Worse yet, he would be out of the country, nowhere near if she needed him.

He tried not to remember what had happened to his own sister. How he'd been in Mexico when Katie was killed. Not that he could have prevented it.

Still...

The smell of coffee reached him, brought him up from behind his desk. He headed for the stairs, then ambled down the hall toward the kitchen.

"I made it stronger," Amy said proudly, handing him a mug of the steaming dark brew. "I hope you like it."

"Thanks." He took a sip. Not nearly strong enough for him, since the stuff he made would straighten nails, but a helluva lot better than before.

"I borrowed some Bisquick from Ellie and baked a coffee cake for breakfast. I figured it would hold us over till lunch, though it's so late this kind of is lunch. At any rate, it's almost done." Leaning down, she opened the oven door and the aroma of brown sugar and cinnamon filled the air.

Johnnie inhaled deeply. "Oh, man, that smells good."

"My grandmother's recipe. All of the Brewer women are excellent cooks."

Johnnie's stomach rumbled. They sat down at the kitchen table and drank coffee and ate the delicious cinnamon crumb cake.

Johnnie sighed contentedly as he leaned back in his chair. "You really are a good cook."

One of her golden eyebrows went up. "Are you kidding? If you had anything in the house to cook with, I could make you something really impressive."

He eyed her over the rim of his cup. "Yeah, like what?"

"Let's see…bacon and egg casserole with green chiles and salsa. Or maybe some sour dough waffles with fresh strawberries and cream."

Johnnie's mouth watered. "That's just cruel," he grumbled, knowing she was going back to her apartment at the club and he wouldn't have any more breakfasts with her for a while.

Amy laughed.

He stood up from his chair. "The food was great, but I'd better get going. I've got some things to do and I need to pack. I'm flying out tonight."

Amy stood up, too. "I need to do that, too."

He eyed her sharply. "You're packing your stuff to go back to the club, right?"

She just smiled. "I'm packing for the trip I'm taking to Belize."

"Bullshit."

Amy set her coffee mug very carefully down on the table. "Belize is a tourist destination, Johnnie, not the edge of the world. They even speak English there. I'm going. With or without you."

His jaw tightened as he fought to hang on to his temper. He should have known last night was too easy.

"Exactly what do you think you're going to do once you get there?"

"The same thing you plan to do—ask questions and hope to get answers."

"No."

"You can't stop me. You don't own me, John Riggs. You can't tell me what to do."

He forced his jaw to unclench. "You'd need contacts, people to point you in the right direction. Aside from that, do you have any idea how dangerous this could turn out to be?"

"I'm aware of what might happen. I would definitely be safer if I went down there with you, but—"

"I swear to God, Amy—"

"I'm going, Johnnie."

He fought for control, felt it slipping away. "The flight is probably full."

"If it is, I'll get another one and meet you there."

"You don't have a passport."

She gave him a fake smile. "Actually, I do."

He made one last try. "I thought you had to work."

"I called Tate this morning. I told him I needed a few more days off and he said it was okay."

Johnnie wanted to keep arguing, tie her up to keep her safe if he had to, but the way she'd been asking questions all over town, she might be in danger right here in L.A. He thought again of Katie. He couldn't handle it if something happened to Amy because he wasn't there to protect her.

And she was just flat-out wearing him down. Rachael was her sister; Amy was determined to find her. One thing he had learned—it was hard to say no to Amy.

"What airline?" she asked, pushing him, knowing she had him beat.

"United," he growled. "It was too late to catch the early flight. This one departs tonight, 12:30 a.m. out of LAX, stopover in Houston."

"May I use your computer?"

His shoulders felt tight as his mouth curved up in a sarcastic smile. "Why not?"

Amy grinned. "I'll be right back."

She wasn't gone long and her grin was still in place when she walked back into the kitchen. "All done. I didn't know your seat number so we won't be sitting together, but that's okay."

His patience thinned once more. "Nothing about this is okay."

"I'll need to go by my apartment before we leave. Can we do that sometime today?"

"Sure, we've got all the time in the world. After all, you'll need your bikini since we're going on vacation."

Amy sliced him a glance but ignored the sarcasm, just hurried off down the hall to load her clothes back

into the overnight bag she had brought with her. Johnnie followed, his own packing to do, his mood even
grimmer than before.

He was going to Belize. Amy was going with him.

How that had happened, he still couldn't quite figure out.

Chapter 20

Amy sat in the back of the plane next to Johnnie on the second leg of the trip. They had arrived from LAX at George Bush International Airport at 5:31 a.m. Houston time. They'd made the best of the three-and-a-half-hour layover, mostly dozing upright in one of the terminal chairs, then had breakfast and climbed aboard a flight leaving for Belize at nine-thirty that morning.

As soon as the captain had turned off the fasten-seat-belt sign, Johnnie had stormed down the aisle and rudely demanded the man sitting next to her trade him seats and move to the front of the plane.

"My bag is stowed back here," the man protested, reluctant to make the switch.

Johnnie nodded toward Amy and said, "Look buddy, you'd be doing me a big favor, know what I mean?"

Realizing the big, barrel-chested man towering over

him wasn't taking no for an answer, the passenger pushed his horn rim glasses up on his nose and gave in.

"All right, fine," he said, making a show of pulling his carry-on out of the overhead bin and dragging it up the aisle.

Johnnie plunked down in the seat beside her.

Amy cast him a sideways glance. "You know you were terribly rude to that man. You could have asked him nicely."

"I'm not in the mood to be nice." He'd been angry and sullen since they left his house. He didn't want her to go, but he was stuck with her and both of them knew it.

"Well, it wasn't your finest moment."

Johnnie sighed, scrubbed a hand over his face. "Okay, you're right. It wasn't that poor joker's fault you're heading into a situation that might get you killed."

"Or...this whole thing might be nothing but a wild-goose chase."

"True enough."

Amy glanced away. "I hope not."

Johnnie reached over and laced his fingers with hers. "So do I."

Amy smiled and Johnnie relaxed against his seat. "All right, you're here. From now on I'll try to make the best of it."

"That's good. And maybe I'll be more helpful than you think."

He flashed her a look. "Yeah, right."

Amy ignored the remark, just opened the Dean Koontz thriller novel she had been trying to read since the night before they left and buried her nose in the pages.

Johnnie tipped his head back and immediately fell asleep.

As tired as she was from their late departure and her inability to sleep in the terminal, Amy wished she could do the same. She didn't realize she had actually drifted off until the landing gear locked into place, jolting her awake, and the plane began its final descent.

She turned to Johnnie, who was wide-awake and watching her sleep. "We're here," she said, both excited and a little fearful. "I didn't think to ask before…have you ever been to Belize?"

"I was here when I was in the Rangers. At the time, we were involved in some…unofficial business in Honduras. Belize was just a short hop away. My buddies and I caught a ride on a supply plane, came on down to do some diving."

"Well, that's bound to be helpful. I looked up some information on Belize when I was on your computer. It's supposed to be a little-known tropical paradise. You know until today, the only time I've been out of the country was a trip with some friends to Canada. That's when I got my passport."

Johnnie rolled his eyes. "Great."

Amy reached over, closed her fingers around his biceps, felt it bunch. "I won't be any trouble, Johnnie. I promise."

A little more of his tension eased. "The truth is, I don't really blame you. If there was a chance in hell my sister was still alive and I thought maybe I could find her, I wouldn't let anything between heaven and earth stop me from trying." As the plane touched down on the tarmac and rolled toward the terminal, he leaned over and brushed a light kiss on her lips. "You ready for this?"

Amy nodded, took a deep breath. "I'm ready."

Johnnie didn't say more as they grabbed their bags out of the overhead bin. They had each brought a carry-on but no checked luggage so they headed straight for Customs and passed through easily. Thank God, she had thought to toss her passport into her suitcase when she had packed for L.A.—in case of an emergency, which this certainly was.

From Customs, they made their way toward the exit.

Johnnie stopped at the currency window and exchanged some U.S. dollars for Belizean money. "Most places take American," he said. "Two Belize dollars for one U.S. This is just in case."

"Shouldn't I get some, too?"

Johnnie handed her some bills. "Let's go. Wheeler's contact should be waiting. We'll see what intel he's been able to scrounge up for us."

As they shoved through the glass door leading out to the street, Amy started to tell him she was keeping her fingers crossed, but the instant she opened her mouth, a wave of hot wet air hit her like a damp rag over a blowtorch and she couldn't say a word.

Her head spun. "I—I can't… I can't breathe."

Johnnie just kept walking. "Hotter than a bitch, the tropics in the summer." As Amy gasped for breath, he didn't even slow down, just set his hand at her waist and guided her toward a tall black man in his mid-thirties wearing a short-sleeved blue-flowered shirt and a wide-brimmed straw hat.

"Nathan Dietz?"

"Yes, I am Dietz." He spoke in a deep voice with a crisp British accent tinged with a trace of the Creole spoken in the Caribbean.

The men shook hands. "You know why we're here," Johnnie said.

Dietz nodded. "Agent Wheeler's email contained the information you sent him regarding the missing woman, as well as a photograph."

"Rachael Brewer. This is her sister, Amy."

She ignored the squares dancing in front of her eyes and dragged in another lungful of humid air. "It's very nice to meet you... Mr. Dietz."

"It is just Nate or Dietz." He tipped his head toward the parking lot. "My van is over there. We can talk on the way to the plane."

Johnnie just nodded as if he knew exactly what was going on.

"What plane?" Amy asked. "We just got off the plane."

Dietz talked to her over his shoulder. "We are flying into Placencia. Ortega's villa is a few miles south. It is less than a hundred miles away, but the roads in this country are primitive. Flying is far more efficient."

They started toward the parking lot, tugging their rolling bags behind them over the uneven asphalt. Palm trees waved along the streets in front of the airport but the breeze did nothing to cool the air.

Dietz slid open the van door. Johnnie helped her climb into the backseat, and the men climbed into the front. The vehicle had to be a hundred and twenty degrees inside. The air conditioner was already cranked to high as Dietz started the engine, but the wind blasting out of the vents was even hotter than the air outside.

Perspiration soaked through her clothes. She had never felt anything like it.

"What kind of intel have you been able to dig up on the girl?" Johnnie asked. "Can you confirm Rachael Brewer was on Ortega's jet?"

"I have very good sources…people who can be trusted. One of them recognized her photo as one of the passengers who arrived on Ortega's last trip. She is very beautiful, the sort of face a man remembers."

Amy's heart started pounding. Oh, God, Rachael was here. Or at least she had been.

"How about Manny Ortega? Was he on the plane?"

"Carlos was among the passengers. No one knows if his son was with him."

"What else?"

"The woman left with Ortega and the others on the private plane he uses to get him to his villa. I can only assume that is where they were going."

"You know whether the girl was on Ortega's jet when it left Belize a week later?"

"My people say only Ortega and two other men left on the plane. The woman may have left at a later date, I do not know. That is all I was able to find out. There hasn't been much time. Until I received Agent Wheeler's message, I knew nothing about the woman's disappearance."

Amy forced herself to breathe. Her sister had been there. They still couldn't be sure, but it looked as if she hadn't returned with the plane. If that was so… She refused to finish the thought. "If you know my sister came here with Ortega, we should go to the police, get them to start searching for her here."

"I am afraid that is not possible. There is no real

proof. The word of an airport worker against a powerful man like Carlos Ortega, the police will do nothing.
All you will do is put Ortega on alert."

"He's right," Johnnie said. "If Rachael is here and
still alive, going to the police would only put her in
danger."

Amy's chest squeezed. Johnnie and Dietz were right.
If Ortega hadn't killed Rachael already, he might do it
now if he found out people believed he was involved
in her disappearance.

Amy fixed her eyes on the road ahead. It was lined
with palm trees, and the asphalt in front of them seemed
to melt into the sand, which was everywhere. As they
neared Belize City, she saw that it sprawled across a
flat plain bordered by endless water.

The van turned off the main road and began winding its way through the narrow, crowded streets and her
attention sharpened. Whatever she had expected, this
wasn't it. The buildings were shabby and run-down.
The signs on the stores were faded, and laundry hung
from ropes tied between salt-corroded balconies. She
reminded herself this was a third world country, but
she had never been to a third world country, and she
wasn't really prepared for the level of poverty or the
way people lived.

Still, they seemed happy. Most were smiling as they
walked the streets, black-skinned women in colorful
sarongs, little children in ragged clothes playing kick-
ball and laughing, dogs barking as they ran along beside the van.

Dietz kept driving until they were on the opposite
side of town. A little ways farther along the road, a
private airstrip loomed off to the left. Dietz pulled the

van through the gate of a chain-link fence and drove up beside a small single engine plane.

Amy eyed the plane with trepidation.

"Another first, I gather," Johnnie said.

"Well, yes. I've never flown in a plane this size." Amy steeled herself. "But I'm sure it will be an interesting experience."

Johnnie smiled knowingly as he stowed her bag and his own, and Dietz stowed the bag he had carried out of the van.

Amy leaned toward Johnnie, speaking softly. "I know this can't be cheap. As I said, I've got a little money in the bank, not much, but my mom has some money from Dad's life insurance policy. I know she'd loan me some. I can call her when we get back."

Dietz must have heard her. "The plane is at your disposal. Agent Wheeler says he owes you."

"We'll worry about all of that later," Johnnie said, and urged her toward the tiny red-and-white plane.

Johnny led Amy to a spot in the shade under the wing of the aircraft. Her pretty face was flushed, her white shirt and navy shorts soaked clear through with perspiration. The blond hair she had pulled into a ponytail hung limply down her back. She was hot and sweaty and miserable, but he had to give her credit. So far she hadn't complained.

"This is Marcos Westby." Dietz appeared beside them with the pilot of the little Cessna 180, a man with skin even darker than Dietz's. "He will get us safely where we need to go."

"Do not worry," Westby said to Amy, his accent a

mix of British and Creole. "It is a very short flight and the plane is well maintained."

Johnnie wasn't sure she believed it, but she gamely climbed into one of the four worn leather seats. Dietz climbed in beside her, the pilot slid in behind the controls, and Johnnie sat in the copilot's seat.

In minutes they were taxiing down the runway, the wheels lifting off the ground. Amy's hand went to her middle as if she tried to calm the butterflies in her stomach.

"You okay?" Johnnie asked, speaking loud enough for her to hear.

She looked down at the ground falling away as the plane went higher, the short strip of tarmac shrinking to the size of a narrow black ribbon. "I'm fine, I'm just... it takes a little getting used to."

He'd been in the air so many times he didn't give it much thought, but it didn't seem to take long for Amy to forget her fears and become fascinated with the flight.

"It's beautiful," she said. "You can't appreciate the view from thirty thousand feet the way you can from here."

Johnnie settled back in his seat while Amy stared out the window at the vast stretches of green below, tropical forest interspersed with rivers, and the wide expanse of turquoise ocean off to the east side of the plane. Hundreds of tiny islands and cayes sprang up in the water along the coastline of Belize, some inhabited, most of them not.

The trip to Placencia wasn't long and soon the plane began its descent.

Dietz leaned toward him, speaking over the roar of

the engine. "We will do a flyover, give you a look at the Las Palmas compound."

Johnnie nodded. The plane swooped a little lower and he could make out a huge, yellow, two-story villa shaped in a U that fronted the sea. A road snaked toward it through a patch of jungle, turned into a gated approach. The place was entirely fenced but only a couple of gardeners and the guard in the gatehouse could be seen.

"When Ortega is not in residence, the security is somewhat relaxed."

Johnnie gave another nod and the pilot swung away, buzzing a short way to the north, then descending again toward a small, local airport. Dietz had a rental car waiting, a nondescript brown four-door Ford. They tossed their stuff into the trunk and the car made the short drive to a place called The Orchid Inn. The building was pink stucco with white trim, two stories, with a walkway beneath the roof around the second floor providing access to the upstairs rooms.

"It is not fancy," Dietz said, "but here you will be unremarked among the tourists, though they are much fewer this time of year. And the property is surrounded by the sea, and open land on either side. I reserved only one room. Will you need another?"

Johnnie flashed a look at Amy. "No," was all he said.

He opened the car door, letting in a fresh round of heat. Though the sea was an inviting blue-green and the sand a sugary white, the sunlight was blinding and the temperature as sizzling as it had been since they stepped off the jet in Belize City.

It wasn't high season in paradise.

Dietz handed Johnnie a room key. "Number twenty-two. That is upstairs. I have the other items you requested, as well."

"Fine, let's take the gear inside." Johnnie took Amy's carry-on and his own and started up the stairs, while Dietz carried the black vinyl bag he had brought aboard the plane. The room looked like a shabby version of a Motel 6, stripped of even the smallest luxury, just a queen-size bed, a dresser and two nightstands. Two wooden chairs sat across from each other at a small round table.

But Amy wasn't looking at the room, she was standing in front of the big plate glass window, staring at the spectacular view of the sea. As far as he was concerned, the best view was the curve of her pretty little backside. And the best news was, the air conditioner was humming away, the ceiling fan rotating over the bed, making the room feel almost chill.

Dietz slung his black vinyl bag onto the table and unzipped it, then stepped back out of the way to let Johnnie inspect the contents.

Standing next to him, Amy's eyes widened as he pulled out a shiny black handgun. "Sig Sauer P250, 9 mil." He popped the clip, saw it was fully loaded, and shoved it back in place with the flat of his hand. Lifting the weapon, he aimed it toward the door, then slowly brought it back down. "Nice choice."

"There is an extra clip and ammunition in the bag."

There was also a shoulder holster. Johnnie pulled it out and set it on the table. He'd asked for a backup weapon. There was a lightweight revolver, Ruger LCR .38 Special in the bag, housed in an ankle holster.

"This'll do just fine," he said, stowing the weapon back in the bag. There was a SoG knife, four-inch blade, which he drew out of its sheath, slid back in and shoved into the top of his high, lace-up boot.

When he glanced over at Amy, he saw that her face was pale.

"Odds are I won't be needing any of this," he said just to put some color back in her cheeks. "But you never know."

"Better to be armed," Dietz said. "This country can eat you alive if you are not careful."

Johnnie turned his attention to the map Dietz rolled out on the table.

"Ortega's villa, Las Palmas, is well-known here," Dietz said. "You have seen an aerial view of the house and grounds. There is an envelope in the bag with a map of the area, aerial photos and directions to the house, which is back down the peninsula road on the mainland."

Dietz took out the envelope and handed it to Johnnie, satisfied he had given him the information he needed.

"I'll take you back to the airport," Johnnie said to Dietz. "Around dusk I'll take a drive by the property." He wanted to see the compound from the road, take a look at possible approaches. He'd like nothing better than to get inside, but unless he had reason to believe Rachael might still be in there, it wasn't worth the risk. "Anything else I should know?"

Dietz shook his head. "I wish I had more. But as I said, time has been short."

"We haven't come up with much on our end, either. This is the first real lead we've had."

"Is there anything more I can get you?" Dietz asked.

"I'll let you know if there is."

"The phone service here is not good."

Johnnie tipped his head toward his carry-on. "Satellite phone. Not a problem."

"When you are ready to return to Belize City, give me a call. And be careful, my friend. Ortega…he is a businessman first, but also extremely ruthless, a man with no conscience."

"Which is why he's been so successful."

"This is true." Dietz handed Johnnie the keys to the rental car. "I will take that ride you promised."

Johnnie turned to Amy. "It's only a mile or so back to the airport. I won't be gone long."

Amy just nodded as he and Dietz headed out the door.

"Don't let anyone in," Johnnie said to her. And from the fear in her pretty blue eyes he figured this time she would do what he said.

Amy's heart was pounding. Somehow the danger Johnnie had warned her about had seemed a distant possibility. Never had she imagined it could mean weapons and death. She thought of Rachael, thought of men who carried guns and knives, and shivered.

She forced a breath of frosty air into her lungs. After the scorching heat outside, the room felt icy cold. She was glad for the bracing chill that chased away a little of her fear. Few people knew they were in Belize, she reminded herself. Ortega was thousands of miles away and he had no idea they had discovered information that would link him to Rachael's disappearance.

She flicked a glance toward the tiny bathroom. She needed to shower and change into fresh clothes—not that it would do much good once she walked back out the door later.

Johnnie planned to drive by Ortega's estate and she meant to go with him. She wanted to know as much about the place as she could. Rachael might be in there. There was no way to know if she was still alive, but Amy had been given a fresh surge of hope and she refused to consider the alternative. And whether Johnnie believed it or not, she could be useful. She was smart and she was determined. And she was a teacher, so she learned very fast.

Amy opened her carry-on and pulled out a pair of khaki shorts, a pink tank top and a pair of sandals to exchange for her sneakers.

With a fortifying breath, Amy headed for the bathroom and a much needed shower.

Chapter 21

It started raining, pouring out of the sky in buckets. Johnnie stepped through the door and saw Amy sitting on the bed, combing her damp blond hair. Amy had showered and changed. Just looking at her made him want her.

"It's the rainy season now," he said, ignoring the hard-on he was getting, walking instead to the window. "June to November. It's the same in the rest of Central America."

"You were there, you said, with the Rangers?"

"I was there...but I wasn't, if you know what I mean."

"It means you can't talk about it, right?"

"Right." And he didn't really want to. He did his best not to think about some of the things he had seen, some of the things he'd had to do. Heading for his carry-on, he took out a small notebook computer, set it up on the table.

"Do they have wireless service here?" Amy asked, the brush stroking down through her long, sleek hair. He wanted to go over there and run his fingers through the silky strands, set his mouth on the side of her neck. He wanted to do a lot more than that but now wasn't the time.

"I'm on satellite," he said, sitting down at the table. "I tether the computer to the sat phone. I drove the length of the peninsula on my way back, took a quick look around. I want to find out a little more about the area."

"Dietz said Placencia is the closest town of any size to Las Palmas."

"That's right. Farther down the road, there's a string of restaurants, motels and shops." He smiled. "There's even a day spa. You can get your toes painted."

Amy shot him a look. She wouldn't be going to any day spa, that look said. She was there to find her sister.

Setting the brush aside, she walked up behind where he sat at the computer reading the info he'd brought up on Southern Belize, a history of the area that went all the way back to the Maya, through pirates and Puritans to the present-day government. The language was primarily English except for the Garifuna spoken in parts of the south. The local flora included hundreds of varieties of orchids. There were giant iguana lizards, and toucans were the national bird.

He Googled *Placencia*. "Population six hundred," he read. "Not many people, but the entire country is largely unpopulated."

He searched until his brain was stuffed with what

was likely useless information, then turned off the computer and stripped off his T-shirt. "I need a shower," he said, walking toward the bathroom naked to the waist. Amy's gaze fixed on his chest and didn't move away.

A corner of his mouth edged up. "I wish I had time to do something about that look in your eyes, but it'll have to wait."

Her cheeks turned pink and she glanced away.

"The afternoon's nearly gone. I want to be at the villa by nightfall. Since we haven't eaten all day, we'll get something to eat now, then I'll head for Ortega's."

Her pretty mouth tightened. He recognized her mulish I'm-going-with-you expression and he knew he was in for trouble.

The rain had stopped by the time they left the motel. At a place called The Blue Lagoon that overlooked the water, they ate conch soup and fresh lobster. In cooler weather, the walls of the building were opened out to let in the breeze and diners ate al fresco, sitting at tables out in the open air.

Too damn hot for that now, Johnnie thought. The AC was running full blast but it was only moderately cool at the battered wooden table. But the food was worth the discomfort.

"I'm stuffed," Amy said, shoving her plate away. "I can't eat another bite."

Johnnie pulled her dish to his side of the table and finished off the rest of her lobster and cole slaw. As soon as the food was gone, he asked for the check, paid the bill and took a look at his watch.

"Time to go." It was an eighteen-mile drive up the road to the mainland, a little farther on to Las Palmas.

He wanted to be settled somewhere out of sight while there was still enough light to see.

They reached the car and he settled her inside, then backed out of the lot and drove toward the motel.

"Remember how you said on the plane that you were going to make the best of my being here?" Amy asked.

He cast her a sideways glance. "Yeah, what about it?"

"I don't want to fight with you about everything we do."

"Then we won't."

She shifted in the seat to face him. "So you'll take me with you tonight."

He inwardly groaned. He had figured this was coming. Damn it, he wanted her safe, not staking out some drug lord's house. "You promised me on the plane, you wouldn't be any trouble."

"And I won't be. I want to go. I might see something, think of something that would help."

"I'm not coming right back. I'm staying there, doing surveillance."

"I don't care. If I go, I can help you. We can take turns watching, that way both of us can get a little sleep."

He wanted to say no, but he knew how important this was to her. From what Dietz had said and what he had seen from the plane, with Ortega out of the country, security at the house was lax. Being there wouldn't be completely without risk, but if something didn't look right, he could leave.

"All right, you can go."

Her eyebrows went up in surprise. "Really?"

"Really. But you'll have to do what I say."

"I will, I promise." She looked so excited he was almost glad he'd let her come with him.

He pulled the car into the motel parking lot and made a quick trip up the outside stairs to the room to retrieve the gear he needed. He returned with the bag, the semi-auto in the shoulder holster under a red-flowered shirt, the ankle gun hidden by his khaki pants. The knife was already in his boot.

They drove the paved road up the peninsula, turned slightly inland and pulled onto the gravel road shown on Dietz's map. The lane ran parallel to the ocean, passing the entrance to the villa marked by a big spiked wrought iron gate. The road beyond it leading to the villa was paved.

Johnnie drove by the house, continuing past the service entrance a little farther down the gravel road from the main entrance. He made a U-turn, waited a few minutes, then drove back to the place he had spotted where he could back the car into the foliage out of sight. From there they could watch both entrances and not be seen.

Johnnie turned off the engine. "You might as well relax," he said, pushing his seat all the way back. "It's gonna be a long night."

There was no one driving the stretch of gravel road that passed the house. From the air, Amy had seen the commanding two-story residence built in a U-shape that backed up to the sea. She had also noticed a swimming pool in the huge yard that sloped down to the beach, a long white dock with what appeared to be a sailboat and a big, fancy cabin cruiser tied to it. There was also some kind of boathouse. Except for the beach and the dock behind the villa, the house and gardens were entirely surrounded by wrought iron fencing.

As they sat in the car with the windows rolled down, trying to ignore the heat, dusk settled around them, and the night sounds began. Insects chirping, monkeys chattering in the trees, scuffling noises in the foliage hiding the car.

The air was so hot and thick it was hard to drag a breath into her lungs. Amy figured it must not cool off in Belize until the fall, but without the direct sun, it was bearable. When she slapped at a mosquito, Johnnie turned around and unzipped the bag he had tossed into the backseat. A can of mosquito spray appeared in one of his hands.

"Malaria can be a problem down here. Close your eyes."

She did as he said, wrinkling her nose at the acrid smell as he sprayed her body and even her clothes. Then he sprayed himself and settled back to wait. She had never thought of Johnnie as a patient man, but clearly he was used to this kind of work.

"What should we be watching for?" she asked.

"Anything or anybody moving around out there."

Which hadn't happened so far, since there didn't seem to be a soul in the area except the guard in the gatehouse. But the small structure sat off the main road, halfway up the paved road leading to the villa.

Amy checked her watch. It was a few minutes past nine o'clock when a battered old pickup drove down the service road away from the house. The vehicle stopped in front of another iron gate, which automatically swung open, and the pickup drove through, followed by a dinged-up ancient yellow car with a shiny red fender, apparently a replacement for one that had been wrecked. A rusty flatbed truck was last in line before the gate swung closed behind them.

"They're heading home," Johnnie said. "It's the end of their shift."

"Employees? That's who they are?"

"Kitchen staff, housekeepers, gardeners, maybe. Anyone who isn't live-in."

Amy watched the ragged-looking vehicles drive past, a man and woman in the pickup, four women in the battered yellow car, and two men in the flatbed truck, the wheels bouncing along the uneven road toward the tiny village of Riversdale or on to Placencia.

"It would take a lot of people to run a place like this," Amy said. "I wonder if the kitchen help does the shopping."

"Probably," Johnnie said absently.

"I saw a couple of grocery stores in Placencia when we went to supper. There are stands that sell fresh vegetables and fish, but the cook would still need staples like flour and sugar, and of course, cleaning supplies."

Johnnie looked at her with something a little more substantial than indulgence. "Good thought. Riversdale's too small for a real store. Has to be Placencia. Something to keep in mind."

An hour passed. The guard in the gatehouse was relieved by another man, both of them wearing short-pants uniforms that appeared to be white, but it was getting too dark to tell for sure. Amy fell asleep a little later, then woke up with a start when Johnnie lightly shook her shoulder.

"Easy. Everything's okay. It's late. I want to take a look around." Pulling up his pant leg, he jerked the revolver she had seen earlier out of the holster strapped around his boot. "I don't suppose you have any idea how to use one of these things."

She straightened. "I do, actually. My dad and I went deer hunting all the time. I mean, I never actually shot a deer or anything, but I know how to do it."

"Good. So you've used a rifle. How about a handgun?"

"Target practice. Daddy owned a .38 revolver. It looked a lot like yours. He showed me how to use it. It's been a long time, but I think I can remember."

"There's an empty chamber beneath the hammer." He put the gun in her hand, wrapped her fingers around it. "Just hold it in front of you, keep your arms straight, cock it and fire. Then just keep firing."

Her mouth felt dry. "I remember."

"Listen, you aren't going to need it, but if something doesn't look right, pull off a shot and I'll come running. Okay?"

She managed to smile and hoped it didn't look wobbly. "I'll be fine."

Johnnie reached up and pulled the bulb out of the overhead light. He rifled through his bag and took out a pair of binoculars.

"Night vision," he explained, looping the strap around his neck. Quietly opening the door, he rounded the car to her side, leaned through the window and pressed a hot, hard kiss on her mouth. "I'll be back as soon as I can."

Amy watched him disappear soundlessly into the underbrush, barely moving a leaf. Insects hummed and darkness closed around her. There was no moon tonight, which was probably good, considering they were out there spying on a drug lord. Amy fixed her eyes on the house. Only the low lights illuminating the path to the front door burned through the night. She sank down in the seat, cradling the pistol in her lap.

Praying she wouldn't have to use it.

Johnnie circled the exterior of the compound. The iron fence was over seven feet high with spikes along the top. It wasn't electric, but was undoubtedly hooked to a sophisticated alarm system. He'd spotted a man patrolling the grounds. Another walked the long stretch of beach behind the house. Both were currently out of sight.

He looked at the fence, wishing he could get into the compound, but he didn't have the equipment to disable the alarm system, and it wasn't really worth trying to get in if Rachael wasn't in the house.

He moved along the fence line. There were no lights shining through any of the windows, no sounds coming from inside. There were probably a few live-in employees, but by now they'd be asleep.

Johnnie didn't like the conclusion he was coming to. He couldn't see a man as powerful as Ortega taking the risk of holding a woman prisoner in his villa, not with servants and guards, and the visitors Ortega often entertained. If Rachael had been brought to the house and hadn't returned on the plane, likely she was dead.

Not a theory he intended to share with Amy. Not yet.

He reached the beach, careful to stay out of sight in the dense foliage and palms along the shore, noted the location of the guard patrolling the area, waited until the man disappeared out of sight, then made his way to the boathouse. It was solidly locked, but looking through the window, he could see a big, white cigarette boat. They were fast—and Jesus, this one was a beauty. More expensive toys to bolster Ortega's ego? Or was it used for something else?

Satisfied with his preliminary observations, Johnnie left the dock area and began making his way along the fence line back to the car. He approached quietly. Stopping a few feet away from the vehicle, he reached down and picked up a pebble, tossed onto the hood on the opposite side from where he stood. Amy's gun came up, pointed straight out the window.

Good girl, he thought. "It's me," he said softly before he came closer. "Don't shoot."

She relaxed against the seat, lowered the gun back into her lap.

Johnnie slid into the driver's seat and started the engine.

"Did you see anything?" Amy asked anxiously as they rolled quietly off down the road.

"Two additional guards besides the guy in the gatehouse. There's probably a couple of live-in servants, but for now, that's it."

"Can you get inside?"

"I'd have to disable the system and I don't have what I need to do that. And to tell you the truth, I don't think she's there."

"Why not?"

"Not enough activity. We've been here for hours. Nothing looks suspicious. And Ortega is a very careful man. It's not his style to leave a loose end like your sister, and that's what she'd be if he was keeping her prisoner in his house."

"Maybe she's there voluntarily."

Johnnie raked a hand through his hair. "It's possible, I suppose. If she's Manny's girlfriend and he brought her down here. But if that's the case, why hasn't she called?"

Amy glanced away. They needed more information, needed to know if Rachael was still in Belize, and finding out wouldn't be easy.

Nor would finding Rachael Brewer's body if she was dead—which was becoming more and more likely.

Rachael would have called. Amy didn't doubt it for an instant. Which meant that if she were still in Belize, she was being prevented from calling her family, held against her will.

Or she was dead.

Amy's heart twisted. She wasn't ready to accept that, not yet. They had only been in the country one day.

She rested her head against the window, which was once again rolled up and the air conditioner blasting. The jungle rushed past in the darkness. As Johnnie turned the rental car onto the long strip of asphalt leading back to their motel, the ocean appeared as a vast black stretch of nothing.

It didn't take long to reach the parking lot and a few minutes later they were climbing the stairs to their room at The Orchid Inn. All the way home, Amy's chest was squeezing. They knew now that Rachael had actually been in Belize, been a passenger aboard Carlos Ortega's jet. Ortega was a notorious drug lord, a man with a brutal reputation.

What had he done to her sister?

As they walked through the door of the room, Amy brushed a tear from her cheek. Johnnie moved silently

past her across the room. He unbuttoned his shirt and
removed his shoulder holster, took off his ankle gun
and set the rest of his gear down on the table. Feeling
sad to her bones, Amy walked over to the window and
stared out at the dark swatch of ocean.

"You bring that bikini I mentioned?" Johnnie asked
from behind her.

She turn to face him, shrugged. "It's the Caribbean.
I brought it. Too hot to sunbathe, that's for sure."

"Not too hot for a swim." Sitting down on the edge
of the bed, he removed his ankle gun and knife, un-
laced and pulled off his boots.

"Come on. You need a distraction." A familiar gleam
appeared in his dark eyes. "I plan to give you one."

Amy just looked at him. She was tired and de-
pressed, worried that her worst fears for her sister were
about to be confirmed. And yet when she looked at
Johnnie, standing there in the trunks she hadn't noticed
him putting on, she felt a tingle of desire she hadn't
expected to feel.

Maybe if he made love to her, she could stop thinking of Rachael and what might have happened. For a
while, maybe she could forget.

She pulled out a yellow bikini from her bag, stripped
off her clothes and put it on. Her fingers seemed not to
be working and for a moment she had trouble hooking
the top behind her back.

"I'd offer to help you," Johnnie said gruffly, "but if
I do, we'll never make it to the water."

She managed a smile. Johnnie grabbed one of the
big beach towels the hotel provided, the only luxury
that came with the room, and they headed for the door.
They padded toward the water, Amy curling her toes in

the warm, soft sand, Johnnie holding on to her hand. It felt good to have him there beside her.

Too good.

He always seemed to be there when she needed him, always seemed to know what to do to make her feel better. She didn't want her feelings for him to grow any deeper than they were already, but she couldn't seem to stop it from happening.

Amy sighed. She would worry about all of that later. Tonight she needed him to touch her, make love to her, make her forget.

And because he was Johnnie, he seemed to know.

Chapter 22

Johnnie unfolded the beach towel and spread it on the sand at the edge of the water. They had walked a ways away from the motel and as dark as it was, there was little chance of being seen. He glanced over at Amy, who stared out at the ocean, her thoughts a million miles away.

Though he couldn't see her face, he could read her thoughts as clearly as if she spoke them. She was thinking about her sister. She was thinking exactly what Johnnie was thinking: that if Ortega brought Rachael to Belize and didn't take her home, she was probably dead.

The *why* was the part he couldn't figure—unless Ortega was protecting Manny from a woman he didn't see as good enough for his son. But bringing Rachael all the way to Belize seemed like a lot of trouble when he could have just gotten rid of her in L.A.

Johnnie reached out and caught Amy's hand, tugged her down the slope into the surf and out into the sea. She needed to forget about Rachael and for a while he could make that happen. Leaning over, he gave her a soft, deep kiss, turned and dove under the water. A few seconds later, he popped up, wiped water from his face and raked back his hair.

"Feels great," he said. "You're gonna love it, I promise." The ocean was warm, more like swimming in a bathtub than the sea.

Amy dove in and disappeared beneath the surface. He felt a tug on his leg, a small hand trying to knock him off balance. Grinning, he let her drag him under. She came up laughing and Johnnie surfaced beside her, a fake scowl on his face.

"You'll pay for that one, sweetheart."

Amy shrieked as he scooped her into his arms, lifted her high in the air, then dropped her into the water. They played like kids, splashing and laughing, forgetting for a while the reason they were there. It was after three in the morning. Not a soul around. Johnnie caught her hand and tugged her toward a little dock that protruded into the ocean. A stack of kayaks sat on top, waiting for eager tourists to rent them.

He turned to Amy, bent his head and kissed her, softly at first, then more deeply. "Baby, you're wearing too many clothes." Unfastening the hook that held her bikini top in place, he slipped it off and tossed it up on the wooden dock. A tug on the strings holding the bottom in place, and he tossed it up next to her top. His trunks joined them.

He could easily touch the sandy bottom, though Amy

was a little too short and had to keep her arms around his neck to stay afloat.

Perfect.

God, he loved kissing her. She tasted so sweet, so female and so damned sexy. Her nipples tightened against his chest as he lifted her, wrapped her legs around his waist. He kissed the side of her neck, nibbled an ear, claimed her mouth again. The water lapped around them, warm and seductive. The night was dark and erotic, kicking his lust into high gear.

With her long hair streaming over her breasts and her lips pouty from his kisses, she was a mermaid escaped from the sea. His erection throbbed. From the moment he had first seen her dancing as Angel Fontaine, he had wanted her more than any other woman.

His tongue slid over her plump bottom lip, testing the fullness, the sweetness. He kissed her softly this time, he wasn't sure why, and Amy made a funny little sound in her throat. Reaching beneath the water, he ran a hand along her thigh, found her sex and began to stroke her. He wanted to be inside her so bad he ached, but he didn't want to rush her.

Instead, he deepened the kiss, caught her soft little moan in his mouth. She was trembling, squirming in his arms, as ready as he was. The condoms he'd brought were lying on the beach towel. Cupping her luscious little bottom in his hands, he started sloshing through the water toward the shore.

The beach towel was spread at the edge of the sand. Careful to keep his weight off her, he lowered her onto the towel and came down on top of her, kissed her hotly, took her deeply with his tongue. Those delicate, pink-tipped breasts beckoned him to taste them. Amy moaned as he took the fullness into his mouth, tugged and laved until she squirmed beneath him.

"Johnnie...please...." Her soft pleas made him harder still.

"Soon, baby." Ripping open one of the foil packets, he sheathed himself, then turned onto his back and lifted her up to straddle him. "Damn, I want you."

She felt featherlight as she adjusted herself, took him deep inside. Her eyes were closed, her golden hair wet and falling like a curtain around her shoulders.

She was magnificent.

Something sweet settled inside him, something he had never felt before and didn't want to feel now. He steeled himself against it, felt her rock against him, concentrated on making it good for her.

"That's right, baby. This time you're the one in control."

A sweet smile touched her lips. Amy arched her back, thrusting her pretty breasts toward him. Her head fell back and wet strands of long blond hair teased his thighs. When she began to move, it took all his will not to explode right then and there. But he had promised to let her explore her sexuality, and he wanted to watch her when she came. As he kneaded her breasts, Amy moved faster, up and down, up and down, little mewling sounds coming from her throat, driving him crazy.

When she started to come, he gripped her hips and drove himself deep, thrust into her again and again, reached his peak just an instant after she did.

Amy slumped onto his chest and for long seconds he just held her. She was so small, so sweet. His throat felt tight. He wanted to hold her forever. It was crazy.

Insane. He wasn't the guy for Amy. He wasn't the guy for any woman.

He eased her off him, settled her beside him. For a while, they looked up at the stars, a spray of diamonds against the black night sky.

A feeling of contentment settled over him he didn't want to feel. He released a slow breath. "We need to go in, try to get some sleep."

Amy just nodded.

For several long moments, neither of them moved. Slowly he rose, reached down and pulled her to her feet. Arm in arm, they walked back into the warm sea to cleanse themselves and put on their bathing suits for the trip back to the motel.

Neither of them spoke on the way.

There was nothing either of them could say and too much on their minds.

Amy lay in bed pretending to sleep as Johnnie dressed in loose-fitting khaki pants and a navy blue T-shirt, grabbed his gear bag and left the motel room. He had written her a note and left it on the table. Scrambling out of bed, she grabbed the note and quickly read the words.

Gone to the villa for more intel. Home before supper. Stay out of trouble. Johnnie.

Johnnie was gone for the day. She smiled.

Perfect.

There was an idea she wanted to explore and she was afraid he wouldn't give her the chance. Writing him a note in case he came back early, she took a quick shower and put on a pair of tan shorts and a loose-fitting yellow T-shirt.

Her stomach rumbled. After supper last night, they had bought some bakery goodies for breakfast and Johnnie had set the bag out on the table. It was still early. They'd only had a few hours' sleep. Shoving her feet into her sandals, she picked up her purse, grabbed a sweet roll out of the bag and headed for the door, ready to put her plan in motion.

Yesterday, she had noticed a shuttle that ran along the beach carrying tourists from their motels into the village. There were shops, restaurants, bars and boutiques all along the ocean.

And the grocery store where she was headed.

There were several in the village, but the Paradise Market looked like a place the locals would shop. Standing in front of the motel, she waited for the shuttle to approach, finally spotted it trundling down the road, waved it over and climbed aboard.

It was early. There were only two other passengers aboard, a couple of tourists from the way they were dressed and the camera hanging around the man's neck. A long stretch of sandy beach ran all the way into the village. Though there weren't as many tourists this time of year, the beaches and warm clear water, perfect for diving, helped the motels and restaurants stay in business.

Amy got off the bus a little ways from the store, stopped in one of the open-air boutiques and bought herself a wide-brimmed straw hat, then stuffed her long blond ponytail up underneath. With a pair of big white sunglasses to cover her eyes, she figured she looked like any of the tourists exploring the town.

And she wouldn't be all that recognizable after she left.

From the boutique, she made her way to the coffee shop next door to the market. Last night, three vehicles full of Las Palmas employees had left the villa. If any of them showed up in the parking lot, she would talk to whoever was in the car.

It was a long shot. But so was everything that had led them here. It was how detective work was done, she imagined, following hunches, running down leads, looking into whatever information could be found. She went to the counter and ordered a cup of thick, dark Belizean blend, then sat down in front of the window to wait.

An hour passed. She went next door and bought a magazine to read to pass the time. Another half hour had passed when a rusty flatbed truck pulled into the parking lot. For an instant, her heartbeat quickened. But there was something off about the truck, something that didn't look right.

She knew cars. This wasn't the truck she had seen last night. Her shoulders sagged. It was a stretch to think she would be in exactly the right place when someone from Ortega's villa arrived to do the shopping. But around here, she figured people shopped for fresh fruit and vegetables nearly every day, and if someone did come to town from the villa, they would probably shop early and they would come to the Paradise Market.

She glanced at the slender black woman working behind the counter. There was no one else in the coffee shop and with the heat and the laid-back attitude of the people, no one seemed to care that she still sat at the rickety wooden table sipping a drink—an iced tea now that she had finished her coffee.

Mentally, she decided to wait another hour. At ten o'clock she would give up and go back to the motel.

It was a quarter to ten when the dented yellow car with the red front fender pulled into the lot. Amy shot up from the hard wooden bench she'd been sitting on and moved closer to the window.

Two dark-skinned women got out. One went over to an open-air fruit stand, the other went into the market. Only a single vendor worked at the fruit stand. Amy headed in that direction.

Johnnie lay on his belly, hidden in the foliage outside the fenced compound of Las Palmas, a pair of binoculars focused on the house.

All day, the servants had been going about their business, the gardener pruning and clipping the plants and blooming flowers: pink, orange, purple, beautiful white orchids. A guard patrolled the grounds while another walked the beach behind the house.

No sign of any guests, or anyone other than Ortega's employees. Johnnie timed the rounds the guards were making, a twenty-minute pattern they seemed to follow consistently. He wished he could get past the alarm system and into the house, satisfy himself that Rachael wasn't there.

She wasn't. He was almost completely convinced. And getting inside wasn't going to happen. Not without the equipment he needed.

The crunch of car wheels churning up the gravel road caught his attention and he turned to see a newer model silver pickup heading for the service entrance. The gate swung open and the pickup drove toward the house. Through the binoculars, Johnnie could see two men in the truck, a pale, skinny blond, and a man who looked like a local. The bed of the truck was filled with crates and boxes.

But the truck didn't stop at the back of the villa to unload. Instead, it continued down to the dock. The men jumped out of the truck and began to lift the boxes out of the bed and carry them into the boathouse. Johnnie scanned the area, saw no other movement, and returned his attention to the activity in and out of the boathouse.

Something was up.

Propped on his elbows, Johnnie glassed the boathouse and prepared to wait.

Amy approached the bone-thin woman with a woven basket on her hip picking vegetables from the stand. She was dressed in a red-and-white-flowered sarong, an orange-checked turban around her head. Amy almost smiled. Caribbean people were nothing if not colorful.

Amy waited until the woman finished her transaction, bartering in thickly accented English for corn, carrots, peppers, onions and tomatoes. Once the basket was full and she started to walk away, Amy moved up beside her.

"You work at Las Palmas," Amy said pleasantly. "I drove by the villa yesterday. It's a very beautiful place."

"It is a lovely place," the woman said.

"I have a friend who visited there recently." She pulled Rachael's photo out of her purse. "I was wondering if you might have seen her when she was there."

The woman's gaze ran over the photo and something flickered in her eyes, an instant of recognition, Amy was sure. Then her features tightened and she firmly shook her head. "I have not seen her. Please leave me alone."

"She's my sister," Amy pressed. "She's been missing for weeks and I'm trying to find her. I was hoping—"

"Go away!" the woman snapped, and stalked off toward the fish stand across the way.

Amy let her go. *No help there,* she thought, though she believed the woman had indeed seen Rachael. She was frightened, that much was clear. Which made Amy even more frightened for her sister.

Pulling a Kleenex out of her purse, Amy blotted the perspiration from her forehead and headed for the market, where the second woman had gone. The aisles were crowded with foodstuffs: sacks of flour, bags of sugar, paper goods and cases of bottled water. She spotted the second person she had seen getting out of the yellow-and-red car, a thin, older woman with skin so black and shiny it was almost iridescent. Amy walked directly up to her, blocking her escape.

"Hello. My name is Amy." She smiled. "You work at Las Palmas, don't you?"

The woman lifted a bag of rice into her cart. "I am one of the cooks."

"It's a beautiful place. So big, though. It must be hard to take care of."

The woman smiled, showing crooked teeth. "It takes a lot of hard work."

"A friend of mine was there for a visit recently. I wonder if you might know her?" Amy dragged the photo out of her purse and held it up for the woman to see. "Her name is Rachael Brewer."

The woman's whole body tightened. When she just kept staring at the picture, Amy rushed to continue.

"Rachael is my sister. I've been looking for her for weeks. I know she was here with the man who owns the villa, Carlos Ortega. She was here, but she never came home."

The woman trembled. "You must leave this place. I warn you. It is not safe for you here. If Señor Ortega finds out you are looking for your sister, bad things will happen."

Amy's chest clamped down. "What do you mean?"

The woman swallowed, the whites of her eyes a little too prominent as she glanced around to make sure no one could hear. "You are in danger. You must go now." She pushed the cart forward, but Amy refused to budge.

"Please...if there is anything you know that will help me, please tell me. I'll never tell anyone, I promise."

The woman's black eyes darted around the store. "If he finds out what you are doing, he will take you away as he did your sister. As he did my daughter, Tayla."

"Where did he take them?" Amy asked softly, urgently. Frightened now herself, she followed the woman's frantic gaze, but the man behind the cash register was a good distance away and busy with a customer.

"To the island. A very bad place. He took my Tayla there, and others. None ever return. It is too late for your sister. Go back where you came from before it is too late."

The woman shoved the cart forward, determined now, forcing Amy out of the way. Inside her chest, her heart was pounding an erratic tattoo. There were islands and cayes all along the coast. Many were privately owned, she knew from the book on Belize she had bought at the airport in Houston.

If Ortega had taken Rachael to a private island, maybe she was still alive and maybe they could find her.

By the time Amy hurried out of the store, the yellow car with the red fender was gone. The shuttle was just arriving. Ignoring the heat beating down on her, she ran toward the vehicle idling in the lot and hurriedly climbed aboard.

Chapter 23

The heat was making him drowsy. It was the hottest time of day and even in the deep shade of the thick tropical foliage it was sweltering. It was the heavy rumble of an engine that had his head jerking up, and Johnnie realized he had almost fallen asleep. He trained his binoculars on the boathouse and saw the big, white cigarette boat being slowly eased out and into the water. The men from the silver pickup were aboard, the skinny blond man at the helm. The crates and boxes were stacked around them, but nothing indicated what was inside.

Swinging the keel of the boat toward the open sea, the driver increased the throttle and the boat began to build up speed. Johnnie watched it head out to sea, moving faster and faster, until it finally disappeared from view.

What the hell was Ortega delivering? And where?

Johnnie couldn't imagine Ortega risking a drug deal this close to one of his private homes, but there was no way to know for sure.

Forcing himself to ignore the heat, Johnnie settled in to wait for the boat's return. When it didn't come back within the hour, he packed up his gear and headed for the car he had hidden down the road. A few minutes later, he was driving back to the motel, a little more eager to get there than he wanted to be.

When he got there, Amy wasn't in the room. Next to the note he had left for her that morning was a second piece of paper.

Gone to the village. Back before supper. Amy.

Son of a bitch. Maybe she had just gone to get something to eat. A sweet roll wasn't enough food for the day. If she had, she should have been back by now.

Johnnie crumpled the note in his fist. He had specifically told her to stay out of trouble. But Amy's middle name was Trouble. If she wasn't back in the next half hour, he was going after her.

Twenty minutes later, he was pacing the floor, contemplating the notion of paddling her sweet little ass. A rush of relief hit him when he heard the key in the lock. The door swung open, and Amy walked in.

She slammed the door and ran toward him. "Johnnie! Oh, thank God you're here!"

"Yeah, well, you won't be glad when I get finished with you."

She just rolled her eyes.

"I told you to stay out of trouble. Where the hell have you been?"

"I've been doing exactly what we came to do. I found out where they took Rachael."

"What?"

"That's right. Ortega owns an island somewhere along the coast. He's taken other women there and that's where he took Rachael."

"How the hell did you find that out?"

"I went to the market this morning. Remember last night I was thinking that one of the servants in the house probably did the shopping in the village?"

He frowned. "So you went there and started asking questions."

"And I got lucky. I recognized the yellow car from last night, the one with the red fender. There were two women inside. One of them recognized Rachael's picture. She said Ortega took her to his island. The woman warned me that I should leave before something bad happens to me, too."

That was exactly why he hadn't wanted her involved in this. "Asking questions that might get you killed—that's your idea of staying out of trouble?"

"I'm here to find my sister, Johnnie. All we have to do is find the island Ortega owns."

"That's all, huh?" But her information could be right on the money, he had to admit. It fit with the boat full of supplies he'd seen leaving the dock. If Ortega owned an island, that's where the crates and boxes were likely headed. "What makes you think this woman was telling you the truth?"

"Because Ortega took her daughter there—Tayla, she said. Because Tayla never came back. She was terrified, Johnnie, but she didn't want to see the same thing happen to another girl."

Johnnie sank down on the bed, ran his hands through his hair. "Christ."

"We have to find that island."

"Then what?" he asked, glancing up. "If she's there, we need a way to get her off. We'd need men, equipment, weapons."

Amy's shoulders slumped. "We *have* to find a way," she said softly, desperately.

Johnnie's chest tightened. Then his sat phone started ringing, saving him from having to reply.

He dug it out of his pocket, pushed the button and pressed the phone against his ear. "Riggs."

"Got some intel for you." Jake Cantrell's deep voice boomed over the line. Jake was a longtime friend, a former marine sniper and Force Recon, one tough son of a bitch. He'd been part of the job with Dev Raines down in Mexico. He was now back in Texas, working with Trace.

"Fire away," Johnnie said.

"Before he and Maggie left for Australia, Trace filled me in on your missing persons case. Sol flagged the tail numbers on Ortega's jet for any new flight plans his pilot might file. A few minutes ago, one popped up on the screen. Tomorrow morning, Ortega's on his way back to Belize."

Johnnie hissed a curse.

"You there now? Trace said you might be headed down there."

"I'm here. We're about twenty miles from Las Palmas—that's Ortega's villa."

"We?"

"Amy Brewer is with me. Rachael's sister."

"So I heard. Guess you finally got her in bed."

"Fuck you, Cantrell." Helluva thing when his buddies knew more about his love life than he did.

Jake just laughed. "Come up with anything?"

"We got a lead on the girl," Johnnie said. "Amy was able to get close to one of Ortega's servants. Looks like he might have taken Rachael to an offshore island. I'm guessing he owns it. We need to find the location but even if we do, it's gonna take time to put a rescue operation together—assuming the girl's still alive," he added quietly, for Amy's sake.

"Sol can find the location. I can help with the other. I'm only a two-hour flight away. I've got a friend, ex-SEAL. Could come in handy for the kind of operation you're facing."

"Might be a wild-goose chase. We're pretty sure he took her out there. We have no idea what's happened to her since."

"I'll get Sol on it and call you back."

"Thanks, Jake."

Johnnie paced the room for an hour while Amy busied herself reading. Johnnie stole a glance at where she stretched out on the bed with a pillow beneath her head and tried not to think of what had happened on the beach towel last night. If he did, he was in trouble.

He smiled. Both of them were in trouble.

He glanced at the clock. It could take hours to find the island. It hadn't shown up on any of the intel Johnnie had seen about Ortega, or been able to dig up on his computer. Hell, the ownership was probably so buried even the whiz kid couldn't find it. His stomach rumbled. He hadn't eaten anything but a sweet roll all day.

"You hungry?" he asked Amy.

She sat up, set the book on the nightstand. "Starving."

"Let's drive into town and get something to eat."

"Great."

But just as they headed for the door, the sat phone started to ring.

"We found it," Cantrell said into the phone. "Took a while, Ortega's good at hiding information, but Sol's even better at finding it. The island is owned by a company called Genesis, which is owned by a company called Encore. Encore's corporate officers include a guy named Raymond Dominguez. Dominguez is one of the men in Ortega's inner circle."

"Where's the location?"

"About twenty-three miles due east of Las Palmas. Satellite map shows heavy vegetation, some kind of structure near the center of the island."

"I'll check it out." He could find the preliminary info he needed on Google Earth. It was a different world these days.

"There's a flight out of here in the morning," Jake said. "We'll be on it. We'll figure things out when we get there."

"I'll have our contact waiting for you when you get here. Name's Nathan Dietz. He can get you down to Placencia. What about weapons?"

"You armed?"

"Yeah."

"I've got connections in the area. I'll take care of the rest of the weapons and ammo and whatever equipment we'll need." Mexico, Central and South America were Cantrell's specialty, though he'd also done some work for the Saudis over the years.

"All right then," Johnnie said, "looks like we're a go."

"I'll see you tomorrow. Tell your lady to keep the faith."

"She isn't my—ah, hell, never mind."

Cantrell signed off and Johnnie hung up the phone.

Amy stared at him, unconsciously biting her lip. "Your friends are coming to help us?"

"Looks that way."

"I don't...don't have much money, but I'll find a way to pay them. I'll do whatever it takes."

Johnnie walked over, settled his hands on her shoulders. "Listen, baby, a lot of this is payback, some of it's quid pro quo. Some of it's just because we're friends. Don't worry about the money. None of us are hurting."

She looked up at him, big blue eyes sparkling with tears. "We're going to find her, I know we are."

"Maybe. Cantrell says to keep the faith."

She smiled but a tear rolled down her cheek. "I think I'm going to like him."

Johnnie hauled her into his arms and very thoroughly kissed her.

"Just don't like him too much," he said.

It was still early morning when Rick Vega turned down the long paved driveway off Highway 1 along the Malibu coastline into the entrance of the Moore Estate. Behind the main house, a single-story bungalow overlooked the sea. Rick drove farther up the lane, parked his unmarked brown Chevy in a guest parking spot and turned off the engine.

Following a gray stone walkway to the front door of the bungalow, he knocked and took a step back. A minute later, a man's deep voice came from the other side of the door.

"Who is it?"

"Police. Open up."

The dead bolt slid back and the door swung open. Manny Ortega stood across from him.

"Detective Vega, Mr. Ortega, LAPD. I've got a few questions I need to ask you."

Ortega looked over Rick's shoulder, searching for more police, but he was the only one there.

"How the hell did you find me?" Manny was a good-looking twenty-five-year-old, tall with black hair and dark brown eyes. He was wearing a pair of baggy navy blue swim trunks and flip-flops, no shirt, and the kid was ripped.

"I called in a few favors, found out David Moore's son is a friend of yours. I put two and two together. I need to ask you a couple of questions about a woman named Rachael Brewer."

Unlike his dad, Manny wasn't good at hiding his emotions. Clearly he knew who Rachael was. "I talked to the cops about this already."

Interesting. No mention in any of the reports he'd seen. "Just a couple more questions. Mind if I come in?"

Manny stepped back letting Rick walk past him into the living room. The bungalow was small, just a living room, kitchen and bedroom, but the view was spectacular, with windows overlooking the cliffs onto the beach and an endless stretch of ocean.

The sight of a petite, black-haired Hispanic girl walking out of the bedroom in a bikini beneath a gauzy cover-up wasn't bad, either.

"This is my fiancée, Chrystal Sanchez. Hon, this is Detective Vega."

"Nice to meet you," Rick said.

"You, too," the girl said.

Rick thought of Rachael, a stripper from the Kitty Cat Club, and the relationship she might have had with Manny. "Is there someplace we can speak in private?" he asked.

"Like I said, Chrystal's my fiancée. I don't have anything to hide, you can ask your questions in front of her."

"All right. I came to find out if you had a relationship with Rachael Brewer."

"No, absolutely not."

"Rumor has it the two of you were seeing each other."

"Not true. I never took her out, never took her to bed. Nothing like that."

"But you knew her."

Manny glanced away. "I saw her a couple of times in the Vieux Carre."

"Who with?"

Manny licked his lips. Rick waited for the lie. The kid was a lousy liar.

"I don't remember. Just some guy. What matters is it wasn't me."

That part was true. Watching him, Rick was fairly certain. "I need to know who she was with. I'd like to see your security tapes for the two-week period leading up to her disappearance."

"We don't have security cameras at the Vieux Carre. Our clientele is adamant about their privacy."

Which was probably also true—a lesson learned from Daddy.

"Is there anything at all you can tell us that might be of help?"

"Not a thing."

"Rachael Brewer was last seen departing your father's jet after it landed in Belize." Information Johnnie had confirmed when he'd called this morning—the reason Rick had volunteered to make another attempt at finding Manny.

Well, one of the reasons. The other was he hadn't been able to get Rachael Brewer out of his head.

The kid just stood there staring, looking as if he had just been poleaxed.

"I wouldn't...wouldn't know anything about that. My father and I rarely see each other."

But clearly he knew something about the connection between Rachael and his dad. From the look of panic on his face, Manny didn't, however, know Rachael had been on his father's plane.

"Sure you don't have anything else you want to tell me?"

The kid just shook his head.

Rick handed him a business card. "If you come up with anything that might be helpful, give me a call."

The kid swallowed, nodded.

"I should remind you that aiding and abetting criminal activity is a felony. If you know something, now is the time to say so."

Manny shook his head. His fiancée wrapped her fingers gently around his arm.

"Manny isn't like his dad," she said. "He does his best to stay clear of all that."

Rick nodded. In a way he felt sorry for the kid. It had to be tough being the son of a notorious gangster.

"Think about what I said." Rick turned to leave,

wishing he'd found out more. As soon as he reached his car, he called Johnnie's satellite number.

"It's Rick. Manny wasn't involved with Rachael. It was someone else. At least that's my take."

"Where'd you find him?"

"I did a little digging. He was staying at a friend's place in Malibu. I think Manny knows who Rachael was seeing, but he isn't saying. And he didn't know about his dad hauling Rachael off to Belize."

A sigh whispered out on the other end of the phone. "That still leaves us with a question mark as to how she got involved with his father, but at least we're pretty sure where he took her. Sol located an island owned by the Genesis Corporation. If you dig deep enough—and I mean deep—you come up with a link to Ortega."

"You think Rachael's still on the island?"

"In one form or another," Johnnie said, and Rick knew he meant she was there somewhere—either alive or dead.

Rick's jaw felt tight. "You going in?"

"Cantrell's flying down with a buddy. We'll recon the place, figure a way to get in and take a look around. What we'll find, I don't know."

Rick knew what they would likely find—nothing at all—not without dragging half the Caribbean Sea. It gave him a headache to think of it. "Well, good luck, my friend."

"Thanks, and thanks for the intel." Johnnie hung up and so did Rick.

He'd found out a little, not enough.

Rick walked back into the station and found Lieutenant Carla Meeks waiting, and got his ass chewed for inserting himself in a case he wasn't working.

He wondered if it was worth it.

Chapter 24

The air conditioner roared, sending a stream of cold air into the motel room. Amy stood at the window. Outside, the late morning heat and humidity were building, the sun blazing down on the white sand beaches, a light breeze pushing the sails of the boats out on the water.

Johnnie finished his call and set the satellite phone down on the small round table in the corner. "That was Vega," he said. "Manny wasn't seeing Rachael."

Amy felt a sweep of relief. Until it struck her. "Oh, my God, so it wasn't Manny after all. It was Danny, just like her hairdresser said."

Johnnie started frowning. "I guess that's probably right. So who the hell is Danny?"

"If Rachael's on that island, she'll be able to tell us."

"Yeah," Johnnie said, but Amy could see he wasn't convinced. Johnnie believed Rachael was dead. It was the logical conclusion. Rachael had been missing for two full months. If she was alive, she would have called, tried to contact her family in some way. Amy tried to prepare herself, but her chest squeezed painfully.

"Cantrell ought to be here soon," Johnnie said. "We'll get things figured out once he's here."

Amy looked over at the phone. "I hate to ask, but would it be all right if I called my mother? I don't want her to worry."

Johnnie cast her a glance. "Yeah, no need for her to worry. Her daughter's in Belize for a couple of days—tracking down a notorious drug lord. No problem at all."

Amy drilled him with a glare.

"Go ahead and call her."

She put the call through, and she and her mother talked briefly. Amy didn't mention she wasn't in L.A.

"I wish you'd come home," her mother said as she always did.

"I will, Mom, soon. I promise." As she ended the call and set the phone back down on the table, she glanced over at Johnnie and felt a soft pang in her heart. One way or another, all of this would soon be over. It would be time for her to go back to Michigan, time for her to end her charade as Angel Fontaine and her summer fling with Johnnie Riggs.

A summer fling that didn't feel like a fling at all.

She reminded herself she had known from the start it couldn't go further. John Riggs was who he was—a sexy, dangerous man who made her heart flutter with a single glance. And she was who she was—a kindergarten teacher from Michigan.

The phone started ringing. Johnnie picked it up. Nodded at something that was said. "I'm on my way."

"They're here?"

"Plane just landed at the airport. Let's go."

"It's only a mile down the road. I'll just wait for you here." *Where it's nice and cool,* she thought.

"Not gonna happen. You forget about your little trip to the grocery store? People know you're looking for your sister. Get your purse and let's go."

He was right, of course. The woman in the grocery store wouldn't say a word—she was too frightened. But the first woman—the one she hadn't mentioned to Johnnie—she might tell someone, and if she did...

Amy grabbed her purse and headed out the door.

The plane was on the ground when they got there. Johnnie waved to the pilot of the little 180 as it turned at the end of the tarmac and started taxiing back the way it had come, revved its engine and prepared to take off. Jake Cantrell strode toward him across the asphalt, six foot five inches of solid muscle.

Johnnie glanced at Amy to see her reaction. She was staring wide-eyed but not the way Angel Fontaine had looked at Johnnie when he'd first walked into the Kitty Cat Club.

That was one helluva relief.

She gave the man walking beside Jake a once-over, but nothing more. He was dark-haired like Jake, with the same blue eyes, but his were ice-cold, his face more ruggedly carved, a good-looking man just the same.

"Johnnie Riggs meet Ben Slocum," Jake said. "And I presume this is Amy Brewer."

"That's right."

Ben reached out to shake Johnnie's hand. "Riggs." Johnnie shook. "Slocum."

"Hello," Amy said a little shyly. "It's nice to meet you both. Thank you so much for coming."

"Car's over here," Johnnie said. The men threw their gear bags into the trunk and climbed in for the brief drive back to the motel.

"Dietz ordered the pilot to fly over the island before we landed. Didn't see much security. Ortega's arrogant enough to think no one can connect him to the island. He probably feels safe there."

They reached the motel and Johnnie tossed Jake a key to the room two doors down from his. Jake and Ben carried their gear inside the double room and Johnnie and Amy followed.

"You able to get what we need?" Johnnie asked.

Jake unzipped one of the bags he'd picked up in Belize City after Dietz had met them at the airport. "A couple of handguns, some heavy artillery—AR-15s, and my personal favorite—"

"A hand grenade?" Amy asked, her eyes wide as she stared at the device.

"Flash grenade," Jake corrected. "Big boom and bright light. Creates a diversion."

Johnnie grinned. "Came in handy last time."

"Last time?" Amy asked, looking even more uncertain.

"Long story," Jake said.

"I got us a boat lined up," Johnnie said, bringing them back on track. He had gone out early that morning and found what they needed. "Guy who owns it gives speedboat rides to tourists. I gave it a trial run and, man, that baby is fast."

"Long as it gets us there and back," Slocum said darkly. Being an ex-SEAL, he'd been around plenty of boats, probably not that picky as long as it didn't sink and got the job done.

Jake pulled a map out of his gear bag and unrolled it. With three big men circling the table, Amy all but disappeared. Still, Johnnie could see her peering between their shoulders, closely following everything that was going on.

So far, she'd been a real trouper. But then, she still believed her sister was alive. Odds were, even their trip to the island might not give her the answers she wanted. Ortega was careful. They might not find a damn thing.

The hours slipped past. The men wouldn't leave for the island until after dark. Amy watched them in awe. They were all ex-military, true professionals. She couldn't help but be impressed.

While they took a break from their planning, Johnnie made a food run. He returned from the village with bags of deep-fried fish and chips, Cokes, burgers and a thermos of coffee.

They dug in as if they were starving.

"We've got a little problem," Johnnie said, between bites as the men wolfed down the food. He tipped his head in her direction. "We can't afford to leave a man behind to protect Amy and I don't like leaving her here alone. Not after she's been sniffing around, asking questions about her sister."

"Getting answers, too, as I recall," Jake reminded him, and Amy gave him a warm little thank-you smile. After all, she was the one who'd found out about the island. She'd been helpful, even if Johnnie didn't want to admit it.

"Maybe so," he grumbled, "but we need to find a safe place to stash her while we're gone."

"We'll move her down the road to another motel," Jake suggested.

"Yeah, that's what I was thinking. I still don't like it, but I can't see any other way."

"She wouldn't be able to use a weapon by any chance, would she?" Ben Slocum's ice-blue eyes slid over her coolly. She might as well have been a lamp on the bedside table.

"I'm right here, guys," she said a little tartly. "I can hear every word you say, and I can shoot a gun if I have to."

"I'll leave her my ankle gun," Johnnie said. "She knows how to handle a .38."

Jake looked impressed.

Amy sipped her Diet Coke and glanced at the clock. It was only 9:00 p.m.

"It's been a long day," Johnnie said. "Why don't we crash for a couple of hours, be ready to leave at midnight."

"Sounds good," Jake agreed.

Slocum walked over and stretched out on one of the double beds. "I could use a little shut-eye." He was sound asleep by the time Johnnie led her out the door and Jake locked it behind them.

It had been a long day and Amy was tired, but tonight the men were going on a mission to find her sister and her nerves were strung too tight to think about sleeping. She turned the light on and jerked to a stop just inside the door.

"What is it?" Johnnie pulled the pistol out of his shoulder holster.

"Someone's been in here. My bag wasn't zipped all the way. Now it is."

He reached out an arm and eased her back against the wall. "Stay here."

Her heart was beating too fast. Holding the gun upright against his chest, Johnnie checked the closet, then silently made his way toward the tiny bathroom. He flattened himself against the wall, turned the knob and shoved open the door. Bringing the gun into position in front of him, he disappeared inside.

He came out an instant later, looking relieved. "Nobody here."

Amy's heart began to slow. She headed for the bathroom, walked inside to take a look around. "I left my makeup bag on the right side of the counter, but it was closer to the sink."

Like most women, she knew immediately if any of her things had been disturbed. In her apartment she knew where every dish went, every pot and pan. Someone had definitely been in their motel room.

"You sure?" Johnnie asked.

"Positive."

"Let's take a look, see if anything's missing." Both of them went through their bags.

There wasn't much besides their clothes in the room. Her passport was with her in her purse, along with her wallet and money. Johnnie was carrying his weapons. He had tossed his gear bag, which held the extra ammunition, into the trunk of the car when they had left for the airport.

"I don't think they took anything," she said.

"Wasn't much to take," Johnnie said. "Maybe it was the cleaning staff."

"We left a do-not-disturb sign on the door. They wouldn't have come into the room."

"Probably not."

"Could have been a burglar looking for money."

"Could be, but I doubt it." He took another glance around. "Ortega's at the villa by now. Maybe his people got wind of our activity. Maybe they're trying to pin down who we are. If that's the case, they didn't find out much." Johnnie fixed her with a look. "Pack your stuff. When we leave we won't be coming back."

A little chill went through her. They were leaving The Orchid Inn.

Amy said a silent prayer that before they left Belize and headed back to the States, they would find Rachael. Or at least find out what had happened to her.

She closed her eyes and tried not to think what that might be.

Chapter 25

"We got everything?" Johnnie asked as he waited for the men to file past him out of the room onto the balcony that led to the stairs.

"We're packed and ready." Cantrell hoisted his duffel bag over his shoulder and starting walking.

Johnnie had interrupted the men's brief nap with the news that his room had been tossed and the motel was no longer safe, which meant all of them were leaving. But even if Ortega had found out Amy Brewer was in Placencia looking for her sister, he wouldn't know they had located his island and that there were three armed men ready to invade his private domain.

Amy spoke softly from beside him. "It's my fault we have to leave. I was asking questions about Rachael. I talked to two different women. I told them I was her sister. I should have figured someone at the villa would find out."

She looked so miserable Johnnie wrapped an arm around her shoulders and pulled her against his side. "You don't get answers without asking questions. We wouldn't know about the island if it weren't for you."

"You did what you had to," Jake said as they reached the car. "It does, however, pose a problem." He looked over at Johnnie. "You aren't gonna like this, buddy, and I'm usually the last guy to go for something like this, but I'm thinking we should take her with us."

Johnnie's whole body tightened. "No way."

Slocum was nodding. "Good idea. We leave her with the boat or somewhere safe on the island, go in and see if we can locate her sister, then pick her up on the way out."

"It's too damn dangerous," Johnnie argued. "Something happens to us, she's left in Ortega's hands."

"We leave her here without protection, she's liable to end up dead," Slocum said flatly. "Or we'll be looking for two missing women."

Amy squeezed Johnnie's hand. "Ben's right. I'm safer with you than I am without you. And if you…if you find Rachael, she might need me."

A muscle tightened in Johnnie's jaw. "Damn it!"

Jake reached for the door handle, opened the front passenger side of the rental car and settled Amy in the seat next to the driver. "Time to go, boys and girls."

Ducking his head, he slid into the backseat behind her, while Slocum rounded the car and climbed in on the opposite side. Johnnie slid behind the wheel, the three men filling the car completely.

Reluctantly, he started the engine, knowing the guys

were right. He didn't have time to arrange protection for Amy and even if he did, he wouldn't trust someone else to keep her safe.

Instead of driving farther down the road to another motel, Johnnie pointed the car toward town and the small private dock he had found yesterday. Both sail and motor boats drifted in their slips, most of them available for tourist excursions, or half- or full-day rentals. Near the end of the dock, the boat he had paid way too much to rent for the next two days bobbed beneath its canvas cover.

Jake opened the trunk of the car. "You got anything dark to wear in your bag?" he said to Amy.

"Navy blue T-shirt."

He unzipped her bag and stepped out of the way. "Put it on."

"Fuck," Johnnie grumbled, thinking that taking her on this mission was the last thing he wanted.

The men turned their backs as Amy changed from her white cotton blouse to the loose-fitting T-shirt. She was already wearing a pair of navy shorts. Not exactly the stuff for a midnight outing in the jungle, but Amy hadn't figured on coming along, either.

"Okay, I'm ready."

Jake unzipped his bag, pulled out a black baseball cap and jammed it on her head. It came all the way to her ears. "Put your hair up underneath."

She tucked her long blond ponytail up out of sight and tightened the band on the cap so it almost fit her.

The men set their gear bags down on the dock and Jake and Ben pulled the canvas cover off the boat.

"Wow!" Amy said. "Donzi 28 ZX with twin Merc 370s. Sweet."

Jake just stared.

Ben Slocum actually grinned.

"What?" Amy looked over at the men. "I'm from Michigan. We've got water on three sides."

"Her dad was a mechanic," Johnnie explained. "Liked fast cars…boats, too, looks like." He jumped into the cockpit, then reached up to catch the gear bags as Ben tossed them down.

"Definitely a nice ride," Jake said, giving the boat a thorough inspection. It was candy-apple-red with orange flames running the length of it. "Good thing it's a dark night." It was near moonless, just a sliver of light mostly hidden beneath a thin layer of clouds, nothing to outline the boat on the water.

"Tops out at around a hundred," Johnnie said, giving the wheel a loving pat. "Guy charges seventy-five bucks a head for a twenty-minute ride." He reached up and helped Amy aboard.

"I wonder what else he uses it for," Ben said darkly. Drug smuggling was a big problem in Belize. Silver or lead was the saying. Take the money and keep quiet or end up with a bullet in your head.

Slocum unfastened the line and jumped into the boat and they settled themselves in the black-padded vinyl seats.

Johnnie fired up the big Mercury engines and idled the boat away from the dock. As soon as they were a respectable distance from the shore, he pushed the power lever forward and the boat picked up speed.

The Donzi was as quick and powerful as its owner had boasted, hitting the top of the waves then settling in and skimming over the flat, calm sea.

Johnnie eased the throttle a little faster, the wind

rushing past his face, pressing his black T-shirt and camo pants against his body.

There was no adrenaline rush like speed.

From the corner of his eye, he caught Amy's grin.

She loved to go fast, always had. Amy allowed herself to enjoy the thrill of racing through the darkness, the boat skimming effortlessly over the smooth Caribbean Sea.

It was the rise of an island in the distance sometime later that shattered her brief tranquility and brought her crashing back to reality. They were on a deadly mission. Whatever happened tonight, they had come to the end of their search.

"Fifteen degrees to port," Jake said, reading the map and the GPS coordinates as Johnnie piloted the boat.

"Isn't that it?" Amy asked, pointing toward the island that was now disappearing behind them.

"Not the right one."

There were dozens of islands out there, some little more than sandbars, others mountainous and completely covered with vegetation. From the Google Earth satellite photos Johnnie had shown her on the computer, Ortega's mountainous island was mostly tropical jungle.

The boat continued its adjusted course and a few minutes later, Amy spotted another island on the horizon. They were still some ways away when Johnnie slowed the engines.

"The dock's on the leeward side," Jake said. "We need to come in windward."

Johnnie turned the wheel, heading the boat in that direction as per their plan, circling the island and coming in from the side facing the open sea.

As the engine slowed and the boat drifted closer, Ben stood up and peeled off his shirt. She had noticed he was the only one wearing a swimsuit and not camouflage. She had also noticed the guy was totally ripped. But then all three of the men, each built a little differently, were prime examples of the perfect male body.

Slocum slipped silently over the side of the boat and disappeared beneath the surface of the water, barely causing a ripple.

"Where's he going?" Amy asked.

"He's checking things out," Johnnie explained, "making sure it's safe to go ashore."

"The lagoon's dead ahead," Jake said, looking down at the map.

Johnnie idled the boat a safe distance away, waiting for Slocum's signal. The night was on their side, only a faint rim of white around a fingernail moon that was mostly hidden by passing clouds. Along the shore, a tiny light flashed three times.

"That's the signal," Jake said, and Johnnie eased the throttle forward.

Every second it took to reach the lagoon seemed like an hour to Amy. She had seen stuff like this in movies, men on combat missions armed with automatic weapons, but she had never thought she'd be smack in the middle of something like this.

As the boat drifted toward the beach, her nerves kicked up another notch. Her mouth was dry but her palms were damp. Johnnie shut down the engines, and he and Jake jumped out and pulled the boat up onto the sand beneath some overhanging foliage. Jake started hauling out their gear while Johnnie lifted her out of the boat. The men broke off some big leafy branches and covered the parts of the boat that were exposed. While they worked, Ben appeared and hurriedly changed into his cammies and then the men assembled their gear.

"I want you to wait for us here," Johnnie said, crouching in front of where Amy stood half hidden beneath a low-growing palm. His black T-shirt, wet and clinging, outlined the powerful muscles across his chest. He was wearing black face paint and he wiped some off and drew marks down her nose and across her cheeks. All of them smelled like the mosquito repellent they were wearing.

Amy stared up at Johnnie, who had never looked tougher or more completely male. He pressed his .38 revolver into her hand.

"I want you to stay out of sight. Anyone comes, just stay hidden until we get back. If you get in trouble, fire off a round. Can you do that?"

She just nodded, her throat too dry to speak.

"God, I hate leaving you here." And then he caught her chin between his fingers, bent and pressed a hot, hard kiss on her mouth.

"Be careful," she managed to squeak out, still tasting him on her lips. Other words crowded her throat. *I love you, Johnnie.* Amy didn't say them. She was aghast to realize she had even thought them. She couldn't afford to love a man like John Riggs. One look at him in his flak vest and camouflage pants, a long-barreled automatic weapon slung across his chest, a pistol in his shoulder harness, and a knife strapped to his leg, and it was clear he wasn't the man for her.

"I'll be back as soon as I can." Johnnie reached out

and gently touched her cheek, and then he and the other two men disappeared into the dense tropical foliage.

Ignoring the sound of insects and the small animals scurrying around nearby, Amy settled herself deeper in the greenery to wait.

And prayed with all her heart that the men would find Rachael and return to her safe.

They spotted two guards moving in opposite directions. Ben continued scouting ahead; Jake went after the guard heading north, while Johnnie took the one patrolling the south end of the island. Dressed in a khaki uniform, a slouch hat pulled low on his head, and carrying an automatic weapon, the man moved easily through the jungle.

For several minutes, Johnnie studied his quarry, noting his movements, the slow, easy strides that said he was used to the routine. The wiry guard paused for a moment, yawned behind his hand.

The guy wasn't expecting trouble, which was exactly what Johnnie planned to give him.

Circling quietly around in front, Johnnie crouched beneath the flat leaves of a giant elephant ear plant. When the guard reached the spot directly to his right, he sprang out of hiding, came up behind him, wrapped an arm around the man's throat, pressed a forearm against the back of his neck and squeezed. His struggles weakened as his air supply faded, and then he went out like a light, slumping down on the path.

Johnnie took the guard's automatic weapon, popped the clip and tossed it one way into the foliage, tossed the weapon in the opposite direction. He used a plastic zip cord to bind his wrists, another to bind his feet, gagged him and dragged him off the path.

He checked his watch. Time to head for the rendezvous point. With any luck, he'd get there right on schedule.

The night sounds faded into an ominous silence. Amy's heartbeat quickened as she caught the shuffle of something moving through the foliage in the darkness, heavy footfalls walking a nearby path in the jungle. She eased farther back into the shrubs and dense growth of plants and flowers, hoping she could make herself invisible to whoever was out there.

The shuffling sounds halted. From where she hid, all she could see was a pair of men's lace-up boots. They didn't belong to Johnnie, Jake or Ben, and fear slid through her.

Her pulse accelerated into a pounding roar in her ears. Her fingers tightened around the pistol in her lap. But Johnnie and the others were out there trying to find Rachael. She'd be damned if she would fire a shot and call them back unless she absolutely had to. Unfortunately, as the thud of a second set of footfalls began to reach her, she realized she might not have another choice.

Please, God.

Amy held her breath, afraid the men might hear the whisper of air passing in and out of her lungs. Something was said in Spanish and then the second man started walking away. She dared a slow breath, praying both of them would leave, that they wouldn't spot the boat hidden a few feet away among the leafy bushes.

She could no longer see the second man and for

an instant, she was sure the man in front of her was going to walk away. Then the leaves erupted behind her and strong hands grabbed her around the waist. Amy struggled as he dragged her backward. When the man in front of her shoved the bushes aside and reached for her, too, Amy thrust her arms straight out in front of her and cocked the pistol.

Chapter 26

It didn't take long to reach the rendezvous point they had chosen. Trying not to worry about Amy, Johnnie did a belly crawl up to where Jake lay in the foliage propped on his elbows, studying the house fifty yards away through a pair of binoculars.

"House sits right at the top of the hill just like in the satellite pictures," Johnnie said, zeroing his own binoculars in on the house.

"I don't think Ortega figured on Google Earth when he built the place."

The open, white, single-story residence wasn't large like the villa, but it was fashioned in an elegant, Spanish style with wide red tile decks off the living room and each of three bedrooms that looked out over the sea. The lights were on inside and soft lights illuminated the decks, making it easy for them to see through the huge plate glass windows, but so far there had been no sign of Rachael or any other woman, just a houseboy and a couple of other male servants.

"No problem with the guard?" Jake asked him.

Johnnie grinned. "He's napping peacefully. Yours?"

"Decided he'd rather sit this one out."

Johnnie chuckled. "Smart move." So two of Ortega's soldiers were out of commission. Slocum was still doing recon and hadn't yet reached the rendezvous point.

"That's Ortega," Johnnie said, recognizing the man moving around on the other side of the windows from the photos he had seen. "Two men with him."

"They aren't protection," Jake said. "Dressed more like guests." Both Caucasian, one blond, one dark-haired, both in Bermuda shorts and short-sleeved sport shirts.

Carlos Ortega was lean and fit with thick, silver-tinged black hair. He was wearing a turquoise silk shirt, loose-fitting ivory slacks and a pair of sandals.

Jake checked the time. "Plane must have gotten in late. Doesn't look like they've been here long."

Johnnie focused on the house. "You're right. Bottle of rum on the bar is almost full."

Jake glanced around. "Ben should be back any minute…unless he ran into trouble."

So far, they'd only seen the two guards, but Slocum might have encountered more. Still, it wasn't the small army Ortega surrounded himself with at the villa. He definitely felt safe here.

The SEAL returned as silently as he had slipped off into the jungle. "I didn't see anyone else. Some sign, though. Could be another man out there, maybe more.

Not good. Amy was on the island. If one of Ortega's men spotted her, she was in trouble.

"There's another building on the leeward side," Slocum said. "Kind of a bungalow. It's hidden back in the foliage, maybe a hundred yards out."

Johnnie caught movement inside the house. "Something's going on." Training his binoculars on the men, he saw them walking toward a glass door at the far end of the living room. Ortega slid it open and stepped out onto the deck.

"Looks like they're heading out," Johnnie said as Ortega stepped off the deck and started leading the men down a path into the jungle. A man they hadn't noticed before fell in behind the group, big brawny, civilian clothes, but the way he moved, the way he surveyed his surroundings without actually looking, marked him as a professional. "Let's see what they're up to."

Staying low, Johnnie had just begun to move out when the distant crack of a gunshot split the air. It sounded as if it had come from the beach down by the lagoon where they'd hidden the boat.

"Amy." His gut clenched as a jolt of adrenaline shot through his blood.

"Go. I'm right behind you," Jake said. "Ben can keep an eye on things here."

Johnnie didn't hesitate. All he could think of was getting to Amy. But the darkness made speed impossible. He wouldn't be much good to her if he wound up falling into some ravine. Keeping low and out of sight, he moved farther into the jungle, Jake a few steps behind. A little ways down the hill, they split up, both of them heading for the lagoon from different angles.

Johnnie reached the beach first, headed straight for

the spot he'd left Amy. The ground around the place she had been hiding was churned up, indicating a struggle.

But Amy wasn't there.

A knot twisted hard in his gut. Johnnie pulled in a deep breath, steadying himself. Using his little four-inch LED light, he checked the area, spotted a pair of men's boot tracks in the mud on an overgrown path leading away from the lagoon.

He looked up as Jake appeared, coming in from the other direction. "Boat's where we left it," Jake said. "Where's Amy?"

Johnnie just shook his head. His chest was clamping down so hard he could barely breathe. The shot had been Amy's signal for help. She was in trouble and he hadn't been able to reach her.

He steeled himself, pointed into the undergrowth. "Two sets of boot prints. There's a game trail leading up the hill. They must have taken her with them."

Jake followed his gaze up the path. The darkness had been their friend when they had arrived, now it was their enemy.

"So let's go find her," Jake said calmly, words that helped him push past his fear.

In the blackness, the overgrown meandering path was hard to see. As the better tracker, Jake started up the trail in front of him. The clouds had thinned, helping them a little. At the first turn in the path, Jake paused, pointed to the footprints that moved along ahead of him. "One set of tracks is deeper. Either he's a lot heavier or he's carrying something."

The knot in Johnnie's stomach tightened. He was carrying something, all right, and Johnnie knew what that something was.

The men fell back into step, moving silently. The clouds floated apart for a moment and a thin ray of moonlight illuminated the way. Then Johnnie's light flashed over a drop of something shiny on a leaf overgrowing the trail. He reached out and touched it, rubbed the wetness between his fingers, smelled it.

"Blood," he said, and rage boiled up inside him.

"Take it easy. We don't know it's hers."

"It better not be."

Jake started forward, moving as silently as the heavy foliage would allow. They needed to find Amy, disarm the men as quietly as possible and complete their mission. But if they hurt his woman, they were dead men.

The rope binding her wrists cut into Amy's flesh. The gag in her mouth tasted like sweat and tobacco as she bobbed along, and the guard's meaty shoulder dug painfully into her belly. Her baseball cap was long gone, her hair loose from its ponytail. The other man walked behind them, holding his bleeding arm, his rifle slung across his back. He swore at her through gritted teeth, calling her foul names in Spanish.

She had shot him, though she hadn't really done it on purpose. She'd been hoping she could warn him away and signal Johnnie at the same time. Instead, she'd nicked his arm.

Not that she felt bad about it.

These were the men who'd brought Rachael to the island, Ortega's men. She shuddered. And now they had her.

Fear curled in her stomach. She prayed Johnnie had heard the shot and that he would come for her, told herself all she had to do was stay alive until he got there.

As the man who carried her reached a fork in the trail and started upward again, she spotted a building ahead, a house, she saw, white, single-story, elegant, with lots of windows facing the sea. The men continued past it, walking rapidly down the narrow, nearly invisible path.

Leaves and branches slapped at her face as they pushed through the foliage. Behind the gag, her mouth was cotton dry. A little ways farther down the trail, the faint outline of a second, much smaller structure appeared in the darkness, and the men increased their pace, eager to reach their destination.

The next thing she knew she was being carried inside the building, dumped onto a sofa in what appeared to be the living room. A guard stood inside the door, wearing the same beige uniform as the others. Another man, big and powerfully built, stood next to the bar. Dark hair, dark eyes, wearing tan slacks and a sport shirt, he might have passed for a guest if it weren't for the cold look in his eyes and the hard lines of his face.

Amy swallowed past a lump of fear as a well-dressed Hispanic male approached where she lay on the sofa, still bound and gagged, staring up at him.

"Señorita Brewer, I assume."

She couldn't reply with the dirty rag tied over her mouth, and in a way she was grateful, since she had no idea what to say. The man motioned for the guard who had carried her inside to untie the gag. The one with the injured arm had wrapped a towel around it. Apparently, he wasn't hurt all that badly.

Unfortunately.

Even after the gag was removed, her mouth felt bone-dry.

He eyed her coldly. "I know who you are. I heard you were in Placencia asking questions. I am your host, Carlos Ortega." The edge of his mouth curved into a smile that wasn't. "It is my property upon which you trespass. I assume you are here to visit your sister."

Her eyes widened. "She's here? Rachael's alive?"

One of his silver-tinged black eyebrows went up. "Why wouldn't she be? Quite a beautiful young woman, your sister. Killing such an exceptional creature would be a waste...do you not agree?"

"Yes, but..." She wanted to believe what the man was saying. Wanted it with all her heart. But looking at Ortega and the hard-faced soldiers he employed, she failed miserably.

"Who brought you here?" Ortega continued pleasantly. He held a crystal bar glass filled with ice and a light amber liquid. A bottle of rum sat open on the counter. She recognized the Angostura label from when she had worked at the club. "I asked you a question, *chica.*"

Amy moistened her lips. She was still trying to process the news that Rachael might actually be here on the island.

His features tightened. "Do not make me ask you again."

Amy took a steadying breath. She'd had plenty of time to think of an answer to the question she knew she'd be asked. "My boyfriend brought me. We found out my sister was planning...planning a trip to Belize. We thought if we came down here we might...might be able to find her."

"Your sister mentioned my name?"

No choice but to continue to bluff. "That's right. She

said a man named Ortega had a villa down here and she was...she was coming for a visit."

"How did you find the island?"

She swallowed, prayed she looked frightened— which she was—and sincere, which she wasn't. She didn't want to put the woman who had helped her in danger.

"It was mostly just luck. A man in the village heard we were looking for a woman named Rachael Brewer. He said if we paid him, he would help us. We gave him money and he...he told us about the island."

Ortega's lips thinned. "Do you remember this man's name?"

She shook her head. "He never...never told us. We never asked. We only wanted to be sure she was all right."

"I see." He swirled the ice in his glass, took a slow sip, as if he savored the taste. "Where is your boy-friend now?"

"I—I don't know. He was going to do some explor-ing, see what he could find out. He was supposed to come back for me but...but he didn't."

Ortega turned to the guards who had brought her, said something to them in Spanish and they laughed. Clearly they weren't afraid of the man she had come with. Amy thought of Johnnie in his flak vest, auto-matic weapon slung over his chest, and black-painted face. *Big mistake.*

"Antoine, take a look around outside, find out if the problem has been resolved. If not, you and the others take care of it."

The black guard who had been standing by the door turned and disappeared out of the house.

"Do you want us to go with him?" the man with the injured arm asked.

"You two stay here, just in case."

The guard nodded and positioned himself by the door. Down the hall, Amy could hear men's voices, what might have been those of women, and the occasional lewd remark coming from what appeared to be a row of bedrooms. She glanced around the living room, which was decorated with lurid paintings of naked women. There were carved erotic objects, phallic symbols and people making love in different positions.

Her stomach churned.

Dear God, where was Johnnie?

Ortega sipped his drink. "So you and your boyfriend came all the way out here alone?" Ortega continued, baiting her, hoping to catch her in a lie.

"We just…just came to check things out, see if the information we got was true."

"Is that so? Well, then I think it is time you found the answer to your question." He walked over, stroked a hand over her hair, bent and wiped a smudge of grease paint off her cheek. "I believe, once you are clean, you may be as beautiful as your sister." His feral smile made her stomach roll with nausea.

"In the meantime, I am sure my men will find your friend and bring him here to join our little party." Ortega took a long, slow drink of his rum. "In fact, most likely they already have."

Chapter 27

Too fucking late. They'd been so close, just seconds behind Amy and the soldiers who had taken her. But close only counted in horseshoes. Instead, Johnnie had reached the second structure just in time to see the men they had been following disappear inside the house, one carrying Amy over his shoulder. It took all Johnnie's self-control not to charge in after them.

At least she's still alive.

Jake eased up beside where Johnnie crouched in the foliage watching the bungalow. There were windows in the front facing the sea, but they weren't big enough to see much of what was happening inside. Through the binoculars, every once in a while, he caught a glimpse of Amy, saw her bound and lying on the sofa.

"We know the two we followed are inside," Jake said. "Might be more."

"Along with Ortega and his friends."

"That's right and one of them looked like his body-guard."

"Yeah, and now he knows someone's on the island. He'll be pressing Amy for answers. We've got to get in before he hurts her."

Johnnie started to move, but Jake caught his arm. "Not yet. Taking out the guards isn't the problem. The trick is getting in without getting Amy killed."

Johnnie's stomach clenched. All he could think of was getting to Amy, but he knew Jake was right. They couldn't rush in like a herd of stampeding bulls. They needed to check things out, move in slowly, make sure Amy was out of the line of fire.

The front door opened and a big uniformed black man, a local, most likely, walked out of the house, jogged off down the trail. Johnnie watched him disappear into the jungle, his nerves stretched thin as they waited for Slocum, hoping he had fresh intel.

A few minutes later, the soft call of a bird let them know the SEAL was approaching. Silently, he slipped up beside where they hunkered down in the jungle not far from the house.

"Ortega's inside," he said, "along with the men who came with him from the main house." His ice-blue eyes glinted and his mouth lifted in a hard-edged smile. "You don't have to worry about the guard who just came out."

So the big Belizean was out of commission. Slocum was good, Johnnie thought. Damned good. "We found blood on the trail."

Johnnie shoved down a fresh stab of worry and fixed his attention on the bungalow, low-roofed, rectangular in shape, soft interior lights illuminating what appeared to be a main room with a long hall running off it. He wished they could just charge in, shoot the bastards and get Amy out of there.

But it didn't work that way.

"Ortega's two guests headed down the hall not long after they got here," Slocum said. "Looks like a row of bedrooms. Far as I can tell, the men are still in there."

"Lots of folks," Jake said.

Johnnie's fingers tightened around the AR-15 slung across his chest. "Let's get close enough to find out what they're doing."

Staying low and deep in the foliage, he moved off toward the house.

Ortega motioned to his man. Amy's heart raced as the guard jerked her up off the sofa, lifted her into his arms and strode off down the hall. She struggled against his hold, but with her arms bound behind her and her ankles tied, there wasn't much she could do.

Ortega opened one of the bedroom doors and the guard strode past him and tossed her onto the bed. Standing in the doorway, Ortega nodded and the man pulled a knife from the sheath at his waist. Amy tried to scoot backward away from the blade, but the man just laughed. Reaching down, he cut the bindings on her ankles, turned her around and freed her wrists.

"There is a basin over there." Ortega pointed to a sink against the wall. "Use it to wash your face and cleanse yourself. Tonight, you and I, we are going to get much better acquainted." He smiled lewdly.

Ortega glanced over at the dark corner behind the bed. "Perhaps your sister will join us."

Her gaze shot to the corner. "Oh, my God! Rachael!"

Ortega's smile widened. As Amy scrambled off the bed and rushed to the slender, dark-haired girl curled into a ball on the floor, he stepped into the hall and closed the door.

Amy's eyes filled. "Rachael... Oh, my God, what have they done to you?" Her throat closed up at the sight of her sister's pale face and vacant eyes. "It's me, Rachael, it's Amy."

Rachael just stared.

"Oh, Rachael..." Amy gently shook her. "Look at me, sweetheart. It's your sister, Amy." She started to say that she had brought friends who were going to get them out of there, but Carlos Ortega was ruthless and powerful. There was every chance the room was bugged, a chance he was watching them, listening to every word.

Nausea rolled through her.

What if something had happened to Johnnie? What if he and the other two men had been captured or killed?

He'll come for us, she told herself. *He heard the shot and he'll come.* She trusted Johnnie to protect her, trusted him more than any man she had ever known.

She thought of the heavily armed guards who had taken her prisoner, and fresh fear gripped her. Amy pushed it away.

"Look at me, Rachael." She tipped her sister's head up, forcing Rachael's eyes to meet hers, but when she let go, Rachael's head slumped back down on her chest.

The lump in Amy's throat grew bigger. She remembered the roofie Kyle Bennett had given her and looked more closely at her sister. Rachael had clearly been drugged. She had lost weight and her eyes were sunken and hollow. Dark circles marred the skin below her thick dark lashes, and there was a bruise on her temple. Dear God, she had been here two months, obviously been beaten and possibly kept on drugs for weeks.

Amy tried not to think what else Carlos Ortega might have done to her, but when she looked at Rachael, dressed in nothing but black lace underwear and a black push-up bra, she couldn't block thoughts of what her sister must have endured.

Fresh tears washed down her cheeks. "I won't let him hurt you," Amy whispered, cradling her sister's head against her shoulder. "I promise I won't let him hurt you again."

And since Johnnie wasn't there to see her cry, she gave in to her terrible fear and the wracking sobs she had been fighting to hold inside and prayed that he would come.

They split up, Johnnie flattening himself against the wall at the front of the house, Jake and Ben going around to the back. Dim lights lit all three bedrooms along the front. The narrow windows at the top of each room weren't big enough to crawl through, but they weren't meant for escape. It was a setup he'd seen before—in brothels in Honduras and Guatemala. He clamped down on the fear and anger he struggled against.

Moving swiftly, he crept along the row of bedrooms, listening for the sound of her voice. There weren't any screams, no shouts for help, only men's laughter coming from two of the rooms, but it didn't sound much like a party.

Someone was talking in the third bedroom, her

voice soft and low. Relief hit him so hard he felt light-headed. *Amy.* He listened for a moment to be sure she was all right, couldn't make out what she was saying but thought she was talking to another woman.

Whatever was happening, for the moment, she was out of the crossfire.

Just stay there, baby, I'm on my way.

Johnnie crouched and ran along the wall toward the front of the house. He spotted Jake moving toward him, signaled that Amy was in a safe place. Making their way toward the door, they moved in on the house together. Johnnie checked his wristwatch, counting the seconds. Slocum was in position by now, ready to come in through the back door they had spotted earlier.

Jake held up three fingers, two, then one. Together they spun and fired a burst of automatic rifle fire through the door, splintering the wood. Then Johnnie kicked it open and they swung back out of the way, the deadly return fire whizzing past them, a thunderous roar and dense rain of lead that battered the jam and sent bits and pieces of wood flying into the air.

Jake tossed a flash grenade into the room, they covered their ears and closed their eyes against the blasts and blinding light.

They were in the room an instant later, firing their AR-15s, Jake's shot taking one of the guards in the shoulder and spinning him around. The other guard fired wildly, blinded by the flash, the shot cutting the air past Johnnie's ear. He ducked and rolled, dove and brought the man down as Slocum charged into the room.

Johnnie wrestled the gun from the guard's hand and tossed it away, noticed the bloody rag wrapped around the guy's upper arm, thought of the blood he'd seen on the path, thought of Amy. *That's my girl.*

He jammed his 9 mil beneath the guard's chin, and the man's arms shot up in surrender. Across the room, the bodyguard stood in front of Ortega, hustling him backward, trying to get out the front door.

He made the mistake of snapping off a barrage at Slocum, who fired four lethal rounds from his big Heckler & Koch in return. The shot took the bodyguard square in the chest but the powerful slug kept going, slamming into Ortega, and both men went down.

Both guards huddled on the floor with their arms raised. Ortega and the bodyguard were down and bleeding.

"I've got this covered," Jake said. "Go get her."

Johnnie took off down the hall, Slocum right behind him. They each took a bedroom, kicked open the door. A young woman lay on the bed, her eyes closed and her mouth slack. Johnnie looked at the piece-of-shit excuse for a man beside her, naked and huddled on the floor, and forced himself not to pull the trigger.

"Second man's in here," Slocum said. "Since he's wet himself, I don't think he'll be a problem. Get your woman and let's get out of here."

Johnnie didn't hesitate. Just grabbed the door handle to the third bedroom, turned the knob and shoved open the door.

"Johnnie!" Amy jumped to her feet and bolted toward him, threw her arms around his neck and just hung on. "I knew you'd come. I knew nothing would stop you."

"Nothing but dying, baby." And then he kissed her,

hard and deep, and his heart throbbed painfully, and all the time he was thinking, *Man, I am so in love.*

And I've got to be the dumbest SOB on the planet.

They were hurrying, anxious to leave the house. While Jake bound the guards' hands and feet with wire ties, Amy gathered what little clothing she could find and dressed her dazed sister in cut-off jeans and a T-shirt, shoved her feet into flip-flops.

In a small closet in the bedroom, she found Rachael's purse. Inside was a comb and brush and small makeup kit. Next to it was her passport.

One less problem. Amy breathed a sigh of relief.

They left the house a few minutes later, heading off down the trail, Amy walking close behind Johnnie, Ben Slocum carrying Rachael, whose head slumped against his chest.

As they neared the boat, Amy saw Johnnie pull the sat phone out of his pack.

"Dietz, it's Riggs. We're on Ortega's island. We've got a situation here. A couple of Ortega's guards wounded or otherwise disabled, two women drugged and raped. Ortega and his bodyguard are dead."

Dietz said something Amy couldn't hear.

"Yeah, we found her," Johnnie said. "She's in pretty bad shape, but she's alive."

Amy turned to look at her sister and her heart squeezed. Dietz must have asked for the location of the island; Johnnie rattled off the coordinates. "We'll need that plane in Placencia as soon as you can get it there."

Apparently Dietz agreed.

"I'll call Wheeler," Johnnie said, "fill him in. I'm

sure he'll be in touch. In the meantime—we were never here."

While Jake pulled the palm fronds and foliage off the boat, Johnnie phoned the DEA agent who had been helping them and repeated the information he had given Dietz. When he finished, he shoved the phone back into his pack.

"Wheeler's getting us a ride," he said. "Company jet should be at the airport by noon."

"They want to debrief us," Slocum said.

"You got it." Johnnie turned and slid an arm around Amy's waist. "You doin' okay?"

She nodded, thought that she was doing fairly well… considering.

Jake jumped into the boat, reached up to collect Rachael and settled her in one of the seats. Amy looked down at her sister, whose eyes were closed in a drug-induced stupor. "I just… I feel so sorry for her."

Johnnie cupped Amy's cheek. "If it weren't for you, Rachael would still be in that house. You saved her, baby. And now you'll do whatever it takes to make sure she'll be okay."

Her eyes burned with tears. She managed a half-hearted smile. "Thank you…for everything."

Johnnie made no reply, just jumped into the boat, reached up and caught her waist, and swung her down beside him. Slocum pushed the nose of the boat off the sand and jumped aboard, and Jake fired up the engines.

In minutes they were heading into the open sea.

Amy looked at Johnnie, sitting on the seat beside her. "I found her passport," she said. "If she knew she was leaving the country that night, why didn't she tell anyone?"

Johnnie drew her against him. "In time, she'll be able to tell us what happened. Till then, none of that is important. What's important is that your sister's alive, and that we're going home."

He took the hem of his T-shirt and used it to wipe the remaining black paint off her face, bent and lightly kissed her. "There, that's better."

He wiped his own face clean, then leaned back against the seat. They were leaving Placencia as soon as the plane arrived. With Ortega no longer in control of his organization, which played a key part in the San Dimas cartel, none of them knew what would happen, and they didn't want to chance running into more trouble.

And Rachael needed medical attention. They didn't want to risk taking her to a Belizean hospital, but as soon as they got back to L.A., she would get the care she needed.

The good news was the DEA was sending a private jet to take them home. They wanted to know everything the men had found out about Ortega and what had happened on the island.

As the boat skimmed over the water, Amy closed her eyes and let the warm wind rush past her face. So many questions remained unanswered.

Why was Rachael in Belize? Who had arranged for her to be brought there? What was her connection to Ortega?

Exhaustion washed over her. She didn't realize she had fallen asleep until the boat bumped into the dock in Placencia and her eyes popped open.

"Come on, baby," Johnnie said gently. "Let's get your sister someplace where she can sleep off some of those drugs. Maybe the rest of us can get a little shut-eye, too."

She nodded.

Still wary, the men took watches standing guard. The next thing she remembered was waking up in a motel room near the tiny Placencia airport, lying on top of the mattress asleep in her clothes, her sister asleep in the bed next to hers. Johnnie dozed in a chair across the way.

As if he had sensed her watching him, his eyes cracked open. A glance at the clock and he was on his feet.

"Time to go," he said, striding toward her.

It was still dark outside, the sun not yet up. "Do I have time to shower?" she asked.

"If you make it fast." He gave her a long, slow perusal. "Maybe we could save a little time by taking one together."

Desire curled through her. Maybe it was the danger they had faced last night, maybe just seeing him there in the room, remembering all the hard muscles beneath his black T-shirt and camouflage pants, remembering how good it was when he made love to her.

Amy glanced over at her sister, who looked more unconscious than asleep, and her heart twisted. "We better not. If Rachael wakes up, I need to be here."

Johnnie nodded. He tipped his head toward the bathroom. "Go on. I'll sit with her till you're finished."

"Thanks." Amy started for the shower, cast a wistful glance back at Johnnie. Forcing her mind in a safer direction, she walked into the bathroom telling herself to think how good it was going to feel to be wearing perfume again—instead of bug spray.

Chapter 28

Johnnie turned his sat phone back on as the bureau jet taxied toward the executive terminal at the Houston airport, a stop on the return to drop off Ben and Jake, who were being debriefed by an agent in their area.

Johnnie looked at the phone, saw a message waiting. He recognized the number and returned the call from Dev Raines.

"Hey, Johnnie," Dev said. "You still in Belize?"

It was amazing the way his friends always seemed to know his comings and goings.

"At the airport in Houston," he said, "dropping Slocum and Cantrell."

"Do any good?"

"We found the girl. She's pretty messed up, but she's breathing."

"That's good news. Listen, I called because your boy,

Brodie, found the chop shop—an abandoned warehouse in East L.A. We went in last night."

"What the hell? I thought you needed backup?"

"Figured you might be busy for a while. Talked to Cantrell before he and Slocum left to join you. Besides, Brodie's a marine, said he could handle the job and he was right. He did real good…for a jarhead."

Johnnie smiled, though Dev couldn't see. "Good to know. So the guys you busted…anyone I might know?"

"The ring was being run by a guy named Arturo Vasquez. We think Jack Romano, the guy who worked in design at General Motors figured how to disable the alarms. The cops are on it."

"Sounds good."

"Here's the interesting part…all of the cars were late model, high-end vehicles—Mercedes, BMW, Porsche. We even found a Lamborghini and an Aston Martin being stripped down and refitted. The thing is, one of the cars in the shop was older, not valuable at all but completely redone. Looked like they were using it to run errands, stuff like that. It was a '98 Toyota Corolla, Johnnie. Ring any bells?"

"Oh, yeah." According to the police report, it was the kind of car Rachael was driving the night she disappeared.

"Brodie says it fits the description of the car he's been looking for, the one owned by Rachael Brewer. And here's the rub. Arturo Vasquez rolled over on a guy named Hector Sanchez. Sanchez has been linked to Carlos Ortega."

"That fits. They took the girl and hid her car in plain sight. Interesting. By the way, it isn't for publication, but Ortega's dead."

Dev whistled. "I'm not asking how that happened."

"Tripped and fell on a 9 mil."

"I'll just bet. Listen, I won't be in L.A. when you get back. I'm headed for Scottsdale. If you recall, I've got a wife and daughter waiting and I'm in a damned big hurry to see them."

Johnnie chuckled. "I don't blame you."

"Give my best to Amy."

Johnnie just grunted. He was way past the denial stage. "Will do." He had no idea what to do about it, knew deep down it could never work out. But for now, she was his and he was going to enjoy every minute for as long as it lasted.

He ended the call and looked up to see Amy watching him.

"Looks like they found your sister's car," he said.

The jet was rolling to a stop. Amy straightened in the deep leather seat beside him. "Where?"

"Warehouse in East L.A. Been stripped and re-painted, numbers probably filed off, but it's her make and model and there's a link to Ortega, so odds are it's hers."

Amy looked over at her sister, asleep in the seat across the aisle. "Why in the name of God would Rachael get involved with a man like Ortega?"

"Good question," Johnnie said. Just then the plane rolled to a stop and a few minutes later the cabin door swung open. Cantrell and Riggs grabbed their gear and headed down the aisle.

Jake paused next to Amy. "Bye, sweetcheeks. Take care of him, okay?"

Amy came out of her seat, ducked into the aisle and threw her arms around Jake's muscular neck. "I'll never be able to repay you for what you've done—never." He hugged her and her eyes welled. "Thank you."

Jake just nodded and headed off down the aisle toward the door.

Slocum came next. He got the same treatment, and for once his ice-blue eyes warmed up. "I'm just glad we could help."

Amy went up on her toes and kissed his cheek, which was dark with a night's growth of beard. "I'll never forget you."

"You just get your sister home and well."

Amy swallowed, nodded.

Johnnie followed the men off the plane. "I owe you guys big-time. You need me, just let me know and I'll be there."

The men shook hands, then Cantrell and Slocum started across the tarmac toward a lanky, dark-haired DEA agent named Richard Haskins that Wheeler had said would be debriefing them. They had all agreed to full disclosure but no recorders. They had to maintain plausible deniability.

With a final wave, Johnnie returned to his seat next to Amy. Across the aisle, Rachael continued to doze off and on, never staying awake for more than a few minutes at a time.

He hoped it was just the drugs, that she wasn't injured in some other way. Wheeler had promised to have an ambulance waiting at LAX when they got there. Amy had decided not to call her mother until her sister had been examined and they knew exactly what they were dealing with.

For Amy's sake as much as Rachael's, he prayed the girl would be all right.

* * *

Amy sat at Rachael's bedside in the West Hollywood Medical Center. Though they had only been there a few hours, the room was filled with flowers—from Jake and Ben, from Dev and Lark Delaney, Molly and Clive Monroe. Johnnie had bought the bouquet of pink roses, Rachael's favorite, that Amy had picked out at the gift shop downstairs. The flowers, with both their names on the card, sat in a vase beside her bed.

She looked over to where her sister lay pale and sleeping as she had since their arrival that afternoon. An IV tube dripped liquids into her arm and a vitals monitor beeped, checking her pulse was normal.

Rachael had been tested for HIV and other sexually transmitted diseases. Someone—she thought perhaps Agent Wheeler—had pressed for a rush on the results and they had come back a few minutes ago—all negative, thank God. A rape kit had been done, but no signs of recent sexual intercourse had been found. Which didn't eliminate the possibility of an earlier rape.

Amy remembered the way Ortega had looked at Rachael as she huddled nearly naked in the corner of the bedroom, and didn't doubt for a moment he had intimate knowledge of her body.

But he had only returned to Belize that day, to the island a brief time before they got there. Amy wondered if Ortega might have considered Rachael his personal property, which would explain why he hadn't invited his two sleazy friends to abuse her.

Lieutenant Meeks had been in and out of Rachael's room. The policewoman had come to question her, but so far, Dr. McMahon, a thin man with buzz-cut gray hair, had refused to let the woman anywhere near his patient.

"She hasn't regained consciousness yet," he'd said. "Rachael's dehydrated and still under the influence of heroin and OxyContin, and a couple of other prescription drugs. She needs time," Dr. McMahon had explained.

Lieutenant Meeks had glanced over at the bed. "Call me as soon as she wakes up." She'd pressed a business card with her phone numbers into his hand.

"I'll let you know," the doctor had promised.

Agent Wheeler, who had helped them from the start, had also been at the hospital. In a private room, he had interviewed Johnnie at length, then brought Amy into the room and questioned her, as well. By the time he left the hospital, he had seemed satisfied with the information he had received.

Amy looked up at the sound of a light knock at the door. Expecting to see Johnnie, Amy was surprised to see Detective Vega standing in the open doorway, his olive complexion and near-black eyes at odds with the bright yellow spring bouquet he held in one dark hand.

Amy smiled and walked toward him. "Detective Vega. How nice of you to come." She stepped out of the way, inviting him into the room and took the vase from his hand, setting it on the window sill with the others. "I'm sure when Rachael wakes up she'll be cheered by all the pretty flowers."

His black eyes moved toward the bed. "How is she?"

Amy's smile faded. "They aren't sure yet. She opened her eyes a couple of times but only for a second and she hasn't said anything yet."

"She owes you her life…you and Johnnie." Vega's

gaze remained on the woman in the bed. "The police never came up with a thing."

"We still don't know what happened. We're hoping she'll be able to tell us when she wakes up."

Amy's cell phone rang just then. She looked down at the number. It was Johnnie. "Excuse me, I need to take this." She stepped out into the hall, leaving the detective still staring at Rachael.

"Hi."

"Hi, baby. You holding up okay?"

"I'm okay."

"How's your sister?"

"Still asleep."

"Have you called your mother yet?"

"Not yet." She'd been waiting for word from the doctors. "I was hoping I'd be able to tell her something besides her daughter is alive."

"Call her. At least she'll have that much to hang on to."

"You're right. I'll do it as soon as I hang up."

"I've got a couple more things to check out. I'll be down there as soon as I'm finished."

"Detective Vega's here. He brought Rachael flowers."

"I talked to him this morning. Rick's a good guy. I'll see you soon."

Amy hung up and dialed her mother, took a deep breath for the conversation ahead.

"Mom?"

"Amy, thank God you called. I was really starting to worry."

She hadn't meant for that to happen but considering everything that had been going on, there wasn't much she could do. "I've got news, Mom. Maybe you should sit down."

"Oh, my God…"

Amy's heart jerked. "No, Mom! We found her! Rachael's alive, Mom. She's in the hospital. A lot has happened. There's a lot to tell you."

"She's alive?"

"That's right."

Her mother's voice broke. "Then just tell me she's going to be okay."

"She is, Mom. We don't…don't know how long it's going to take, but—"

"I'm coming to L.A.," her mother said, her voice firming again. "I'll be on the first plane out of Grand Rapids."

Amy felt a rush of relief she didn't expect to feel. She was a grown woman, after all, but some things never really changed. Her mother was coming. Everything was going to be all right.

"Just let me know what time you're getting in and I'll pick you up." Of course she didn't have a car, but she was sure Johnnie would drive her.

Her mother's voice clogged with tears. "Tell your sister…tell her I love her."

A lump rose in Amy's throat. "I will, Mom."

Then the phone went dead and Amy just stood there, fighting to pull herself together. When she stepped back into the room, Detective Vega was standing at the foot of Rachael's bed, his gaze on Rachael's face.

"Did you know she got that part she tried out for?" Vega turned to Amy.

"What part was that?"

"A new TV series. *LAPD Blue.* The director said she was perfect for the role she read for."

Amy's eyes filled. "Oh, God."

"Let her know, will you? After she went missing, they had to recast the part, but the director was really impressed. I think she'll have a good chance of getting something else."

The tears in Amy's eyes spilled onto her cheeks. She wiped them away with her fingers. "I'll tell her."

Amy watched the detective leave, her throat aching for all that Rachael had lost. As she turned to walk back to the chair next to the bed, Rachael's green eyes slowly opened. This time there seemed to be more in them than hazy dullness.

"Rachael!" Amy rushed toward her. "Just take it easy." She reached out and took hold of her sister's icy hand. "You're in the hospital. You're back in Los Angeles and you're safe."

Rachael blinked several times. She stared at Amy, her eyebrows drawing together. "Los Angeles?"

"That's right. Mom's on the way. Everything's going to be okay."

Rachael just stared. "Who...who are you?"

"You don't know me? I'm your sister... It's me, Amy."

Rachael swallowed, her head moving back and forth on the pillow. "I—I'm sorry, I don't...don't remember you." She looked up, and Amy could see the panic in her face. "I don't remember anything. Not even...not even my name."

Chapter 29

Johnnie stood with Amy and Dr. McMahon outside the door to Rachael's room. It was dark outside, getting toward the end of a very long day that had started early that morning thousands of miles away.

"The bruise on her temple gave us some concern, but the CAT scan showed nothing that could account for the memory loss."

"What about a concussion?" Amy asked.

"No sign of anything like that."

"Then what is it?" Johnnie asked.

"It may be nothing more than a form of post-traumatic stress. From what we know, Rachael was abducted, drugged and probably raped. She's just beginning to feel the withdrawal symptoms of the opiates she was given on a daily basis. She may be blocking, unwilling to face the things that have happened to her."

Amy's hand trembled where she held on to Johnnie's arm. "Will the memory loss be permanent?" she asked, her face still pale.

"It's possible, but not likely. Odds are, as time passes and she feels safe, her memory will slowly return."

"When can she go home?" Amy asked.

"Whether she's here or somewhere else, she'll have to deal with the withdrawal symptoms. The drugs she was on were opiates so the recovery will be faster, but she'll still suffer periods of anxiety and insomnia. There'll be sweating, runny nose, then it will start to get worse. She'll experience nausea, abdominal cramps, diarrhea, vomiting. We've got medications that can help the withdrawal, but it won't be easy. It never is."

Some of the color returned to Amy's cheeks, along with a look of determination. "So she can go home?"

"If there's a place she can receive the proper care."

"My mother's flying in. We'll find a place. Between the two of us, we can see she gets the care she needs."

Johnnie looked up just then to see his landlady, Ellie Stiles, striding down the hall in her usual jogging suit, silver hair neatly combed, a basket of violets in one hand.

"I can help with that problem," Ellie said, having a knack for eavesdropping on other people's conversations. "Nobody can afford a long stay at the hospital these days and I've got a great big house and no one in it. You can have the whole guest wing to yourselves for as long as you need."

Amy looked stunned. "Oh, Ellie, that's so kind of you, but we couldn't possibly impose on you like that."

"Why, yes you can. Johnnie's family. You're his girl,

so you're family, too. Family helps each other when they need it."

Amy's eyes glistened. "I don't know…it seems like an awful lot to ask…"

"Go ahead," Johnnie said. "I'd just as soon have Rachael close by until we figure out her connection to Ortega." He had hoped Rachael would be able to tell them how she'd wound up on the island, but for now that wasn't going to happen. He figured with Ortega dead, any threat to her safety was slim. Still, he didn't have the whole story yet. He'd feel better after he tied up all the loose ends.

He looked over at his landlady and friend, his mind returning to the part where Ellie had said that Amy was his girl. She was…sort of. But the more they were together, the harder it was going to be to let her go.

And he'd have to. He was who he was and she was who she was. A not-so-ex-Army Ranger and a kindergarten teacher.

Just another of God's little jokes.

Amy refused to leave the hospital that night, choosing instead to sleep in a chair one of the nurses brought into her sister's room. Johnnie went back to the clubs on Sunset to do a little digging, see if he could pick up any rumors that might help him find out how Rachael Brewer managed to wind up in Carlos Ortega's jet on her way to Belize, but wound up with the same big fat zero as before.

He went home to get some sleep. It was funny how empty the house felt now that Amy was gone. No one to share a cup of coffee with in the mornings, no soft, sweet woman to share his bed. He hadn't noticed his lonely existence before. Now he did.

He told himself he'd get over it, that things were just the way they were and there was nothing he could do to change it. He figured in time he'd go back to normal. He showered and dressed, then heard a knock at the door as he headed for the kitchen and a last cup of coffee.

In a pair of jeans and a clean white T-shirt, Tyler Brodie stood on the porch. "I heard you were back. Thought I'd better check in."

Johnnie stepped back and let Brodie in.

"Want some coffee?" Johnnie asked.

"Sounds great."

They headed for the kitchen. Johnnie poured coffee into a mug and handed it to Ty, then emptied the pot into his own mug.

Johnnie took a drink. "I heard about the raid. Dev said you did real good."

"The thing was we couldn't go to the police. We pieced enough intel together to know what was going on, but there wasn't enough evidence for a warrant."

"So you went in and took 'em down."

"That's right." Ty shot him a boyish grin. "It was almost too easy."

"Yeah, right." It was never easy taking down a gang of professional thieves but the kid was still at the gung ho, hoorah, stage of his life. Johnnie had passed that phase long ago.

"After we subdued the subjects," Brodie continued with glee, "Dev made an anonymous call to the police explaining the situation. A couple of the cars hadn't had the VIN numbers filed off yet. We left the big roll-up doors open, the cops showed up and hauled the bad guys off to jail."

Johnnie took a drink of his coffee. "Dev needed backup and I wasn't here. I'm glad you were able to handle it."

The kid nodded, grinned. "So have you got anything new for me?"

"Maybe. I still haven't figured the connection between Rachael Brewer and Carlos Ortega. Rick Vega talked to Manny. He doesn't think Ortega's son was involved. At least not directly."

"Which leaves us pretty much where we were before you left."

"Except for the part where the girl came back alive."

"Yeah, that's really great. So I'll start digging again, see if anything new turns up."

Johnnie nodded. "That's what I plan to do. Maybe we'll get lucky this time."

"Maybe." Ty finished his coffee and set the mug down on the table, calling over his shoulder as he left the house, "Thanks for the coffee." The door closed softly, Johnnie drained his mug and headed for his car.

During the morning, he ran a couple of errands, then returned to the hospital. That afternoon, he drove Amy to LAX to pick up her mother.

He had tried to imagine what Hannah Brewer would be like but couldn't come up with much of a mental picture. When the woman pushed through the United Airlines baggage claim door, he saw an attractive fifty-plus woman, a little overweight with Amy's blue eyes and golden-blond hair cut in a shoulder-length style.

Johnnie grabbed her bag off the curb and tossed it

into the trunk of the Mustang while Amy made the introductions.

"Mom, this is Johnnie Riggs. He's the man who saved Rachael's life."

Hannah turned to him and gave him a smile. "Well, then, I owe you a very great deal. It's nice to meet you, Mr. Riggs." But the way she sized him up, his jaw already dark with an afternoon's growth of beard, he thought that she didn't think it was nice meeting him at all.

"It's just Johnnie. And it's Amy you need to thank. It was her persistence that saved your daughter. If it hadn't been for her, we never would have found her."

He tried not to look at Amy, knew the heat in his eyes would be hard for a mother to miss. "Let's get you both back to the hospital," he said to distract her, "so you can get Rachael out of there and comfortably settled at Ellie's."

Better to move the girl before the withdrawal symptoms got worse. And Ellie was right. Neither Amy nor her mother could afford the massive bills a long hospital stay would incur.

The nurses had Rachael up and mobile by the time they arrived. She was sitting in a chair, talking but not saying much.

Amy and her mother watched from the open doorway, Hannah Brewer eager to reach her daughter, yet beginning to understand the situation Amy had explained to her on the way from the airport.

"So you're saying you don't remember anything," Carla said. "Not how you got there, not what happened in Belize. Nothing."

"No."

"Not even who you are."

Misery washed into Rachael's face, still pale and thin but unmistakably beautiful. "No…" The answer came out as a whisper, and Carla rolled her eyes. She planted her hands on her hips.

"If that's all you're going to say, then I guess for now we're through. But make no mistake. I'll be back. And if it turns out you're lying—"

"That's enough!" Hannah Brewer charged through the door like a lioness protecting her cub. "If my daughter says she doesn't remember, then she doesn't remember."

Carla's lips thinned. "I've got a job to do, Mrs. Brewer. Whether you like it or not—I intend to do it."

Hannah stayed where she was, guarding the space between Meeks and her daughter. Turning, Carla strode across the room, casting Johnnie a warning glance along the way, and disappeared out the door.

Johnnie breathed a sigh of relief. As soon as he'd returned to L.A. he had phoned the department and told them the story he and Wheeler had come up with. The DEA had found Rachael in Belize City and brought her back to the States. He didn't mention Ortega or the villa or the island or anything that had happened. It wasn't LAPD jurisdiction and the DEA wanted it kept quiet. So did Johnnie.

Carla wasn't happy about it. When she pressed Johnnie for more information, he referred her back to Wheeler, who told her the rescue was DEA business and that was all she needed to know.

By now it was international news that Carlos Ortega was dead. According to word on the street, no one knew which man the cartel leaders would be putting in charge of his operation. Hopefully the men would be more concerned with keeping their illegal businesses running smoothly and the cash flowing in than finding the men responsible for what had happened in Belize.

Standing next to Rachael's chair, Hannah reached for her daughter's hand. "Sweetheart, I don't want you to feel bad if you don't recognize me, all right?"

Rachael just nodded.

"I'm your mother. I'm here to help you get back on your feet."

Rachael swallowed. Her nose was running, her skin glistening with perspiration. She was clearly anxious, the withdrawal symptoms getting worse. Her mother plucked a tissue off the bedside table and wiped away the wetness beneath her nose.

"I wish I could remember you," Rachael said. "I wish I could remember Amy, but I don't." Tears welled in her pale green eyes. "It's all just… Everything is a blank spot in my mind."

Hannah's smile never wavered. "You'll remember. It's just going to take a little time."

"Amy told me you were flying out from Michigan. Thank you for coming."

Hannah leaned over and kissed her daughter's cheek. "Oh, dear heart. Of course I would come. Whether you recognize me or not, I'm your mother. I'll always come when you need me."

Standing next to Johnnie, Amy made a soft sound in her throat.

"Come on," he said a little gruffly. "Let's give them some time. We'll go downstairs, finish the paperwork and get Rachael out of here."

Amy looked up at him. "I don't know what to say

to you, how to thank you for everything you've done. I love you, Johnnie. I know I shouldn't say it, especially not here. I know I'm not what you need and I don't expect you to say anything back. But you're just the most amazing man and as hard as I tried not to, I couldn't help falling in love with you."

Johnnie just stood there. His throat moved up and down in an effort to form some kind of reply but nothing came out. Instead, he pulled her into his arms and just held her.

There was nothing to say. Amy was sweet and brave, intelligent and beautiful. And she was right. She wasn't what he needed.

He didn't need anyone.

He never had and he never would.

They were settled in the guest wing of Ellie Stiles's fabulous Hollywood Hills home. Apparently in his day, her deceased husband, Harry, had been a bigtime movie mogul, a producer with a long list of boxoffice hits. Amy hadn't paid much attention to the house next door to Johnnie's; it was kind of off down the hill, mostly just the rooftop showing.

Like the guesthouse, it was contemporary in style, at least eight thousand square feet, with high ceilings, twelve-foot doorways, granite floors and massive plate glass windows that overlooked the rectangular swimming pool out into the valley.

"It has pretty much everything I need," Ellie said as she gave them the tour, then guided them down the wide hall to a row of large, beautifully furnished bedrooms in the guest wing. "Except a gym, which is over at Johnnie's." She grinned. "Gives me an excuse to go over and check on him."

Amy smiled. She liked Ellie Stiles, liked that she looked out for Johnnie. She knew he valued his independence, but everyone needed a friend who cared about him and Ellie thought of Johnnie as a sort of adopted son.

Two days slipped past and still Rachael had no memory of her family or what had happened. Both days she had been violently ill: stomach cramping, diarrhea, nausea and vomiting, but the drugs—clonidine and Subutex—that the doctor had prescribed were helping, and Amy believed her sister was on the road to recovery. At least physically.

The first and second days they were there, Lieutenant Meeks stopped by, determined to grill Rachael for information, but she still had no memory and she was feeling so ill the detective left her alone.

On the third day, Rick Vega showed up at the house. This time he brought a prettily wrapped box of dark chocolates.

He extended the chocolates to Amy. "I thought it might help with the craving once the nausea has passed."

Amy smiled. "She's feeling a lot better today. Why don't you give them to her yourself?"

Vega's dark features brightened.

"She's sitting out on the deck. It's this way."

"Beautiful house," he said as they made their way down a wide hall to the huge sliding glass doors leading outside. Along the way, they passed a line of elegant Miró sculptures. A big, colorful Lichtenstein hung on one wall.

"I've been at Johnnie's a lot over the years," Vega said, taking in the glamorous surroundings. "Ellie was there off and on, but I've never been in her house."

"Isn't it gorgeous?" Amy said. "Ellie says she gets lonely, though. I think maybe she should sell it, move into a retirement community, the kind of place where people get to know each other."

"She does that," Vega teased, "some guy will snap her up."

Amy smiled, thinking how attractive the woman was at age seventy, the smart, vibrant person she was, and figured he was probably right.

Perhaps Ellie would find someone. Amy tried not to think of Johnnie, to remember the moment she had told him she loved him. She tried not to wish he had said the words in return, told her he wanted them to be together.

She had known from the start that wasn't meant to be.

Amy walked Rick out onto the deck. A soft breeze lifted strands of her hair and though a slight haze hung over the city, the view stretching out as far as the eye could see was spectacular.

"Rachael, this is Detective Vega. He's with the LAPD. He was one of the people who helped us find you. He's also a friend."

Rachael looked up at him from where she sat reading in a comfortable chaise lounge. "The pretty yellow flowers," she said. "Your name was on the card that came with them."

"That's right."

"They're still beautiful. I have them in my bedroom." She suddenly looked nervous. "Are you here to ask me questions?"

Vega shook his head. In a perfectly tailored fawn-colored suit, his black hair combed back, and with his intense black eyes, Amy thought he was amazingly handsome. "This is a personal visit, nothing to do with work. I just… I did a lot of digging when we were trying to find you. In a way I feel as if I know you. I hope that doesn't sound weird."

Rachael smiled. "Not at all. Since I can't remember anything, maybe you could help me learn a little about myself. Do you have time to sit for a minute?"

"Sure."

As Rick sat down in the chair next to Rachael, Amy eased back toward the house, leaving them alone. Though Amy couldn't hear what he said, when Vega started talking, for the first time since they had come to the house, Rachael laughed. The sound was so sweet it made Amy's heart hurt.

Her mother came up beside where she stood watching her sister with the handsome detective. "Rachael's doing better every day," her mother said.

"This morning she remembered something about Daddy. A trip we went on to the lake. She said the memory only lasted a couple of seconds, but I think it gave her hope."

Her mother's eyes strayed to where Rachael sat on the deck. "It's hard to look at her and know she doesn't have the faintest idea who I am."

"I know it is, but if a memory of Daddy came back, I think in time she'll remember everything. I really think she's going to be all right."

Her mother's blue gaze swung to Amy. "What about you, honey, are you going to be all right?"

Amy looked up at her. "What do you mean?"

"You and Johnnie. It's clear you have feelings for him. It's also clear he isn't the man for you, and I think you know it."

Amy ignored a stab of pain. "I love him, Mom. He's the most incredible man I've ever met. If I thought I could make him happy, there's nothing that could keep me away from him. But you're right. His life is just too different from mine. And there's no way I would want him to change."

Her mother squeezed her shoulder. "You've always been the sensible one. I'm glad you're willing to see the truth."

Amy made no reply. The truth was glaringly there for anyone to see. He wasn't for her and she wasn't for him. It didn't make her love him any less.

Rick spoke quietly to Rachael. She was even more beautiful than her pictures, with the color returning to her cheeks and her dark hair gleaming in the sun. And softer, more vulnerable. He couldn't imagine the woman in front of him dancing onstage at the Kitty Cat Club.

From beneath thick-fringed lashes, she looked up at him. "Amy said I worked as an exotic dancer." Words that mirrored his thoughts. "She says my mother doesn't know. But you do, don't you?"

"I've seen you dance. To tell you the truth, I was there on police business. At the time, I didn't pay that much attention."

She seemed somehow relieved. Her shoulders relaxed and her pretty lips curved into a smile. "Wasn't I any good?"

His mouth edged up in return. "There were other

things about you I found more interesting—not that you don't look great in a silver G-string."

Rachael laughed. She let her head tip back against the chaise she was resting in. "So what was it you found interesting about me?"

"Well, you're involved in charity work at the Dennison Children's Shelter. You often went to see a little boy named Jimmy whose mother wasn't around very much. You were a very good actress—or so Marvin Bixler, the director I talked to, told me."

"Amy said you told her I would have gotten the part in *LAPD Blue* if I hadn't…hadn't…if I hadn't…"

Rick reached over and gently caught her hand. "Take it easy. You've locked away the memories of what happened, but they're still in there, rolling around inside your head. In time, I think you'll remember. When you do, it's going to be painful. On some level, I think you know that."

She swallowed. "Amy told me some of it…how they found me in that…that house on the island. I know I went to Belize with a man, a drug dealer. What kind of a woman would associate with a man like that?"

"Not the one I know. I don't think you went willingly, Rachael. I think he forced you."

Her eyes teared up and she glanced away. "I guess somehow that makes it better."

"We'll figure it out, Rachael. I promise you. Once you remember, you'll be able to tell us how you ended up with Ortega."

Her gaze swung back to his. "You won't say anything about the rescue? I don't want to get Johnnie and the men who saved me in trouble."

"John Riggs is a very good friend. He's a bit of a

renegade, but he's one of the best men I've ever known. What he tells me stays between him and me. It's the same with you, Rachael. You can say whatever you want and you don't have to worry."

Rachael squeezed his hand. "Thank you, Detective."

"It's Rick, okay?"

She smiled. "Rick." He noticed she was beginning to perspire, the withdrawal hitting her again.

"I think I'd better go in," she said. "All of a sudden, I'm not feeling so well."

"Here, let me help you." He eased her up from the chaise then helped her cross the deck to the big glass doors. What possessed him to bend down and kiss her cheek as they stepped inside the house he would never know. "You take care of yourself, all right?"

"I will. Thank you for coming."

"If it's all right with you, I'll stop by again."

Her eyes met his. "I'd like that," she said softly. "I'd like that very much."

Looking into that arresting face, Rick felt something he had never felt before. Something that made his chest feel tight and scared him half to death.

Still, he'd be back. There wasn't a chance in hell he could stay away.

Chapter 30

He sat in his wood-paneled office, the walls lined with gold-embossed diplomas and certificates. The door was closed, giving him the privacy he needed.

His fingers tightened around the disposable phone he used for calls like these. "I can't believe this."

"You shouldn't have let your conscience get in the way," said the voice on the other end of the line. "You should have done what Ortega told you. You should have let him kill her."

"He was supposed to get her out of the country, take her someplace safe and keep her there."

"Well, now she's back. What are you going to do about it?"

He licked his lips, which suddenly felt bone-dry. "You said she's lost her memory. If she doesn't remember anything, how can she be a threat?"

"The doctors think it's only temporary, just a matter of time till it all comes back."

He took a deep breath, steadied himself, slowly released the air trapped in his lungs. "Can you handle it?"

A moment of silence on the line. "I know someone who can."

He'd weakened before. He had feelings for Rachael Brewer. If she hadn't been a goddamned stripper they might have had a future together.

If she'd stayed in the bedroom that night, instead of walking into his study when he was in the middle of an important meeting, she wouldn't need to die.

But life had a way of changing the best laid plans. Dan clenched his jaw. "Do it," he said.

The following night Johnnie sat at a table at the back of the Kitty Cat Club, sipping a bottle of Bud. Tate Watters spotted him and took a seat beside him.

"Haven't heard from you or Angel for a while. What's going on?"

Johnnie set his beer down. "We found Rachael. I can't give you the details. The important thing is she's back and the doctors think she'll be okay."

Relief and then worry flickered in Tate's eyes. "How bad is she?"

"She's in pretty rough shape, Tate. Until she's well enough to handle visitors, I need you to keep the news under your hat. Not even Babs can know."

"Understood."

"It's DEA business so how it actually came down isn't going to be in the papers."

"Even if it was, running off at the mouth has never been my style."

Johnnie picked up his beer, took a long swallow. "Another thing.... Angel's finished. She's nursing her sister. You'll have to find a replacement."

Tate eyed him with speculation. "You don't have to look so damned happy about it. She was one of the customers' favorites. Maybe I should talk to her, offer her more money."

Johnnie set his bottle down a little too hard on the table. "Bullshit, it's over. Consider this her official resignation. She's out and that's the end of it."

Tate laughed. "I was kidding, all right?"

Embarrassment burned the back of his neck. He was glad it was dark in the club. "Sorry."

"No problem. She's a really nice girl. If I were you, I'd—"

"Don't say it. She's going back to Grand Rapids as soon as this is over."

"That's too bad."

Johnnie looked over Tate's head. Honeybee was on the stage, jiggling her oversize breasts and tossing her mane of red hair.

"Listen, I stopped by to fill you in, but there's something else. We still haven't figured the link between Rachael and Ortega. We know his men took her the night she disappeared, but we can't figure the why. You hear anything...anything at all, you let me know."

"I'll keep my ears open."

Leaving his beer half finished, Johnnie rose from the table and picked his way through the crowded club, and out to the parking lot. He'd make his usual rounds, see if anything new turned up. Then he'd go home and climb into his empty bed.

And do his damnedest not to think of Amy, knowing

she was in the house next door and he couldn't touch her. Do his best to convince himself it was better to end things now, just stay friends.

Tell himself he didn't want her just as much as he had the first night he had seen her onstage, dancing as Angel Fontaine.

Amy couldn't sleep. For a while, she lay beneath the sheets staring up at the ceiling, thinking of Johnnie, missing him, wishing things could be different.

Wishing she was in his bed and they were making love.

With a sigh, she finally gave up and tossed back the covers, hoping a glass of milk would help. Pulling on her robe, she tied the sash and padded down the hall toward the kitchen. She passed her mother's room and paused at Rachael's door, thinking maybe she should pop in for a quick check on her sister to be sure she was sleeping all right.

Quietly turning the knob, she eased open the door and her breath caught. A man dressed completely in black slid open the glass door leading out to the deck and stepped into the bedroom. As he moved toward the bed, a sliver of moonlight glinted off the pistol in his hand, the barrel pointed at Rachael, soundly sleeping beneath the covers.

Amy let out an ear-piercing scream and bolted toward the attacker, praying she could sidetrack the man long enough for her sister to get out of the way.

Johnnie pulled his Mustang into the garage and turned off the engine. As he cracked open the car door and reached beneath the seat to retrieve the 9 mm Beretta he carried on nights like these, a shrill scream cut through the air. Cold fear washed over him. A rush of adrenaline had his instincts kicking in. Gripping the pistol in his hand, Johnnie started running toward Ellie's house.

He knew where that scream had come from, knew it had to be an assault on Rachael, damned himself for thinking the danger was over. Scanning the grounds for any additional threat lurking in the darkness, he raced toward the back of the house, bolted up the steps leading onto the deck and ran for the guest wing.

One of the sliders was open. Inside the room, he saw Amy struggling with a man in black, a ski mask over his face, fighting to wrench the gun out of his hand. She kicked a leg out from under him and they landed hard on the carpet, the pistol going off with a deafening roar.

"Hold it right there!" Johnnie's pistol pointed directly at the gunman, but there was no way he could pull the trigger, not with Amy tangled up with his target.

The gunman swung the barrel of his pistol up to Amy's head. "Back off—unless you want her to die."

Johnnie's fingers tightened around the grip of his weapon. If he'd had a clear shot, the guy would be dead. "Let her go," he said softly. "Let her go and I won't kill you."

The intruder hauled Amy to her feet, his gun pressed hard against her temple, an arm locked around her neck. "You're not the one in charge here."

From the corner of his eye, Johnnie saw Rachael backed against the wall, tears streaming down her face. Even without looking their way, he knew Ellie and Hannah Brewer were standing in the open doorway.

A shitload of women and a shooter in the mix.

He wondered if things could get worse.

Hannah gave a soft sob and he thought, *Oh, yeah, a whole lot worse.*

"Step away from the door," the gunman warned. Johnnie did as he was told, easing backward out to the deck, opening what appeared to be a path of escape.

"Look, just let her go and get out of here," he said. "By the time the cops get here, you'll be long gone."

"Put down the weapon."

Johnnie shook his head. "Not gonna happen." If he did, people would be dead. He took another step backward, but kept the intruder in his line of fire. "All I care about is the woman. Just let her go and you'll have a chance to get away." Not much of one but he didn't say that.

The gunman made the mistake of turning his pistol away from Amy and pointing it at Johnnie. Her eyes locked with his an instant before her hands shot out to the side and she slapped her palms hard over the gunman's ears.

"Fuck!" The man staggered and nearly fell. The women screamed as Amy dropped to the carpet and rolled out of the way. The gunman fired wildly and Johnnie fired back.

One, two, three shots, dead center in the shooter's chest. The guy crashed backward onto the bedroom floor, twitched a couple of times, then lay still.

Shit. He needed the bastard alive but the guy hadn't left him any choice.

The women burst into the bedroom, Hannah rushing to Rachael, Ellie moving quickly toward Amy. Johnnie got to her first, hauled her up from the floor and straight into his arms.

He could feel her trembling. His hold tightened. "Damn, you were good," he said, and when she gave him a wobbly little smile, he bent his head and kissed her—right there in front of her mother and Ellie. Right there in front of God and the rest of the world and he didn't give a rat's ass whether they liked it or not.

Amy was clutching his shoulders when he came up for air. Ellie was giving him that look that said this wasn't the time, which he ignored.

"I called 9-1-1," Ellie said. "The police are on the way."

Johnnie nodded. Amy looked dazed, her hair a tangled mess around her shoulders, her robe torn and hanging open, giving him a tantalizing look at her pretty little flowered shortie nightgown. He glanced away

"I—I need to see if Rachael's all right," Amy said. She reached up and touched his cheek, her fingers gentle against the roughness along his jaw.

Johnnie stepped away, letting her go, though he didn't really want to.

She straightened her robe, retied the sash and went over to her sister. "Rachael, are you okay?"

Rachael shook her head, her cheeks wet with tears. "No…but…but I will be. I just… I need a minute."

Her mother gave Rachael a heart-wrenching glance and turned her attention to Amy. "Sweetheart, are you all right?"

"I'm okay, Mom. A little shaky, but I'm okay."

Johnnie thought she was more than a little shaky. The guy had knocked the crap out of her. He hadn't missed the bruise blooming on her cheek, figured she'd be stiff and sore all over by morning.

His jaw tightened. He wanted to shoot the prick all over again.

Instead, as the echo of sirens drew near, he took a deep breath and went over to the intruder. A quick search of his pockets gave up a pack of Camels and a Bic cigarette lighter. No ID, no wallet, no cell phone. A silver money clip held a wad of hundred dollar bills, partial payment for the hit, Johnnie figured.

He lifted up the ski mask. Lifeless brown eyes stared back at him. White guy in his thirties, earrings in his ears. He tugged the mask a little higher, saw the guy's head was shaved. A skinhead. He'd been thinking gangbanger, someone Ortega's people might have on the payroll. Nothing about this case made sense.

He made a quick check for tats, saw nothing but a couple of generic lightning bolts, dragons and skulls and the rest of the usual bullshit all over his neck and arms, probably under his T-shirt.

Police cars were careening up the drive. Ellie must have opened the gate because they came roaring up to the house.

Digging his tiny LED light out of his pocket, he took off down the hill before they reached the front door. He needed to find out how the guy had gotten up to the house, probably climbed up from the road below. The only fence was a five-footer that separated the house from the neighbor's property, and there wasn't any perimeter alarm system.

He'd been hounding Ellie to upgrade the fifteen-year-old system inside the house. Maybe now she'd listen. Course, he couldn't say much since he didn't have an alarm system on his place, either.

He continued on down the hill, hoping to find the guy's car, find something inside that could identify the shooter. Picking his way between rocks and shrubs, he made his way to the road below. Of course, the guy could have had an accomplice who had already fled the scene, but Johnnie didn't think so.

In the bushes along the winding street, he found what he was looking for. Harley-Davidson. Expensive custom job, blue and silver with skulls and dragons in the design work. Whoever did the painting was good. Real good. And that kind of talent could be tracked. He dug out his cell phone, flashed his light on the fuel tank, and snapped a couple of photos.

A black leather saddlebag hung across the back of the bike. Inside he found a wallet and extra ammunition. The driver's license gave the name Wes Henley with a home address in Anaheim. His cell was in the pouch. Johnnie was only interested in the calls received since they brought Rachael back to the States but the list was too long to check. The police would run the numbers. He'd get Vega to find out if anything turned up.

He looked at the recent calls made. The last two went to the same number. He hit the redial button, heard the sound of a young woman's voice on the other end. Girlfriend, he figured and mentally stored the number.

Johnnie headed back up the hill. The cops wouldn't be happy if they knew he had tampered with a crime scene, which they'd figure out if they ran the wallet or phone for prints, which they probably wouldn't since the info they needed was all right there. In the meantime, he had something to go on, something that could lead him to the man or men who wanted Rachael Brewer dead.

If he was lucky, he'd also find the why.

Amy sat next to her sister at the round, glass-topped table in Ellie's kitchen. It was still dark outside, but the first faint light of dawn had begun to purple the horizon. Ellie was brewing a second pot of coffee, its bracing aroma filling the air. Police still swarmed the house, which was now a homicide crime scene.

The cops had found the motorcycle parked below the house so they knew the assailant's name, something Johnnie had already discovered. Being a homicide detective with the Hollywood police department, Rick Vega was working the case. He had arrived on the scene just minutes after the police cars starting rolling up the driveway.

"I heard the call on my scanner," he explained to Rachael as he sat down in a chair beside her. "When I recognized the address, I knew it had to be you and it scared the hell out of me. I'm glad you're okay."

Rachael's eyes filled. "I wish I could have done something. When Amy screamed, I was so scared I could barely move. I didn't even try to help her. If she hadn't gone after that man—"

"Easy…" Rick reached over and caught Rachael's hand. "You've already been through more than most people endure in a lifetime. You can't expect to be thinking clearly right now."

"Detective Vega's right," Amy said softly. "You've suffered a terrible trauma. When that man came after you, part of you was reliving what happened before."

Johnnie walked up just then, apparently finished giving his statement to the police. He pulled out a chair, spun it around and sat down facing the table. "Rachael's going to need protection," he said flatly. "After what happened tonight, until we figure out how she was involved with Ortega, her life is clearly in danger."

Vega blew out a breath. "I thought with that scum out of the way, she'd be okay. Obviously I was wrong."

"You weren't alone," Johnnie said darkly. "We need a safe house. Someplace we can watch her 24/7."

Vega shook his head. "I've already talked to the department. They aren't convinced the abduction and what happened tonight are connected."

"What? That's crazy. Of course they're connected. Ortega abducts Rachael to get her out of the way. Now she's back and someone's trying to kill her. I figure she knows something—something she doesn't remember. They want to make sure she forgets—permanently."

A chill slipped down Amy's spine. She thought of that night on the island, the sort of men they were dealing with. Ruthless men who would stop at nothing to protect their own interests.

"I think people in the department are pissed the DEA left them out of the loop," Vega said. "They're saying Wes Henley has a history of using and selling. They're working on the theory it was just a drug-related burglary gone bad."

"That's so much crap and you know it."

"We both know it, but it's not going to change anything. Maybe the DEA will step in."

Amy's eyes found Johnnie's. She knew he could read the worry in her face.

"I'll talk to Wheeler, see what he can do."

The coffeepot chimed, signaling the pot was done brewing. Ellie poured a mug and set it in front of the detective, who wrapped his fingers around it.

"In the meantime," Vega said, "who besides us knew Rachael was staying here?"

"Yeah, that's what I've been asking myself." Johnnie leaned back as Ellie bent over to refill his mug with some of the fresh-made brew. "People at the hospital knew. We used Ellie's address on the release forms. Wheeler knew. He talked to her here a couple of times."

"So did several people in the department," Rick said, "including me."

"It wouldn't be hard to figure. I talked to Tate Watters. He knows I've been seeing Amy. Guessing Rachael was here wouldn't be much of a stretch."

"You think Watters is involved?"

"Not likely. He's a straight shooter, always has been."

"What you're saying is it could be anyone."

Johnnie took a sip of his coffee. "Yeah, that about sums it up."

Rachael stared into her untouched cup. "I wish I could remember. Every time I try, my mind just shuts down."

Vega took her hand and laced his fingers with hers. "I don't want you to worry. I promised you we'd figure this out. I gave you my word. What happened doesn't change that. It just means we have to move faster."

Rachael looked into his eyes. "I believe you. I don't know why, but I trust you." Something passed between them, something Amy could almost feel.

Vega squeezed Rachael's hand. "I won't let anything happen to you, Rachael. I swear it."

And Amy thought that whatever undercurrents were moving between them, Rick Vega would lay down his life for her sister.

Chapter 31

Johnnie talked to Special Agent Wheeler early that morning about arranging DEA protection. If Rachael's memory came back, she could be a valuable asset in a grand jury investigation into the drug smuggling operation formerly run by Carlos Ortega.

Or at least that was the premise Wheeler had used to get the okay.

And after the attack last night, it was beginning to look like a real possibility.

Rachael knew something.

Unfortunately, even she didn't know what it was.

The bad news was the agency's budget was stretched way too thin. Without any solid way to justify the expense, the DEA could only offer protection for a limited time. Unless Rachael's memory returned, unless she could provide some kind of evidence against Ortega's organization, two, maybe three days was all Wheeler could guarantee.

They needed to act fast, needed a lead to follow that would break the case open.

Johnnie looked past the agent with the pale complexion and receding hairline. Along with Wheeler, another two agents were there at Ellie's house, sitting in a big black SUV, ready to drive Rachael and her family to the DEA safe house. As the ladies rolled their luggage down the front steps toward the car, Wheeler walked over to load their bags into the back. One of the agents got out to help.

Johnnie's gaze swung to Amy. He figured this would pretty much be the end for them. Ever since the night of the shooting he had tried to steel himself. Unfortunately, from the dark mood he found himself in this morning, he knew it hadn't worked. He watched her now, wondering what he could possibly say that would let her know how special she was to him. He was surprised to see her tugging her little rolling bag past the other women over to where he stood.

With her hair swinging loose around her shoulders and a soft smile on her face, she looked so damn pretty his chest tightened. Even with the bruise on her cheek, she was beautiful. He straightened, worked to slow the painful thudding of his heart.

"So I guess this is goodbye," he said with a slight catch in his voice, "at least for a while."

Amy just smiled. "I'm not going anywhere. Mom's going with Rachael. She's been telling her things about her life, trying to help her remember. She'll make sure Rachael's okay. We talked it over this morning and since no one's trying to shoot me, I'm not going with them."

Worry filtered through him. "You need to go to the safe house, baby."

"I'm not the one in danger."

"Probably not, but—"

"If I stay, I can help. And don't say I can't. I found the island, didn't I? I did the ear thing last night. I can help and you know it."

He tried not to smile. God, he wanted her to stay so bad he ached. Still, it was the wrong thing to do.

"Ellie's house is a crime scene. She's going to be living in a hotel until the police are finished."

Amy just shrugged. "Then I guess I'll have to stay with you."

He ignored the way his heart was pounding inside his chest. He wanted to kiss her, just lean down and capture those plump pink lips. He wanted to drag her down on the grass, rip off her clothes and bury himself inside her.

"Your mother wouldn't like it."

"That's the thing… I'm not a little girl anymore so I don't have to worry about what my mom has to say. Besides, Rachael won't be safe until we find out who's after her."

He gave it one last shot. "We both know it's not a good idea."

She looked him straight in the face. "Don't you want me here?"

He told himself to lie. It was better if things ended now. "I want you here. Hell, I just plain want you."

Amy smiled so wide he felt like someone kicked him in the stomach.

"Then it's settled. I'm staying."

He couldn't think of anything to say, so he just pulled her into his arms and kissed her, not as long and deep as he wanted but that could wait until later.

"Fine," he said gruffly.

Amy left her suitcase and walked back to the car to say goodbye to Rachael. "You're sure you'll be all right?" Amy asked.

Rachael nodded. "I need some time to get myself together. And this way, Mom and I can talk."

Amy reached up and hugged her. "I'll see you soon."

Rachael wiped a tear from her cheek and even from a distance, Johnnie could see the sheen in Amy's eyes. She turned and hugged her mother, who cast Johnnie a cool look over her daughter's shoulder. Next Amy paused to hug Ellie, who was nodding and grinning.

Women. He should have known from the start he didn't stand a chance.

Wheeler took off in his own car. The black SUV was getting ready to pull out when Amy spotted a maroon convertible pulling up the drive, a Chrysler Sebring, not that expensive but a classy-looking car. The vehicle came to a stop and the engine fell silent.

Rick Vega cracked open the door and stepped out wearing a pair of perfectly pressed jeans and an Izod knit shirt instead of his usual tailored suit. The clothes looked really good on him.

Amy and Johnnie both started toward him.

"What's up?" Johnnie asked.

"They pulled me off the case. Said I was too personally involved."

"You gotta be kidding."

"They knew I was following Rachael's missing persons case, feeding you information. They found out I talked to Manny Ortega."

"They ought to be glad to have you on this."

"Truth is, in a way, I'm glad. I'm taking a couple of weeks of personal time. I talked to Wheeler, told him I'd help his guys keep an eye on things at the safe house. He said he was stretched pretty thin, glad for the extra manpower."

"I have a feeling Rachael's going to feel better knowing you're there," Amy said.

"I hope so. I know I'll feel a whole lot better."

Johnnie eyed him with speculation. "I think maybe for once the department is right. You *are* too personally involved."

"Maybe, but then so are you, so let's just leave it at that."

Johnnie flicked a sideways glance at Amy. "I see your point."

Across the drive, the SUV rumbled to life. As Vega walked over, the driver rolled down the window.

"I assume Wheeler told you I'll be staying at the safe house," Rick said to him.

The agent nodded.

"I'll see you there in half an hour."

"Make sure you aren't tailed," the agent warned.

Vega cast him a glance. "You do the same."

The car pulled away and Rick walked back to where Amy and Johnnie were standing. "Before I left, I took a look at Wes Henley's record. He's been in and out of jail, arrested for assault, charges dropped and arrested for the murder of a drug dealer named Benny Camacho but the prosecution couldn't make it stick."

"I knew last night the guy wasn't a pro. And if the hit had been ordered by someone in Ortega's circle, they wouldn't have sent just one man. If they had, it wouldn't have been a loser like Henley."

"My partner's running down the phone numbers on Henley's cell."

Mitch Lansky, Johnnie recalled, the older guy who'd transferred in a couple of months ago. The two men hadn't been working together long. Johnnie wondered if Lansky would be willing to go against orders to help them.

"The number you got last night off Henley's phone— the last two calls he made—belongs to a girl named Patty Wilkins. She does manicures at a salon on La Cienega called Epiphany. When I called her, she said she and Henley went out a few times, said he wasn't her type and she dumped him. He'd been hassling her ever since."

"Sounds like a great guy."

"Another thing… Rachael's passport was a phony. Her real one was logged as part of the stuff they found in her studio apartment."

"Which means Ortega had a forgery made, probably a hurry-up job. He'd know people who could handle that kind of thing."

Amy looked up at Johnnie. "Then Rachael had no idea she was leaving the country that night."

"No," Johnnie said. "She definitely wasn't planning to take off with Ortega."

"So who wants Rachael dead?" Rick asked.

Johnnie just shook his head. "I've got something I want to check out. If it comes to anything, I'll let you know."

Vega nodded. "I'd better get going." He handed Johnnie a slip of paper with a number written on it. "It's a throwaway. No way to trace the call to the safe house."

Johnnie pulled out his cell and entered the number. I'll keep you posted. In the meantime, don't underestimate these jokers."

"Find 'em, Johnnie. Do that for me, will you?"

"Count on it," Johnnie said.

As soon as Detective Vega left, Amy and Johnnie headed for the guesthouse.

"I need to find out who did the work on Henley's bike," Johnnie said as they climbed the front porch steps. But he was looking at her with those hot brown eyes and she knew he was thinking about more than just the case. It seemed forever since they had made love. Nights she had lain in bed yearning for him.

They made it only as far as the entry when he turned her into his arms and his mouth came down over hers. Heat, need and desire all poured through her, collected low in her belly.

"Johnnie…" Parting her lips, Amy deepened the kiss, gave in to the feel of his big hard body pressing against her. Reaching down, she cupped the heavy bulge in his jeans, felt the power of him pulsing in her hand.

"We don't have time for this," Johnnie said against her mouth.

"I know…" But they were both past stopping and Amy didn't want to. Johnnie walked her backward into the living room. She came up against the sofa that looked out through the big glass windows. The next thing she knew, he was lifting her up and setting her on the couch, unzipping her jeans and pulling them down. Her sandals dropped onto the floor as he tugged the jeans down her legs and her panties followed.

"Next time we'll go slow," he promised. She felt him stroking the wetness between her legs, then he opened his fly and he was inside her.

Amy breathed a sigh of relief.

For several moments, Johnnie just stood there, his hands on her hips, his hardness deep inside. "God, I've missed you."

Amy leaned in and kissed him. "I've missed you, too."

He filled her completely, and when he started to move, she forgot everything but the pleasure, everything but Johnnie and how much she wanted him. How much she loved him. It was impossible. Loving him was breaking her heart, but in that moment, she didn't care.

He took her fast and hard and it was glorious. Amy felt a clenching low in her belly and then she was coming and so was he. They clung to each other, absorbing the pleasure, letting it swirl around them, then slowly drifting down.

She ran her fingers through his short dark hair. "We...uummm...forgot to use protection," she said.

He just smiled. "I'm safe and I'm sure you are." She nodded and he brushed a thumb across her cheek. "If something happens, we'll deal with it."

That something was a baby, and her heart squeezed. Nothing would please her more than having Johnnie's child.

He kissed her softly. "I've got to go. I won't be long."

Amy recognized the protective gleam in his eyes and

preyed on it. "I'm not sure I should stay here alone. I'd feel safer if I went with you."

"I'm riding my bike."

Her eyes widened. "Your Harley?"

He grinned. "Maybe you're right. I'm not crazy about leaving you here. You like speed. Maybe you'd better come along."

She had never ridden a motorcycle. But she was definitely game. "Give me a minute and I'll be right with you." Grabbing her jeans and panties, she dashed down the hall to the bathroom, then returned a few minutes later, her hair pulled into a ponytail and her clothes all back in place.

Johnnie caught her hand. "Come on, let's go."

Johnnie set his spare helmet on Amy's head and tightened the strap beneath her chin. It was way too big, but it would protect her if something happened.

He swung onto the bike, supergloss black like his car, semicustom, not too far over the top since he used it for work and he didn't want something easily recognizable.

He pulled on his black helmet. "Just hold on to me and lean the way I do."

She nodded, slid her small arms around his waist. He could feel her breasts pressing into his back.

Damn, the woman drove him crazy.

Forcing his mind back onto the job he needed to do, he cranked the powerful engine to life. "Hang on." Then he slammed his boot against the kickstand, gunned the accelerator, and they shot off down the drive. The police were still roaming the estate so the gate was open. He pulled the bike into the street and headed down the hill.

The first stop was a place he knew in Hollywood, a shop on a side street that specialized in custom paint jobs, Bill's Precision Auto Painting. Johnnie left Amy outside with the bike and went in to question the owner, Bill Meadows, a longtime acquaintance.

Bill shook his head at the photo Johnnie showed him on his cell phone. "Wish I could help but the work doesn't ring any bells. I know a couple of other places you might try."

Johnnie thanked him and headed back outside.

"Any luck?" Amy asked as he climbed onto the seat in front of her.

"Bill gave me a few more places to look. Shops that do the quality painting done in the photo. We're just getting started."

They'd be riding the bike most of the day. Through her face mask, Johnnie caught Amy's grin.

She had figured the motorcycle ride would be great. She loved speed and she loved Johnnie and the combination was potent. He was wearing a black leather jacket over the gun in his shoulder holster. Though it was early July, it was a perfect day, sunny, not too hot, not too cold.

Amy was going to miss the California weather when she went back home.

Home. Back to Grand Rapids. She tightened her hold around Johnnie's waist, pressed her cheek against his broad back. As he leaned into a turn, she told herself not to think about leaving, that the only important thing right now was finding the people who wanted her sister dead.

The hours ticked past. The afternoon was waning when they pulled up in front of the fourth body shop on their list which, like the last one, was in a less than respectable neighborhood. The buildings along the street were run-down, some of the windows broken. Papers and trash filled the gutters, and loud rap music boomed from a car parked nearby with a man inside and the windows rolled down.

"Come on. I'm taking you with me this time."

Amy didn't argue, just pulled her helmet off and tucked it under her arm as he led her toward a building made of corrugated steel with the name Custom Paint and Airbrushing on the sign above the door.

Just inside, she stopped next to Johnnie, her nose wrinkling at the acrid smell of paint and thinner in the air. On the concrete floor, two cars, a van and two motorcycles were in the process of being painted. The picture on the side of the van was spectacular, a desert scene with ghosts hovering in a purple sky above. *Ghost Rider* was the name scrolled beneath the painting.

"Hey, Johnnie!"

He looked over at the skinny black man walking toward him, his kinky hair graying at the temple. He wore a paint smock over a pair of worn, faded jeans. "How you doin', man?"

"Lavon! Hey, good to see you, man, I didn't know you worked here."

"Are you kiddin'? I'm in charge round here. The rest of 'em just amateurs."

Johnnie smiled. "You do the van?"

"Course I did."

"It's wonderful," Amy said, swinging Lavon's attention to her.

"This your lady?"

Johnnie looked down at her, a warm, possessive gleam in his eyes. "She's mine, yeah. Amy this is Lavon Jeffers. He's one of the best artists in the business."

"You do beautiful work," Amy said, smiling up at him.

"Thanks. Always nice to be appreciated." He turned back to Johnnie. "So what you need done, man? Your car? Put a nice design on the hood, make it look real special. Or maybe your bike. That baby could use a little somethin' to spice it up. How 'bout some orange flames on the tank, or maybe a fire-breathin' dragon?"

Johnnie just smiled. "Actually, I'm here on business." He pulled his phone out of his pocket and flashed the photo of Henley's tank showing the silver skulls on the blue background. "I'm looking for the guy who did the work on this. Quality is way above average. I'd say the design is unique. Any idea who might have done it?"

Lavon studied the picture, his thick eyebrows drawing together. "He ain't in any trouble, is he?"

"No, nothing like that. I'm just hoping he might be able to help me with a little information."

"I didn't do it, but I know who did. That's him right over there."

Johnnie turned and so did Amy. "That's my son, Darius." He grinned. "Got him followin' in his old man's footsteps." He turned and called to the young man working on one of the motorcycles, painting designs on the tank in red and gold. "Hey, boy, come over here a minute. I want you to meet some friends of mine."

In his mid-twenties, Darius Jeffers was taller than his dad and even skinnier. He wiped his hands on a rag, tossed it on the counter and ambled over. Lavon made introductions, Darius stuck out his hand and the men shook.

Darius turned to Amy. "It's nice to meet you," he said.

"Nice meeting you, too," Amy said.

Johnnie showed Darius the photo on his cell. "You do this work?"

Darius nodded. "I painted it."

"Who for?"

He flicked a glance at his dad, who nodded.

"Guy named Wes Henley."

"What can you tell me about him?"

Darius shrugged. "Not much. I did some work for a friend of his, fella named Dickie Talbot. Talbot recommended me. I showed Henley some of my work and I got the job."

Johnnie was frowning. "Dickie Talbot. Why do I know that name?"

Lavon answered. "He's a punkass from down in Orange County. Mid-level drug dealer, fancies himself a real player. Makes plenty of money, pretty well-connected, I hear. Likes his toys, pays us to make 'em look special."

"Yeah, now I remember him. Anything else?" Johnnie asked.

Lavon shook his head. "I ain't seen neither of them in a while."

"Well, you won't be seeing Wes Henley. I shot him

last night when he tried to take out a friend of mine. What I'm trying to find out is who paid him to try to kill her."

Lavon's eyes widened. He scratched his wooly head. "Coulda been Talbot, I guess. If he had a reason to want her dead. Like I said, he's got plenty of cash and he's connected."

"Who to?"

"That I don't know."

Johnnie stuck out his hand. Lavon and his son both shook. "Really appreciate your help."

Lavon grinned. "Think about what I said. Black is beautiful, but black and red is mean, man."

Johnnie laughed and Amy smiled.

They left the shop. "So you know this guy Talbot?" Amy asked as they reached the bike.

"I know who he is. I need to talk to Wheeler, see what the DEA knows about him, see if there's some way to connect him to Ortega. First I'd like to talk to Patty Wilkins, the girl Henley was calling the night he died."

"She works at Epiphany, right? Vega said it was on La Cienega."

Johnnie checked the time. "Too late to catch her. Shop'll be closed by now." He cast Amy a glance. "Neither of us got any sleep last night. What do you say we go home?"

Home. Amy's heart pinched. The word shouldn't have sounded so right, but it did. Her gaze found his. She recognized the heat, but there was something more, something that made her heart beat faster.

"Sounds good to me."

Amy hung on to Johnnie as he cranked up the bike and they roared off down the street toward the house on the hill that felt way too much like home.

Chapter 32

The night sky was streaked with intermittent clouds so only a trace of moonlight streamed through. Inside the small, suburban track home the DEA was using as a safe house, Rick Vega sat in the living room. George Henderson, one of the agents assigned to guard Rachael, patrolled the perimeter of the house. An agent named Freddie Flores was getting some sleep before it was time for his shift.

The house was basic: besides the living room, just a kitchen, three bedrooms and two baths. The decor was equally simple—a sofa and chair, end tables, lamps and a coffee table sitting on brown shag carpet. Framed posters of palm trees running along the streets in Beverly Hills, and of a sunset on Santa Monica beach hung on the walls.

Rick sat with his iPad in his lap, a gift he had bought

himself for his thirty-sixth birthday. He slid his finger across the screen, turning the pages of *Time* magazine he was only half reading. The TV was on but no one was watching.

He glanced toward the kitchen, where Hannah Brewer was saying good-night to her daughter. Hoping to jog Rachael's memory, she'd been telling her stories about her life in Michigan as a young girl before she had moved to L.A. Hannah had even admitted that at times, the two of them had had trouble getting along.

"I didn't want you to go to Los Angeles," Hannah had said. "I wanted you to stay home and finish college. It was such a long way from home and such a big city. I was afraid something bad would happen."

Rachael glanced away. "Looks like you were right."

Hannah shook her head. "I was wrong. You were looking for something you couldn't find back home." Her mother smiled sadly. "Amy said you would have gotten that part you wanted in a new TV show. You would have succeeded, Rachael, just the way you always thought you would. It may take a little more time, but I'm convinced you'll do it again."

Rachael's answering smile looked forlorn. "Thank you… Mom."

They were getting to know each other all over again and Rick thought that when this was finished, Rachael and her mother would be closer than they had ever been before.

He watched the older woman heft herself out of the kitchen chair where she had been sitting. All of them were exhausted and the brief naps the women had taken that afternoon hadn't been nearly enough.

"Are you sure you aren't ready to go to bed?" Hannah asked her daughter. "You didn't get much sleep last night."

Rachael managed to smile. "Not quite yet. I'll be there in a little while."

Hannah nodded and walked away. As soon as she was gone, Rick went into the kitchen and sat down at the table next to Rachael.

"You doing okay?" he asked.

She looked up at him for several long moments, then her eyes filled with tears. "I guess so, but... No, not really."

Rick felt a tightening in his chest. "I know how hard this must be. Why don't you tell me what's going on."

Her eyes remained on his face. She picked up the glass of water in front of her and took a drink. "Last night...after that man broke into my room I... I remembered something about...about what happened."

Beneath his breastbone, he could feel his heart beating faster. "You ready to talk about it?" He kept his voice even, hoping she would open up to him, wishing she didn't have to.

She moistened her lips. He noticed that they were trembling. "I remembered being in this room. I think it was the bedroom Amy found me in on the island. I remembered..." She broke off, took a steadying breath.

"Just take your time."

She shifted in her chair. "I remembered waking up. I was lying on a bed. The sheets were all rumpled around me. And there was this man... He was...he was on top of me. He was...raping me." She swallowed and the tears in her eyes spilled over onto her cheeks.

"Easy. You don't have to say anything until you're ready."

"I want to tell you. Maybe it will help the police find out what happened."

He nodded, reached out and took hold of her hand. Her skin was cold, and faint tremors moved through her body. He hated the agony he saw in her lovely green eyes. "Do you remember what the man looked like?"

She took a sip of water. "Dark skin, dark hair touched with gray. I might have thought he was handsome if…if…he hadn't been…hadn't been…" She bit her lip and glanced away.

"It's all right. Take as much time as you need."

Rachael breathed deeply. He could see she was fighting for control. "I remember I tried to push him off me, but my arms and legs felt too heavy. Just moving seemed impossible. I tried to scream, but when I opened my mouth, no sound came out. I started crying and he slapped me. He told me to shut up if…if I wanted to live." She looked up at him, her eyes filled with a sorrow that touched him deep inside. "I don't remember much about the attack. I think he raped me more than once but they were giving me drugs every day and most of the time I was more asleep than awake."

"They were giving you heroin…among other things."

"That's what the doctors said." She managed to smile through her tears. "I'm feeling better now."

Rick squeezed her hand. "Your withdrawal symptoms are over. You're a strong woman, Rachael. You'll get past all of this."

"I remember one more thing… I remember talking to the other women in the house. They said the man's name was Ortega. They said when he chose a woman, he kept her for himself until he got tired of her. Then he shared her with his friends."

Fresh tears pooled in her eyes. "The night Amy and Johnnie found me, I knew he'd returned. I knew he would come to my room and rape me again. If they hadn't gotten there when they did—" Her voice broke and she started crying.

Rick came up from the table, lifted her into his arms and carried her into the living room. He sat down in an overstuffed chair, cradling her in his lap, her head on his shoulder.

"It's over now, Rachael. Ortega is dead. He can't hurt you anymore."

"I know." He handed her a handkerchief and she dabbed it against her eyes. "I haven't told anyone what happened. I can't tell my mother."

Rick forced himself to smile. "I'm glad you chose me."

"After what happened, I should be afraid of any man who comes near me. But there's something about you. I knew I could trust you the first time I saw you."

"I won't hurt you, Rachael. I'd never do anything to hurt you." He lifted dark strands of hair away from her face, gently looped them behind an ear.

Rachael laid her head back down on his shoulder. "I'm beginning to remember my childhood," she said. "Scenes flash into my mind, memories of my mother and my sister. Stuff about my dad."

He hated to press her, but her life depended on finding answers. "Do you remember anything about the night you were taken? Or maybe something that happened during the weeks before it happened?"

She shook her head. "I don't even remember working at the Kitty Cat Club."

"Does the name *Danny* mean anything to you?"

She sat up in his lap. "Danny?" She bit her lip, her dark brows pulling together. She shook her head. "Just for a second, something flashed in my mind. But it's gone."

"It's all right. It's all going to come back. It's just going to take some time."

"I don't think I'll ever remember much about what happened after they started giving me drugs."

"Maybe it's better that way."

"Yes… I think so, too."

She eased herself out of his lap, and Rick stood up beside her.

"I didn't mean to cry all over you." Her hand shook as she wiped away the last of her tears. "I know you're just doing your job."

Rick ran a finger gently along her jaw. "I'm way past just doing my job. I'm here for you, Rachael. Any time you need me, I'm here."

She leaned over and brushed a soft kiss on his cheek. The faint scent of her perfume filled his senses. "Thank you. For everything."

He just nodded. "Good night, Rachael."

"Good night, Rick." Turning, she walked off down the hall.

Rick watched the place she had been long after she disappeared inside the bedroom.

It was almost ten in the morning. Seated behind the desk in his walk-out basement office, Johnnie grabbed his cell phone as it started to ring.

"Riggs."

"Hey, buddy, just thought I'd check in, see how

things are going." Jake Cantrell's deep voice boomed over the line.

"Not so good at the moment. Night before last, someone broke into the house and tried to kill Rachael."

Jake whistled. "She okay?"

"She's fine. Believe it or not, Amy helped me bring him down."

Johnnie could almost see Jake's grin. "Pretty amazing lady you got there."

"She is that. I'm really gonna miss her."

"From what I saw, it looked like you two had a pretty good thing going."

"Yeah, well, I'm lousy husband material."

"Maybe. Maybe not." An instant of silence and then Cantrell asked, "So what's the deal? I figured with Ortega dead, Rachael would be safe."

"We all did. Intruder was a guy named Wes Henley. Unfortunately for Wes, I was next door when he got there. He won't be a problem anymore."

"But someone else might be."

"Yeah. Wheeler's got her in a safe house while I'm trying to figure out who the hell wants her dead."

"What about the cops? They come up with anything?"

"Vega's off the case and the police are calling it a burglary gone bad."

"That's nuts."

"Don't I know."

"Doesn't sound like they're gonna be much help. Anything I can do?"

"I don't know...maybe. I got a name, Dickie Talbot, mid-level drug dealer, might be the guy who hired Henley. He's gotta have a rap sheet an arm long but with

Vega out of play, I can't get access to his file. I don't suppose the whiz kid—"

"He can do it. The question is can he do it and stay out of jail. I'll find out and get back to you."

"Thanks, Jake." Johnnie ended the call and looked up to see Tyler Brodie coming down the stairs.

"Hey, boss."

"Hey, kid, what's up?"

"Heard about the shooting. Nice work. Word on the street is a guy named Dickie Talbot paid one of his dealers to take out the Brewer girl."

"Wes Henley. Heard he and Talbot were friends, probably the guy who hired him. The question is why. You wouldn't have any idea where I can find Talbot?"

"That's what I came by to tell you. I was able to dig up his address. He's got an apartment up in the hills off Franklin. I figured you'd want to talk to him, and if so you might need some backup."

Johnnie nodded. Grabbing his shoulder harness off the back of his chair, he headed for the stairs, Brodie right behind him.

As they made their way down the hall, Amy walked toward him across the living room. "What's going on?" she asked, her gaze going to Brodie.

"Ty Brodie, meet Amy Brewer."

"Hi, Amy."

"Hi, Ty."

"Listen, baby, I've got an errand to run."

"What kind of errand?"

"Just a guy I need to talk to." He turned to Brodie. "Okay if we take your truck?"

Ty shrugged. "Sure."

Amy's eyes widened when Johnnie tossed her his

car keys. "You've been wanting to go see Mrs. Zimmer, visit little Jimmy."

"You're letting me use your Mustang?"

"I figure you can make it that far without wrecking it."

Amy closed the distance between him and threw her arms around his neck, gave him a smacking kiss on the mouth. Her big blue eyes sparkled with mischief. "I'll show you how grateful I am when I get home," she whispered in his ear.

Hell, even if she demolished the damn car it would be worth it.

"Stay out of trouble," he said gruffly, trying not to think of the last time he'd said that and how she had gone to the village and started asking dangerous questions.

"I will, I promise."

Johnnie just grunted. All of them walked outside. Johnnie started toward the passenger side of Ty's snazzy little red Toyota pickup, a Texan's idea of a city car, but stopped before he got there.

He turned to look at Amy, his mind filling with worry. "I changed my mind," he said, suddenly recalling Wes Henley's gun barrel pointed at her head. "There's always a chance whoever's behind this might try to use you to get to Rachael."

"I'll be fine," Amy argued, clutching the keys against her breast as if they were solid gold.

Johnnie turned to Ty. "I'm just gonna ask Talbot some questions. You stay here with Amy."

Amy's pale eyebrows shot up. "Wait a minute—"

"I want you safe," Johnnie said. "I don't want to leave you alone."

Amy tossed him the keys, turned and stormed back into the house. Ty eyed him strangely. "Dev said you really liked her. Said his wife liked her, too. Looks to me like you're in love with her."

Johnnie just shrugged. "Doesn't matter. It wouldn't work out. Amy's smart enough to know that."

"Sometimes smart isn't all it's cracked up to be."

Johnnie couldn't think of anything to say so he just kept his mouth shut.

"I've got an idea," Ty said. "Why don't I take Amy over to visit her friend?"

"That'd be great. Make her happy and keep her busy till I get back."

"Hey, Amy!" Ty called out to her. "Come on, we'll go see that friend of yours." He winked at Johnnie. "I'll even let you drive my truck."

Amy raced back outside, her gaze shooting to Brodie's hot little pickup. "You mean it?"

"Johnnie trusts you to drive his Mustang." Ty tossed her his keys. "I guess I can trust you with my truck."

"I'll let you drive another time," Johnnie grumbled, not liking the way she was smiling at Ty.

Amy nailed him with a look. "I'm gonna hold you to that."

Johnnie turned and started walking. He had almost reached his car when he heard feminine footsteps racing up behind him. When he turned, Amy threw herself into his arms.

"Be careful, okay?"

"I'm always careful," he said a little gruffly, and kissed her quick and hard. Then she was running back to the pickup, holding up the keys and jiggling them in the air.

Johnnie watched her drive away, trusting Ty to take care of her. As the truck disappeared, he forced his mind away from Amy and focused on finding the man who wanted her sister dead.

On a street above Franklin, Dickie Talbot's duplex apartment was built into the side of a hill overlooking the city of Glendale. It was only noon on a workday, but a bright yellow Stingray sat in front of the single car garage attached to Dickie's unit.

As Johnnie climbed out of his Mustang, he noticed a brown, unmarked police car parked on the opposite side of the street a little ways down the block. Looked like the cops were there. He'd only made it halfway to the door when a series of gunshots shattered the quiet and sent him into action.

Johnnie yanked the pistol out of his shoulder holster and cautiously made his way toward the apartment. A guy in a brown suit, young and blond, ran around the corner of the house.

"Police officer!" he shouted, his gun pointed at Johnnie's chest. "Put down your weapon!"

Johnnie raised his hands, his Beretta dangling from his fingers. "John Riggs. I'm a P.I." Very slowly, he bent and rested his pistol on the sidewalk, straightened and lifted his hands into the air. "Your partner might need help. Let me get my ID."

The young detective kept his gun pointed straight at him, but his gaze swung toward the house. "Kick the pistol away and get down on the ground."

Johnnie used the toe of his boot to slide his weapon out of reach. "Just let me get my ID and you can go help him."

The kid glanced anxiously toward the door. "Go ahead."

Reaching into the pocket of his jeans, Johnnie eased his identification out of his pocket and flipped it open.

The young cop breathed a sigh of relief. "Looks okay. I gotta go."

"I'll go round back," Johnnie said as the kid turned and ran to the door. Retrieving his pistol, Johnnie took off toward the back of the duplex, but before he reached the side yard, Mitch Lansky, Vega's partner, walked out of the house. He looked even thinner than the last time Johnnie had seen him and the little fringe of gray around his bald head did nothing to improve his skeletal appearance.

Johnnie holstered his weapon. "What's going on, Lansky?"

"Talbot was a suspect in a homicide. He resisted when I tried to bring him in for questioning, pulled a gun on me. I didn't have any choice."

"Tell me he's not dead."

"'Fraid so."

Johnnie clamped down on his temper, but not quite enough. "Goddamn it."

Lansky's young partner came out of the house and walked toward them, relaxed now that the incident was over. "Gun is still in his hand. Won't be any doubt it was a righteous shooting."

"Riggs, this is Detective Brian Mears," Lansky said.

"We met," the kid said.

"Why didn't you go in with Lansky?" Johnnie asked, trying to put the pieces together and when he did, not liking what he saw.

"Mitch sent me round back. I planned to come in

from the rear, but then I spotted you coming up the walk."

On the surface that made sense. Not much else did. "You need me to make a statement?" Johnnie asked the older detective.

"Not at the moment. I've called it in. Uniforms will be here any minute. If we need you, I know where to find you."

"Mears filling in for Vega?" he asked because it was obvious the young detective was as green as grass.

"That's right. Anything else you'd like to know?"

"Yeah, I'd like to know why the hell Dickie Talbot wanted Rachael Brewer dead."

"That's what we came to find out. Looks like it's a moot point now."

"Yeah," Johnnie said darkly. "Just like everything else."

Chapter 33

The muffled sound of a cell phone ringing drew Dan's attention. He grabbed his laptop case off the floor and set it on his desk, unzipped the side pouch and dug out the disposable phone.

He was expecting this call.

He pressed the phone against his ear. "Give me some good news."

"The good news is the secondary problem is resolved. They can't get to you through Talbot."

"I never had any connection to Talbot."

"No, but I did, and if I go down, you're going with me."

Beads of perspiration popped out on Dan's forehead.

"We need to get rid of the girl," said the voice on the other end of the line. "So far, everything that's happened to her points to Ortega. They'll think his people wanted to keep her quiet. Once she's out of the way, we're in the clear."

"How do you figure?" Dan asked. "Talbot has no connection to Ortega and he's the one who hired Henley."

"Talbot's a lowlife. He was shot resisting arrest. And it was only speculation that he had anything to do with the attempt on Rachael's life."

"What about Henley?"

"Henley dealt drugs. He could have been one of Ortega's underlings. We just need the girl out of the way."

"Where is she?"

"DEA has her stashed someplace safe."

"Then how do we get to her?"

"That's the good news. Like everybody else, the agency hasn't got much money. They won't be able to protect her for long. At least not unless her memory returns."

"So we just sit around and hope it doesn't?" Dan didn't like where this was going.

"Unless you can figure some other way to get to her."

Dan's stomach churned. Could he use his position to find the girl without raising suspicion he was somehow involved?

"Think about it. Either way, with any luck it'll only be a couple more days until our problems are over."

Dan's jaw tightened. "You'd better hope so. That warning you gave me goes both ways."

The caller hung up the phone.

Amy sat in the kitchen of Mrs. Zimmer's cozy little Culver City home, Ty seated across from her. Since

Amy couldn't tell Mrs. Zimmer about Rachael's safe return, "Angel" had offered to take little Jimmy to the Baskin-Robbins a few blocks away.

"Jimmy likes to go just about anywhere," the gray-haired woman said. "It doesn't seem to matter. He just loves riding in the car."

Ty grinned. "He's not the only one." He tipped his head toward Amy, who just smiled.

Mrs. Zimmer's lips twitched. After introductions had been made, she had brewed a fresh pot of coffee and poured each of them a cup. "I'll get Jimmy ready to go." She reached down and took hold of the little boy's hand. "You'll find some chocolate-chip cookies in the jar. Help yourself."

Amy brought Ty a couple and he finished one of them off in a couple of bites. "Man, I'm likin' this job better all the time." He polished off the second cookie in record time and drained his coffee mug.

Amy walked over and set their empty mugs in the sink. "Jimmy's really excited about going to the ice-cream shop. You don't mind taking us?"

"I like kids. Not a problem."

A few minutes later, Mrs. Zimmer led Jimmy back into the living room. Dressed in clean blue jeans and a yellow T-shirt with a hot rod on the front, he dashed across the room toward Amy.

She caught hold of his small hand. "Are you ready?"

Jimmy grinned and vigorously nodded.

"Wait till you see Ty's truck. You're gonna love it."

Jimmy tore loose and raced toward the door. When he saw Ty's snazzy red pickup, his eyes widened. "Can I drive?" he asked.

Ty laughed. "Not quite yet, buddy, but someday

you'll be old enough." He swung the boy into the air, propped him against his shoulder, and they headed out the door.

At Baskin-Robbins, they placed their order, then sat at a small round table licking double-scoop ice cream cones. Ty lapped at a mint chocolate chip while Amy and Jimmy ate rocky road.

"I love ice cream," Jimmy said. "This is so good."

Ty reached over and ruffled the little boy's red hair. "It sure is, partner."

When his cell phone started ringing, Ty stood up and dragged it out of the pocket of his faded jeans. "Hey, Johnnie." He started frowning and then he was nodding. When the call ended, he didn't look pleased.

Amy grabbed his arm. "Is it Johnnie? Is he all right?"

"He's fine." Ty glanced down to make sure Jimmy was busy with his cone and spoke quietly. "Talbot's dead. Cops shot him for resisting arrest. Johnnie doesn't like the way things are coming down. He wants us to head back home."

Amy's nerves kicked up. She turned to the little boy. "We're gonna take these home with us, okay?"

Ty looked at the sloppy cones they would be taking in his nice clean truck and grimaced.

Amy laughed. "You let me drive so I owe you. I'll clean up the truck."

"Deal," Ty said.

It didn't take long to reach the Zimmer house. With the amount of napkins Amy had taken from the ice cream shop, the mess was minimal. By the time she led Jimmy up the steps and across the porch to the door, the boy was finished eating. While Ty waited on the porch, Amy took Jimmy inside and washed the chocolate off his hands and face.

"I've got to go but I'll be back," she told him. "I promise."

Mrs. Zimmer walked into the kitchen, catching Amy's attention, and Jimmy dashed away.

"Something's come up and I have to go," Amy said. "I think Jimmy enjoyed the ice cream."

Mrs. Zimmer smiled. "I'm sure he did."

"Tell him goodbye for me, will you?"

"Oh, look, here he comes."

Grinning, the little boy raced toward her, something clutched in his hand.

"I got you a present." Shyly, Jimmy held out his hand.

Amy's eyes widened when she saw it was a cell phone. She looked at Mrs. Zimmer for an explanation, but the older woman looked as surprised as she was and just shook her head.

Amy knelt in front of Jimmy. "Where did you get this, sweetheart?"

"I found it on the floor by the sofa. I think it's Rachael's."

Amy's pulse kicked up. She gently took the phone from the little boy's hand. "Thank you, Jimmy. I'll take very good care of it until Rachael gets home." She looked up at Mrs. Zimmer. "This could really be important."

"Take it. Maybe it will help them find her."

Amy leaned over and hugged the older woman, bent down and hugged little Jimmy. "Thank you for the present, sweetheart. I'll see you again soon."

So excited her heart was racing, Amy ran out onto

the porch. "Ty! Jimmy found Rachael's cell phone! We need to find a Verizon store and buy a battery charger."

Ty shoved away from the railing, grinned and pulled out his iPhone to find the nearest location. "No problem."

A few minutes later, they were flying down the street, Ty behind the wheel, driving even faster than Johnnie.

Johnnie had a stop to make on his way home—the call he had wanted to make last night. Patty Wilkins, the girl Wes Henley had called the night he died, a manicurist who worked at a salon called Epiphany.

The bell above the door at Epiphany salon rang as Johnnie shoved it open, and the smell of ammonia hit him. The sound of hair dryers merged with the chatter of women. He walked over to a buxom blonde who was cutting a woman's wet black hair.

"I'm looking for Patty Wilkins. You know where I can find her?"

The woman turned, eyeballed him top to bottom, flashed him an interested grin and pointed to a redhead with pretty blue eyes. "That's her right over there."

Patty smiled at his approach.

"You're in luck. I just had a cancellation." She grabbed his hand and examined his nails, which he kept short and fortunately were clean. "You want a full manicure? Or would you rather just have a buff?"

Johnnie eased his hand away. "Thanks, but not today." He pulled his ID out of his pocket. "I'm John Riggs. I'd like to talk to you about Wes Henley."

Her gaze shot to his face. "Wes is dead. The police called me already, a detective named Vega."

"You know you were the last person Wes talked to the night he was killed."

"That's what the cop said, but at the time I didn't know. Wes called me twice that night, but the truth is we hardly knew each other. That's what I told the detective. We went out a couple of times and I broke it off. I'm not really into his type."

"What type is that?"

"I don't know…guys who shave their heads and cover themselves with tattoos to make them feel macho. A man whose favorite topic is himself."

"So what did you and Wes talk about that night?"

"Not much. That's what I told the police. But later, I got to thinking… I remember he told me he was into something big. Said he was going to make a nice chunk of money. I had a feeling it was something illegal."

"He wasn't worried about getting caught?"

"I asked him that. He said he had it covered, said the guy who was paying him had connections so he didn't have to think about that."

"What did you say?"

"I said if I'd had any doubt he wasn't my type, I didn't anymore and then I hung up."

Johnnie pressed a twenty into her hand along with a business card. "Thanks, Patty. If you think of anything else, give me a call."

She smiled, stuffed the twenty and the card into the pocket of the smock she wore over her jeans. "Call me when you're ready for that mani."

He smiled back. "Yeah, I'll do that."

Johnnie was halfway home when his cell phone started ringing. He recognized Amy's number and pressed the phone against his ear.

"We've got Rachael's cell!" Excitement rang in her voice. "Little Jimmy found it on the floor at Mrs. Zimmer's. We're charging it in the truck on the way back to the house."

"Oh, baby, that's good news. I'll meet you there." Johnnie closed the phone and stepped on the gas.

They all poured into the house together. They went straight to the kitchen, pulled out the chairs and sat down around the table.

"It should be charged enough to use. Where do we start?" Amy handed Johnnie the phone.

"We could look at the calls Rachael made the night she was abducted," Ty suggested. "Vega should be able to track down who they went to."

Johnnie flipped open Rachael's phone. "First, let's take a look at her address book. Most call lists go by first names. Let's see if we can find a Dan listed in there."

"Great idea!" Amy said excitedly. "Maybe he's right there in her phone book." Jumping up from her chair, she came around to lean over Johnnie's shoulder as he brought up Rachael's address book and started looking through it.

All of a sudden the name appeared. *Danny Turner.*

"Oh, my God, there he is!"

"Only one number listed," Johnnie said. "Probably his cell."

"Jesus," Ty said. "You think this is the Danny we've been looking for? Can't be that easy."

"Call him, Johnnie! If Rachael's number is in his cell, he'll think she's the one who's calling."

"I guess we'll find out." Johnnie pressed the send

button and the phone started ringing. When a man answered, he handed the phone to Amy, then leaned close so that both of them could hear.

Amy took a deep breath. "Hello... Danny?"

A long pause, the tension on the other end of the line seemed almost tangible. "Who...who is this? Who's calling?"

"This is Rachael. I've missed you, Danny."

"Rachael?" The man's voice rose a notch. "You don't...don't sound like yourself. Is this...is this really you?"

Amy looked up at Johnnie. He nodded for her to continue.

"Why did you do it, Danny? You knew the way I felt, how much I cared about you."

"I... I can explain everything...sweetheart." His voice firmed. "Why don't we meet someplace and talk things over? We'll straighten everything out."

When Amy paused, Johnnie reached over and took the phone from her hand, broke the connection.

"He's our guy. He didn't come forward when Rachael disappeared, now he figures she's got her memory back and he's screwed."

Johnnie pulled out his phone and called Rick Vega at the safe house. "We found Rachael's cell. The name of the guy she was seeing is Danny Turner. We need a GPS location for the call he just received." Johnnie rattled off the number.

"I'm on it," Vega said. "I'll call you right back." The line went dead.

"It may be a disposable," Ty warned.

Johnnie shook his head. "She was just a girl he was dating. At the time, she wasn't a threat. Until he got that call, he probably didn't even remember he was in her address book."

"He knows we're on to him now," Amy said. "What if he tries to run?"

"He might," Johnnie said. "But if he's the link to Ortega, he's high enough on the food chain he's got a lot to lose. I think he'll make a last-ditch effort to get rid of the problem."

The minutes ticked past. When everyone began to fidget waiting for Rick's call, Amy got up and grabbed some soft drinks out of the refrigerator. Pop tops cracked open all around.

Then Johnnie's phone rang.

"The call went to 210 North Figueroa," Rick said. "That's the D.A.'s office, my friend. Organized Crimes Division. Daniel Turner's a deputy D.A."

"You don't fucking say?" Johnnie blew out a breath. "That's it then. Turner was in Ortega's pocket. Rachael found out something she wasn't supposed to know and Turner handed her over to Ortega.

"We've got to be careful with this," Vega warned. "Ortega's dead but his reach may go a whole lot deeper than Turner. If that's the case, anyone involved will be trying to save his ass."

"I don't know if you've heard, but your partner just blew away the one guy who might have been able to lead us to Turner."

"Lansky? Damn. It's possible he's involved, I guess. We've only been working together a couple of months. I know his wife left him for another guy. He was always talking about winning her back. Maybe he figured the money he made from Ortega would do the trick."

Johnnie's jaw hardened. "I want Turner." He flicked

a glance at Amy, thought of all she and Rachael had suffered. "I want him bad."

Vega's voice roughened. "We both do. But the evidence just isn't there. Let me talk to Rachael. Her memory's been coming back in bits and pieces. Let's see if Turner's name rings any bells."

Johnnie's fingers tightened around the phone. "Do it."

Chapter 34

Rachael sat on the sofa, staring at a game show on TV. Rick didn't think she was actually watching. Hannah was in the kitchen, busy chopping onions and tomatoes—some of the groceries she had convinced one of the agents to get for the lasagna she wanted to make.

Rick had called Johnnie from the bedroom so Rachael wouldn't hear. Afterward, he had used his iPad to dig up as much information as he could on Daniel Turner. He wasn't looking forward to the task ahead. He just prayed it would work.

"Rachael?"

Her gaze swung to his and for the first time seemed to actually focus. "Yes?"

"I need to talk to you a minute. It'd be better if we could speak in private."

She flicked a glance at her mother, who was busy

working away, and walked over to where he stood in the entry. Rick took her hand and led her down the hall into the bedroom he was using.

She stopped and looked up at him. "What is it? You look worried."

He urged her to sit down on the bed then picked his iPad up off the dresser and sat down beside her. "Actually, I'm hopeful. I think we may have found something that will help us end all of this, and there may be a way you can help."

Her eyes found his. She had the loveliest pale green eyes he'd ever seen. "What can I do?"

He set the iPad in his lap. "You've been remembering things. This morning you remembered a little about being on Ortega's plane. It was just a glimpse, you said. So far you haven't remembered anything that happened before your abduction."

"I know. I'm sorry."

"I think maybe it's just too painful for you to recall. But the thing is, we need to know why Ortega took you to that island." He turned the iPad so that she could see the photograph on the screen, a picture of Deputy District Attorney Daniel Turner in a newspaper article he found on the internet.

"Do you know who that is?"

She studied the photo and her breathing grew shallow. "I—I'm not sure."

"Does the name Daniel Turner mean anything to you? You called him Danny."

The color leached out of her face. Her lips trembled. She ran her tongue across them. "Danny?" She looked back down at the screen. "Danny. Oh, my God, Danny." And then she burst into tears.

Great sobs shook her and a keening sound broke from her throat. Rick's chest clamped down so hard he could barely breathe. He reached for her, eased her into his arms.

"Rachael...honey, it's all right. Everything's going to be okay." He held her, let her weep against his shoulder, made no effort to stop her, just tried to absorb the shaking of her body and lend her the comfort of his own.

They sat that way for several minutes, until her crying began to ease, then finally subsided. She took the handkerchief he pulled out of his pocket, wiped her eyes and blew her nose. A few moments later, she started talking.

"I remember. I was in love with him," Rachael said. "At least I thought I was. I thought he loved me, too." She swallowed. "We were going away together. He had a friend, he said, a man who owned a villa in Belize. It was beautiful, he said, and I was so excited. But Danny... Danny worked in the district attorney's office and I was an exotic dancer. I was going to quit my job at the club, but until I found something more respectable, we had to keep our relationship secret."

She paused, wiped away fresh tears and dragged in a shaky breath.

"Go on, honey," Rick softly urged.

"I used to stay the night at his house whenever we could make our schedules work, but I always left early so no one would know I was there. Then one night...it was late and something woke me, and Danny... Danny wasn't in bed. I could... I could see a light under the door coming from down the hall so I put on one of his shirts and wandered down the hall toward the study.

When I realized he wasn't alone, I... I stopped just outside the study door."

Rick took her hand and gave it a reassuring squeeze, urging her to continue.

"There was a mirror on the wall inside the room and I could see two men inside. Danny was talking to them. It took a minute for me to realize they were discussing a shipment of drugs that would be coming into the harbor. They were worried about...about the DEA." Her throat moved up and down. "They said they needed to know if there was a raid coming down. They needed Danny to warn them so they could make adjustments. That's what they called them. Adjustments."

"What did Danny say?"

She looked up at him and those beautiful green eyes flooded with tears. "He said they didn't have to worry. He'd make sure to get them the information they needed. When he told them it would cost them extra, they just...they laughed. One of them said money wasn't a problem."

The tears spilled over onto her cheeks. She mopped them up with his handkerchief. "That's when I knew... I knew the truth about him. I must have made some kind of sound because the next thing I knew, the men were grabbing me, dragging me into the study and telling Danny they would have to kill me."

"But they didn't," Rick said, his jaw clenched so tight it was hard to speak.

"Danny didn't want them to kill me. They talked about it, decided what to do. Danny gave me to Ortega, instead." She leaned toward Rick, slid her arms around his neck. "I would rather have been dead."

Rick wrapped her in his arms and just held her, his heart aching for all she had suffered.

He knew if he got the chance, he would kill Dan Turner with his own bare hands.

As soon as the call came from Vega relaying his conversation with Rachael, Johnnie called Kent Wheeler.

"I've got what you need. Where can we meet?"

"You're at home?"

"That's right."

"I'll be there in twenty minutes."

The lanky agent arrived right on time and Johnnie led him into the kitchen. Amy made a pitcher of iced tea and poured glasses for Wheeler, Johnnie, Ty and herself. They sat back down around the table.

"So what have you got?" Wheeler asked, taking a drink of tea.

Johnnie told him about finding Rachael's phone and making the call to Turner, repeated Vega's conversation with Rachael, explained that her memory was returning. He told Wheeler the reason for her abduction, who was behind it and why.

"Sounds like we've got more than enough for search warrants for Turner's home and office," Wheeler said. "If we're lucky, we'll find enough to link Danny boy to Rachael's abduction. We've been looking for a leak for weeks. We never thought it would be so close to the top. I'll talk to the district attorney, myself."

"It doesn't stop with Turner," Johnnie said. "I think Mitch Lansky's involved."

"I heard about the shooting. Lansky's been on our radar since before he was transferred out of missing persons. He always seemed to be in the wrong place at just the right time."

"I wonder how Lansky hooked up with Turner? Seems an unlikely partnership."

"We'll figure it out." Wheeler turned to Amy. "I don't want you to worry about Rachael. We'll keep her in protective custody till all of this is straightened out."

Amy smiled with relief. "Thank you. You've been wonderful about everything."

Johnnie caught Amy's hand, brought her fingers to his lips. "It's almost over, baby."

Wheeler drained his iced tea and set the glass down on the table. "I've got lots to do. I'll keep you posted."

"Thanks, Kent."

"I've gotta run, too," Ty said, finishing his tea and carrying the glass over to the sink. Johnnie walked the men out the front door. By the time he returned, his phone was ringing again.

Jake Cantrell's deep voice boomed over the line. "Sol got into that police file, got the info you wanted on Dickie Talbot."

"Talbot's dead. Police shooting. Detective named Mitch Lansky. Claims Talbot resisted arrest."

"Pretty convenient."

"Too convenient. Good chance Lansky's involved."

"I'll take a chunk of that wager."

"We found Rachael's connection to Ortega. A deputy D.A. she was dating named Daniel Turner."

"So we were right... Rachael overheard something she shouldn't have, and Turner got rid of her."

"Yeah. Turner was in love so he wouldn't let them outright kill her."

"Nice guy. You might be interested to know there's

nothing in Talbot's file that connects him to Ortega. He was arrested a half-dozen times, drug dealing mostly, served time for that. Once for assault, once for attempted kidnapping. Charges were dropped."

"Kidnapping?"

"Yeah, why?"

"Missing Persons would have been involved in that. Lansky was transferred to Homicide out of Missing Persons. That must be how he knew Talbot."

"Actually—" Johnnie could hear paper shuffling "—a lieutenant named Meeks was in charge of the investigation."

And with that last bit of information, the puzzle pieces all fell together. "Listen, I gotta go. Thanks for the info."

"Keep me posted."

"Will do." Johnnie hung up the phone. He stood up, pulled Amy into his arms and kissed her. "Guess who Dan Turner was working with?"

"I thought you said it was Lansky."

"Not exactly. Carla Meeks handled Dickie Talbot's case, got him off an attempted kidnapping charge in exchange for his services. When Rachael came home, Meeks went to Talbot for help and he hired Henley to kill her. When that went bad, the lieutenant had to get rid of Talbot so no one would make the connection between the two of them."

"What about Lansky?"

"Meeks was Lansky's boss. He's her stooge. Meeks was paying Lansky out of the money she was getting from Turner. Meeks is the reason your sister's disappearance was being glossed over by the department. The lieutenant works for Turner. Turner needed to get rid of Rachael because she found out he worked for Ortega."

"Oh, my God."

Johnnie phoned Wheeler. He gave the agent all the information without saying how he'd found it, since he didn't want the whiz kid going to jail.

"I'm not telling you I've seen Talbot's file, you understand, I'm just saying if you look at it, you'll find the connection isn't Lansky, it's Lieutenant Carla Meeks."

"I'm on it. With Rachael's cell phone and her statement of what went down, along with Lansky shooting Talbot, we've got enough to bring them in. Good work, my friend."

"Keep me posted." Johnnie hung up the phone. He turned to Amy. "Wheeler's going to let us know as soon as they've been taken into custody. In the meantime, I'll call Vega and bring him up to speed."

"So it's finished."

"Just about."

Amy gave him a halfhearted smile. "That's really great news." She glanced away but not before he caught the resignation in her face. He knew she was happy for her sister. Rachael would be safe and all of this would be over.

But it would also be over for them.

Johnnie figured the sadness in Amy's pretty face was reflected in his own. For now, they were together, but a few days from now, she would be heading back to her life in Grand Rapids.

He looked at her and his insides tightened. Love for her echoed in his very bones.

If they just weren't so different...if they weren't so

damn far apart. But they were, and it would never work between them. He knew it and so did Amy.

He spent most of the next hour tying up loose ends, making calls, then waiting while Amy talked to her mother and sister. She was smiling, but he could see she was fighting back tears.

When she hung up the phone, he went to her, eased her into his arms. She was so tiny she fit well beneath his chin. He wanted to tell her how much she meant to him, how much he cared, but it wouldn't be fair to either one of them.

Instead, he bent his head and very softly kissed her, hoping he could show her without words the feeling in his heart. Amy went up on her toes and kissed him back. He could feel her trembling and drew her more tightly against him, kissed her even more deeply.

A noise sounded behind them, finally penetrated the haze of his growing need and he broke away.

"Well, now…isn't that touching." Carla Meeks stood in the kitchen doorway, her Glock 9 mil pointed at Johnnie's chest.

Johnnie silently cursed. He should have counted on Turner tipping Carla off to their phone call, should have known she wouldn't go down that easy.

Johnnie eased Amy behind him. "What's this about, Carla?" As if he didn't know. The woman hated his guts. She'd been willing to kill to keep her secrets and now she was there to kill him for destroying her life.

Carla sneered. "Don't give me that crap. You know what's goddamn going on. Dan called. He told me he got a call from Rachael, but I knew it had to be you and your little whore. I take it you found Rachael's phone."

"We found it. Turner's going down and so are you

and Lansky. It's over, Carla. You might as well put down the gun." He had to keep her talking. He needed time to think, try to find an angle. His knife was in his boot, but getting to it wouldn't be easy.

He eased toward her, hoping he could get close enough to knock the pistol out of her hand before she could get off a shot.

"Hold it right there." Her fingers tightened around the trigger. "Move again and I'll fucking kill you."

He'd only made it a couple of inches. It wasn't enough. "What are you doing, Carla? Along with everything else, you want to face murder charges, too?"

"I don't care. If I'm going to prison, killing you might just make it worthwhile." The gun wavered. She steadied it. "This is all your fault. You and that little tramp of yours. If you'd just left things alone, just let Rachael Brewer disappear, everything would have been fine."

"Fine, Carla? You think people being kidnapped and raped, taking drug money from criminals for not doing your job...you think that's fine?"

"Why shouldn't I have it? It's not like I'm stealing it from someone. People want drugs. They're willing to pay for them. That isn't going to change."

"Let me have the gun, Carla." He started forward, stopped at the vicious gleam in her eyes.

"Just keep coming," she taunted. "We'll make this end right now."

Amy was right behind him. If he didn't do something, Carla Meeks was going to kill them both.

He heard the front door swinging open.

"Yoo-hoo! Johnnie, are you and Amy in there?"

For a heartbeat, Carla's gaze swung toward the door

and Johnnie launched himself across the kitchen, taking her down, the gun flying out of her hand and slamming into the wall as she hit the tile floor beneath him. She struggled like a wildcat, tried to claw his face, tried to knee him in the groin, but he had her by at least seventy pounds, and with his training, had her pinned in seconds.

Amy rushed forward, unfastened the handcuffs attached to Carla's belt and handed them over. "Here, Johnnie, take these."

"Thanks, baby." He rolled Carla over, dragged her arms behind her back, and clamped the cuffs around her wrists. As he climbed to his feet, he saw that Amy was shaking, but she seemed to be all right. Ellie stood in the kitchen doorway, hands propped on her hips, looking pleased with herself.

"You bastard!" Carla hissed. "I hate you! I regret the day I ever let you into my bed!"

Amy flashed him a look.

Johnnie shook his head. "It was a long time ago."

The sound of sirens ended any further discussion, saving him at least for the moment.

Ellie strolled toward them. "I remembered who she was. I saw her go inside your house. Guess your door wasn't locked."

Carla struggled against the cuffs.

"I came over to see what she was up to, and when I looked through the window, I saw her with the gun pointed at you. I had my cell so I dialed 9-1-1, but I knew they wouldn't get here fast enough. I decided to see if I could distract her."

"You were great," Amy said.

As the sirens drew near, Johnnie dragged Carla over and propped her against the wall.

"She must have come up the hill the way Henley did," Ellie said. "Guess it's time I put in that alarm."

"Past time," Johnnie said.

"I'd better go open the gate so they can get in." As she walked toward the door, Johnnie stopped her, leaned over and kissed her cheek. "I guess that keeping an eye on things works both ways. Thanks, Ellie."

"My pleasure." She paused in front of Amy, winked and patted her cheek.

A few minutes later, the police were there, black-and-white units roaring up, uniforms rushing into the house. They headed straight for Carla, dragged her to her feet.

"There was an APB out on her," a heavyset cop explained. "Whoever called it in mentioned her name so we pretty much knew what was going down." One on each side, the cops hauled Carla out the door.

Kent Wheeler came in behind them. "Heard the call come through, hoped like hell you'd be okay. You'll be happy to know Lansky's also been arrested. So has Turner."

Johnnie looked over at Amy. Her face was pale but she seemed oddly calm. He thought of how Carla had come here to kill them and his stomach knotted. "Could have gone the other way."

Wheeler followed his gaze to Amy. "I don't think so. I think you'd have done whatever it took to keep your lady safe." Wheeler smiled, showing the gap between his teeth. "The good news is we've got enough to put them all away for a very long time. We can use Rachael's testimony, of course, but the truth is we've got plenty of evidence without it. As soon as Lansky and Turner realized what was happening, they turned on each other like rabid dogs. And they both rolled over on Meeks."

Johnnie drew Amy against his side. "It's over, baby. Rachael's safe and now…" He forced himself to say it. "Now you can go home."

Amy turned into his arms and just hung on.

Chapter 35

Amy was exhausted. The events of the day had drained her. That, and knowing she would be leaving Johnnie.

The police were gone. Ellie was back in her house. It was dark and late and they were finally alone. Standing next to Johnnie in front of the windows in the living room, she stared at the tiny specks of glittering light that seemed to go on forever.

"You okay?"

She just nodded. She wasn't okay at all, which Johnnie seemed to know. His dark eyes found hers and his hands slid into her hair. Tilting her head back, he kissed her long and deep. She could feel the desire pumping through him, feel his hunger, and an answering hunger swept through her.

"You have any idea how much I want you?" He

kissed her again, deep, taking kisses, then softly, almost reverently. Lifting her into his arms, he carried her out of the living room, down the hall to his bedroom, and set her on her feet.

"It seems like forever since I've had you. God, I ache with wanting you."

Amy thought how good it always was between them. She thought of what it would be like when he was gone from her life, and closed her eyes so he wouldn't see how close she was to tears. "Johnnie…"

He kissed her softly, slowly, a kiss that went on and on. Her tongue tangled with his and her body heated, turned soft and liquid.

He took his time undressing her, removing each piece of clothing, kissing the places he bared. Amy reached up and pulled his black T-shirt over his head, then reached for his belt buckle and slid down his zipper. He helped her undress him, didn't try to hurry her as she ran her hands over all his beautiful muscles.

His body was as hard as granite, sculpted in all the right places, his shoulders wide and his chest banded with muscle. She bent and brushed her lips over a flat copper nipple, ran her tongue around the rim and a shudder rolled through him.

Bending his dark head, he took her breast into his mouth and suckled deeply, the sweet pull tugging low in her belly. He ministered to the other breast, returned his attention to her mouth for a slow, deep kiss, lifted her and settled her on the bed, then followed her down.

The thick down comforter felt cool against her bare skin while his body burned wherever they touched. His erection, hard and pulsing, pressed like a hot iron against her, letting her know how much he wanted her, promising how good it would be.

Wet, hot kisses followed. Deep drugging kisses that had her squirming beneath him.

"Johnnie...please. I need you so much."

"Not yet. I'm not hurrying, baby...not tonight." And the gruffness in his voice told her why.

Their time together was over. Tomorrow, the next day. It wouldn't be long now. He was saying goodbye to her tonight, making memories for both of them.

Her throat closed up. She loved him so much.

His mouth moved over her skin, trailing hot, moist kisses along her neck and shoulders. He took her breasts again, slowly savored each one, tugged on the diamond hard tips. Moving lower, he laved her navel, settled himself between her legs and made love to her with his mouth and tongue.

Her body pulled taut and a fierce climax shook her, sucked her deeply under. She surfaced sometime later when he started kissing her again, began to ease himself inside. They had never made love this way, with so much emotion seething between them. Johnnie took her with a quiet desperation Amy felt clear to her soul.

She loved this man, loved him in a way she would never love another. And she believed he loved her.

It didn't change things. From the start, it was never meant to be, not for a schoolteacher and a hard man like Johnnie.

She felt him moving inside her, wrapped her arms around his powerful neck and hung on, loving the feel of his heavy weight on top of her, his hardness filling her so completely. She didn't want to leave him, knew that if he asked her to stay she would.

But Johnnie would never do that and she would never press herself on him, force him into a life he didn't want.

She loved him too much for that.

So she blocked her mind to the emptiness ahead and let her body respond to him as it always did, let him carry her higher and higher, until she burst into the sunlight, tasted the pleasure, the sweetness. An instant later, she felt his hard body stiffen as he followed her to release.

Amy clung to him as they spiraled down and hoped he wouldn't see the tears in her eyes she worked so hard to hide.

A week passed. A hectic week that brought Rachael and her mother back to Ellie Stiles's house, where Amy was now also staying. After the night she'd spent with Johnnie—sexually amazing but emotionally heartbreaking—she needed some time to herself, time to prepare for the painful separation ahead.

Johnnie must have felt the same.

He didn't argue when she told him she was moving back into Ellie's with her mother and sister until it was time for them to leave. He just nodded and said it was probably for the best.

It was time to go home. She and her mother were leaving, but both of them were worried about Rachael.

"Are you sure you'll be okay?" her mother had asked as they sat in Ellie's kitchen, drinking mugs of chamomile tea. "You have a lot to face, a lot to get through in the next few months. If you need me to stay you know I will."

Rachael leaned over and hugged her. "I'm staying

in Ellie's guest wing—what could be nicer than that? I'm seeing a counselor to help me deal with everything that's happened. Mr. Bixler thinks he may have some TV work for me, and Rick... Rick is here."

As for the last, Rick Vega was clearly in love with Rachael.

Though her sister wasn't ready for a relationship, Amy had a feeling Rachael was at least half in love with the handsome detective who had been there when she had needed him so badly.

Yesterday, Ellie had loaned Amy her car so she and Rachael could go down to the Kitty Cat Club for what turned out to be a surprisingly tearful goodbye.

"I'm so glad you're okay," Babs said, hugging Rachael hard, her cheeks wet and glistening. Honeybee had thanked Rachael and Amy for helping with little Jimmy, and Rachael had promised to visit him as often as she could.

Tate Watters had walked them back to the car. "I'm going to miss you both." Leaning over, he kissed Rachael's forehead. "Whatever you end up doing, I know you'll do great. Linda and I wish you the very best."

"Thanks, Tate."

He looked over at Amy. "So you're heading back to Michigan."

She nodded. "Mom and I are flying out in the morning."

"What about you and Johnnie? The way he feels about you, I can't believe he's letting you walk away."

Amy's heart twisted. She forced herself to smile. "It was just a fling for both of us."

Tate scoffed. "Could have fooled me," he said, clearly not believing it. But Amy had known how the relationship would end the first time she had seen John Riggs—sitting in the back of the Kitty Cat Club, looking like a hungry lion who wanted to eat her up.

And so the week passed. She and her mother were packed and ready to leave in the morning. She hadn't seen Johnnie in days, had tried not to listen for the sound of his Harley roaring up the drive. She tried not to wish he would come for her, carry her off and never let her go. She tried not to ache for him.

How much worse would it be, she thought, when he was thousands of miles away instead of right next door?

Seated in the chaise lounge out on the deck, the floppy straw hat she had bought in Belize perched on her head to keep out the sun, Amy tried to block him from her mind. She had to get over him, had to look toward the future. It was a summer fling, nothing more. It had to be.

Still her heart ached with the need to see him, to feel his arms around her. But Johnnie was a loner, a man who needed no one and would never allow that to change.

She wiped away a stray tear and looked up as her mother approached.

"Hello, sweetheart. Can we talk a minute?"

Amy pasted on a smile. "Sure, Mom."

In a pair of navy shorts and a red knit top, her mother sat down in the chaise next to hers.

"So…are you looking forward to going back home? You've got a good job waiting for you. And I'm sure you've missed your friends."

Amy glanced away. "It'll be nice to see them again."

"But it would be far nicer if you could stay right here

in Los Angeles with Johnnie. Isn't that right, honey? Isn't that what you're thinking?"

Her throat tightened. "I love him. That hasn't changed. But we both know it wouldn't work."

Her mother reached over and caught her hand. "That's what I thought, too…in the beginning. But after seeing the two of you together, after knowing what the two of you have faced together, I don't see it that way anymore."

"Why not?"

"From the day you met John Riggs, you've stood shoulder-to-shoulder with that man. You convinced him to help you find your sister. You went all the way to Belize to bring her home. You carried your own weight with the toughest sort of men, and I would bet that you won their respect. I know you think you'd be a liability to Johnnie, that you would somehow be in his way. But that just isn't true. John Riggs would be the luckiest man on earth to have you by his side. And I think you should tell him so."

Fighting to hold back tears, Amy shook her head. "I couldn't, Mom. He's never even said he loves me."

"I've seen the way he looks at you. That man would lay down his life for you. He loves you. I know it." Her mother pressed a fist over her heart. "I know it right here."

Amy wiped a tear from her cheek. "What if you're wrong? What if that isn't the way he feels about me at all?"

"Then you'll finally know the truth, and you'll deal with it." Hannah stood up, and Amy stood and went into her arms. "I tried to stop your sister from doing what was right for her. I won't do that to you. Think about what I've said."

Amy nodded. She'd think about it. She hadn't been able to stop thinking about Johnnie Riggs since she had seen him in the back of the Kitty Cat Club.

Johnnie heard a knock at his door. A key grated in the lock and the door swung open. *Ellie.* He looked up from where he sat on the sofa staring out the windows, seeing nothing but the haze that hung over the city like the pall hanging over his heart.

Sitting there with a beer in his hand he hadn't even started to drink.

"So here you are, home at last." Ellie walked toward him, sat down in the chair beside the sofa.

"I had some work to do in my office."

"Really? I've heard that Harley of yours racing off early every morning. You've been staying out half the night and from the looks of you, you aren't getting any sleep."

He rubbed the three-day growth of beard along his jaw. "So I've been busy."

"Rubbish. You've been pining away, running around on your Harley trying to escape your own foolish self, hanging out in the bars so you don't have to think about the woman next door."

"Fine, if that's what you want to believe."

"Oh, that's what I believe, all right. I think you're crazy in love with Amy and too damn stubborn to do anything about it."

He sat up a little straighter, raked a hand through his disheveled hair. "I know you're trying to help, Ellie, but the truth is it wouldn't work out. Both of us knew that from the start."

Ellie stiffened. She had a way of looking down her nose at him though she was shorter than he was. "Why ever not? In case you haven't noticed, that woman is perfect for you. She marched through the jungle with you and your soldier buddies, didn't she? And I'll bet she never once complained. She helped you save Rachael from that no-good Wes Henley. She loves your car and riding with you on your Harley. I'd venture to say the two of you are matched just as well in bed. Am I wrong?"

The tips of his ears burned. "None of your damn business."

"No, but your happiness *is* my business. I love you, Johnnie. You're the son I never had and I know you better than you know yourself. Why are you so afraid to take a chance?"

Frustration filled him. "She's a kindergarten teacher, for chrissake, Ellie. Look at me." He stood up, his dark hair rumpled, his black clothes wrinkled, the eagle tattoo standing out on his arm. He looked like the mercenary he'd once been. "She loves kids. If we...if we were together, she'd want some of her own. What kind of father would I be?"

"Probably a great one, since your dad was such a loser. You won't want to make the same mistakes with your own family."

Something tightened inside him. Secretly, he'd thought about having children. He just never really believed it could happen, not for him.

"Amy loves you," Ellie continued, beating at him

harder than any drill sergeant he'd had in the Rangers. "Surely you know that."

His voice roughened. "I know."

"Then damn it, do something about it before it's too late. You're never gonna get another chance, Johnnie. Not with a woman like Amy."

He swallowed past the tightness in his throat, sank back down on the sofa, tipped up the bottle in his hand and noticed the beer was warm.

Ellie stood up from her chair. "For God's sake, Johnnie, at least think about it!"

Johnnie made no reply. He'd think about it. He had no choice. Ellie was right. He was in love with Amy, over the top in love. And because he loved her, he couldn't take the chance he'd hurt her. He was better off leaving things alone.

Chapter 36

Amy looked up at the clock on the wall, saw it was almost midnight. First thing tomorrow morning, Johnnie was driving her and her mother to the airport. Ellie was supposed to do it, but something had come up and she had asked Johnnie to take her place.

Her heart squeezed. Their final goodbye would be at LAX, one of the busiest airports in the world. Thousands of people milling around, jostling them, giving them not an ounce of privacy. Amy couldn't bear it. She had to see Johnnie one last time and it had to be tonight.

Her mother was right. She couldn't leave without letting him know the way she felt. She couldn't go back to Grand Rapids without making her feelings clear. What Johnnie would say, she couldn't begin to guess.

He was home, she knew. In the past week, she had

become so attuned to his comings and goings she knew every time he left the house, mostly on his Harley.

Dressed in jeans and a white cotton blouse, a pair of gold hoops in her ears and sandals on her feet, she headed for the guesthouse. Her mouth felt dry but her palms were damp. Inside her chest, her heart was throbbing dully, aching with every slow beat.

There was a light on in the living room, the soft glow leaking from the windows over the kitchen sink. Gravel crunched under her feet as she determinedly headed for the stairs leading up to the porch. She didn't know what she would say to him, only knew that the moment she saw him, her heart was going to crumble. She was nearly to the stairs when the door swung open and Johnnie walked out. His jaw was clean-shaven, his hair damp and shining from a recent shower, a clean black T-shirt stretched over his powerful chest. He looked so handsome and dear, so beloved, she almost lost her courage, turned around and ran back to the house.

She straightened her spine and forced herself to smile. "Hi," she said lamely.

"Hi." His voice sounded gruff. In the light creeping out of the windows, she could see something in his eyes she had never seen there before. It was uncertainty, she realized. And something she thought looked like pain.

"I wanted...wanted to talk to you," she said, frozen where she stood, working to keep the smile in place. "If...if you have time."

"Sure, I ummm... Truth is, I was on my way over to your place. I...ummm...wanted to talk to you, too."

She tried not to hope. Hoping was a dangerous, heartbreaking thing to do. "You were?"

He nodded, his eyes moving over her, returning to

her face. "There were some things I wanted to say, things I should have said before, but I... Ah, hell..." Her eyes widened as he came down the stairs, strode over and hauled her into his arms.

Amy clung to him, trembling, wishing so hard that she could make him change his mind, make him want to be with her as much she wanted to be with him.

She broke away, took a step backward. She had to say it now or she would never say it at all. "I've been thinking, Johnnie. I know you think we're too different, that it couldn't work out between us, but—"

"I think it could work," he said, his eyes still on her face. "I think it could work, you know, just fine. Better than fine. I think it could be terrific."

Her heart slowed, seemed to stop. "You do?"

"Yeah, I do."

She made a little sound in her throat as he scooped her back into his arms and just hung on.

"I love you, baby," he said against her cheek. "I love you so damn much."

Her eyes filled. "Ask me to stay," she blurted out, surely the wrong thing to say but she couldn't keep the words locked up inside. "Oh, Johnnie, please ask me to stay."

His hold tightenen around her. "Stay with me," he said gruffly. "I don't want you to leave. I don't ever want you to leave."

The tears in her eyes slipped onto her cheeks. "I'll never leave. Not ever. I love you too much."

He was trembling. She couldn't believe it. He eased back a little and brought his hand up to cradle her cheek.

"Marry me," he said softly. "Will you, baby?"

Love for him swamped her. A smile bloomed on her lips and fresh tears spilled over. "I'd love to marry you, Johnnie."

He cupped her face in his hands and kissed her, the sweetest, sexiest, most tender kiss she had ever known. Amy let the thrill of it wash through her.

By the time the long kiss ended, everything seemed to have settled back into its rightful place. She looked up at him, her heart filled to bursting. "I can get a teaching job out here," she said, smiling and wiping her eyes. "I know you have to work nights a lot, but I don't care. I'll wait up for you. I'll be waiting when you get home."

He kissed her again, more softly this time. "I don't have to work late that often. I just do it because I get lonely."

An ache slipped through her. Going up on her toes, she planted soft kisses all over his face. "Not anymore, Johnnie. You'll never be lonely again."

"We can have kids if you want. I don't know what kind of father I'd be, but—"

"You'll be a wonderful father—the best."

Johnnie kissed her. "Your mother isn't going to like it."

Amy laughed. "Coming over here was her idea."

He grinned. "You're gonna marry me, right?"

She laughed. "Right."

"How about tomorrow?"

Her throat ached. "Are you sure?"

"I've never been more sure of anything. What I can't understand is why it took me so long to figure things out."

Amy went back into his arms and Johnnie just held

her. She didn't know what had happened to change his mind, but she wasn't going to question fate.

Johnnie swept her up and carried her back inside the house. Instead of dreading tomorrow, she was looking forward to the future as she never had before. Amy reached up and pulled his head down for another slow-burning kiss.

Epilogue

Johnnie slowed his Harley and pulled off the dirt road beneath the gnarled branches of an old oak tree. They were taking a day trip up the coast. He had a friend who owned a piece of property in the hills above Santa Barbara, the perfect spot for a picnic. They'd been married two weeks. The best two weeks of his life.

He and Amy climbed off the Harley. She pulled off the bright red helmet he had bought her, along with a set of black leathers. Damn, she looked sexy.

He opened one of the saddlebags on the back of the bike, took out a blanket and tossed it to Amy. "You pick a spot and I'll bring the lunch stuff."

"Don't forget the wine," she said, smiling.

He'd brought a bottle of chardonnay, though he'd rather have beer, and didn't drink much anyway when he was riding. They'd enjoy the wine with lunch, and have time for a nap and a little lovemaking.

Johnnie smiled. They'd gotten married at Ellie's, out on the deck on a perfect Saturday a week after his hasty proposal. Hannah had changed her flight plans and the women all pitched in to get things ready on such short notice. They did a bang-up job, setting up an arbor, then decorating it with white orchids and roses, and finding Amy the prettiest white lace dress he'd ever seen.

As she'd stood there beside him, he'd felt such a swell of love for her, he almost couldn't get the "I do" past the lump in his throat.

The guests were a motley crew. Tate Watters and his wife, Linda; and the girls from the Kitty Cat Club. Mrs. Zimmer and little Jimmy. Special Agent Kent Wheeler.

Trace and Maggie Rawlins had flown out from Texas. He'd been surprised when Jake said he was coming, too.

"Are you kidding? This is monumental," Jake said. "I was hoping you'd wake up and come to your senses."

Dev and Lark were there, Dev acting as his best man. Madman couldn't make it. Molly went into labor and Clive was beside himself. Molly had the baby the day after the wedding, a little boy named Clive, Jr. Mother, father and baby were all doing fine.

Ty Brodie was there, grinning like a jackass and giving him an I-told-you-so look.

Rick Vega stayed close to Rachael, who seemed to be loving every minute of having him there. Johnnie had a feeling down the road there'd be a Vega/Brewer wedding.

He and Amy made it through the ceremony, both of them grinning at each other as if they shared some private joke, which they did, since it was a wedding that wasn't supposed to happen and both of them were as happy as kids that it was. Amy tossed the bouquet. Ellie caught it and all of them whistled and cheered.

A surprise came as they finished opening their gifts when Ellie walked over and pressed an envelope into Johnnie's hand.

"What is it?" he asked.

"This property is actually divided into two separate parcels. That's the deed to the guesthouse. Now it belongs to you and Amy."

"Oh, Ellie," Amy said. "We couldn't possibly accept something so valuable."

Ellie just shrugged. "I left it to Johnnie in my will, so all I'm doing is giving it to him a little early." She grinned. "Besides, with the two of you around, life will never be dull." Everyone had laughed and the women exchanged tearful hugs.

"Thanks, Ellie," Johnnie managed a little gruffly. The lady was really something and he was grateful to call her a friend.

As for Rachael's abduction case, everything they'd pieced together turned out to be true. In an effort to cut a deal, Lansky admitted to planting a throwaway gun on Dickie Talbot after he'd shot him, and Meeks and Turner were singing like birds. The district attorney was prosecuting the case himself, which meant they were all going down hard.

It came out that Dan Turner had taken Rachael to the Vieux Carre a couple of times for dinner. It was likely Manny Ortega knew about Turner's connection to his father, but the kid was doing his best to stay out of trouble, and nobody wanted to press charges.

"Where's that wine?" Amy asked, dragging him from his thoughts. "I'm dry as dust over here."

Johnnie laughed and started walking, a bottle in one hand, a sack filled with cheese, different kinds of Italian sausage, olives, crackers, a fancy French pâté that Amy picked out, fresh strawberries and chocolate éclairs for dessert, though they looked a little worse for wear after riding in his saddlebags.

Johnnie sat down cross-legged next to his tiny wife and set the food out on the blanket in front of them. He reached for her, dragged her into his lap and kissed her deep and thoroughly.

"Thank God you married me."

"Why is that?"

"Because I'm crazy in love with you and I wouldn't want to have to go all the way to Michigan to bring you back home."

She looked up at him. "Would you have done that?"

"Probably. I can't stand to think of the alternative."

Amy laughed. It was the sweetest sound.

"I love you, baby."

"I love you, too, Johnnie Riggs."

And he kissed her again, and all seemed right with the world.

* * * * *

Also by Brenda Jackson

Madaris Family Saga

Tonight and Forever
Whispered Promises
Eternally Yours
One Special Moment
Fire and Desire
Secret Love
True Love
Surrender
Sensual Confessions
Inseparable
Courting Justice
A Madaris Bride for Christmas
Best Laid Plans

HQN Books

The Protectors

Forged in Desire
Seized by Seduction
Locked in Temptation

The Grangers

A Brother's Honor
A Man's Promise
A Lover's Vow

Harlequin Desire

The Westmoreland Legacy

The Rancher Returns
His Secret Son
An Honorable Seduction

And don't miss the first book in the Catalina Cove series

Love in Catalina Cove

For additional books by *New York Times* bestselling author Brenda Jackson, visit her website, brendajackson.net.

THE OBJECT OF HIS PROTECTION

Brenda Jackson

To the love of my life, Gerald Jackson, Sr.

He catches the wise in their craftiness,
and the schemes of the wily are swept away.
—*Job* 5:13

Chapter 1

"I might as well come in since it doesn't appear that you're busy."

Charlene Anderson didn't need to look up to know who the deep, husky voice belonged to.

Drey St. John.

She did, however, glance over at the small heart-shaped ceramic clock sitting on her desk, the only part of her work area that wasn't buried under paperwork. Drey was early although his visit wasn't unexpected. He was a private investigator and she was a forensic scientist in Houston's coroner's office. It wasn't unusual for him to drop by occasionally to harass her for forensic information that would help with the investigation of his current case.

"If you think I'm not busy, St. John, look again,"

she said, not taking her eyes off the document she was reading. "Now get lost."

She knew he wouldn't go away. He never did. That didn't bother her since she had a weak spot for the rebel private investigator and actually looked forward to seeing him, although she would never admit such a thing to him. His visits were the only high point in her rather dull life. At twenty-seven, she was focused on work, and no matter how you looked at it, dead bodies didn't equate to great dates. Her social life was practically nonexistent, and of all things, she was still a virgin.

While attending Oklahoma State University, she had been too busy making the grades to get involved with anyone and had figured things would change once she finished school and got her career off the ground. She had been convinced, since she looked decent enough, that she would eventually meet some nice guy and get serious. That never happened. For her it always seemed to be all work and no play.

"Don't you ever get tired of messing around with the dead?"

She glanced up. Speaking of dead... Drey was drop-dead gorgeous. Definitely a living-breathing specimen of a sexy male. Tall, dark and ultrahandsome. There was no doubt about the fact that at thirty-three he was every woman's fantasy.

He had skin the color of creamy rich chocolate, and had dark hair and slanted dark eyes. All she knew about him was the tidbit she'd overhead from a group of women discussing him one day at lunch. According to them, his mother was half Chinese. If that was the case, she had passed a strikingly exotic look on to her son. Charlene had also heard that his middle name of Longwei meant "dragon strength" in Chinese. The name suited him because of his well-defined muscular physique.

"Not really," she finally said, taking her eyes off him and attempting to return her focus to the document in front of her. "At least I don't have to worry about the dead giving me a hard time."

"Yeah, I would imagine they wouldn't."

She didn't have to glance up to know he was no longer standing in the doorway but had come into her office. Her heart began beating twice as fast. The man had a way of getting to her. In addition to her erratic heartbeat, there was this unexplainable flush of heat that always overtook her whenever he was near, not to mention the way the air surrounding them always felt charged. He apparently didn't pick up on such vibes, nor did he notice she did. He was too busy trying to pump her for information.

When he halted before her desk, blocking her sunlight, she decided to glance up, but took a deep breath before doing so. "And what got you out of bed so early this morning?" she asked, and immediately she wished she hadn't when a vision of him getting out of bed—half naked—filtered through her mind. It was a nice vision but dangerous ground for her mind to tread on.

"I need your help with something."

She rolled her eyes. "What else is new?"

"You're the best there is," he said, smiling. She wished he wouldn't do that. He was sexy enough without the megawatt smile.

"Flattery will get you nowhere, Drey."

"What about dinner tonight?"

She placed her pen down and leaned back in her

chair. "This must be some case if you're willing to spring for dinner."

She watched the emotions that crossed his face, emotions he rarely let show. He was angry and upset but was holding it in. Something about the case he was working on was bothering him. She could feel it.

"It is," he finally said. "And the answers may very well come from a stiff brought here last week by the name of Joe Dennis."

Charlene turned toward her computer and typed in the name. "Nothing has been done with him yet. He's on Nate's list to do later today." Nathaniel Ganders was her boss. "What exactly do you need to know?"

His tensed features relaxed somewhat when he said, "Anything you can tell me."

She nodded. He understood there were limitations as to what she could share, and she appreciated the fact that he had never asked her to cross the line in doing anything unethical. Not that she would. "In other words, anything out of the ordinary."

"Yes."

"Okay. I'll take a look at the report when Nate's finished. As you know, my boss is very thorough." She cleared her computer screen and turned back to him. "I'll let you know if I notice anything."

"Thanks, and I'm serious about dinner."

"But I'm not." It hadn't been the first time he had hinted at the two of them going somewhere to grab something to eat. She could barely handle her reaction to him now; she didn't want to think how things would be if she had to share a meal with him. Besides, she considered him business and she didn't mix business with pleasure. "Maybe some other time, Drey," she said, knowing it wouldn't happen.

"You said that before."

Not that she was foolish enough to think that it mattered to him. "And I'm saying it again. I'll call you if I learn anything."

"Thanks, Charlie. I would appreciate it."

Charlene glared at him, something she always did whenever he called her that. "Do I look like a Charlie to you?"

He smiled. "Hard to say. That lab jacket's all I've ever seen you wear."

Before she could give him a blazing retort, he turned and left.

The smile remained in place on Drey's lips as he got into his car. For some reason he enjoyed getting a rise out of Charlene. In fact, the thought of seeing her today had pretty much kept his anger at bay, although it was creeping back on him now. He was discovering that being lied to all his life was something he was having a hard time dealing with.

Before starting the engine, he sat still a moment and stared out of the windshield, thinking about the conversation he'd had with his mother, Daiyu Longwei, a few days ago. The conversation had practically shattered his world when she had told him that Ronald St. John was not his father. Instead, the man whom Drey had considered his mentor, Congressman Harmon Braddock, was actually his biological father.

His hands tightened on the steering wheel as his mother's words flowed through his mind.

Sighing deeply, Drey started the engine, thinking

that in essence, he was investigating his own father's death. His own father's *murder,* he immediately corrected, since he was convinced Harmon Braddock's fatal car accident had been deliberate. Someone had wanted him dead and Drey was determined to find out who.

Something else he couldn't put out of his mind was that the very people who had hired him to find the truth were Harmon Braddock's offspring—and his siblings. He shook his head knowing they didn't have a clue as to what his relationship was to them. At some point he would have to tell them, but not now. He wasn't ready to go there yet. It was bad enough that he had to deal with it. Besides, how his own mother played into the investigation was still a mystery since it was well documented that less than an hour before his death, Harmon had tried contacting Daiyu. Hell, Drey hadn't known the two knew each other and none of the Braddocks knew that Daiyu was his mother. He didn't like withholding information of any kind from clients, yet that was exactly what he was doing.

He had known the congressman for a number of years. When Ronald St. John, the man Drey had adored as a father, had gotten killed in the line of duty as a police officer when Drey was fifteen, Drey had taken it hard since the two of them had always been close.

It was during that time that Congressman Braddock took an interest in him. And later on in life when Drey had felt himself getting tired of his own career as a police officer, it had been the congressman who had encouraged him to start his own private investigating firm and had gone so far as to keep him on retainer during those times he'd been trying to make ends meet. He would be the first to admit that over the years, Harmon had become the father figure that he'd lost.

To be quite honest, at first when he'd heard of Harmon's car accident he had no reason to suspect foul play, even when the other Braddocks had. But now Joe Dennis's death was raising his suspicions.

Drey brought the car to a stop at the next traffic light as he replayed the facts of the case over and over in his mind. Congressman Braddock had gotten killed in a car accident. The skid marks on the road had been consistent with a car losing control. It seemed Harmon was heading for the airport, which was another mystery since Gloria Kingsley, the congressman's executive assistant, who'd known Harmon's every move, hadn't known about any planned trip.

Another thing that baffled everyone was why the congressman was behind the wheel when his personal driver, Joe Dennis, usually drove Harmon everywhere he went.

And now Joe was dead and according to the police report there didn't appear to be any foul play. Someone just wanted him dead. Why? And exactly what had been the cause of death?

Drey had a lot of unanswered questions but at least he felt fairly confident the latter question would get answered soon enough, once he heard from Charlene. With that certainty, his thoughts couldn't help shift to the efficient forensic scientist. They might bicker every chance they got, but they understood each other. He was as dedicated to his profession as she was to hers.

In the two years he'd known her, he'd never met another no-nonsense woman quite like her, and he found her to be sharp, intelligent...and definitely beautiful.

The latter he tried not to dwell on too much. Seeing her in that lab coat all the time should have been a turnoff; instead it was a total turn-on because he often wondered just how she looked beneath it.

But what he liked most about her was that she didn't hesitate to give him hell if she thought he deserved it, and that made the verbal sparring with her that much more fun.

For some reason he had felt the need to see her this morning. Of course there had been that matter regarding Joe Dennis, but it seemed once his mother had hit him with the news of his parentage, he needed the light-hearted banter he and Charlene enjoyed to take his mind off things.

Lately, all of his relationships with women had been casual, just the way he wanted. He didn't have time for any type of serious indulgence, and the last thing he needed was a woman getting too clingy. He could tell that Charlene wasn't the clingy type. Besides that, their relationship was strictly professional. He had asked her out to dinner a few times, after the information she had given him had helped him solve a case, but she had refused and he hadn't had a reason to push.

Frowning, he turned the corner onto the road that would take him to his office. Later, he would drop by headquarters to check the police report again on Joe Dennis's death to see if he'd missed anything. Drey was determined to find out anything and everything that he could.

"I'm leaving to attend a meeting, Charlene. Don't stay too late."

She smiled as she glanced over at Nate Ganders as

he slipped into his jacket. "I won't. In fact I intend to leave on time today."

When he tried smothering a cough, she said, "And please take my advice and do something for your cold. You're passing germs and I can't afford to get sick."

Nate's chuckle was the only sound he made before leaving the room. She stretched her legs, trying to recall just how long the two of them had worked together. Three years. He was an easy enough boss, although he could be demanding at times. The city had this thing about doing more with less, and amidst a number of budget cuts, the coroner's office was operating on slim funds that could barely keep up with the number of suicides and suspicious deaths they handled each year. Her only saving grace was that Nate left her alone to do her job, and the nice salary increases she'd gotten each year let her know her hard work and dedication hadn't gone unnoticed.

Nate was a pleasant man, and a good father to two children. And from the conversations Charlene had overheard, he was happily married to a woman he'd adored for over twenty-five years.

Seeing it was almost five o'clock, she stood up after logging off her computer. She then recalled Drey's visit and what he had asked her to do. Deciding now would be the best time since Nate had left for a meeting, she went into the autopsy room to take a look at Joe Dennis's chart. Nate had just finished performing the autopsy on Dennis, and the chart was still lying on the table. She picked it up and began reading.

"Trauma to the head, consistent with an attack from behind, as well as several other bruises to neck and shoulders." She raised her brow at the notation that a key had been removed from the victim's stomach. She glanced over at the key that was on the table. Why would anyone swallow a key?

Deciding that was definitely something worth mentioning to Drey, she left the autopsy room, determined to call Drey once she got home. She was about to exit the room when she heard Nate talking loudly to another man. Odd, she thought, because in the three years she'd worked with Nate, she had never known him to raise his voice. And why had he returned in the first place? Most of the time his meetings lasted for an hour or longer.

She decided it was none of her business. Besides, she'd better leave before Nate found something else for her to do. As she headed for the door, she couldn't help noticing that the voices had gotten louder. She paused. Nate was definitely upset about something, but so was the man he was talking to. His voice was deep and sounded slightly hoarse. She could only assume, since she hadn't been sitting at her desk when Nate returned, that he thought she had left for the day. Not wanting to eavesdrop on Nate's argument any longer, she slipped out the door.

Drey heard his cell phone ring the moment he stepped out of the shower. Wrapping the towel around his waist, he quickly walked out of the bathroom to pick it up off the nightstand next to his bed. "Yes?"

"Drey, this is Charlene."

He felt his stomach churn and immediately thought, not for the first time, that she had such a sexy phone voice. There was just something about it that made goose bumps rise on his skin. Wanting to curb the boost to his testosterone level, he said, "Charlie."

She paused a moment, and he figured she'd done so to blow off a little steam, before saying, "I was able to take a look at Nate's report on Dennis."

The way she said the statement told him there was more. "And?"

"And I noticed a couple of things you might want to know."

"Such as?"

"There was trauma to the head consistent with some sort of an attack from behind."

Drey nodded. Not that the police had been much help, but he had paid a visit to headquarters after lunch hoping to learn something not on paper. For some reason it seemed everyone had closed lips. Usually they would loosen for a former member of their own, but today was not the case. And unfortunately, Detective Lavender Sessions, his former partner while on the force, was out of town. Like Charlene, Drey could always count on him to tell him what he needed to know.

"And there's something else pretty strange about Joe Dennis."

Charlene's statement cut deep into his thoughts. "What?"

"He swallowed a key."

"Excuse me?" Drey said, certain he hadn't heard her right.

"I said he swallowed a key. One was taken out of his stomach."

Drey rubbed his chin thoughtfully. "Are you sure?" Immediately, he knew he had made a mistake in asking her that. In all his dealings with Charlene he had come to realize that she was a professional who knew her business.

"Of course I'm sure. Not only did I read it in the report, but I saw it myself. Nate hadn't removed it from the table."

Drey didn't say anything for a moment; he was too busy thinking. Had Dennis swallowed the key to keep it from getting into someone else's hands? Was the key a link to Harmon's death? Those were questions he intended to get answered. "What sort of key was it?" he asked.

"Too small to be a door key. It was more like the size of a locker key or safe-deposit box key."

He rubbed his chin again, his curiosity igniting. "I need a copy of that key," he said, placing the phone on speaker so he could get dressed.

"That's not possible, Drey. I don't mind passing information on to you if I think it will help your case, but I draw the line at removing anything that could later become evidence."

"And I'm not asking you to," he said quickly.

"Well, what *are* you asking me to do?"

He could hear the agitation in her voice. The last thing he wanted to do was get her teed off, especially now when he needed information about that key. "I'm asking that you provide me a mold of it in wax. I've got a small kit that resembles a ladies' compact."

She didn't say anything for a moment, as if contemplating his request. And then she asked, "But what good is that when you don't know what the key goes to?"

"I'll find out. So will you get an indention of that key?"

"I don't know, Drey...."

"Please." If he sounded desperate, there was no help for it. He needed to know everything about Joe Dennis's death, especially now that he knew it hadn't been from natural causes.

He could hear her deep sigh and felt his heart begin to beat wildly in his chest. Even her sigh was a turn-on.

"Okay, fine," she said.

He couldn't help but smile. If he solved the case and was able to link it back to Harmon's death, then he owed her more than just dinner. "Meet me tonight so I can give the kit to you."

"Where?"

"You name the place. Better yet, if you give me your home address I can drop it off there."

He heard the hesitation in her voice and was about to throw out another option when she said, "That's fine, since I really don't want to go back out tonight. I live in the Rippling Shores Condos."

He knew the area. It was a newly developed subdivision of nice townhomes. "I know where it's located. What's the condo number?"

She rattled it off to him and he saved it in his memory. "I'll be there in less than an hour."

He smiled when, with not even a goodbye, she hung up the phone. For some reason he was looking forward to seeing her without her lab coat.

Chapter 2

Charlene glanced out the window and wondered for the umpteenth time why she had given Drey her address instead of meeting him somewhere. What had happened to her "do not mix business with pleasure" rule?

She was used to seeing him in a business setting, but now he would invade her personal space. The only consolation was that since he was dropping something off she wouldn't have to invite him inside.

Satisfied with that, she glanced down at herself. Okay, so she had decided to change out of the frayed pair of shorts and T-shirt she had put on after coming home into a skirt and blouse. No big deal. It wasn't as though he would see her in them. It was dark outside and all she had to do was poke her head out the door to get whatever he had to give her. Again, no big deal. She sighed deeply, thinking she was definitely making a lot out of things she considered to be no big deal.

When she heard a car door slam, her breath caught and for a moment she didn't move. She inhaled deeply, trying to control her racing pulse. There was no reason to get nervous and jittery. Drey St. John wasn't the first guy to come to her house…but she had to admit he was the first one in over a year, if you didn't count the serviceman who dropped by a few weeks ago to take a look at her computer when it had gone on the blink.

She didn't want to think about Carlos Hollis, the guy she had dated nearly two years ago. They had met at one of those financial seminars and she had taken him up on his offer to go somewhere for drinks afterward. They ended up going on a couple of dates after that, and when he began hinting that he wanted to sleep with her, she felt it was only fair to let him know up front that she was a virgin. He informed her that most guys were turned off by any virgin over the age of twenty-two, and to prove his point he never called her again.

Charlene heard the knock on the door and for a brief moment she contemplated not answering, which made absolutely no sense. *There is simply no reason for you to be nervous,* she told herself firmly as she headed toward the door. She reached for the doorknob and paused before turning it, convinced that even through the thickness of the wood that separated them she could breathe in Drey's scent. At least it was the scent that she always associated with him, robust and definitely manly. Drawing in a deep breath, she opened the door slightly and saw how the glow from the porch light lit his handsome features before she acknowledged him. "Drey."

"You shouldn't have opened the door until you were absolutely sure it was me, Charlie."

She thought about closing the door on him but decided she was a lot more mature than that. Instead, she opened it a little wider to place her arms across her chest and glare at him, or at least she tried to while attempting to downplay the heated sensations flowing through her. "The name is Charlene and I knew it was you."

"And how did you know that? I note you don't have a peephole in your door."

There was no way she would tell him that his scent had been a dead giveaway for her. "I just did. Now, if you don't mind, please give me what you drove all the way over here to deliver." She reached out her hand.

Instead of placing anything in her hand, he took her hand into his and looked at it. The moment he touched her she felt a slow sizzle move up her spine and she kept her body still, not to let him know the effect of his touch.

"You have pretty hands, Charlie."

She tensed at the compliment before pulling her hands from him. "Thanks, and how many times do I need to remind you that it's Charlene?"

Drey then glanced back at her and noted her stance and felt his temperature rise. There was just enough light from the lamppost to see her outfit. The skirt and blouse looked cute. No, they looked exquisite, in a subtle sort of way. His gaze moved down to her long, shapely legs.

His eyes met hers then as he decided he owed her an explanation for his intense scrutiny just now. "This is the first time I've seen you without a lab coat and you look different."

She lifted an arched brow. "Different how?"

"Different as in nice. Not that you didn't look nice before, mind you." *Nice* was too mild a word but he felt it would be out of place for him to say anything else. He doubted he could ever call her Charlie again without thinking how much like Charlene she now looked.

Whenever he dropped by the coroner's office she would be sitting behind her desk and wearing her lab coat with her hair twisted on top of her head in a ball. Now she was standing up and wearing a skirt and blouse with a mass of long light brown hair flowing around her shoulders. In his opinion the entire package was sexy.

Desire flowed hot and heavy through his veins and he downplayed his rapid breathing when he said, "So, what's a nice-looking girl like you doing home on a night like tonight? Why don't you have a date?"

Charlene's glare deepened. It was the same question her mother had asked her when she'd called earlier tonight. Nina Anderson-Smallwood-Caldwell-Olson actually thought a woman's life centered on a man. But after four marriages Charlene wasn't surprised her mother would think that. Her father was just as bad with wife number three. Since her parents seemed happy with their lives, she left them alone to do as they pleased and reminded them of their pledge on her twenty-first birthday to do likewise with her.

"I don't have a date because I don't want a date, so now give me the wax kit before I change my mind," she said, extending her hand back to him, hoping he didn't pull what he had before and take her hand again. His touch evoked feelings within her, unfamiliar feelings, feelings she could very well do without. When she was around him, a keen physical yearning seem to overtake her common sense, but she always fought to ignore it.

"Okay, here," he said, placing the item in her hand. She glanced down at it. He was right. It did resemble a small makeup compact.

"You want me to show you how to use it?"

She looked up at him. Was he looking for any excuse to come inside? She immediately dissed the thought. Why should he? Besides, she was certain she wasn't his type anyway. "No, I think I can handle it. It should be easy."

"It is. But even if it weren't I have a feeling you'd be able to handle it. In fact, Charlene Anderson, I think you can handle just about anything and anyone."

Another compliment—one laced with sexual innuendo? Or was she imagining things? Letting her mind jump to all kinds of conclusions? No, she decided after looking into his eyes, she wasn't imagining things. She might be a virgin but she wasn't naive. They had a routine of giving each other a hard time, but she was smart enough to recognize the sexual tension that existed between them.

Even now.

Was he throwing out a challenge? Could she handle him? She wanted to wrap her arms around herself to ward off the yearning she felt, but then she quickly decided that she had a right to experience these things. She was a woman, after all, and Drey was definitely a man who could make an impression on a woman. She didn't know any female who wouldn't be affected by the sheer maleness of him. He was dressed casually in a pair of jeans and a T-shirt. Both showed off an ultrafine body, one that probably spent a lot of time in a gym messing around with all kinds of machinery with the sole purpose of staying in shape. She could tell that whatever clothes he wore he was well-toned and filled them out with masculine perfection.

She suddenly felt the need to retreat, instinctively aware of a need to protect herself from him and from the things he was making her feel. But then another part of her wanted to explore those feelings, to discover—up to a point—all the things she hadn't experienced yet. Was she prepared for such a discovery?

"If you're certain I don't need to show you anything, I'll be going."

His words flowed through her mind, and her body picked up on the sensuality that laced his words. Again she wondered if she was imagining things. She studied his eyes. The slant in their shape made them look sexy and— Was that desire she saw in their dark depths? She shook her head, certain she was imagining things now. But then...

"Would you like to come inside for a drink, Drey?"

She inwardly flinched at the question, sure he had been asked that a thousand times by different women. He probably recognized it as the old "hit" line it was, one that had played out years ago, and was likely wondering if that was the best she could do. Unfortunately, it was. She didn't want to give the impression that she was anywhere close to being promiscuous or an easy mark, because she was far from it.

"I'd love to come in and share a drink with you, Charlene."

It hadn't gone unnoticed that he had called her Charlene this time instead of Charlie. His words, spoken in what she thought was an overly sexy tone, reeled in her thoughts and caused her to focus once again on his eyes. He was staring at her intensely, as if she was a puzzle he was determined to figure out. The thought bothered her until she felt surprised he was even taking the time to do so.

On their own accord her eyes then lowered to his mouth. When she thought of that mouth pressed against hers, a warm sensation flowed low in her belly.

Without saying anything, she took a step back inside the house and he followed.

Drey found himself drawn to Charlene's alluring sensuality as he stepped across the threshold into her home. With each step he took he felt something happening to him, something that could be perilous to his well-being as well as to his state of mind. Yet he was at a loss to stop it even with all the caution signs flashing at him.

He was used to women inviting him inside their homes with all kinds of intent and had always been careful to make sure it wasn't a setup of the worst kind. When it came to his sex life he maintained control. There was never a discussion on the matter. He chose his bed partners as meticulously and carefully as he chose anything else. He wasn't one to take anyone lightly. He could spot ulterior motives a mile away, and with the keen sense of a man who could most times read a woman like a book, he could figure out—even long before they could—if they wanted him.

Charlene wanted him but for what reason he wasn't sure. He wasn't even certain if she knew. There was something about her, something about her invitation to come in for a drink that made him smile. Most women he knew just came right out and asked at the end of the date, "Would you like to come in for sex?" They didn't beat around the bush about anything and usually by the time the door closed behind him they had stripped naked.

He glanced across the room at Charlene. She was fully clothed and the thought flitted through his mind that he would give anything to see her naked. Seeing her without her lab coat was an eye-opener. Removing her clothes was a boner just waiting to happen. Even now he could feel desire flowing through him. Heated lust that was increasing the flow to his brain up north and a certain other body part down south. Whether Charlene knew it or not, she was an extremely desirable woman. Why had she kept it hidden?

"So, what would you like?"

Her words pulled in his thoughts and immediately a vision flashed across his mind. Sexual imagery, hot and enticing, shot through his brain and threatened to short-circuit his nerve endings.

"What would I like?" he asked, shooting the question back at her, pausing to fully enunciate, sensually articulate every single word. He watched her tense as she realized she had unintentionally set herself up for that one.

She tilted her head at an angle he thought was sexy and glared at him. "What would you like to drink?"

He smiled, tempted to tell her sipping on her would satisfy him rather nicely, but decided not to do so. He might be wrong, way off base, but he had a feeling she was trying to downplay a certain innocence about her, while at the same time trying to prove something. What? And to whom?

"I'll take anything you have," he finally got around to answering. "But I prefer a beer if you have one."

She nodded. "Yes, I have one. I'll be back in a second."

He heard panic in her voice and when she left the room he shook his head. Did she think he would pounce on her the first chance he got? She had been the one to invite him in.

He smiled thinking he might not pounce on her right away, but he intended to kiss her before he left. For a long time he had wondered how her lips tasted and he intended to find out tonight. Her lips had always intrigued him, had always turned him on even when they had been discussing dead bodies.

Dead bodies.

He remembered one in particular. Joe Dennis. His concentration should be focused on working his investigation and not working Charlene. He sucked in air, trying to get a grip. Instead he got a whiff of Charlene's scent. It was all over the place. Jasmine.

He moved to the center of the room and looked around. She had a cozy place, nicely decorated, not overly furnished and crowded. It looked lived-in in a feminine way with splashes of pastel colors blended with the boldness of some darker shades. He noted that her preference in style leaned toward Early American while his remained staunchly Asian. He thought it was an interesting contrast.

"Sorry I took so long."

He turned to face Charlene and swallowed hard, while fighting back the sensations that suddenly engulfed him. Compared to him she seemed to be a tiny thing, no taller than five three if that. His six-four height seemed to all but tower over her. And then there was the way she filled out her skirt and blouse. She was just as shapely up top as she was around the hips. Usually, he didn't make a habit out of sizing up a woman's breasts, but with the way hers filled her blouse he couldn't help doing so. He had seen her many times, but because of the way she normally wore her hair, he hadn't noticed the red highlights in her hair and what they did to her medium brown complexion.

"No problem," he answered as he took the beer bottle from her, deciding he needed to remember the reason he was there and take care of it and leave. There was no need wasting time thinking about how good she looked or just how delicious he figured she would taste. He had an important case to solve and didn't have time for anything else, especially anything involving a woman.

"You have a nice place," he said before popping the cap off the beer bottle and taking a long, needed gulp. It immediately quenched his thirst but did nothing to wipe away his desire. He had focused on her mouth too many times not to know a sampling of her taste was what he really needed.

"Thanks. It's just right for me. Not too big and not too small."

It was then that Drey noticed she hadn't grabbed a beer for herself. "You aren't drinking anything?"

She shook her head. "No, I don't drink much."

He licked his lips, aware more than ever of her femininity. And just to think seeing her without a lab coat and wearing regular clothes could have this sort of effect. "So, what else don't you do, Charlie?" There, he figured calling her by the name she disliked would get her dander up and put back up the space he wanted between them. Thinking of tasting her all over wasn't a good thing.

Charlene glared at him and said, "I definitely don't do guys who can't seem to get my name right."

Too late Charlene was aware of how that sounded, which was pretty bad considering she'd never done a guy at all. But Drey didn't know that. The way his brows rose indicated he was evidently intrigued by her statement.

"So," he said, dragging out the single word and looking at her with those deep, dark, slanted eyes that made heat stir in the pit of her stomach. "Do you *do* guys who get your name right?"

Charlene's glare deepened. The last thing she would admit to him was that she didn't do guys at all. Carlos's abrupt departure proved what guys thought of overaged virgins. "That's none of your business."

He placed the beer bottle on the table beside him before taking a step closer to her. The heat she felt earlier intensified into a hot flame. "And what if I were to tell you, Charlene, that I intend to make it my business?"

Charlene swallowed. He had taken that step with such confidence and style that if she didn't know herself as well as she did, she would be tempted to believe him, especially with the way he said her name whenever he did get it right. She hadn't realized just how close he was standing until she tilted her head and met his gaze, trying to ignore the strong, masculine shoulders the top of her head barely hit. "If you were to tell me that, Drey, then I would warn you that you would do better sticking to solving your cases since you have a better chance there," she said, not wavering when she looked into his eyes.

A smile touched his lips and she knew he didn't intend to heed her warning. "Are you saying that I don't have a chance with you?" he asked.

She rolled her eyes. She'd had enough of his game playing. "Do you honestly think I'm gullible enough to believe that you even want one?"

She gasped when suddenly she was pulled into his strong arms and her body was pressed against his hard, solid frame. She thought she would melt right then and there when his eyes bored down at her. Why did he always manage to get such a strong reaction from her?

"There's nothing gullible about it, Charlene," he said, leaning down just inches from her lips. "It's what most people call sexual attraction. We got it. We've had it from the first. Now the big question is, what are we going to do about it?"

"Nothing." She whispered the word from lips that suddenly felt dry.

"I disagree," he said, smiling confidently with a challenging glint in his eyes.

And then his mouth swooped down on hers, snatching her next breath and replacing it with a demanding, hot mouth. She heard herself moan and tried not to return his kiss but found herself doing so anyway. The moment his tongue touched hers, she could swear her panties got wet. And she was certain that the room was moving. His kiss, intense and deep, was leading her down a road she didn't know. All she knew was that he was taking her mouth with an expertise that had her following, no matter where he led.

Of their own accord she felt her arms wrap around his neck. Lifting her arms caused the tips of her breasts to press deep into his chest. It was as if the material of his T-shirt served as no barrier at all and for all her breasts cared, she was touching bare skin. The touch inflamed her nipples and sent a heated, electrifying charge all the way to the juncture of her thighs. She didn't want to think about that. In fact, she didn't want to think at all. She didn't. She let his mouth have its way, while hers did the same.

Drey deepened the kiss thinking it had been long in coming and was bound to happen sooner or later. He was grateful it was now. He had so much drama going on in his life, disappointments and confusion about a lot of things concerning his birth. But he wasn't confused about this, the way his mouth had latched on to Charlene's, or the enjoyment he was getting from tasting her this way. In his book, she tasted pretty damn good. Too good. Her mouth was a temptation he'd better walk away from here and now. But he didn't want to stop just yet.

The backfiring of a car in the distance took the choice out of his hands. With the sound came the return of his senses, but not before he let his tongue swipe across her lips for one final taste. He smiled. She looked as if she was shocked, not by the kiss but at its intensity. What he felt was resentment—toward whoever owned the damn vehicle that had interrupted them.

"I think you should go now, Drey."

He sighed, not wanting to go but knowing she was right. If he stayed, the next move was to get them both naked. "All right."

To get some sort of normalcy back between them, where he could take his mind off their kiss, he said, "Are you sure you know how to use the kit?"

She nodded. "Yes, I'm sure."

He lifted a brow, surprised she hadn't given him some smart comeback. "Okay, then. I'll check with you tomorrow."

He turned and walked toward the door thinking this was the most excitement his libido had endured in a long time. Over the past year he had been too busy for a social life and Charlene just proved there were advantages to mixing business with pleasure at times.

He stopped when he got to the door and glanced back over at her. She was standing in the same spot staring at him. Just so she would know, he told her what he was thinking. What he had suddenly made up his mind about. "That wasn't the last kiss we'll share, Charlene."

He saw her eyes narrow. "Yes, it was."

He gave her an easy smile. "No, it wasn't. In fact I won't be totally satisfied until I've gotten the chance to taste you all over."

And then he opened the door and left.

Chapter 3

Charlene held the phone tight in her hand as she let the caller on the other end have her say. This was certainly not turning out to be a good day. She had awakened that morning in a bad mood after a sleepless night, not having been able even to close her eyes without memories of Drey's kiss intruding. What on earth had enticed her to go that far with him? And then his final comment before leaving…"I won't be totally satisfied until I've gotten the chance to taste you all over." Sensual shivers shot up her spine whenever she thought about it.

The irritated voice pulled her back to the conversation. Marsha Crenshaw was an attorney from the district attorney's office inquiring about a body whose autopsy should have been completed that morning. It was on Nate's list to do, but for some reason he was running behind schedule. In fact, Charlene had only seen him once that day and he'd seemed somewhat agitated about something.

"I'm sure the report will be finished by the end of the day, Marsha. If not, I'll have Nate give you a call." Charlene quickly hung up thinking the woman was getting pushier every time they talked. Rumor had it that she had lost so many cases that the particular one she was now working on was considered a must-win for her.

With Marsha off the phone and everyone out to lunch, Charlene leaned back in her chair to grab a quiet moment. Once again her thoughts drifted to what had happened last night between her and Drey. She would be the first to admit that the kiss had come as a surprise. She certainly hadn't expected it, nor had she done anything to provoke it. What she had done was give him a smart comeback after he'd said that he intended to make it his business to know whether or not she did guys who got her name right. Things had gotten crazy from there and eventually led to a kiss she couldn't forget.

Something else she couldn't forget was agreeing to make an indention of that key. She had gotten busy earlier and it had slipped her mind. Thinking this would be a good time to do it since Nate was at lunch, she opened the drawer to her desk where she kept her purse. A few minutes later with the wax kit Drey had given her last night she entered the autopsy room where the records were located. She opened the huge file drawer and pulled out a folder with Joe Dennis's name on it and was surprised the key was not in a plastic bag inside the folder. Wondering why, she began reading Dennis's chart.

"What in the world…"

She blinked, certain she wasn't reading the chart

correctly. Nate's report, the one that had been released to the police earlier that day, indicated Joe Dennis had died of a heart attack. The report contained no mention of the trauma to the head or the key that was found in his stomach. And speaking of the key, where was it? she asked herself as she quickly flipped through the chart. And why would Nate release a report that didn't come close to the truth?

"Is there anything in particular you're looking for, Charlene?"

Charlene almost jumped at the sound of Nate's voice, then breathed in deeply. She hadn't expected him to return from lunch so soon. She glanced over at him and noticed he was looking at her rather funny. His smile, she noted, didn't quite reach his eyes. He had caught her snooping in the file drawer containing the cases he had worked and he was probably wondering whose file she had. She saw no reason not to tell him since she was curious as to why he had falsified the information on Dennis's autopsy report.

She cleared her throat. "I was reading your final report on Joe Dennis," she said, placing the report back in the cabinet drawer and then closing and relocking it. She glanced up and saw a frown settle on his features.

"Why would you concern yourself with Joe Dennis's autopsy?"

She heard the tenseness in his voice. She also heard a hardness that had never been there before, except for that one time she had overheard him arguing with some man.

"Just curious," she said, refusing to let him know about Drey's request. He'd seen Drey around but had probably assumed he was dropping by to see her for personal reasons.

"And you were curious because..." he prompted.

She met his gaze. "Because I saw the body, Nate, and I know Joe Dennis didn't die of a heart attack. There was trauma to—"

"There was no trauma," he all but snapped. "Are you questioning my findings?"

Yes, I am, Charlene thought. She *was* questioning his findings because he knew as well as she did that they were wrong. "All I know, Nate, is what I saw. Someone had hit Dennis over the head."

"You are mistaken, Charlene, and that's the end of it," he said with a finality in his tone, while coming close to raising his voice. "And I would appreciate it if you never go checking behind me again."

"I wasn't doing that, Nate."

"Weren't you?"

Charlene really didn't know what to say. All she knew, all she was definitely sure about was that the report Nate had issued to the police was wrong. Why would he do such a thing? Why was he trying to convince her it was right when she knew what she saw? And what about the key that had been taken out of the man's stomach? There was no mention of it. She had a funny feeling about this and the intense way Nate was looking at her wasn't helping. Still, she wasn't dissuaded by his words. She knew what she saw and she intended to get to the bottom of it.

"Great," she muttered as she headed out of the room. "I guess I was mistaken." But she didn't mean it. She needed to talk to Drey right away.

"Charlene."

She stopped and turned to Nate before reaching the door. "Yes?"

"I think you should take some time off. In fact I strongly suggest that you do. You need time to clear your head since you're imagining things."

Charlene held back from telling him all the things that concerned her. She tilted her head and studied him and suddenly felt uneasy. There was a reason he wanted her gone for a while and they both knew it had nothing to do with her imagination.

"And it will be time off with pay," he said, as if that meant something.

It was an effort not to tell him just what he could do with the time off with pay, but she bit her tongue to stop from doing so. Instead she walked out of the room.

A few minutes later after removing the items from her desk that she wanted to take with her she paused before entering Nate's office when she saw he was on the phone. She couldn't help but notice how quickly he ended the call when he saw her.

"Yes, Charlene?"

"I transferred my reports to Miller to work while I'm gone just in case someone needs a follow-up."

"Okay."

She inhaled deeply, then said, "What's going on, Nate? Why are you—"

"I don't want anything about Joe Dennis to go any further. You're wrong in what you thought you saw," he said, cutting in.

Forcing a smile, she said, "Fine. I'll see you in two weeks."

"Make it three and you might want to take the opportunity to go visit your parents while you have the time."

Charlene frowned. Why was he suggesting that she leave town? "That sounds like a good idea, Nate. I'll see you when I get back."

As soon as possible, she needed to talk to Drey.

Drey studied the man who was standing at the window staring out as if he was in deep thought. Drey recalled just what he knew about Malcolm Braddock, other than his most recent discovery that the man was his half brother...something Malcolm didn't know.

Malcolm assumed like his other two siblings—Tyson and Shondra—that Drey had been nothing more to their father than a mentee, someone Harmon Braddock had taken an interest in. They had no idea that their father had had an affair with his mother thirty-three years ago. It was the year before Malcolm had been born.

Although it had never bothered him before, now Drey felt a sense of loss that while he had gotten to know Harmon over the years, he hadn't been given the chance to form any sort of relationship with his siblings. He inhaled deeply thinking there was still a lot of information his mother hadn't told him. After she had dropped the bomb on him a few days ago regarding his true relationship with Harmon, he had left her office both confused and angry. He had deliberately avoided talking to her since that day, but he knew he could no longer avoid her. His questions needed answering. He had a case to solve and it was an investigation that had gone from business to personal. He was anxious to get that call from Charlene about that key.

Charlene.

His thoughts automatically shifted away from Malcolm to her, especially the kiss they had shared last night. He felt a tightening in his groin just thinking about it. Hell, he had barely gotten any sleep last night for thinking about it, replaying every aspect of it in his mind and finally drifting off to sleep with the taste of her still very much a part of his palate. It still *was*. The donut and coffee he'd consumed for breakfast hadn't erased it.

And then there was the way she had felt in his arms, the way her body had automatically adjusted against his, raising his desire to a level it hadn't been at in a while. Because of his workload, he hadn't had time to spend with a woman, and last night Charlene had reminded him just how long it had been. A year, he had determined, was too long to go without female companionship, namely a good, hard roll in the hay.

He decided to get his mind off Charlene and back on Malcolm. He was still silently standing at his office window, evidently trying to make sense of this entire investigation and probably asking himself who would want his father dead.

Drey leaned back in his chair thinking that from the time he'd come to know Malcolm he'd always thought of him as a likeable guy. Drey was also aware of the rift that had existed between Malcolm and Harmon for years, namely because Malcolm thought that Harmon had "sold out" to play the political game. That was something Malcolm could not tolerate because of his ingrained sense of right and wrong. The man was extremely smart and in a lot of ways he reminded Drey of Harmon in that Malcolm was headstrong, he liked to debate and was passionate about his beliefs.

Something else that Malcolm seemed passionate about was the woman he was engaged to marry, Gloria Kingsley. Gloria had been Harmon's executive assistant. Drey knew that Gloria had been instrumental in getting Malcolm to assume a leadership role in the Braddock family as well as to run for his father's now-vacant seat in Congress.

The special election was to be held at the end of the month, and recent polls showed Malcolm was ahead of his opponent, Clint Hardy, who was running a negative campaign. With the election so close at hand, as well as the investigation into his father's death, Malcolm pretty much had his hands full. No wonder he was standing at the window staring out, and had been that way since Drey had arrived almost ten minutes ago.

However, no matter the outcome of the election or the investigation, the one thing Drey knew for certain was that Malcolm would be marrying Gloria next month on Christmas Day.

As if on cue, Malcolm turned his head and looked at him, meeting his gaze. Drey wondered if there was anything—his facial bone structure, his strong chin or full cheekbones that would give his secret away and make it obvious to Malcolm that they shared the same blood. Drey knew there was not. Other than his skin coloring and full lips, most of his features were Asian.

"So, you think this key that was taken out of Dennis is connected to Dad's death?" Malcolm asked, coming to sit back down at his desk.

"I would have to say yes since not too many people make a habit of going around swallowing keys."

Malcolm nodded, then leaned back in his chair and made a steeple with his fingers. "I was standing over there trying to recall just when Dennis started working for Dad and if in the past I've ever had a reason to question his loyalty. But then it's not like Dad and I were close over the last few years for me to get to know any of his associates or employees." A smile touched his lips when he added, "Other than Gloria. She used to be quite a sticky thorn in my side."

Drey raised a brow. "How so?"

"As his executive assistant, she thought my old man walked on water, refused to see his faults like I did. And she resented me for walking away from my father and my family."

"Why did you?"

If Malcolm thought the question odd coming from a person who had no connection to the family, who was merely someone that he and his siblings had hired to investigate their father's death, he gave no indication of it. Instead he said, "Despite my privileged upbring-ing, I've always been drawn to those in need and al-ways wanted to help those less fortunate. A few years ago a bill came across my father's desk that would have helped a lot of needy families—a bill that my dad him-self had once championed. I couldn't take any more of him not practicing what he preached."

"So you walked away from the family."

"Yes. Although I kept in touch with my mother and siblings, I couldn't find it in my heart to forgive Dad for what he did by turning his back on so many who needed him to make a difference. I loved him, but I just couldn't accept the political behavior my father was practicing. In my eyes he was becoming involved in the dirty side of politics and I couldn't turn my head and pretend he wasn't."

"What about Tyson and Shondra? Did they break their relationship with your father as well?" Drey asked, thinking that the Harmon Braddock whom Malcolm had just described was not the one he had known.

"Not as clean as I did. And unable to deal with the tension between me and Dad, they threw themselves into their careers."

Drey nodded. "So you and the congressman were not on good terms when he died?"

Malcolm held his gaze. "No, and if your next question is going to ask me if I had anything to do with the accident—"

"No, I wasn't going to ask you that, Malcolm. That hadn't crossed my mind. I was at the funeral, remember? I saw how badly you took the congressman's death. The two of you may have had your differences, but you loved your father."

Malcolm didn't say anything for a moment, and then, "Yes, I did."

Before Drey could say anything else, his cell phone rang and he stood to retrieve it from his pocket and flipped it open. "Excuse me," he said to Malcolm before glancing down at his phone. He was surprised to see his caller was Charlene. He hadn't expected to hear from her until later that day. "This is Drey. What do you have for me?"

"Trouble. Can we meet somewhere and talk?"

Chapter 4

Drey walked into the coffee shop and glanced around, then sighed with relief when he saw Charlene. She had refused to go into any details over the phone, but he had heard the nervousness in her voice.

As he headed toward her table in the back of the restaurant, he knew she hadn't seen him yet, which gave him the chance to study her. Looking every bit of eighteen instead of twenty-seven, she wore dark brown slacks and a beige cotton blouse. He was still finding it odd seeing her without her lab coat, although he was enjoying doing so.

His face went back to hers and he saw she was wearing very little makeup. She didn't need any either. Something nagged inside him, reminding him of their kiss and causing sensations to flow through him. He frowned. Now was not the time to remember how she had felt in his arms or how she had tasted in his mouth. He was in the throes of an investigation that seemed to be getting more complicated by the second and the last thing he needed was thoughts of getting Charlene Anderson in his bed.

He wasn't surprised that he wanted to take her to bed. After all, he was a hot-blooded male who enjoyed sex as much as the next guy. Unlike most guys, though, he wasn't getting any on a regular basis and seeing Charlene was reminding him of that fact.

As if she sensed his presence, she tilted her head in his direction and their gazes met. While lust was probably glinting in his eyes, he saw something altogether different in hers. There was anxiousness there, a tenseness that immediately pushed any thoughts of sex from his mind...for the time being. Instead he couldn't help but wonder what had her so worried.

"Charlie?" he said, sliding into the seat beside her. And he knew whatever was bothering her was massive because for the first time she didn't glare at him for the use of his play name for her. "What's wrong? What kind of trouble were you alluding to earlier?"

She took a sip of her coffee before putting her cup down and giving him her complete attention, turning those intense, beautiful eyes on him. "Nate caught me going through Dennis's file." She paused a second before asking, "Are you aware what Nate stated in the report he released to the police earlier today?"

When he couldn't stop drowning in the allure of her eyes quickly enough to respond, she said, "It said Joe Dennis's death was the result of a heart attack."

That got his absolute attention. "What!"

"You heard me," she said tersely.

He frowned. "Why would he lie about such a thing?"

She shook her head. "I have no idea. I saw Joe Dennis's body, Drey. I saw the bruises and I saw the key. Now the key is nowhere to be found."

Drey didn't say anything but it was clear from what Charlene was saying that a cover-up of some sort was going on. Why had Charlene's boss lied about the cause of Joe Dennis's death?

Drey looked at Charlene. He saw the nervous way she lifted her cup to her lips to take a sip of her coffee. There was more. He felt it. "What did he say when you questioned him about it?" he asked. There was no need to ask if she had questioned him because he knew that she had. It would go against her grain not to do so.

She met his gaze again. "He denied it. He said I'd made a mistake about what I thought was the reason Dennis died. Then he suggested that I take time off to clear my head. Three weeks. And he went on to suggest that I leave town."

She paused for a moment and then added, "Something is going on, Drey, something that I don't like. Nate was acting strange. Creepy. It's like he was warning me off, making veiled threats, alluding that disappearing for a while would be in my best interest. I think we should go to the police."

"No," he said, squashing that idea quickly. "You're right, something is going on, but I don't think going to the police is the answer, especially when they are the ones backing up a faulty report. It can't help but make you wonder if perhaps they are somehow involved."

He saw the way Charlene was looking at him and knew he had gotten her to thinking the way he was doing now. Until they uncovered more information they were on their own. Then another thought entered his mind regarding the veiled threats her boss had made. If there had been foul play in Joe Dennis's death, more than likely that meant Congressman Braddock's death was no accident either. And if someone was out for more blood as a way to keep things quiet, Charlene could very well get caught in the crossfire and he refused to let that happen.

"Are you planning to take your boss up on his offer and leave town?" he asked, taking a sip of the ice-cold water a waitress had placed in front of him.

"No."

He hadn't thought so. "Disappearing for a while might not be such a bad idea, Charlene."

He watched as a frown formed around her lips. They were lips he had tasted last night and would love sampling again today. "What good will disappearing do?" she asked.

He had a quick answer for her. "It might keep you alive. Think about it. Without evidence we don't have proof of anything and who's going to take your word over your boss's? And if there is a cover-up, then whoever is behind it got to your boss somehow, and there's a possibility the police are somehow connected."

She shook her head. "What you're saying doesn't make sense. Why would anyone be interested in what happened to Joe Dennis and why go to that extreme with me, Drey? If there's more to this mystery I would appreciate hearing it."

He knew that was fair enough since, thanks to him, she might have unknowingly placed her life in danger. After the waitress came to take his drink order, he said, "Joe Dennis was the personal driver of Congressman

Harmon Braddock. As you know, the congressman was killed in an auto accident a few months ago. I was hoping that Dennis could shed some light as to why the congressman was driving his own car that night instead of Dennis and—"

"Wait! Hold up. Back up," Charlene said, using her hand to give him a time-out signal. "Are you saying what I think you're saying?"

"Yes. I have reason to believe the congressman's death was intentional."

Charlene didn't know what to say. Like everyone else in Houston, she had read about the congressman's car accident but hadn't had a reason to think much about it. "And is that what you're investigating?"

"Yes. I was hired by his family. When they approached me I was doubtful that I would find anything, but after Joe Dennis died mysteriously I really got suspicious. And now…"

She nodded and waited until the waitress had placed his beer in front of him before saying, "But it's hard for me to believe that Nate could be involved. He's a family man with a wife and children."

"Yes, but what if the person behind all this is using blackmail or threats? Nate warned you to disappear and you would be wise to heed his warning."

Charlene nibbled on her bottom lip. A part of her knew Drey was probably right, but another part didn't want to disappear. She wanted to go to work, continue her life as she knew it. Besides, where would she go? She could go visit her mother and her new husband in Florida, but she preferred not to. And her father's place in Detroit with his wife of three years was a definite no-no since she and Monica could only tolerate each other in small doses.

"Okay, I'm convinced you might be right about me getting lost for a while," she finally said. "Especially now that I remember the argument Nate was having with that man."

Drey frowned as he glanced over at her. "What argument?"

She took another sip of her coffee before answering. "A few days ago. In fact it was the same day I discovered the key. Nate thought I had already left for the day, but I was in the autopsy room snooping around. When I came out I heard Nate and another man arguing. They were practically yelling at each other."

"Do you know what about?"

"No. I didn't stick around long enough to find out. However, at the time I thought it rather strange for Nate to be arguing with anyone since he has a tendency not to get upset about anything. He's always said it's not good to get stressed."

"Did he act upset with you today when he discovered you going through Dennis's chart?"

Charlene sighed deeply as she remembered her and Nate's conversation. "Not as much upset as he was nervous, like he hated me finding out the truth. He was trying so hard to convince me that I was wrong. It was rather creepy seeing him that way."

Drey didn't say anything as he studied her. Yes, her disappearing for a while was for the best considering everything she had told him. If someone was out for more blood, he didn't want it to be Charlene's. The thought of anything happening to her didn't sit too well with him and he wasn't about to take any chances.

He leaned back in his chair. "How long will it take you to pack?"

She lifted her head from studying the contents of her coffee cup and met his gaze. "Am I supposed to be going somewhere?"

"Yes."

She arched a brow. "Where?"

"My place. For your safety, I think it's best for you to move in with me for a while."

Chapter 5

Charlene blinked. "Excuse me?"

Drey knew she had heard him but figured what he'd said deserved repeating so there wouldn't be any mis-understandings. "I said I think it would be for the best if you were to move in with me for a while."

She frowned, actually glared at him. "Thanks, but no, thanks. I have my own place."

He leaned back in his chair and before taking an-other swig of beer he said, "It's not safe to disappear there, Charlie."

She gave him a disapproving glare. "The name is Charlene and I see no reason I can't stay put."

"I can name several reasons and none of them is pretty. In fact all of them are rather dangerous, to say the least. If Nate has mentioned to anyone that you know anything, they'll figure it's best for you to be-come a casualty."

The thought of that happening made her skin crawl. "But why would he do that?"

"For the same reason he gave you a clear warning, which he really didn't have to do. Whatever he's into, he's in it over his head and trying not to get you involved. Think about it, Charlie. We're not talking about the cover-up of just anyone's murder. We're talking about the cover-up of the murder of a well-known politician, a congressman." *My biological father,* he didn't add as he looked down at his drink.

His true relationship to Harmon Braddock was still rather new to him and he still had a number of questions he wanted answered. The only person who could do that was his mother. He had tried calling her that morning and hadn't been able to get a hold of her. He knew she was deliberately avoiding him, trying to evade his questions.

"Did you know him?"

Drey glanced back at Charlene when her question invaded his thoughts. "Who?"

"Congressman Braddock."

Drey didn't say anything at first, tempted to tell her just how well he knew him, but instead said, "Yes, for years he had been my mentor."

"Why?"

He lifted a brow. "Why what?"

"How did you get a U.S. congressman to be your mentor?"

Drey sighed. That was a good question, one he hadn't thought of before. He couldn't help wondering if anyone else was curious about that same thing. The Braddock siblings perhaps? They had known of his relationship to their father, but none of them had ever asked why and how it had come about.

A part of him would never forget that day right after his father had died and he'd been walking home from school when suddenly a big black shiny car had pulled up beside him and come to a stop. Suddenly the back passenger door opened and a man stepped out. It was a man whom he had never seen before, but the man knew him because he had called him by name. That was the day Harmon Braddock had become a part of his life. Drey could truly say that although Harmon had never claimed him publicly as his son, he had done enough for him behind the scenes to engrave his presence and existence into Drey's life. And no matter what, he owed it to the man who was his biological father to bring to justice anyone responsible for his death. Just as he felt he owed it to Charlene to keep her safe.

"Drey?"

Drey realized he hadn't answered Charlene's question. "He had been a family friend," he said simply, hoping she didn't want any more details than that.

"It must be hard on you to investigate his death, knowing how close the two of you were."

"Yes, it's hard. Just like it's hard for me to turn my back on the fact that your life might now be in danger because of me."

"It's not."

"You don't know that for certain. Whoever is responsible for the congressman's death didn't hesitate to kill Joe Dennis, probably because they thought he knew too much. Evidently he did to have put a key in his stomach. I wish there is a way we can get our hands on it. Are you sure your boss had taken it out of Dennis's file already?"

"I didn't see it. He might have passed it on to an interested party or it might be in Nate's office somewhere. He has a habit of getting busy and leaving stuff around at times. That's how I came across the key in the first place."

Drey nodded, very much aware she had not yet agreed to move in with him until his investigation has been resolved. Of course she could very well move in with family or friends, but for some reason he felt he might need her around if he had additional questions about what she'd seen in her boss's original report.

"I can't force you to move in with me, Charlene," he decided to say to bring the matter up once again.

She gave a little laugh, one that he found rather sexy. So sexy he could feel the tightening of his abdominal muscles. "I'm glad you know that, Drey."

His mouth quirked. So she wanted to play hard. He would show her just how hard he could make things. "But I can move in with you." He watched the frown that formed around her lips. Lips he could distinctly remember tasting last night. Lips that he could honestly say he would love sampling again.

"No, you can't."

"Yes, I can, and haven't we been down this road before? I can appoint myself as your bodyguard. If you don't let me stay inside your place, I can always sleep outside in the car just as long as I keep an eye on you. And I hope you'll think twice before calling the police since right now we don't know whose side they're on."

She tilted her chin and he thought it was another sexy

move. "You are so quick to think the worst of them, yet you used to be one of them," she said.

He couldn't help but wonder how she knew he used to be a part of the force, but decided he would find out later after they moved in together. "Because I used to be one of them I know there are good cops and there are bad cops. My father was a good cop. My partner and I were good cops and there are others I can vouch for. But I can't and won't vouch for every one of them, and I don't plan on taking a chance by letting you assume you won't become a target. So I'm going to ask you again. Do you move in with me or do I move in with you?"

"I won't even consider such a thing until we get something straight."

"Like what?"

"Like the threat you made last night."

He had an idea what she was talking about, but he didn't consider those words a threat. He considered them a fact. "And what threat was that?" he asked, feeling an intense thudding of his pulse.

She hesitated, then expounded in a low voice. "The one you made after we kissed. What you planned to do the next time."

"As far as I know there's no law against saying something you intend to make happen eventually. But if it makes you feel better, I promise not to touch you until you're good and ready. It will be your call."

"Then I don't have anything to worry about," she said triumphantly, as if all was well.

"And why do you say that?"

She tilted her head and said in an irritated tone, "Because I've never been that forward with a man."

He shrugged, not the least bothered by her attitude. "You will with me. I'll encourage it."

Charlene snorted. "Encourage what you want, it still won't happen."

He decided to set her straight about a few things so they could move on. "Since the first there has been sexual chemistry between us and we both know it. The reason we bicker back and forth as much as we do is to play it off. All I'm saying, Charlene, is that us being sexually attracted to each other is a fact, just like the fact that your life may be in danger. My main concentration now is to make sure nothing happens to you and to complete my investigation. You have no reason to fear me because I want you. I won't touch you unless you say it's okay and if you're certain you won't be doing that, then there shouldn't be a problem."

He saw the expression on her face and knew she was about to put up yet another fight. She was one stubborn female and at any other time he would have appreciated that quality since he didn't run across many women like her. Most of them, he found, gave in too easily, especially when it came to him.

When time ticked by and she still didn't say anything, he said, "Okay, just don't be surprised when you find me parked outside your house tonight. As of this very minute I become your bodyguard."

Her gaze narrowed. "You can't watch me every minute while investigating the case," she said smartly.

He smiled. "Yes, you're right. I guess I'll just have to drag you everywhere I go."

She pushed her coffee cup aside and threw up her hands. "Fine. I'll move in with you, but I'm not going to like it."

Drey motioned for the waitress to bring him another beer while thinking he probably wouldn't like it a whole hell of a lot either.

A few minutes later Charlene walked into her apartment with Drey following behind. "It'll take me but a minute to pack," she said over her shoulder as she kept moving toward her bedroom. When he didn't say anything she stopped and turned around and was hit with a multitude of sensations, swift and fierce, when she saw him leaning against her closed door staring. "What are you staring at?"

He met her gaze. "You. But more specifically the shape of your backside. I like it."

She crossed her arms over her chest. "Not that I care whether you like it or not, but I prefer you not to think of me as only a sex object."

"I don't. You're smart, intelligent and attractive. You also have a body that I find fascinating. Why were you hiding it behind lab coats?"

"Everyone who works in the coroner's office wears lab coats. At home I dress like any normal person. Until last night you had no reason to see me anywhere other than where I work."

Drey lifted his broad shoulders in a shrug. "You're right, of course," he said smoothly. "Now I'll be seeing you all the time."

"If you're going to have a problem with it, please let me know now. I won't move in with you only to feel uncomfortable being around you," she said firmly.

"I won't have a problem with it and you'll have no reason to feel uncomfortable. I told you where we stood.

However, as a man I find it hard to ignore some things when it comes to a woman, but I'll cope."

Charlene saw the way he was looking at her and wasn't so sure. Her uncertainty blended with apprehension.

"I told you nothing will happen between us until you want it," he tried assuring her. "But I can promise you that when that time comes I will be ready."

His statement caused a deep stirring in her stomach and she fought the sensations, despising her traitorous body for responding to his words, his promise. She sighed deeply. He wouldn't be making such promises if he had any idea just how limited her experience was.

Instead of saying anything else to him she turned and went into her bedroom, closing the door behind her.

Drey watched her departure and shook his head, refusing to give in to the lust that tried overtaking his mind and body whenever he was around Charlene. That wasn't good, especially since she would be moving in with him. Like he'd told her, nothing would happen unless she issued an invitation and with her stubbornness, he couldn't see that happening any time soon, which was fine with him since he needed to get his mind back on the investigation.

That meant he needed to talk with his mother.

Taking his cell phone out of his pocket, he punched in his mother's business number. A few minutes later he hung up after being told she had left work early that day. He tried her cell number but she didn't answer there either. He decided not to leave a message. Maybe he'd make it his business to drop by his mother's home tomorrow so they could continue the discussion they'd started a few days ago. He wanted the whole story about Harmon and he intended to get it. He refused to let his mother evade him any longer.

Flexing his muscles to ease away the frustration he felt, he walked over to the window and glanced out just in time to see a white Maxima slow up when it passed by Charlene's condo. He stood and watched, making sure he wasn't seen. His features hardened. Had Charlene's boss put out the word on her already? The car momentarily came to a stop before moving on.

"I'm through packing."

Charlene's voice got his attention. He turned around and saw the overnight bag she held in her hand. "Am I to assume you were able to fit all your belongings in that?" he asked, pointing at her bag.

"No, of course this isn't everything. I'll come back for the rest at some other time."

"No, you can't."

Before she could gear up to give him the retort that would probably blaze his ears, he asked, "What kind of car does your boss have?"

He could tell his question threw her for a loop.

"What?"

"I asked what kind of car your boss has."

Her brows arched as she considered his question. "A white Maxima. Why?"

Drey glanced toward the window. "He just drove by. It's my guess he needed to see if you heeded his warning or not, so it's a good thing we came in my car."

He looked back at her. "Chances are he was probably concerned as to whether he would have to report to someone what you may or may not know and he was trying to avoid doing that."

He saw the tenseness that filled her eyes and knew it was time for her to realize just what kind of dangerous situation she was in. "I know you don't want to leave here, Charlene, but I hope now you see that until I discover who's behind those deaths that you're not safe staying here."

She jutted out her chin. "But what if you never find those responsible? What if—"

"What if you show a little confidence in my abilities?" he interrupted by saying in a harsh tone. "Now please go back in there and pack like you were supposed to be doing in the first place."

The silence as well as the tension in the room reached a monumental peak. Drey very seldom got angry, but Charlene was trying his patience big time. Between her and his mother he had been encountering more emotions in one week than in all the years since he was a teenager and his father had died.

Her dark eyes blazed at him. "Fine. I'll do as you've requested."

About time. Instead of saying what he felt or the scorching comment that was on the tip of his tongue, he nodded and then walked back over to the window, fully aware of the moment she left the room.

Chapter 6

Mumbling under her breath, Charlene began throwing things out of the drawers and onto her bed. Drey had a way of using a tone of command even when he assumed that he was speaking nicely. He had a lot to learn to master the use of persuasive language.

Jeez! She couldn't believe this was happening to her. First she was forced to take time off her job and now she was forced to move in with the person responsible for her predicament. She was trying hard to control her anger, but it wasn't working.

The only thing working was the achy feeling in the pit of her stomach at the mere thought of sharing living quarters with Drey. Remembering all the words she had spouted earlier, she felt trapped between a rock and a hard place with no way out. More to the point, she felt as if she would be held hostage. Just the thought that he would have his eyes on her, watching her practically every minute, her every move, didn't sit well with her. For crying out loud, it was the most ridiculous thing she'd ever heard...but at the same time just as he'd said, it was the only way to ensure her safety.

Not liking the very thought of that, she crossed the room to her closet and flung open the door. She didn't want to become indebted to Drey for making her the object of his protection, and at the moment she preferred not to feel she owed him anything.

She went through her clothes, wondering what she should take and what she should leave behind. Certain outfits were a must, but then a few others she felt would send Drey the wrong message and she refused to give the man any more ideas than he already had.

A short while later she had loaded everything she felt she needed into the luggage she had taken from underneath her bed. Suddenly everything inside her tensed and she glanced around to find Drey standing casually in the doorway.

She inhaled sharply, trying not to stare. Today he wore boots, a pair of jeans and a blue chambray shirt. His height made him appear taller and his stance exuded lethal sexuality in a way that was heating up the blood flowing through her veins. Earlier at the café when she had looked up and watched him approach her table in a walk that was sexier than anything she'd ever seen, she had been forced to expel a calming breath. She talked with surefire confidence around him when deep down she knew she'd have to watch her guard or she would be in trouble. The last thing she needed was to live under the same roof with a man who got on her nerves one minute and had the ability to cause havoc with her hormones the next.

"Need help with anything?"

Charlene inhaled deeply, forcing herself to relax, but found doing so rather difficult. His deep voice felt like silk across her skin, caressing her in places she rather not think about. She was beginning to regard him as a risk she should avoid taking. The man had all but stated—and in explicit terms—what he would do to her if given the chance. But she was determined to make sure nothing happened between them, no matter how tempting the thought. "No, thank you, I can handle things myself."

He straightened away from the doorway to move into the room, coming to a stop by the bed. "I'm not so sure that you can. This luggage is a lot bigger than you are."

"I can handle it," she said, zipping up the luggage while struggling to keep calm. Sexual chemistry was becoming a constant between them and she wished it would go away, find someone else to torture.

She reached to pull the luggage off the bed the same time Drey did. Their hands touched and she jerked back as if she had been scorched.

"Drey," she said brusquely. "I told you I could handle it."

"Yes, and I recall saying the luggage was as big as you are and that I would help."

Charlene took a step back away from the bed. "Then by all means, flex your muscles. After all, I'm just a weak woman who can't do anything for herself."

Drey cocked his head and stared at her with a bit of hardness in his eyes. "What you can do is remove that chip off your shoulder, Charlene."

With his statement her anger lost some of its punch. Was she acting as if she had a chip on her shoulder? If so, she had good reason. She gave a breathy yet sarcastic laugh. "How would you like to be in my predicament?" she asked in a flippant tone.

"Frankly, I wouldn't. But I certainly wouldn't bite the hand that's trying to help me every chance I got."

She finger-combed a lock of hair behind her ear and exhaled, putting up a good fight between being defiant and being reasonable. "Look, my day hasn't gone like I had hoped and I'm in a bad mood. Sorry if it seems that I'm taking it out on you, but being forced to leave my home wasn't what I'd counted on when I woke up this morning."

"And I understand and feel somewhat responsible for that. However, our situation is as it is, and to make the most of it I think we need to at least try to work together and not snap at each other at every opportune moment. Don't you agree?"

Grudgingly, she said, "Yes."

"Okay then, I believe this calls for a truce," he said, offering his hand to her.

Charlene paused a moment before accepting his hand. The moment she touched it she knew why she had resisted doing so. Instead of shaking her hand and releasing it, he held on to it, closed his fingers around hers.

"I told you last night that you had pretty hands. What I didn't get the chance to say is that there's something about your hand that I find irresistible."

He turned her hand over and then fingered the lines in the palm, studying them as he did so. She tried to ignore the sensations that raced through her with his touch and was tempted to pull her hand from his as she had done last night.

Moments later, he raised his head and met her gaze. "Do you know anything about Chinese palm reading?"

"No, do you?" She tried not to respond smartly, but it came out that way anyway.

But for once he didn't seem to mind her tone and actually chuckled. "Yes. My mother is half Chinese and as a child I got a chance to visit her family in China for an entire summer. My great-grandmother explained that Chinese palm reading is an ancient art passed down from generation to generation. By reading the lines in a person's hands a skilled palm reader can find out everything there is to know about that person."

"So now you're claiming to be a palm reader, Drey?"

"Somewhat."

He sounded serious and she wasn't sure whether to believe him or not, but she decided to call his bluff. "Okay, what does mine say?"

He closed her hand before releasing it. "I'll make a point to tell you one day."

She lifted a brow, wondering if he'd seen something she should be concerned with, then decided he was probably pulling her leg. "Whatever," she said, rubbing her hands together, trying to rid them of the feel of his touch that seemed to linger and wouldn't go away. "I'm ready to leave if you are."

"Okay."

She then watched as he effortlessly lifted the luggage off the bed, and followed him from her bedroom. When they got to the living room he glanced over at her phone. "You might want to leave a message giving the impression you've left town for a while, just in case anyone is curious enough to check."

Knowing he had a point, she quickly crossed the room and within minutes had done what he had suggested. When she returned to where he stood and glanced up at him, she noticed how his eyes had darkened and were filled with an intensity she had immediately associated with him. *Desire.* And she knew the cause of it. He had watched her walk across the room, checking out her rear end with every step she had taken.

She frowned. "You have a problem," she said, knowing he was aware of what she was talking about.

A wry smile curved his lips. "Some men are leg men, others prefer breasts. Personally, I have a fetish for the hind part." And without waiting for her to comment, he walked off.

Charlene watched him go, thinking since fanny-watching seemed to be fair play, she might as well check out his. *Umm, not bad.* In fact she thought he had a real nice-looking tush.

He stopped when he got to the door and looked over his shoulder at her and gave her a smile that only heightened his sexiness. "Like what you see?"

She could lie and say no, she didn't like it, but decided this was one time she would be honest with him… up to a point. "Possibly."

He chuckled. "Fair enough. And to answer your question from earlier, about what I see in your hands…. One thing I found interesting is the fact you are a very passionate woman."

A passionate woman? Who was he kidding? "If you say so."

"I do and one day I intend to prove it to you."

* * *

His ultimate goal, Drey thought, was to finish the investigation and make it possible for Charlene to return to her home—but not before he had taken her to bed. He glanced over at her, saw the way she avoided looking at him by keeping her eyes focused on the scenery outside the car window, and wondered what she would think of his plans if she knew them, especially the part about him sleeping with her.

He didn't mind letting her know that he wanted her. It would be hard keeping something like that a secret anyway while they lived under the same roof. But she didn't have to know she was at the top of his to-do list. He had given her fair warning, but for some reason she didn't believe him.

He'd even left it up to her as to how she would handle him and the situation. However, for some reason she assumed she could keep sexual urges, tension and good old chemistry at bay by doing nothing and pretending they didn't exist between them. What planet had she been living on most of her life?

Any hot-blooded adult knew the best way to handle red-hot lust was to work the person out of your system and move on, which was something he intended to do. He could handle her bouts of anger just as he would be able to handle whatever degree of desire she had the ability to whip up within him. As he had told her earlier, she was a passionate woman. Not only could he feel it in her hands, but he had tasted it in her kiss and he could even pick it up in her scent. The way he was doing now.

"Tell me about your family, Drey."

Her words cut into his thoughts and he glanced over at her. For reasons unbeknownst to her, his family was the last thing he wanted to talk about. He brought his car to a stop at a traffic light, inclined his head and said, "How about telling me about yours?"

From her expression he could tell she hadn't expected that. It was obvious she preferred not talking about her family, but since she had been the one to bring up the subject, he figured that eventually she would respond.

It took her a while and then she said, "My parents divorced when I was ten. I took their divorce hard until I realized they were happier living apart. Neither of them liked the idea of being single so they remarried quickly, and before you ask, no, not to each other. My mother is into her fourth marriage and Dad is involved with wife number three. I'm the only child they had together, but I have a number of stepsisters and stepbrothers."

"And do you get along with them?"

She shrugged. "Most of the time. But then there have been occasions when they avoid me like I avoid them."

She glanced over at him when he stopped the car to another traffic light. "What about you? Are you an only child?"

He thought about her question and decided to answer it the way he felt best. "Yes. My father was a cop. He died when I was in my teens. My mom is still alive and in good health."

"How did your dad die?"

"In the line of duty," he said, remembering that day so clearly in his mind.

"Sorry."

"So was I," he said automatically, noticing how his voice had lowered, how he still felt pain after all these years. And then he added, "We were close." After saying those words he wondered why he had told her that.

His relationship with his father had never been up for discussion with anyone other than his mother.

"Is that why you became a policeman?"

"Pretty much," he said evenly, knowing that *had* been the reason. "Dad was a good cop and I wanted to be like him. I was on the streets a few years before I decided I didn't want to put up with all the beauracacy that went along with it."

"So you became a private investigator instead?"

"Yes." He remembered how much Harmon had played into that decision and the support he had given him. "And I've never regretted it, although the first few years were hard. Clients were scarce." He chuckled. "And it took me forever to solve my first case."

"Tell me about it."

Drey glanced over at her. She seemed truly interested and wasn't just asking for conversation's sake. He didn't say anything for several long moments and then he began talking and was surprised how easy it was to open up to her. He remembered the case as if it were yesterday when Sharon Mosley had shown up at his office and hired him to get the goods on her cheating husband. It hadn't been the type of case he'd wanted starting out, but it had eventually paid the bills. When it had come to adultery, Kent Mosley had covered his tracks well, refusing to let his wife of thirty-something years get anything on him that could entice her to take him to the cleaner's. His luck finally ran out when Drey captured on film the man making out with the wife of one of his business associates.

Over the next few minutes Drey talked and Charlene listened; she even asked him a few questions every now and then. He wasn't surprised by her intelligence or how quick she was in figuring out things. Pretty soon they were pulling back into the parking lot of the café where they had left her car.

"You can follow me back to my place. It's not far from here," he said, bringing his car to a stop next to hers.

"Okay," she said, unsnapping her seat belt and turning to open the door.

Drey glanced in his rearview mirror, something he'd done several times to make sure they hadn't been followed. He glanced back at her in time to see one smooth thigh when she descended from the vehicle. And again when she got into her car. His mouth hardened. That hadn't been what his already horny body needed to see.

He only began driving away when he was certain she was following him.

It was then that he decided to try contacting his mother again. Pulling his cell from off his belt, he flipped it open to punch in his mother's number only to be met with the answering machine again. This time he left a message.

"Mom, this is Drey. We need to talk. I would appreciate if you'd call me later."

He hung up the line wondering how soon she would contact him and whether he was ready to hear what else she had to say.

Charlene was quiet as she listened to the soft jazz sound on the radio while following behind Drey. She couldn't help wondering what she had gotten herself into. She knew moving in with him on a temporary basis was the smart thing to do, but that didn't mean she had to like it.

He had surprised her when he had opened up and told her about the first case he had taken on as a private investigator. She had found it interesting, but more than anything she had admired his diligence in solving the case. She figured getting him to talk would ease some of the heated tension between them. It had for a while, but she had felt his eyes watching her every movement when she had gotten out of his car. It was if he'd been undressing her with his gaze. How in the world would they manage to live under the same roof? She had never felt this desired by a man in her entire life.

Of course she knew it was a passing fancy for Drey. She couldn't allow herself to get caught up in what was probably one of his testosterone moments.

She followed his car into a gated community and as she pulled in directly behind him, she glanced around at the large town houses that made her place look like a dollhouse.

A smile touched her lips. Drey's first case might have been the pits, but evidently he had recovered nicely. She nearly jumped when her cell phone went off in her purse and she eased it out and flipped it open after seeing the caller was her mother. "Yes, Mom?"

"I called your house and there's a message on your phone indicating you're out of town. You didn't mention coming to Florida, so does that mean you're visiting your father?"

Charlene rolled her eyes. Another issue she had with her parents was their constant competitive nature where she was concerned. Her mother did not like her father's third wife and wanted to make sure Charlene didn't like her either. "No, Mom, I'm not visiting Dad. I just need to get away for a while."

"Why?" her mother demanded, as if she had every right to know.

"Things are crazy at work," she said truthfully. "So I thought I'd take a few days off, go somewhere and enjoy myself." *Enjoy herself?* She had to be kidding. She watched as Drey parked his car and got out, saw how nicely his jeans covered his tush and knew she *was* kidding. Inexplicably, a heated sensation flowed through her.

"Better do it now before you stress yourself out," her mother said. "Stress isn't good. That's why I stopped working."

Charlene frowned. She'd never known her mother to work outside the home. At fifty, Nina was still a beautiful woman and would be a trophy on any man's arms. When Charlene saw that Drey had turned and was waiting for her to get out of the car, she quickly said, "Okay, Mom, I need to go. Someone is waiting for me."

"It's a man, right? Tell me that you got away with a man."

Charlene's mouth tightened. Why was her mother so obsessed with her finding a man? "Yes, Mom, I'm spending some time with a man," she said, giving in to what she knew her mother wanted to hear. "I'll touch base with you when I return."

"You haven't said where you are."

No, intentionally, she hadn't. Charlene glanced around and noticed the name of the community and saw the huge water fountain close by as well as the well-tended landscaped yard. "It's called Kindle Wood Lakes and it's near the water." Okay, so she was stretching the truth a little bit.

"Sounds like a real nice resort. Have fun and don't make any babies until after the wedding."

"Mom!"

"Don't Mom me since I was young once. Besides, I'd like to have a son-in-law while I'm young enough to appreciate him."

Yes, Charlene thought, she knew that, had accepted it and most of the time just plain ignored it. "Goodbye, Mom."

"Goodbye, sweetheart."

Drey leaned back against his car and watched Charlene get out of hers with a frown on her face. He had seen her cell phone plastered to her ear and had wondered who she was talking to. Whomever it was evidently had gotten her a little annoyed. Had her boss tried contacting her? His protective instinct automatically kicked in, and when she reached his side he asked, "Are you okay?"

She glanced around, looking everywhere else but at him when she said, "Yes, I'm fine. I just finished talking to my mother."

He knew damned good and well he shouldn't care one iota about her relationship with her mother but heard himself remarking anyway, "You were frowning."

She looked at him. "I usually do whenever I talk to either of my parents. Sometimes they forget our agreement."

"Which is?"

He would not have been surprised if she had told him it was none of his business, because truly it wasn't. So she sort of stunned him when she answered, "Considering their numerous marriages, they promised me on my twenty-first birthday that they would stay out of my business if I stayed out of theirs. Staying out of theirs is a piece of cake, but they still find it a challenge to stay out of mine. Especially Mom. She's constantly reminding me that my biological clock is ticking and wants me to do something about it."

Drey laughed. "So in other words, she wants grandchildren." He'd heard the same request a number of times from his own mother.

"She wants me to find a husband before I start populating the earth and gets quite annoyed with me by my lack of interest."

Lack of interest? He couldn't help but remember she had gotten quite annoyed with him last night when he'd asked why she didn't have a date.

"My mother thinks we're having an affair."

"Excuse me?" Staring down at her, he could clearly see the red highlights in her hair, although she was wearing her hair pinned up in a knot on her head. He preferred seeing it down the way she'd worn it last night.

"She called my apartment and got my message about me going out of town. I couldn't tell her the truth, so I fabricated a story for her that included a trip away for a few days, and of course she assumed it was with a man."

"And she's okay with that?"

"Overjoyed, actually. Like I said earlier, she thinks my biological clock is ticking."

He watched as she glanced around again. "Nice community. Have you lived here long?" she asked.

"A couple of years." He pushed away from his car. "Are you ready to go in? I can come back for your stuff later."

He then smiled when he saw the look of apprehension on her face. "Will it make you feel better if I promise not to jump your bones as soon as I get you over the threshold?"

She narrowed her gaze. "I'm glad one of us finds all of this amusing."

Drey held up both hands in a defensive pose. "Hey, don't get uptight on me. I don't find the thought of your life being in danger amusing. What I do find amusing is your reaction to the idea of living with me for a while. I take it you've never shared quarters with a man."

"Of course not!"

"Any reason why?"

She didn't answer immediately, so he figured she was thinking about his question. "I'm nitpicky."

"So am I, but I have a feeling we'll get along just nicely."

She opened her mouth as if to say something, then quickly closed it, leaving him wondering just what was on her mind. "Get it out, Charlie. Say whatever you want."

Her eyes narrowed at him and then she asked, "Just in case one of your lady friends shows up and wonders who I am, what should I tell them?"

"I doubt that will happen, but if it does the simple thing is to tell them you're my girl."

She shook her head. "No way would I lie like that."

"Then if it will make you feel better, tell them you're my long lost sister, although I doubt they'll believe you."

Determined to end this topic of conversation before he would be forced to tell her that she would be wearing the title of "Drey's lover" before long, he began moving toward his front door. She walked at a leisurely pace next to him and for the first time in a long while he liked the thought of a woman by his side.

Another thought that flashed through his mind was that Charlene was used to handling dead bodies. There was nothing dead about him and soon enough she would discover how it was to handle a living, breathing. hot-blooded man.

going next to him and now that her gaze has long while see them the moment she would be looking at the Analyzed bringing the haunt when she would hide said where there was beauty standard dead body entire a dull aboration and reverse accomplished would the eye remain to the middle personal of to be multiple into the small frame.

Chapter 7

Charlene froze the moment she stepped over the threshold in Drey's home, finding his taste in furniture and decorating utterly exquisite. Her gaze was immediately drawn to the numerous selections of Asian artwork he had on his walls. Even from a distance she found them intriguingly unusual and definitely exotic.

She crossed the room, immediately smitten with one painting in particular. She couldn't help but study the richness of the colors the artist had used as well as the selection of a mahogany-trimmed leather frame. It was a painting of a beautiful Asian woman, drenched in a multicolored robe as she walked through a flower garden with a shimmering pond in the background. The expression on the woman's face was both exotic and erotic.

"I see you like this one," she heard Drey say, coming up behind her. She tensed, immediately feeling his heat, which made her totally aware of his masculinity. Those thoughts made her even more determined to keep a tight rein on her control as well as her common senses while around him.

"Yes, it's different, although I'm surprised to find such a painting in your living room. It seems more fitted for the bedroom."

Drey chuckled. "Yeah, probably, but I prefer to have it out here."

"She's beautiful."

"Thanks. When I see her I'll tell her you said that."

Charlene spun around, her eyebrows arched. "You know her?"

"Yes. I know her. That's my mother."

Charlene blinked before turning back at the picture, amazed. "Your mother?"

Drey smiled. "Yes. She was only twenty-three when it was painted and she gave it to my father as a wedding gift." He didn't say anything for a while, then added, "I recall it was one of Dad's most prized possessions."

Charlene could clearly see why. As she'd said earlier, the woman was beautiful. Although he had told her about his parents, he hadn't said a lot about his mother, other than the state of her health. He'd mostly spoken of his father. She wondered if his relationship with his mother was strained for some reason.

"Come on, I'll give you a tour of the place and then I'll show you to the room that you'll be using while you're here."

The tour made her realize even more just what a beautiful home Drey had. His kitchen, with stainless steel appliances, was to die for, large and spacious. He told her he enjoyed cooking and spent a lot of time in the kitchen. She could tell just from looking around that like her, he was neat and tidy and liked nice things. She could also tell that his tastes included the exotic and she figured they were mainly because of his background.

He worked from his home, so the room he considered as his office reflected such. It wasn't cluttered although a number of files were open on his desk. He told her that he had a woman come in a couple of days a week to file and manage the books.

The guest room was neatly decorated although he told her that in the three years he lived there she was officially his first guest. The view out of her bedroom window faced the lake. The only problem she had was the proximity of her bedroom to his. It was directly across the hall.

Overall, she liked the layout of his home. It was rather spacious for one person, but he indicated he didn't like the feeling of being cramped.

He had just placed her luggage on the bed when his cell phone rang. He pulled it out of his pocket, glanced at who was calling and then flipped it open. "Yes, Mom?"

A few moments later he said. "Good. I'm on my way."

He glanced over at Charlene as he put his cell phone back in his pocket. "I need to go visit with my mother for a while. Will you be okay here while I'm gone?"

She waved off his question. "Of course. After I unpack I intend to sit outside on the patio. "You have a beautiful view."

"Thanks."

She studied his features, saw the dark look in his eyes and the way his nostrils flared. He was staring at her and the look at that moment was so blatantly sexual, she felt chills run up and down her spine at the same time blood raced through her veins.

"If you get hungry before I return, I have a loaded refrigerator."

She straightened her shoulders. "Thanks."

He suddenly took a step forward and on instinct she took one back, but not quick enough to stop him from reaching out and letting his fingers gently grab her wrist to bring her close to him. "Where do you think you're going?" he asked in a husky tone.

She stood close to him. More than ever she could feel his heat. Standing this close was causing all types of emotions to bombard her inner being. She tilted up her head and met his gaze. "I was trying to get out of your way," she said, trying not to look into the darkness of his eyes. "I'm not here for this, Drey."

A smile touched his lips. "Here for what?"

"To be a live-in woman who is available for you."

He didn't say anything, but she could tell her comment had him thinking and she had a feeling whatever it was, wasn't to her advantage. "I really hadn't thought of you as such, but now that you mention it, Charlie…"

She tried pulling her arm away; instead he pulled her closer with his full concentration on her mouth. "Don't get irritated with me, but before I leave there is something I need from you," he said in a deep, throaty voice.

She gave him a quelling look. Her chin went up. "There is nothing that you could possibly need from me."

"Want to bet?" He released her arm and reached up and let the tip of his finger caress her lips, as if he was fascinated with their shape. Without his hold she had the perfect opportunity to bolt, but she found herself rooted to the spot, held prisoner by the heated look in his eyes.

Looking down at her, he said in a whispered tone, "The shape of your mouth fascinates me."

It was on the tip of her tongue to say the shape of his mouth fascinated her, as well. But she didn't. Instead she continued to watch him while intense heat seemed to flood every part of her body.

"I want to kiss you, Charlene."

His words had her swallowing deeply. They had every nerve ending in her body on fire. "If I let you kiss me, it will give you the wrong idea."

She watched the corners of his lips tilt into a smile that nearly took her breath away. "Or it could give me the right one," he answered.

She signed deeply. "You mother is waiting," she said, deciding to remind him he had more pressing matters to take care of.

He still didn't move. "Drey," she said softly. "I think that—"

"Shh, don't think at all for a second," he whispered, removing his hand from her face to place it at her waist. "Just close your eyes and experience the taste."

He leaned in closer and lowered his head. His breath felt hot and wet against her lips, "Will you do that for me, Charlene?"

There was something in the way he asked that touched a part deep within her, persuading her to give in to his request. And just that easily she closed her eyes and within seconds, she felt his mouth on hers as he began kissing her in a slow, yet deep connection that devoured her with each stroke of his tongue.

It was like taking a sip of a bubbly drink in a highly

charged room. That was the only way she could describe the feelings that were overtaking her senses. Just once she didn't want to think that this was a kiss with a purpose or one that wasn't meant to happen. Instead she catered to needs she'd never encountered before and let herself be swept away by a multitude of feelings. Grudgingly she conceded that she wanted to indulge in this type of kiss as much as he did. It was a stimulant to her senses, a boost to her hormones and a must-do to her brain cells.

The kiss was everything it should be and more. And it reminded her of what she'd been missing out on for a long time. A life filled with long hours at work without any type of social life had led her to this. She didn't understand why they were drawn to each other, but she couldn't deny they were and had been from the first, although they'd tried downplaying it.

The kiss turned greedy, almost shamefully erotic, as he shifted his stance to take as much of her mouth as he could. His arms tightened around her like a band of steel and she was pulled even closer into his tight embrace.

For a split second she came close to moaning deep in her throat, but held it back and shivered under the impact of what he was doing to her mouth. She felt the physical evidence of his desire pressed against the apex of her thighs. It both frightened her and elated her that she had the ability to elevate his desire and bring him to this point.

He slowly released her mouth but not before taking his tongue and licking her lips from corner to corner, then sliding it back into her mouth for one final intense mating. She clung to his tongue with her own, feeling the strength in it, while her body quivered in the rush of sensations passing through her.

The moan she couldn't hold back any longer came out in a soft whimper, and at the same time her knees weakened under such intense passion. When it came to the art of kissing, Drey was an expert. He had the ability to take it to a level she had never experienced until now.

He finally pulled back from her mouth and lifted his head. The dark eyes staring into hers almost made her dizzy and she watched as his eyes lowered from hers to flick over her lips once again.

"I'd better go before I kiss you again," he said in a low, deep voice. "If I keep it up I'll make good my threat."

She swallowed, knowing just what threat he was talking about. The one about kissing her all over. If he did make good his threat, she was doubtful she would be strong enough to resist.

"I'll be back later. Just make yourself at home."

And then he released her and smiled down at her. It wasn't a smile of victory, but one of contentment. She could tell from the expression on his face that he had needed that kiss as much as she had and the enjoyment of it was mutual. That kiss had been the turning point for her and she admitted at that very moment that she wanted to get to know Drey St. John on an even deeper level.

Chapter 8

As much as he wanted to, Drey could not dismiss the impact on his senses of the kiss he had shared with Charlene. He felt a tight squeeze in his chest when he thought about what she was doing to him. And he didn't like it one bit.

He hadn't been able to walk out the door quick enough. Temptation had been nipping at his heels to go back inside of his home and pull her into his arms for another round. It had taken everything he had to get into his car and drive away. Even now he was fighting the urge to turn around and go back.

When was the last time a woman had taken such a toll on his libdo? Probably never. He had invited Charlene into his home, totally unprepared for the degree of attraction he had for her. He'd been very much aware that he wanted her before, but what he hadn't been prepared for was his lack of control around her, where at every opportune moment he wanted to drag her into his arms and kiss her senseless. He was not one who easily succumbed to passion, but he had today. If he could have had his way he would still be kissing her.

No, he would have escalated things to another level by now. At some point she would have made it to his bed and he would be inside her this very moment. The mere thought had intense desire flooding all parts of him, especially one that was destined to explode if it didn't get some relief.

It didn't take long to reach his mother's house, and for a few highly charged moments he remained in his car, trying to bring a semblance of control back to his body. After taking several deep breaths he cut off the ignition and calmed the wild flutterings in his stomach.

He had an investigation to complete and he could not lose sight of the fact that somehow his own mother might be involved. The last time he had been here she had dropped a bombshell that had rocked his entire world. And now he wanted to know everything, hear the entire story. He wanted her to explain just how thirty-three years ago she had gotten involved with a married man.

Drey had done the math. Harmon Braddock had been married at the time he and Daiyu had been involved. For the life of him, Drey could not picture his mother as a home-wrecker. His parents had shared a beautiful marriage. She had been completely dedicated to his father. She had taken Ronald St. John's death just as hard as he had and over the years since then, she had not gotten serious with another man, although he had known there had been a few who'd been interested. Just as Charlene had stated, his mother had been and still was a very beautiful woman.

He glanced around. The approach of winter hadn't stopped his mother from spending time outdoors in her garden. The last time he was here the plants had looked a little sickly. Now they looked alive and vibrant, which meant although his mother had avoided him for the past few days, she had managed to tend to her garden.

He thought about why he was here. It seemed the one woman he loved most in the world had been keeping secrets. Secrets he was slowly unraveling.

Getting out of the car, he moved up the walkway toward the Cape Cod-style house as his mind filled with memories of other times he'd taken this same path. It wasn't unusual for him to drop by on occasion to see how she was doing or to see if she needed his assistance. His mother was an independent woman and although he always offered his services, she preferred doing things for herself. He'd always admired that about her.

Taking the keys out of his back pocket, he let himself in as he'd always done. At any other time his mother would be at work, but she had called and said she wanted to finish their conversation, which meant she'd be waiting for him to arrive.

He walked through the house and went straight to the kitchen. He found her there, sitting at the table with her hands crossed on top of it. Her long dark hair hung past her shoulders, and like his, her eyes were dark and slanted over high cheekbones and a rounded face. She was an Asian beauty who looked like thirty-five instead of fifty-five.

"I heard your car pull up," she said, tilting her head back to look up at him.

He crossed the room to give her a peck on the cheek. "Hi, Mom."

"Drey. If you're hungry, I can make—"

"No, I'm not hungry," he said, taking the chair across from her and thinking that he didn't want to put anything in his mouth just yet that would diminish Charlene's taste. He wanted to savor it for a little while longer.

He glanced around the kitchen and saw all the pots on the stove. "You've been busy," he said, when it was quite obvious that she had been. She once told him that she did a lot of cooking when she was nervous about something.

Evidently that was the case now.

Deciding to get to the heart of the matter, he said, "Mom, the last time we talked you shared some things with me. However, I left before you could finish telling me everything."

He knew that was putting it mildly since he hadn't given her a chance to tell him anything else. The dam had burst once she had admitted that Harmon Braddock was his father. It was pretty obvious how upset he'd gotten that day upon hearing it. He had walked out angry, mad at the world, especially at her for not being truthful with him for all those years.

"All right, where do you want me to start?" she asked, her voice low and shaky.

"From the beginning. I want to know how you and Harmon Braddock met."

She said nothing for a moment while studying the teacup. Then she began speaking. "As you know I came to this country at the age of twenty as part of an international exchange program with Stewart Industries."

"Yes." He had heard that part before a number of times.

"Well, one week I got to attend a conference for Stewart Industries. Harmon was staying at the same hotel. We met at the hotel bar and I thought he was the most handsome and charismatic man I'd ever met. That week we became involved in an intense affair."

"Did you know he was married?"

She met his gaze. "No, I didn't know, at least not at first. Apparently he and his wife were having marital problems. However, once he told me the truth, that he was a married man, I threatened to break things off."

"But you didn't." He wished his words hadn't sounded so accusatory.

"No, I didn't break it off. I was convinced that he would leave his wife to be with me."

"Did he tell you that he would?"

She shook her head. "No. I just assumed that he would. I was young, inexperienced and in love and I thought that he would leave his wife because he was unhappy at the time. He didn't. After about a few months he ended things between us, and said he and his wife were going to try and make their marriage work." His mother paused for a moment before adding. "Not long after that I discovered I was pregnant."

Now it was Drey's time to pause to absorb everything his mother had said thus far. Then he asked, "Did you tell him you were pregnant?"

"No. I was scared to tell him so I kept it a secret. It was during that time, not too long after me and Harmon broke up, that I met Ronald. He wanted to take me out and I told him up front that I was pregnant, but that didn't matter to him. Ronald had fallen in love with me and wanted to make my child his own."

Drey didn't say anything but he sat there, looking out the window at her flower garden. His gaze returned to hers when he asked, "But Braddock eventually found out about me." He figured as much since the man had sought him out.

"Yes. I ran into him one day and he saw me pregnant. He put two and two together and realized the child was his. I was still hoping he wanted me and actually told him that I would end my relationship with Ronald if he left his wife. He said it was too late. His wife was pregnant and he was worried about the potential damage it would do to her if she were to find out. So we decided to cut our losses and move on, go our separate ways. I married your father and worked hard to make him a wonderful wife."

Drey held back his brutal retort that she hadn't given his father anything less than what he'd deserved. Ronald St. John had been a wonderful husband and father. Had his mother only shared part of her love with him? Had the other been for another man who had used her?

"But Harmon always kept up with what was going on with you, Drey," his mother said, breaking into his thoughts.

"And how would you know that?" he asked, wondering if this was where she would admit that she and Harmon had picked back up their affair after she'd married, and that in doing so, she had been unfaithful to his father.

"Because he told me he always would," she replied. "After Ronald was killed and he saw how hard you were struggling with his death, he reentered the picture to be there for you and eventually became your mentor. I wasn't happy about it, but as long as he kept his agreement and didn't tell you he was your biological father, I told him that I wouldn't stop him from building a relationship with you. And he wanted that, Drey. Harmon wanted to get close to you. He felt being your mentor, being there when and if you ever needed him, would be the only way he could have anything close to a father/son relationship with you."

Drey inhaled deeply, trying to keep his control from snapping. He felt as though his entire life hadn't been anything but a lie. He'd always liked the congressman, but now he wasn't sure how he should feel about him. The man had totally used his mother when it had been convenient, and then walked out of her life, only to return years later when his conscience probably had begun bothering him.

And then Drey thought about his siblings. It had been hard to gaze into Malcolm's face earlier that day without thinking that they were brothers. And how would he deal with Tyson and Shondra when he saw them again? And what about Evelyn, Harmon's widow? How would he deal with her as well? Her husband had been having an affair while she was pregnant with their first child.

However, as far as he was concerned, the person who had suffered the most was Ronald St. John. His father had loved his wife deeply, only to be given part of her love in return. Drey thought of all those years he had allowed Harmon to be his mentor when he had no clue he was the man's son. A part of him felt an outright betrayal to Ronald, the only father he'd ever known.

He pushed back his chair and stood, devastated and

unable to hear anything else for now. "Look, Mom, I need to go. I'll talk to you later."

"No, Drey," Daiyu said in a firm tone as she came to her feet. "I won't let you walk out on me again, and I refuse to let you think I didn't love Ronald, because I did. I grew to love him in a way that I could never love anyone else, including Harmon. Ronald was everything to me like he was everything to you. Your father was my whole world. Even now I miss everything about him. I miss his warm and loving nature, the times we shared together, our special love."

Drey pulled in a deep breath when he heard the sadness in his mother's voice. Then he saw the tears that clung to her lashes. He felt like an ass for making her cry. Gritting his teeth, he moved around the table to pull her small frame into his arms.

"I'm sorry, Mom, I didn't mean to upset you. It's just hard finding out Dad wasn't my father."

His mother pulled back slightly and gazed up at him. "But Ronald *was* your father in every way that counted. He gave you his name and his love. He could not have loved you more if you had been his natural child. He said so many times."

Drey believed her. He also knew talking about his father had taken a toll on her, but there was one other question he needed for her to answer.

He eased her away from him slightly but maintained an arm around her shoulder. "Mom, do you have any idea why Braddock was trying to reach you the night he was killed?"

She shook her head. "No, but he called several times that week before finally getting me. Our conversation was short because he had a call come in on his other line. He said he would call me back but he didn't."

Drey met his other gaze. "Can you think of anything else I need to know?" he asked, knowing the question was still out there as to why Harmon had tried calling his mother that night.

His mother lowered her gaze and pulled completely out of his arms. She went back to the table and sat down in the chair she had vacated earlier. "Yes, there is something."

Drey lifted a brow. "What?"

"Evelyn Braddock came to see me last week."

There was a moment of complete silence, shrouded in tension, when Drey came to sit back down at the table. "For what reason?" He leaned closer to his mother.

Daiyu took a sip of her tea before meeting her son's concerned gaze. "She had heard about Harmon's calls to Stewart Industries and knew I worked there."

Drey nodded. "Had the two of you met before?"

"Yes, years before. The night he broke things off with me she was with him. I guess it was their way of showing me they had both come to terms with his affair and were working through it."

Drey could only think that at the time meeting her lover's wife had to have been difficult. "What did she say to you last week when she came to visit?"

"She wanted to know about the call Harmon made to me. I told her that I didn't talk to him. I'm not sure whether she believed me. I could tell she was upset to find out that he had tried contacting me after all these years."

Deciding he wanted something to eat after all, Drey went to the counter and helped himself to a plate of cookies while asking, "Do you know of anyone at Stewart Industries that Harmon was interested in?"

"No. However, I do know that Harmon's daughter took a job there a month or so after his death to find out whose number Harmon called. It's my understanding that she ended up falling in love with Connor Stewart."

Drey also poured a cup of tea. "That's my understanding as well. And they were able to determine the call from Harmon came to you, but no one knows I'm your son."

Daiyu sighed. "Evelyn never knew I was pregnant, so she's unaware that Harmon has another child. Although you know who they are, they don't know you."

Drey intended to keep things that way until he was forced to do otherwise. He wanted to have completed the investigation by then.

"I'm sorry I don't have more to tell you, Drey."

He glanced over his mother and forced a smile. "That's fine. You've told me enough."

Chapter 9

Charlene went inside Drey's home after sitting on the patio for the past hour or so. Although the weather was a little cool, she had enjoyed sitting there watching the ducks play on the water. They appeared not to have a care in the world and she envied them.

Feeling somewhat hungry, she went into the kitchen. She had checked out his refrigerator and pantry earlier and found both places to be well stocked with food. One thing was certain. She wouldn't starve while living with him.

Within minutes she had prepared a sandwich that would make even the people over at the sandwich shop near work jealous.

And speaking of jealous...

She frowned when she remembered the call that had been left on Drey's answering machine. It was from some Karen, who wanted to know if Drey was interested in a fun time, and if so to come over to her place tonight, along with an extra set of clothes to stay for the weekend. The nerve of the hussy!

She turned when she heard the sound of the key in the door and felt a quickening in her chest when Drey walked in. She frowned thinking that this deep attraction for him was not what she wanted. But then she couldn't dismiss memories of the kisses they had shared. Kisses that still had her lips burning in some places.

She could feel her temperature rise when he strode into the kitchen and stood next to her at the counter and stared down at her sandwich. He then looked back at her and smiled. "Hungry?"

She wished he wouldn't smile in a way that made her want to wrap herself around him, cuddle close and hold on to him real tight. His smile always made him look extremely handsome in a totally masculine and sexy sort of way. "What makes you think that?" she asked.

He chuckled. "The size of your sandwich is a dead giveaway. It's enough to feed two people."

She lifted a brow. "Is that a hint that you want half?"

He shook his head. "No, not half. I ate a bunch of cookies over at Mom's. But I'd love to take a bite."

She picked up the sandwich, lifted it up close to his mouth and offered it to him. "Go ahead. I don't mind sharing."

While she held it he took a bite and she got turned on just by watching him chew. It was the methodical, slow movement of his mouth and the way their eyes stayed connected until he had finished. She swallowed, feeling a mass of heat invade her insides.

"It's okay," he said in a husky tone.

She stared at him, feeling her pulse rate increase. "What's okay?"

"The fact that you want me."

He was one arrogant ass, she thought. He was also correct. She wondered how he had known. Probably from the sound of her breathing. Instead of denying what he'd said, she looked away out his French doors and saw the ducks were still on the pond. She was then reminded of the phone call he had received earlier.

Placing the rest of her sandwich back on the plate, she grabbed her glass of iced tea and sat down at the table before throwing over her shoulder, "Oh yeah, by the way, Karen called."

He stared at her, as if not comprehending. "Karen?"

"Yes. Karen. She's invited you to her house for a sleepover."

"You answered the phone?"

"No, she left a message." And then Charlene added, "I imagine you're sorry that you missed her call."

"Yeah, I'm all broken up about it."

Charlene looked at him, not sure if he was serious or not. She tried not to glare at him when he came over to the table and sat down. He was a free man to do whatever he wanted. "You can call her back. She left her number."

"No need. I know it by heart."

"Figures," she said under her breath.

"Did you say something?"

"No."

He pushed his chair back from the table. "I'll let you eat in peace while I go over some reports."

She wondered if he was really going to go over any

report or if he was rushing off to return Karen's call. He glanced at his watch and then asked, "What time do most of the people leave at the coroner's office?"

"Around seven. Why?"

"No reason. I'll check you out later."

She then watched as he quickly walked off toward his office.

As soon as his office door closed behind him, Drey leaned back against it and pulled in a deep breath. Talk about bringing sexy back. Hell, Charlene Anderson took the icing off the cake. What was there about her that made him want to get her naked each and every time he saw her?

When he had walked into his kitchen and seen her standing there at the counter, in the direct path of the sunlight that was streaming in through the window, his heart began beating at a rapid pace. There was something about her standing in his kitchen, as if she had every right to be there, that had actually turned him on big time.

He had never taken a woman on his kitchen counter, but a few minutes ago he had come close to doing so. There was something about Charlene that tempted him to take her on the kitchen counter, the table, the bar stool. She brought out the wild side of him, a side he seldom showed. Maybe the reason was that she seemed to understand absolutely nothing about the opposite sex. For example, for an entire year the two of them had relentlessly bantered back and forth. He had understood why and accepted that the underlying cause was this deep sexual attraction they were trying to fight. For the longest time he felt she hadn't had a clue. She'd never picked up on the fact that he had been sexually attracted to her at all, nor that each and every time he saw her in that lab coat, he had undressed her with his eyes. Nothing had changed. She was no longer wearing her lab coat, but he was still undressing her with his gaze every chance he got. Wondering what she had on underneath her clothing gave him a boner each and every time, which was something else she never even noticed.

Shaking his head, Drey moved away from the door to his desk thinking that it wasn't an easy thing to admit that any one woman could blow your mind. Karen had nothing on her...other than experience. There was something about the way Charlene had returned his kiss the last two times they'd kissed that had made him wonder just how knowledgeable she was in the art of kissing.

She had been reluctant to put her tongue in his mouth until he had grabbed hold of it with his own and began mating with it. That only made him even more curious as to how often she had actually engaged in a French kiss. Would she carry that same level of inexperience into the bedroom?

A man could tell a lot about a woman's experience with a kiss, and right now he would rate Charlene's experience level to a single digit. Not that he was complaining. He had no qualms about showing her what her last lover had evidently failed to do. Meeting a woman who wasn't all that experienced, one he could introduce to new things in the bedroom, was rather refreshing. In fact he looked forward to doing so.

Drey glanced around the room, and not for the first time he admired the setup of his office. Large, light and airy, because of a huge window that overlooked the pond, it was the only room in the house besides the kitchen that didn't have any carpeting. Instead he had put in hardwood floors that fit in perfectly with the contemporary office furniture.

Knowing it was time to focus on work, he pulled a file out of the drawer, thinking that he needed to see the original autopsy report on Dennis, and if he could get his hands on that key, it would help tremendously. With Charlene no longer working at the coroner's office for the time being, there was only one way for him to get the items he needed. Forced entry.

Drey sighed with frustration. If there was another way, he couldn't think of it. In fact he was having difficulty in computing that Nate Ganders had changed the autopsy report and that some members of the police department might be involved. That made him even more determined to find out the truth. He had a meeting with the Braddocks in a few days and he wanted to be able to tell them something positive that he'd uncovered.

He wasn't sure just how long he had worked, going over the documentation he had collected, reading the police report on Harmon's accident and studying in detail again all the phone records and information Gloria had shared with him. Suddenly something outside his window caught his attention.

He crossed the room and saw Charlene. She was standing by the edge of the pond, throwing in bread crumbs to the ducks. His gaze focused in on her. She had put on a jacket and had swapped her skirt for a pair of white denim jeans. Not for the first time, and he doubted it would be for the last, he zeroed in on her backside, thinking just how much he liked it, wanting to cover it with his own body, mate with her from that position where he would enter her womanly core from behind. He inhaled a deep, hot breath, again wondering what there was about her that made his thoughts so sexual.

He observed her for a moment longer before deciding that it would be hard to go back to his desk and refocus on his work now that he'd seen her. Making a quick decision, he moved away from the window and grabbed his jacket off the coatrack and headed out of his office to join her at the pond.

Charlene threw bread crumbs out to the ducks while trying to convince herself that it didn't matter one iota to her that Drey was probably in his office talking on the phone to Karen and planning their hot night together. How many men would give up a chance to be with an eager woman? A woman who evidently had a lot of experience.

A woman who still wasn't a virgin.

For once she would like to come across as a woman in the know, and not get all giddy when being exposed to something new. Like the way Drey always kissed her. She'd been kissed before but not the way he did it. He could heighten her senses just with his tongue. She had only read about that type of kiss. It was the kind of kiss that still had heat sizzling inside you long after the contact ended. Amazing.

"The weather has turned rather chilly, hasn't it?"

At the sound of the deep, masculine voice Charlene turned around so quickly she almost lost her balance. She glanced at Drey, who had come to a stop beside her. "I thought you had a lot to do," she said, deciding not to add "with Karen."

"I've taken care of most of what I plan to do today," he said, shifting his gaze from her to the ducks.

"So, what time are you leaving?"

He looked back to her and raised a dark brow. "Am I supposed to be going some place?"

"Yes, I told you that that Karen person called. I heard the message."

He crossed his arms over his chest. "And?"

"And I figured that, like most men, you wouldn't hesitate to take her up on her offer."

A smile that didn't quite reach his eyes appeared on his face. "Well, today you will learn something new."

"Which is?"

"I'm not like most men. And I don't take advantage of every opportunity being offered. Some you learn to stay away from."

"And is Karen one of those opportunities?"

"Afraid so. She's looking for a husband but she won't find one here."

Charlene studied him. "Does that mean you're not looking for a wife?"

"Yes, it means I'm not looking for a wife. Just a temporary bed partner. It's better for me that way. I don't do well with long-term affairs. The short ones work a whole lot better with my lifestyle."

Charlene wondered if he was throwing out hints. If he was, then he was wasting his time. Once he discovered she was still a virgin, he would hightail it in the opposite direction real quick.

"So, what would you like to do tonight, Charlene?"

She didn't fail to note Drey had said her name with just the right amount of sugarcoating to spike her hormone level up a notch and couldn't help wondering if it was deliberate. A man with as much skill and experience with women as he possessed had to know when he'd hit the jackpot.

She decided to call his bluff to see just how far he would take this and if he was trying to break down her defenses. "I don't know, Drey. What do you have in mind?" she asked in a voice so soft and seductive it didn't sound like her own.

She watched his eyes darken a little and saw the smooth smile that formed on his lips. "Something that might get the both of us in trouble. But I'm willing to take the chance."

Yeah, I bet you are.

"Think you're interested?" he asked her.

Deciding to play along for a while, she said, "Possibly."

His smile widened and he showed beautiful white teeth. "Good." He glanced down at his watch. "You need to go into the house and change into something dark."

Charlene lifted a brow. He said dark but not sexy. Did he have a fetish for dark clothes? "Why do I need to wear something dark?"

"So you can't be seen."

Now she was confused. Why wouldn't he want to see her? She thought naked skin turned most men on. She met his gaze and saw the mischievous glint and wondered...

"Excuse me, are we talking about the same thing?" she decided to ask.

He gave her a half smile. "I don't know. Are we?"

She didn't have time to play guessing games with him. "Am I wrong or did you suggest we do something tonight that might get us into trouble?"

"No, you aren't wrong. I did suggest that." He leaned in closer, so close she could blatantly feel the heat off his body that seemed to suddenly block the cool air from coming her way. What other reason would her body suddenly feel as if it were burning up inside?

"And I'm curious to know what you thought I was referring to," he said, leaning in even closer. She was tempted to take a step back, but a part of her refused to do so, afraid if she moved even an inch all those vibrations that were slowly thrumming through her body would get even stronger.

"No, you go first," she said, nervously licking her lips and watching his gaze follow the movement of her tongue. "Tell me what you were talking about."

He reached out and placed his hands at her waist and her body immediately reacted, shooting sparks of fire to every nerve ending. "Okay, what I was talking about us doing tonight, where we might get into trouble, is…"

"Yes?" she asked softly, curiosity eating away at her, especially in some very sensitive places.

"Breaking into the coroner's office to find your boss's original autopsy report on Dennis as well as that key."

"What!" She would have jumped back in shock, but the moment her mouth opened to exclaim that one word, he was right there on it. And that was the last part of their conversation that she remembered.

Chapter 10

She moaned.

The sound made Drey delve into her mouth that much deeper. He had no business kissing her this way out in the open where any of his neighbors could observe, but at the moment he didn't care. The only thing he cared about was kissing Charlene, tasting her.

He ignored the warning bells, he disregarded the danger signs. All his body and mind could comprehend was both need and greed. Warmth was spreading all over him, shooting right to his groin area. He wanted her. That fact he understood. And whether she knew it or not, she wanted him too. He could tell in the way she was kissing him back. All they needed was a bed… and, oh yeah, a little privacy.

He quickly remembered again just where they were and grudgingly pulled away from her mouth. "Come on, let's go inside," he whispered hot in her ear while taking her hand in his.

He could tell the instant she regained her senses. She pulled her hand away from his. "Why? No. We can't. We need to talk."

He couldn't help but smile at all the words that tumbled out of her mouth. A mouth he wanted to devour again. "Okay, let's go inside and talk. Anything in particular you want to discuss?"

She looked at him as if he were dense. "You're suggesting breaking and entering and you want to know what in particular I want to discuss? What about the thought of being arrested? How does that sound for starters?"

He began walking and noted that she was moving beside him. "Not good. You're right. Forget the idea."

"Now you're sounding reasonable," she said, nodding.

"It's something I can do on my own. You stay here until I return."

She stopped walking and swung around and stared at him as if he'd completely lost it. "What! Are you crazy?"

"Don't think so," he said, smiling at the way she got overexcited at the least little thing. He wondered if she showed that same degree of excitement in the bedroom.

When they were back at his place he took the keys out of his pocket to open the door. He followed her inside, closed it behind them and leaned back against it. "Has anyone ever told you how cute you are when you get stirred up about something?"

She took off her jacket and tossed it across a chair

before giving him an irritated look. She then crossed her arms over her chest. "This isn't funny, Drey."

His gaze moved from her face to her chest, more specifically, her breasts. The way her arms were folded lifted the twin globes up, pressing them against her blouse where he could clearly see the nipples. "No, it isn't funny," he said. "I might find a number of things amusing but never what I'm looking at now."

He could tell that at first she didn't comprehend what he'd said, but seconds after she did, she quickly dropped her hands by her sides at the same time he heard her grit her teeth.

He slowly crossed the room to pull her into his arms and kiss her. Surprisingly, she didn't resist him. Moments later he disconnected their mouths and then proceeded to cradle her face in his hands and kiss her again. He didn't know any other woman who in addition to having a high degree of sensuality was capable of igniting his enthusiasm for any little thing. Go figure.

Moments later, he withdrew his mouth from hers thinking he would never get tired of kissing her. The feel of her lips beneath his was a sensation he just couldn't explain. "I think I'll kiss you every time you get pissed off with me about something," he said softly. "Anger must do something to your taste buds. Electrify them. Make them addictive."

He then stepped back and gestured over to a huge book cabinet on one of the walls. "There's a bunch of movies in that top drawer over there if you want to watch one while I'm gone. And if you get bored doing that, you can tackle all those video games that I—"

"I'm going."

He frowned. "No, you're not."

"Yes, I am."

He shook his head. "What you said by the pond made sense. There's no need for the both of us to go to jail, so you stay here."

"I'm going, Drey. You don't know your way around once you get inside. Besides, you won't know what you should look for. You'll need me to identify just what you need."

He stared at her. She did have a point. "Okay, then, let's get moving. Like I said earlier, you need to change into dark clothes."

She nodded and then he watched as she rushed off toward the guest room.

They were both going to end up in jail, Charlene thought as she stood with her body pressed close to Drey's while he used something that looked like a hair clip to force their way inside. And this might not be the best time to think about it, but she thought he smelled super good.

"And you're sure there's not an alarm system?" he asked her over his shoulder.

"I'm sure."

It was dark but she didn't need any lights to see the dangerous yet sexy glint in his eyes. She had noticed them on the drive over. Whether he admitted it or not, she knew he was enjoying this. She could just see the headlines now.

Former Police Officer Arrested for Breaking into Coroner's Office.

She hadn't figured out yet just how they would broadcast her part in it, but there was no doubt in her mind that they would. At that point she would have to kiss her job goodbye. She should never have insisted on coming, but then she couldn't imagine watching a video while waiting for him to come back.

Charlene heard a click and knew Drey had gotten the door open.

"Right or left?" he asked her in a whispered tone.

"Left then straight for around 5 feet and then turn right," she responded. They would not be turning on any lights other than a penlight he held in his hand. They would stop by her desk to get the key that would open the file cabinet where the autopsy reports were kept. They intended to get both Harmon's and Joe Dennis's autopsy records. Then they had agreed to search Nate's office for the missing key.

"Okay, here's your desk."

Charlene nodded and within minutes she had the key to the autopsy room in her hand. "I got it," she whispered. And then she gave him directions on how to get to the autopsy room from where her desk was located.

Reaching their goal was done with little difficulty, but that didn't stop fear from flowing down Charlene's spine. Although the coroner's office didn't have an alarm system, it did have a security guard on payroll who made periodic checks. The key was to get in and out between the security officer's visits.

Drey whispered most of his words while she quickly opened the file cabinet and began thumbing through for the autopsy reports on Harmon and Dennis. The penlight had been replaced by a slim flashlight and within minutes they had retrieved the reports they wanted.

"Where to now?" she whispered close to Drey's ear, trying to ignore the stirrings in the pit of her stomach.

How could she be thinking of wanting him at a time like this?

They carefully made their way from the autopsy room toward Nate's office. At one point they paused when they thought they heard a sound and discovered it was only the hum and click of the air-conditioning system.

Drey and Charlene began searching Nate's office in earnest, making sure to return anything they picked up to its proper place. After a few minutes of searching they still had not found the key. However, they did come across a copy of Joe Dennis's original autopsy report. It was in a folder with other documents labeled "To Be Destroyed."

After searching high and low with no success in finding the key, Drey whispered, "Evidently the key has now changed hands. Let's not waste any more time in here looking for it."

Charlene was about to agree when they heard footsteps coming down the hall. Drey killed the beam from the flashlight immediately and pulled Charlene with him into a small closet in Nate's office.

Charlene was standing behind Drey and clenching his shirt when fear gripped her. What if someone had heard them moving around in Nate's office and had called the police? What if they had guns?

"Relax," Drey whispered. "Your breathing has changed. Take it easy."

That was easy for him to say, she thought as she pressed her body even closer to his back. Panic surged through her and had her clenching his shirt even tighter. From a crack in the closet door she could see it was one of the security men making his rounds. She might have been imagining it, but Drey didn't appear in the least bit nervous. He stood there, cool and ready for action. Silently she prayed that they didn't see any.

The security guard—who had a gun strapped to his waist—seemed to linger in Nate's office longer than necessary. Glancing over Drey's shoulder and gazing through the crack in the closet door, Charlene saw why. The man had taken a seat on the edge of the desk and was using the computer, namely the Internet.

She and Drey watched as the man signed on and went to a pornography Web site. Her view wasn't as good as Drey's but she saw enough to know the man was enjoying looking at the photos of all the naked bodies that appeared on the screen. It was downright embarrassing, Charlene thought, and wished there was some hole she could crawl into.

After about half an hour, it seemed the man finally remembered he had a job to do, and reluctantly signed off the computer. Charlene had been afraid of getting caught the entire time. Fear had clogged her throat at some point, making breathing difficult.

Once they were sure the man had left to go to another part of the building, Drey came out of the closet and pulled her with him. After having stood in the same cramped position for so long, her legs felt stiff and her joints ached.

"Come on," Drey said taking her hand. "We got most of what we came for. Let's get the hell out of here."

Chapter 11

An hour later after taking a shower Drey took the time to remember everything that had happened that night at the coroner's office. It had been like a scene from a James Bond movie. The only difference was that he hadn't had in his possession any of that fancy technology. But he had been stuck in a very dangerous situation with a beautiful woman—a woman who was now probably asleep, dead to the world, after tonight's action.

He hadn't failed to notice that Charlene hadn't said much of anything during the ride home. And once they had gotten here she had said good-night and raced off to the guest room.

While preparing for his shower he had heard the one in the guest bath going. Visions of her standing naked under a spray of water had given him a boner and he'd ended up taking a cold shower before settling down and taking a warm one.

Thinking back on the evening, he realized getting into the coroner's office hadn't been a complete waste of time. He had gotten copies of Harmon's and Joe Dennis's autopsy records, as well as the discarded original autopsy record for Dennis. But they hadn't found the key. Chances were Nate had gotten rid of it by giving it to whomever he was in cahoots with.

Feeling the need of a cold beer, he left his bedroom and was rounding the corner when he heard a sound. He stopped, glanced over at the window and saw Charlene standing there and staring out.

Drey paused and looked at her thinking she was definitely a picture of beauty wearing a long velour white bathrobe. Even from across the room he picked up her just-showered scent that mingled with vanilla.

He couldn't help noticing that she was shaking. The heat was on in the town house so he wondered what was wrong with her. Then he knew. She was having a flashback to what had happened earlier that night. She was probably thinking about what could have happened had they gotten caught. More than likely she was reliving the fear, the excitement and the intensity of the situation they had found themselves in.

"Charlene?"

He said her name softly and she turned. The look he saw in her eyes made him swiftly cross the room and pull her into his arms. "Hey, it's okay. You're safe now. We're both safe."

Inwardly he called himself all kinds of fool for letting her talk him into taking her. As a police officer he had been in such dangerous situations before, but she had not. However, tonight he had exposed her to danger and because of it, she was going through this. An aftershock.

Drey continued to hold her with her face buried in his chest. He whispered over and over that she was okay while her shaking continued. What she needed was something to drink, preferably a glass of wine. But he didn't want to leave her alone for the time it took to fix her one. He just wanted to stand there and hold her.

A few moments later the shivers in her body began to ease. He tried not to think about just how soft she felt in his arms, how nice she smelled or how good her body felt pressed up to his. And most of all, he didn't want to remember just how delicious her mouth tasted.

But he did remember. And when she lifted her head to stare into his eyes, he no longer saw tension in them. He saw desire so thick it made his breath catch. Before he could react in any way, she stood on tiptoe and placed her mouth on his. And then she eased her tongue into his mouth.

He wasn't exactly sure what was driving her, but he knew what was driving him when he took control of the kiss. It was as if something inside him snapped and he wanted to gobble her up. And the way she was returning the kiss let him know that she wanted to be gobbled up. He thought the other kisses they'd shared had been intense, but they couldn't compare to the heat and passion they shared now. There was nothing simple about this kiss. It was the hottest kiss he'd ever endured and he felt his entire body ignite in flames.

He tangled his hands in her hair, trying to keep her mouth immobile while he plundered it in pleasure, and when she pressed even closer to him, molded her body intimately to his, he felt an explosion just waiting to happen. He knew just where he wanted to be when it did.

Inside her.

That thought made him pull back to end the kiss. She wasn't in the right frame of mind for him to have such thoughts, and he refused to take advantage of her. He would do the right thing even if it killed him, and right now it almost was. His entire body was on fire. More than anything he wanted to make love to her. But he wouldn't.

"Why did you stop, Drey?"

He heard her words, felt her confusion and knew he would be honest with her. "Because you aren't in your right mind now. You're thinking that you want something you really don't."

She shook her head, disagreeing with him. Instead of saying anything verbally, she leaned up on tiptoe and took his mouth again and he didn't deny her. What he did do was fight for control, though he found it hard to do. This time it was she who finally pulled back. "I know what I want, Drey. I know what I need," she said in a whisper. "I need you. Now."

He gazed into her dark eyes, saw the desire there. That same desire stabbed him in the chest and he was tempted to pull her back into his arms to taste her some more. To gobble her up again.

He remembered what he'd said after their first kiss and the promise he'd made about not taking his desire for her any further until she gave the word. Although she had just done so, he wanted to make sure she understood what she was asking of him.

"You want us to make love?" he asked, so there

wouldn't be any misunderstanding, no morning-after regrets.

"Yes."

He heard her response but pressed on to make absolutely certain. "I want to get inside you, Charlene. I want to make love to you the way a man makes love to the woman he wants, the woman he desires. I want to take you to the edge and back. I want to hear you scream, and in the end I want to make you come. Again and again. I want to feel it. Taste it. Are you absolutely sure those are the things that you want too?"

She stared at him, and he watched as she nervously licked her lips. She probably hadn't expected him to make things so blatantly clear. He watched her eyes darken and heard her breathy sigh before she said, "Yes, I'm sure that I want all those things. I want to share every single one of them with you."

In one smooth move Drey swept her off her feet and into his arms. He moved toward his bedroom, hoping she knew what she was agreeing to because he planned on keeping his word and making love to her all through the night.

Charlene's heart began beating faster the moment Drey placed her on his bed. A part of her wanted to tell him the truth about her experience level in the bedroom, but then another thought it best not to say anything. She needed him and she wanted him, and she wouldn't tell him that she was a virgin. He would find out soon enough.

Through heavy-lidded, desire-filled eyes, she watched as he stood back away from the bed to remove his clothes. This was the first time a man had

ever undressed in front of her, and she was giving him
her undivided attention. When he dropped his pajama
bottoms, her breath caught. His shaft was large, hard,
thick and ready. She felt the muscles in her womanly
core tighten, either in fear or anticipation.

Would she be able to handle that? Inwardly she
forced herself to relax. She believed what he said. Under
his skillful hands she would experience her first orgasm
and she was looking forward to it. After everything she
had gone through tonight, she needed it. She needed
to be a part of him and wanted him to be a part of her.
Regrets, if there were any, would come in the morning. But not tonight.

She then watched as he reached into a nightstand to
pull out a condom packet. Several of them. The area
between her thighs felt hot and edgy at the thought that
he intended to make love to her more than once and
hoped when he discovered that she was a virgin that
he wouldn't change his mind.

He returned to the bed and reached out, and with
practiced movement he removed her robe and nightgown. When she was completely naked before his eyes,
he began touching her all over, letting his strong fingers
cover her entire body, caressing it tenderly, methodi-
cally, while heightening the desire inside her.

He pressed her back in the bedcovers and stretched
out beside her, allowing his mouth to discover the same
areas his fingers had earlier. He tongued her throat,
down her neck before moving lower to her breasts. She
was aware of the throbbing of her pulse the moment he
captured one hardened nipple between his teeth, lavish-
ing it and torturing it all at the same time. And then she
felt him ease his hand between her legs and she shivered

at his touch. When he began to stroke it with the pad of his thumb, the sensations were so intense that her hips rose off the bed. It had to be the most erotic thing she had ever felt in her life.

She heard a moan and realized it came from deep within her throat, but Drey kept his mouth on her breast while his hand continued to fondle her between the legs.

"Drey."

His name came forth from her lips on a breathless sigh and she had no idea why she was calling it. She didn't want him to stop, but she wasn't sure she could handle the pleasure overtaking her, gripping her in a way she had never experienced before.

He raised his head up to whisper, "Relax, Charlene, and let me take you on a pleasurable journey. There are parts of your body that are more sensitive than others. I plan on touching and tasting every one of them. There is a Chinese way of lovemaking that increases one's sexual pleasure while at the same time stimulating one's mind. I want to use several demonstrations of it tonight. Is that all right?"

"Yes." Somehow she had managed to get the single word past her lips while a ripple of fierce excitement passed through her. He began caressing her body again with his fingertips, and she could feel the heat gather beneath his hand. When it reached her thighs, she felt herself getting wet.

He shifted positions and his mouth took over for his hand. She released a small whimper the moment his tongue touched her there and she reached out, at first to pull his head away but then to hold it there while his mouth did some scandalous things to her womanly core, devouring it as if it was something he had to have. And then she felt a mirage of sensations overtake her, making her entire body appear to be coming apart and exploding in several pieces. She felt as if she were falling into a sea of pleasure that was destined to drown her.

"Drey!"

She screamed his name when an orgasm struck her, flinging her into mindless bliss and intense satisfaction. Shivers rammed through her and she heard herself moan over and over again. Moments later, when the last quake had subsided, Drey lifted his head, licked his lips and then leaned upward and kissed her, letting her taste the essence of her off his mouth.

He pulled back enough to put on a condom, and then he was covering her body with his. She met his gaze, wanting to warn him that this was the first time she had ever been intimate with a man, but afraid if she did so he wouldn't finish what he started. And she would die if he didn't. Her body felt too alive and sensitized for him not to carry this to completion.

She felt him ease her thighs apart just moments before the tip of his manhood touched the entry of her femininity. It felt huge, engorged and hot. It was as if it needed to be inside her to cool off. And then she felt him slowly easing inside her, stretching her and going so far and not being able to go any farther.

Their gazes held and she felt him place his hands beneath her hips just before he leaned forward to kiss her again. Then suddenly, she cried out in his mouth the moment he pushed forward in a hard thrust, going inside her to the hilt. Pain came and went, yet he paused to give her body time to adjust to him and his size. It felt as if he was locked inside her, had completely taken over her lower body.

And then he began moving, slowly, in and out, demonstrating his power and skill with every thrust he made, while at the same time building pleasure within her yet again. Over and over he brought her to the brink of a mind-blowing orgasm, only to snatch it back and make the sensations ripple through her once more. She wondered why he was torturing her this way. She heard her own pleas for release from the tension he was steadily building inside her.

And then it seemed to peak and she screamed at the same time her body exploded, actually broke into a million fragmented pieces, melted into liquid. But he kept moving on top of her, thrusting rapidly, deeply, and on the heels of one orgasm she felt another. And then another. It was as if he was determined to see how many she could have.

Then she felt his body buck on top of her. Heard her name forced from his lips between gritted teeth. She felt him explode inside her. And then as if he had some sort of control over her body, she felt sensations flow between them that triggered more pleasure deep within her, and she felt herself drowning in ecstasy all over again.

He had warned her that he would make her come all night, but she hadn't accepted the truth of his words until now.

Chapter 12

The next morning Drey woke up to find a soft body wrapped around him. He remembered the events of last night and felt his heartbeat kick up a notch.

Charlene Anderson had not only turned out to be a surprising lover; she had been totally different from any woman he'd ever been with. She had been a virgin—something he was definitely curious about—yet she had managed to pull passion and desire out of him that he'd never felt before. And he had kept his promise. He had taken their lovemaking to the max and had made her come not only once, but all through the night. He couldn't remember the last time he had made love to a woman all night long.

She had to be totally exhausted. Chances were she would sleep most of the day. The only time they had taken a break was after that first time when he had discovered she was a virgin. He had taken her into the bathroom and placed her in a tub of warm, sudsy water and had joined her there and held her in his arms. Then after drying them both off, he had taken her back to bed and made love to her again, over and over.

Knowing if he didn't get up he would be tempted to make love to her again, he eased out of bed. As much as he enjoyed being with her, inside her, tasting her, he had work that needed to be done. And the first thing on his list was to go over those autopsy reports they had taken from the coroner's office last night. He would use the time she slept to do so while enjoying a cup of coffee.

But when she woke up…

He felt his body get hard just thinking of how their day might end up. They were lovers now and he couldn't see them going back to business associates or friends. He couldn't bear the thought of not making love to her again. There was so much he wanted to teach her, share with her. Last night proved she was a willing student, and as he had told her before, she was a very passionate woman. He knew the degree of that passion had astounded even her last night. She had wanted more and he had delivered each and every time.

After slipping back into his pajama bottoms he remembered he had a meeting with the Braddocks later today. He intended to tell them everything he knew about the case so far. Well, almost everything. He still wasn't ready to tell them that he knew the identity of Daiyu Longwei and more specifically, her relationship to Harmon Braddock as well as to him.

A half hour later he was in his office concentrating on the autopsy reports. A ripple of pain went through him while reading about the extent of Harmon's injuries, the man who was his biological father. That he had been murdered caused anger to mix with that pain.

He then compared the original autopsy report on Joe Dennis to the new one. Among numerous inconsistencies was one constant—neither report mentioned a key.

The only living relative Joe Dennis had was a nephew who lived in Dallas. Drey had contacted the man by phone and according to him, he and his uncle had not been close and there wasn't much the man could share with him about any friends Dennis might have had.

Typically if a death was ruled a homicide, the police would question neighbors who'd been home at the time. But since, thanks to Nate Ganders, Dennis's death would not be ruled a homicide, no one would be asking questions. At least no one but him. It was time for him to start sniffing around as of today. He would get access to Dennis's home and poke around and see what he could find.

"Drey?"

He didn't have to look up to know Charlene had entered the room. He felt her presence immediately, in every part of him, especially in his shaft. It hardened immediately.

She was standing in the doorway, wearing only his T-shirt which she had evidently taken out of his drawers. That she had gone through his stuff to find the T-shirt didn't bother him. In fact, the thought that she was wearing something of his over her naked skin sent a surge of excitement through him. Mainly because it was skin he knew the taste of, skin that he had rubbed against his own and touched all over.

He started to stand and decided not to. The last thing

he wanted her to see was the size of his erection. No telling what she would think if she saw it. Besides, although she had willingly participated in last night's activities, today was the morning after and he wasn't sure what her attitude might be. For all he knew, she might have regrets about last night. So he would sit right there and follow her lead and hope it was positive. He wasn't sure how he would handle things if it wasn't. He couldn't tell from her expression how things would go. And that made him nervous.

"Charlene, you're awake," he said in a gravelly cautious tone.

"Yes, sorry about that. I should have awakened sooner," she said, still standing in the same spot. He tried to keep his eyes focused on her face and not allow them to travel down the length of her to see beyond where his T-shirt stopped midthigh. She had a nice pair of legs—long and smooth—and he could distinctly recall how he'd felt being between them. The memory made his shaft grow another notch.

"No, you needed your rest," he heard himself say. He leaned back in his chair. Again he tried to keep his gaze on her face but found it straying downward. He cleared his throat when he felt his pulse rate increase. "What are your plans for today?" he asked.

She shrugged her beautiful shoulders. He knew for a fact that they were beautiful because he had seen them last night, bare. "Don't know. It depends on you," she said softly.

He smiled at her, although uncertainty was still eating away at him. "In what way?"

She stepped closer into the room, and he couldn't help it when his gaze lowered and feasted not only on her legs but her hips, thighs, ankles and feet. Seeing the parts of her that he had come into intimate contact with the night before sent a stirring of deep pleasure through him, aroused him even more. "In how do you feel the morning after?" she asked.

That was the same concern that he had for her. Did she hold the same uncertainty that he did? Did she honestly think he would regret what they had shared the night before? "How do you think I should feel?" he decided to ask.

She took another step into the room and he watched her, getting more aroused by the second. "Not sure. I can only go by what I was told," she said.

Now he really was confused. "What exactly were you told and by whom?"

"His name was Carlos and he said that most men had a problem with overaged virgins."

He lifted a brow. "I thought we already covered the fact that I'm not like most men. Besides, you're no longer a virgin. But even if you would have confessed to being one before we made love last night, that would not have stopped me."

Her expression seemed unsure. "It wouldn't?"

"No."

"Why not?"

He couldn't believe she was asking him that, but from the look on her face, he could tell she really needed to know. "Mainly because I wanted to make love to you. Knowing beforehand that you were a virgin only meant I needed to handle you another way. I would have known to be gentler. But make no mistake about it, Charlene. I would not have changed anything else. I would still have taken you as many times as I did and made love to you using those same various positions. Knowing you were inexperienced didn't dull the sensations of being inside you. Last night's sex was good between us and I have no doubt in my mind that it will only get better."

He stood. "Come here and let me show you what I mean."

She didn't hesitate in crossing the room to him but was surprised when he pulled her down in his lap facing him. She felt his body part beneath her, hard and throbbing beneath her naked bottom.

In one swift movement he pulled his T-shirt over her head, and before she could make a startled gasp, his mouth latched on to her breast. Each pull by his mouth triggered an arousal deep in her stomach. He was stirring up desires deep within her, primitive needs and wants.

And then he stood with her in his arms and, placing her on her feet, worked the pajama bottoms from his body, leaving them both totally naked. He lifted her onto his desk, widening her legs to stand between them and aiming his shaft straight for her feminine core. He eased her closer to it and when she felt it there at the entrance, she met his gaze.

Her heart began pounding as he began easing inside her, gripping her hips to hold her in place and accept his entry. She threw her head back when sensations began building inside of her and she closed her eyes.

"No. Open your eyes and look at me. Watch me bring you pleasure."

She did.

He wrapped her legs around his waist and locked

her in. Over and over again he thrust inside her, making pleasure so intense overtake her.

Then suddenly he went still.

She met his gaze and saw shock in them when he said, "I forgot about a condom."

She fully understood what he was saying. "I'm on the pill to regulate my periods," she whispered. "Now, please…" Her body was in a feverish pitch and needed release.

He began moving again, and each thrust into her went deeper, faster, until she couldn't take any more. She screamed out his name as her body exploded and she felt his release, thick and hot, shoot inside her, at the same time.

One orgasm led to another and another and some time later she lay spent on top of his desk with his throbbing member still buried deep inside her. "I think we need to take this to the bedroom now," he whispered, lifting her body in a way that kept them connected.

She wrapped her arms around him thinking she had to be dreaming. Nothing could be this perfect, this sensual, this earth-shatteringly blissful. But she knew once they got to the bedroom, Drey would proceed to show her that it could.

"Let's get dressed. I have somewhere to go and I want you to go with me," Drey said, gently rubbing his hand along her thighs. He'd never been possessive when it came to a woman, not even the least tiny bit. But for some reason he was with her and unashamedly so.

"Where are we going?" she asked, leaning over to nibble his ear.

He knew if he didn't stop her she would take her

newfound sexual confidence to a level of no return for them and she would find herself flat on her back beneath him yet again. They had made love most of the morning and then had showered together only to end up making love again after their shower.

He stood and placed her on her feet. "We're going to meet the Braddocks."

Chapter 13

Charlene knew all eyes were on her when she walked into Malcolm Braddock's office by Drey's side. She knew Malcolm by both name and face since he was currently embroiled in a heated campaign with a man by the name of Clint Hardy. Both were vying for the congressional seat left vacated as a result of Harmon Braddock's death. The special election was to be held at the end of the month and if the recent polls were reliable, Malcolm had a substantial lead.

Malcolm, the oldest at thirty-two, was tall, with coffee-brown eyes and dark brown hair. Charlene thought he was a very handsome man and from what she'd read in the papers a few months ago, he was engaged to marry Congressman Braddock's former executive assistant, Gloria Kingsley. There would be a Christmas wedding at the family estate.

Although she did not know the others, Drey had filled her in as to who would be attending the meeting. Shondra Braddock, the late congressman's daughter, and Tyson Braddock, the late congressman's younger son.

Like Malcolm, Shondra was tall, with long dark hair and dark brown eyes. An attorney, she always had it together and from what Charlene had heard, she was not only beautiful, but highly intelligent. According to Drey, Shondra was so convinced her father's death hadn't been an accident that she followed up on a lead by going so far as to go work for the company where Harmon's last phone call was placed. She met the CEO's son, Connor Stewart, a former jet-setting bachelor. The two eventually fell in love and according to Houston's society's column, Shondra and Connor were Houston's hottest couple.

The middle child, Tyson resembled his siblings. On the drive over Drey had told her that Tyson and his wife had been on the verge of getting a divorce but were now back together and expecting their first child.

Drey quickly made introductions, explaining who she was and why she was there. Malcolm was the first to ask a question. "So, Ms. Anderson, you actually saw this key?"

Charlene nodded and said to the three, "Yes, and I'm Charlene, please. Drey and I were able to get a copy of my boss's first autopsy report indicating trauma to the body before he was able to destroy it."

"And you have no idea why he changed it?" It was Shondra who asked.

It was Drey who answered. "No, although I have my suspicions. I have a strong feeling that Nate Ganders is being blackmailed. Otherwise, why would he warn Charlene off and suggest to her that she take time away from the job? It's apparent he didn't want to get her involved and seems to be doing everything he can to keep her out of it. She's moved in with me for a while for protection."

Tyson leaned against the edge of his brother's desk. "So you're operating on the theory that whoever killed our father is paying a lot of money to keep it covered?"

"Yes, and until we find that person, keep in mind that a murderer is still on the loose and he's struck twice—with your father and Joe Dennis—and he will strike again to keep his identity hidden."

"So what do you suggest that we do?" Shondra asked, agitation very clear in her voice.

"Right now I have a few more people to talk to," Drey said, glancing down at his notepad. "I'm hitting a brick wall at the police station. I hate to say it but I think a few people down there are in on this too. I hope I'm wrong but I have a gut feeling about it. The one guy down at headquarters that I know I can trust—my former partner—is out of town but is scheduled to return this week. I'm hoping he'll be able to check out some things and shed some light on a few inconsistencies I've found."

"And what about that employee at Stewart Industries? The one Connor spoke with? Daiyu Longwei. She clammed up when Connor questioned her about Dad's last phone call to her. Have you spoken to her at all?" Tyson asked.

Drey shook his head. "I've spoken with her, but she didn't have any more to tell me either. I'll keep working on it, though."

Charlene didn't say anything as she racked her brain trying to recall where she'd heard the name before. Daiyu Longwei…

"So, what's next?" Malcolm was asking Drey.

"I plan to talk to the congressman's associates to see if they recall him acting strangely during his last days. There had to be a reason for his unscheduled trip to D.C."

"I suggest you start with Senator Ray Cayman and Judge Bruce Hanlon. They've known Dad for years and are two of his closest friends," Tyson said.

Drey smiled. "I'll certainly do that."

After his meeting with the Braddocks, Drey dropped Charlene off at his place before proceeding to the apartment building where Joe Dennis had lived. He wanted to question the man's neighbors about the night Joe Dennis died.

He spoke first with the elderly couple who lived across the hall, Fred and Eleanor Billings. Mr. Billings was eager to let him in, assuming he was a detective from the police department. When Drey informed the couple he was an investigator, the Billingses were surprised that after several calls to the police station, no one had come out to ask them questions about what they had heard that night. Drey was surprised as well.

According to Mr. and Mrs. Billings they had been trying to watch their favorite television show and couldn't do so for all the loud noise coming from across the hall. Two men were yelling at each other at the top of their lungs. They had gotten so loud the Billingses had been tempted to call the police for disturbing the peace. In less than an hour the noise had stopped and the next day they had heard that Mr. Dennis—who they thought was a nice hardworking man—had died. Even though the recent news update indicated he had died of natural causes, the couple still questioned why no one wanted to hear what they had to say.

Drey visited several more of Joe Dennis's neighbors, but each one said they hadn't seen or heard a thing that night. One lady questioned why he was asking around when the papers said he'd died of natural causes. He had explained that he just wanted to collect all the facts.

It was getting late and he decided to put off contacting Senator Cayman and Judge Hanlon until tomorrow. What he wanted to do more than anything was to head home and mess around with Charlene some more. Memories of how they had spent their night and this morning caused his nerve endings to react. He loved her taste so much that he could bury his head between her legs and stay there. But then he also enjoyed being inside her, moving in and out and feeling her inner muscles clamp tight as they tried to squeeze everything out of him.

There were other things he enjoyed about her that weren't related to sex. He liked the way she went tit-for-tat with him, how she could make some offhanded comment in a way that made him smile. And he appreciated her sense of humor. His face broke into a lopsided grin when he thought of introducing her to his mother. Daiyu would like her.

His mother.

He then remembered how his mother's name had come up during their meeting with the Braddocks. Sooner or later he would have to tell them the truth, but that would be only after he discovered for himself why Harmon had been trying to reach his mother that night. Had he suspected his life was about to end and wanted to leave her with some information? If that was the case, why Daiyu instead of his wife, Evelyn, or one of his kids? Why not his friends Senator Cayman or Judge Hanlon?

There were a lot of questions yet to be answered, but right now the only thing Drey wanted to think about was the sexy woman sharing his condo.

Charlene paced the room deep in thought. Now, where had she heard the name Daiyu Longwei from? It had first struck her as familiar when they had met with the Braddocks, and the nagging feeling wouldn't go away.

She had meant to ask Drey about it, but while Drey had been driving back from Malcolm Braddock's office her cell phone had rung. Her mother had been in a talkative mood. Nina had wanted to know how her relationship was progressing with the young man she had gone out of town with. Charlene felt her mother didn't need to know that things had progressed so well that she was no longer a virgin.

Thoughts of what she and Drey had shared since last night had her heart racing. She never knew a man could have so much energy when making love. Multiple orgasms were common for him, as well as being able to go for long periods of time without stopping. He'd seemed insatiable.

She'd been surprised at the extent of her own stamina. Granted, there had been pain at first, but after that, she had enjoyed his well-timed strokes into her body, the way he wouldn't hesitate to kiss her all over, as well as his knowledge of a woman's pleasure points. He had done everything last night that he'd said he would do. He had tasted her all over, had made her scream more times than she could count, had given her enough orgasms to last a lifetime and had remained inside her body for a long while...even when they had slept.

She had awakened that morning feeling totally rejuvenated and well rested, although she hadn't gotten much sleep. And then later, what they had done in his office, right there on his desk, made her blush. It was simply amazing how a woman could go from a virgin to a naughty sexual vixen overnight.

She was about to go into the kitchen to unwind with a glass of wine when Drey's phone rang. She wondered if it was that woman Karen calling again and figured she would know soon enough if the woman left a message.

"Drey, mail came for you today. I think it's about your high school class reunion. You can drop by and pick it up anytime. Love you."

She smiled knowing the caller was Drey's mom and that he—

Charlene blinked when she suddenly thought of something. Walking quickly into Drey's office, she went straight to a photograph he had framed on the wall. It was a photo of him and his mother on the day he had graduated from the police academy. A gold plate beneath the picture said "Daiyu Longwei and Her Son, Drey St. John."

Confusion began snarling Charlene's thoughts. She studied the photograph again. She wasn't sure exactly how long ago the photo had been taken, but Drey's mother was definitely still an Asian beauty. It didn't look as if she'd aged that much at all from the photo Drey had hanging in his living room.

Another thought popped into her head when she recalled the meeting earlier at Malcolm Braddock's office. She shook her head. Something didn't make sense.

She turned and walked out of Drey's office at the same time she heard the key turn in his door, alerting her that he had returned. The moment he closed the door behind him he glanced over at her and upon seeing her expression he quickly crossed the room and took her hand.

"What's wrong, Charlene?"

She stared at him, the man she had made love with all night. "I don't know, Drey. You tell me."

The brows covering his slanted eyes lifted and he released her hand. "And what do you want me to tell you?"

She held his gaze and asked, "Why didn't you tell the Braddocks that Daiyu Longwei is your mother?"

Chapter 14

Surprise held Drey immobile for one stunned moment and then he threw his car keys on the table. "I saw no need to do so." He then walked off.

Charlene followed and threw up her hands. "That doesn't make sense. You're handling a murder investigation for them and apparently your mother is somehow involved."

He swung around as a deep, angry frown covered his face. "You don't know that."

"Look, Drey, all I know is what I heard earlier. Your mother was the last person who talked to Harmon. She apparently was the last person he tried to contact. Surely you want to know why."

"I've questioned my mother and she doesn't know why," he snapped. "And I don't want to discuss this investigation with you any longer."

She took a step and got in his face. "Fat chance! I had to leave my home because of this investigation. I'm not even sure I'll have a job to return to when all this is over, and you have the nerve to stand here and tell me you won't discuss it?"

He leaned in closer. A cold, hard look appeared on his face. "Yes, that's what I said. I don't want to discuss it."

And then he turned away and went into his office, closing the door behind him.

Drey leaned against the closed door and drew in a deep breath while his heart vibrated relentlessly against his ribs. No one was to know about his mother until he was prepared to tell it. He didn't want anyone asking those same questions that Charlene had just asked.

He gritted his teeth to keep from lashing out and hitting something. The last thing he wanted was to be on bad terms with Charlene, especially when she was right. He did owe her an explanation. Because of trying to help with his investigation she had been forced to leave her home and could possibly have lost her job.

But he wasn't ready to share with anyone how his world had gotten shattered a few weeks ago. He was still trying to work things out for himself. And he needed more time to do so. Problem was that time had run out. Charlene had figured out the truth and wanted answers. Answers she had a right to have. He could tell from the look on her face that he had hurt her feelings, something he hadn't intended to do. He was about to open the door and go talk to her when he heard his front door slam shut.

Damn!

He quickly came out of his office and crossed the room to snatch open his front door, only to see Charlene drive off in her car. Where in the hell was she going? And more importantly he wondered if she would be coming back. Thinking there was a possibility that she wouldn't come back made his gut clench. His chest suddenly felt tight.

He had never waited on a woman to come back to him before, but he would wait on Charlene Anderson.

Charlene had no idea where she was going. All she knew was that she needed distance from Drey. Going into separate rooms hadn't been far enough for her. She hadn't wanted to be under the same roof with the man.

Deciding the best thing to do was to walk off her anger, she headed in the direction of the mall, and then quickly changed her mind. The last place she needed to go was some place where she might be recognized. Instead she thought she would go to a movie at one of those theaters on the outskirts of town.

A part of her wished she could go to her own house and sleep in her own bed tonight. But, was that what she really wanted after having slept in Drey's bed? She knew the answer without much thinking. No. But she also knew she needed more from Drey than sex. She needed him to trust her enough to tell her what was going on. But why would he trust her? She was nothing to him but a temporary bed partner. Wasn't that what he'd once told her was all he needed? Men didn't have to confide in women they didn't intend to keep around. She refused to acknowledge the pain she felt in her heart. Nor could she acknowledge that she had fallen in love with him.

She thought about what he'd said and the degree of anger with which he'd said it. Her thoughts then shifted to last night and earlier that day, when he had made love to her with a gentleness that had almost brought tears to her eyes.

Yes, she loved him. It was her issue, her personal problem. But it would never, ever be her regret.

Drey stopped pacing long enough to glance down at his watch. It had been three hours and it was now dark outside. Where was she? He had tried reaching her on her cell phone a number of times but hadn't gotten an answer. Evidently she was too mad at him to return his call. He had even called her home number on the off chance she'd gone there, though he refused to think she would put herself in danger by doing that.

After he had time to fully think about it, he had called himself all kinds of fool for saying what he had to her. She definitely deserved an apology and an explanation—if she would only return to listen.

His breath caught when he heard a car door slam and automatically he moved to the door. If it was Charlene, she would knock since he hadn't yet given her a key. His heart began racing when he heard footsteps moving up his walkway and he knew it was Charlene. It just had to be.

Too eager to wait for her knock, he opened the door and there she stood, utterly beautiful in the moonlight with a startled look on her face. "Sorry," he said softly. "I didn't mean to scare you."

She shrugged. "No harm done."

His gaze caressed her face before he stepped aside, allowing her entrance. Hoping she was there to stay and hadn't just come to pick up her things. "If you're hungry we can order out," he said.

She walked into the foyer and turned around after placing her shoulder bag on the table. "Thanks, but I'm not hungry. I took in a movie and grabbed a couple of hot dogs while I was there."

"Oh." So that's where she had gone. "Well, if you've got some time I'd appreciate it if we talked."

She placed her hands in her back pocket and tilted her head back to meet his gaze. "What about?"

"What I didn't want to talk about earlier."

Her gaze lowered to the floor. "You don't have to do that."

"Yes, I do." And he honestly knew that he did. He could feel the strain between them, the distance. He didn't want that. He wanted things the way they were last night. He wanted the closeness.

"All right, then. Talk."

"Can we sit down in the living room?"

She shrugged again. "Sure. Why not?"

He watched as she went to sit on the sofa, folding her legs beneath her. With his heart still racing non-stop, he took the chair across from her, when what he really wanted to do was reach out and pull her into his lap and kiss her. But he knew he couldn't do that. He had screwed up and had to backpedal. Get back into her good graces. Literally, he had to do something he had never done with a woman before—bare his soul.

He was a private person. No other woman had ever reached beyond that area of "do not enter" with him. But Charlene had invaded his space. In just a short period of time she had gotten totally and completely under his skin. And last night he had gotten under hers in the most intimate way. He had been inside her, places where no other man had ever gone. He had branded her with his markings all over her body and didn't regret doing so. And if given the opportunity he wouldn't hesitate to do it again.

"First, I want to apologize for lashing out at you earlier, Charlene. I had no right to do that. You deserve to know what's going on with the investigation, every aspect of it."

He paused a moment before continuing. "What I'm about to tell you is something I haven't told anyone yet, especially the Braddocks. But I will eventually tell them because they too have a right to know. I took this case before knowing it myself. While I was investigating, my mother's name come up as the last person the congressman spoke with. My mother says she honestly doesn't know why he called her and I believe her. But something I do know is that the two of them had a history."

"What sort of history?" she asked quietly.

He was silent for a moment and then he said, "My mother and Congressman Braddock had an affair many years ago, before I was born and before she married my father. She was young, inexperienced and thought she was in love, and yes, he was a married man at the time. However, it's my understanding that he and his wife, Evelyn, were going through some things. That does not excuse his behavior or my mother's."

Charlene nodded and then said, "I can see your reluctance to spring that on the Braddocks."

"Yes, but there's more. It goes a lot deeper than that."

She leaned forward in her seat. "Deeper in what way?"

He swallowed and felt a sudden tightness in his chest.

This was the first time he would admit this to anyone. He spoke, hearing the words as he said them. "Congressman Braddock was my biological father."

Chapter 15

A stunned expression covered Charlene's face. "Your father!"

"Yes, my father. However, I didn't find out until I questioned my mother as to why the congressman would call her and just how they knew each other."

Charlene stared at him and immediately she knew that admitting such a thing had been hard for him. "And Ronald St. John? He was your—"

"He is the only father I know. I can't deny it was Harmon Braddock's seed that made me, but it was Ronald St. John's love that shaped me into who I am today. He's the person I remember from the time I was in the crib, who had always been there for me. The person who took me to my Little League games, showed up at every activity I was in while attending school and the person who made me believe I could do anything. Ronald St. John is the man I consider my father."

Charlene eased to the edge of her seat. She could tell Drey still had a hard time accepting that biologically, he was a Braddock. "Didn't you say that the congressman was your mentor?"

"Yes."

"To me that means he wanted to share some aspect of your life."

Drey nodded. "My mother said basically the same thing."

"Don't you believe her?"

He leaned back in his chair. "It's not that I don't believe her, Charlene. I just don't care. Braddock had his family and Ronald St. John had his. I consider myself a St. John."

"But truly you are a Braddock." There, she'd said what he evidently needed to hear. He couldn't deny who he was, not when Braddock blood ran through his veins.

He stood and walked over to the window and glanced out. She knew he was thinking. Moments later he turned to her. "I don't know how I'm going to tell them, but I know I have to. I'm even doubtful that their mother knows about me. It's my understanding that she's aware that Harmon had an affair and with whom, but she doesn't know that a child had been conceived out of it. I don't want to do anything to tarnish her husband's memory."

Charlene didn't know what to say because that was a good possibility when Mrs. Braddock discovered the truth.

He interrupted her thoughts by saying, "And then the siblings might be resentful."

She wondered if he was afraid that would happen. Was he concerned that his siblings would reject him because of what their father and his mother had done thirty-three years ago? "I don't know, Drey. I met them today and they seem a pretty confident yet wholesome trio."

"They are close."

"Yes, I can tell they are," she said slowly. "But that doesn't mean they won't let you in or that—"

"I might not want to get in."

He did, Charlene immediately thought. Otherwise he wouldn't be carrying so much on his shoulders. What would it take to make him see that no one could blame him for the congressman's and his mother's actions all those years ago?

Suddenly, something hit her. *Drey needed her.* She wasn't sure just where that thought or idea came from; it was just there, in her mind and in her heart. It was still strange how quickly things had progressed between them, but they had. And although he might never admit to any feelings for her, she knew at that moment she had to have meant something to him for him to have shared that with her. Okay, she wasn't about to operate under any false illusions. In all honesty, she knew exactly where she stood with him. But for her, it didn't matter. She loved him and would always love him and would be there for him until he said it was time for her to go. She would love to share more with him, but he had a wall erected, one she doubted she could scale.

She slowly walked over to where he was standing. For a long moment she stood silently beside him and looked out at the same pond, saw the same ducks and for a little while felt the same sense of peace.

"So now you know," he finally said softly, without looking over at her.

"Yes, now I know. Thanks for sharing." She then stood on tiptoe and kissed him on the cheek.

Automatically, he reached out his hand and captured her around the waist and pulled her closer to him. She felt him, every hard part of him, while she gazed deep into his eyes. He was tall, well muscled and unmistakably male. And she was willing to accept that he would not love her back no matter how much she loved him. But that was okay. She could handle it. Didn't someone say it was better to have loved and lost than not to have loved at all?

"Are you still upset with me?" he asked, and the deep timbre of his voice felt like silk sliding across her skin.

"Not anymore. But promise me the next time that we'll talk through things," she said firmly.

"I promise."

The air between them suddenly felt hot, charged. Sexual tension was building, spreading. She could feel it the longer he looked into her eyes. Desire was vibrating in her veins, causing a ripple effect in her stomach. She watched his gaze shift slowly from her eyes to her mouth, and automatically she licked her lips.

"Let me do that for you," he said in a throaty voice and proceeded to lick her mouth from corner to corner. As she released a breathless sigh, he slid his tongue inside.

Caught, she thought, as she grabbed hold of it with her own and began mating with it, the way he had taught her to do last night. She felt him pull her deeper into his arms as she feasted on his mouth. When she had returned from the movies she had been wound up so tight, and now she was beginning to unravel, right in his arms, under the onslaught of his tongue.

He suddenly pulled back and shut the blinds. He then proceeded to tear his clothes off right there. She followed his lead. He finished undressing before she did and helped her get out of her clothes. The last piece to go was her panties and when he dropped to his knees to help her remove them she had a feeling where such helpfulness would lead.

He backed her up against the closed door for support, spread her legs and then buried his head between them. She heard his manly growl just seconds before his tongue invaded her, going deep and devouring her. She was no longer shocked by how much he enjoyed tasting her this way. She held her breath, fought back an intense scream as sensations tore into her, ripped through every part of her body, fizzled through her veins and electrified her pores.

And then he took his hands and lifted her hips, wrapped her legs over his shoulders so he could feast more. She was a goner. She felt the buildup inside her ready to burst and couldn't hold back any longer.

She screamed as an orgasm of gigantic proportions slashed into her. But that didn't deter Drey from his goal, which was to make her come again.

She did. But instead of screaming she released a deep, gutted moan while he continued to hungrily lap her up. And when she thought there was no way she could take any more, he quickly eased her legs off his shoulders and placed them around her waist just seconds before thrusting hard into her feminine core. He began pumping into her with whiplike speed, making her aware of every throbbing inch of him that was sliding in and out of her, stroking her insides with a skill and perfection that she found astounding.

The warmth of his breath stirred her ear as he whispered just what he was doing to her and how he was doing it. She wrapped her arms around his neck when she felt another orgasm coming on. And when he called out her name, she felt him explode deep inside her, shooting his hot release everywhere. She followed, tumbling into a sea of ecstasy that nearly drowned her.

Moments later, without disconnecting their bodies, he supported her back with the palm of his hand and with her legs still securely wrapped around his waist, he moved away from the door and carried her to his bedroom.

Drey stared at Charlene while she slept.

It was a crazy thing to do but a rather simple one, mainly because he liked looking at her, especially after they'd made love. He liked seeing the perspiration on her skin as well as the passion marks he'd put in various places. He liked seeing the peaceful look on her face and how her lips twitched on occasion while she slept.

To be quite honest, he liked everything about her. Especially the way she gave herself to him, so unselfishly and with a thrill that excited him and heightened his desire for her.

When she shifted in sleep, he tilted his head to the side and gazed at her breasts. The tips of her nipples still looked hard, as if they begged to be licked. Or better yet, sucked. He could imagine her baby doing that very thing.

No, he couldn't imagine it because the baby would belong to some other man rather than him, and the thought that someone else's child would grow in her stomach was unacceptable.

Easing closer to her, he placed a hand on her waist. He wasn't used to feeling possessive, but around her you could call him Caveman Drey and it wouldn't bother him any.

Why?

Why was he so affected by her in a way he had never been by any other woman? The sex was good. Off the chain. But good, off-the-chain sex had never made him feel this way toward a woman. Ever. But then he had to admit making love to Charlene wasn't just good or off-the-chain. It was thrilling, sensational, mind-blowing. It was the kind that made you want to make love all night, all day, every chance you got. It was addictive.

But most importantly, it was theirs.

And he knew he would only feel this way with her, which suddenly made sweat bead on his forehead. He was getting hooked on her and for him that wasn't a good thing. He wasn't a man prone to having just one woman in his life. He didn't intend to settle down, now or ever. He liked having bed partners, not long-term girlfriends or, heaven forbid, a wife. It just wasn't in his makeup.

He would enjoy what they shared for now and then work her out of his system. When she left that would be it. He would bury himself in another case. And he would be fine. He would get over her. He had to.

Charlene woke with the sun shining in through the window. Her head lay nestled in the crook of Drey's shoulder and he was turned slightly toward her with one leg thrown over her thigh and one hand resting between her legs, tangled in the curls covering her femininity.

She glanced up and found him asleep, which was fine. It gave her time to think about last night. He had shared himself with her, and later she had shared herself with him. She had no regrets. All she had was a happy mind and a satisfied body. She couldn't help but smile at that.

"Aren't we just full of cheer this morning?"

She glanced up and looked into Drey's smiling face. He was awake. "Yes, we are," she said, and then almost groaned out loud when his hand between her legs began moving.

"Like how that feels?" he asked in a husky voice. "Do you like for me to touch you this way?"

"Yes, I like it."

"Umm, I like it too. I like it especially when you get wet, like you're doing now. You're getting real wet. You know what that means, don't you?"

"Yes."

"Then ease over here. I want you to ride me this morning."

She slid her body over his, found him hard and ready and looked down into his face. "Is this all you want me to do?"

"For starters."

And then he lifted her up and eased her down on his shaft, connecting their bodies immediately when he slid into her. She began riding him and from the expressions that crossed his face, he was enjoying it. And so was she. She could get used to starting each of her mornings this way, but she knew that was only a dream. For now, though, she could make her dream a reality.

* * *

Drey glanced over at Charlene across the breakfast table. He had a busy day ahead of him. First he planned on meeting with Senator Cayman and Judge Hanlon, before paying a visit to Stewart Industries. There had to be a reason Harmon had been contacting his mother. Was there some specific information he had wanted her to find out for him but had gotten killed before given the chance to reveal it to her? Connor Stewart, who was currently dating Shondra, had welcomed his visit. Connor's father was CEO, but it was rumored the old man was about to step down and would name Connor as his successor.

"More coffee?"

He glanced across the table at Charlene and smiled. "No, but I'd love having more of you."

She chuckled. "You've had enough, thank you. Don't be so greedy."

"Ah," he said with an amusing glint in his eyes, "you of all people have the nerve to call me greedy. You, who have become the multiorgasm queen."

Her smile unashamedly widened. "Yes. You know what they say. Practice makes perfect."

He laughed, not believing the conversation they were having at the breakfast table. "I want you to hold on to that thought until I return later."

"I will." Her expression turned serious then and she asked, "Do you think Congressman Braddock took either Senator Cayman or Judge Hanlon into his confidence and told them anything?"

"Not sure but I won't know until I ask. Once I tell them about my theory regarding the congressman's death not being an accident, I'm sure they'll want to help any way they can."

"I feel certain they will too."

Drey reached across the table and took Charlene's hand in his. "Miss me today."

She smiled and lifted the hand that held hers and kissed the back of it. "I will."

Chapter 16

The look on Judge Hanlon's face was one of shock. "What do you mean you think Harmon's death wasn't an accident?"

Drey knew it was a lot for the judge to believe but he answered anyway. "There are a lot of inconsistencies in the reports. And then there's Joe Dennis's death."

"But I thought Dennis died of a heart attack."

"It seems a lot of people think that as well."

The judge raised his bushy brows. "But you have reason to believe otherwise?"

"Yes, I have reason to believe otherwise." Drey decided not to go into details about the inconsistencies in the autopsy report. To do so meant revealing how they obtained the report. There was no way he could overlook the fact that Hanlon was a judge, one known as

"Hard-time Hanlon." No criminal brought before him got off easily.

"Well, I hope you find the person responsible. Harmon and I go back a long way, all the way back to when the two of us were young upstart attorneys working in the prosecutor's office. That was over twenty years ago and we remained good friends since."

Drey nodded. "I won't rest until I find the person responsible."

"Good, now what can I do to help?"

"I just need to know if the congressman ever mentioned anything to you about Stewart Industries."

The judge rubbed his jaw in deep thought. "Not that I can recall. Why?"

"Because it seems the last call Harmon made was to there."

The judge looked surprised. "Why on earth would Harmon call there?"

Drey stood. "We don't know but that's just one of the many things I plan to find out."

The judge then stood as well. "Well, young man, if you find the person responsible, I want to try him or her in my court. If they're found guilty I promise they will pay for what they did to my friend."

Drey found Senator Cayman on the golf course and had to ride in the golf cart with him to hold a conversation. Now retired, the senator told of his and Harmon's friendship.

"You know," the older man was saying, "in a way I feel responsible for Harmon's political career. After about twenty years as a prosecutor, Harmon accepted a position as my head legal counsel and he was a darn good one. Worked for me for a number of years before deciding to run for political office himself. He was a darn good congressman. But…"

Drey lifted a brow. "But?"

"But even I would have to admit that the bill Harmon voted down a few years ago—one that would have helped a lot of needy families—surprised as well as disappointed a lot of people, especially Malcolm. That's when he walked away from the family."

Drey wondered why the senator was telling him that. Evidently his confusion showed on his face because the senator then added, "There's always a dirty side of politics, son."

Drey thought on his words before asking carefully, "And you think Congressman Braddock wasn't an honest politician?"

"I'm not saying that. The Harmon Braddock I knew was a very honest and upright man. But people can change. He wasn't perfect."

The senator's statement made Drey press on with his questions. "You and Harmon spent a lot of time together, right?"

"Yes. We played golf together at least once a week when he wasn't in Washington."

"Did he ever mention Stewart Industries to you?"

The older man thought on his question and then shook his head. "No, not that I recall. Why?"

The golf cart came to a stop and they got off near a beautiful pond. "We have reason to believe that he made his last telephone call to a person there."

The senator seemed to ponder Drey's words and then said, "Hmm, I find that interesting."

Drey lifted a brow. "And why is that?"

"Because Stewart has been in the news a lot lately. Everyone is wondering when the old man will be stepping down, and more importantly, if he'll make his son CEO when he does. I've often heard that fathers and sons have a difference of opinion when it comes to running a company. Personally, I think Connor Stewart would do a better job. He's smart, intelligent and a natural leader." The senator then gave a low chuckle. "And I understand he's something of a ladies' man."

Drey didn't comment. From what he could see, Connor Stewart's days as a ladies' man were over, since according to the gossip column of the local newspaper, there was speculation as to whether he and Shondra were secretly planning a June wedding.

"I appreciate you taking time to meet with me today, Senator."

"No problem." The senator then eyed him curiously. "How good are you with a club?" the older man asked.

Drey couldn't help but chuckle. "Fair."

"Well, if you ever want to get in any practice time, this is the place to be."

Drey smiled. "Thanks, I'll remember that."

The last person Drey needed to visit was Connor Stewart. A Matthew McConaughey look-alike with blue eyes and long blond hair, Connor worked hard and was all-business. On the other hand, Drey also heard Connor had a wild streak, which was the reason his father hadn't stepped down to make him CEO.

And just as Senator Cayman had said, Connor was something of a ladies' man…or he used to be. It had grown increasingly obvious to the media over the past couple of months that he was strictly wining and dining one woman—Shondra Braddock. Their interracial love affair was getting a lot of attention.

Drey had met Connor before and thought he was a likeable guy. "Thanks for seeing me," he said, taking the seat Connor offered.

"No problem. I know Shondra's mind will be eased when she finds out what really happened to her father and why."

Drey began asking him a series of questions, trying to determine if there was any record of Harmon having any contact with Stewart.

Connor shook his head. "Trust me, if there was, Shondra would have discovered it long ago." He chuckled. "I'm sure you're aware that was her primary reason for taking a job here a few months ago. She was determined to undercover some wrongdoings with the company. She didn't find anything. However, we were able to trace Harmon's calls back to one of my employees, a competent woman by the name of Daiyu Longwei. I understand you've already spoken to her yourself."

Drey shifted uneasily in his chair. "Yes, I have."

"And I'm sure she's told you she doesn't know why the congressman was trying to contact her."

Drey spent the next few minutes going over some of the committees that the congressman was a part of to see if any were connected to Stewart Industries in any way. They didn't discover any.

When Drey stood to leave, Connor said, "I understand that you have a houseguest."

At Drey's raised brow, Connor smiled. "Shondra mentioned it. She likes Charlene and appreciates the information she was able to pass on to you about the autopsy reports."

Drey nodded. "Yes, Charlene finding out about the false autopsy report made it obvious there was some sort of cover-up going on."

"Well, Shondra and I want to show our gratitude by giving you this," Connor said, offering a key to Drey.

At Drey's bemused look, Connor said, "It's the key to my beach house in Malibu. It's free for you to use this weekend. One of my pilots will be at your disposal to fly you there."

Drey reached out and took the key with a huge grin on his face. "Thanks. I'd love to take you up on your offer."

Drey let himself in the house later that day and immediately heard the sound of the vacuum cleaner. Finding Charlene in the hallway, he walked up to her and lightly tapped her on the shoulder. He hadn't wanted to scare her but could tell when she nearly jumped out of her skin that he had done so anyway.

"Why are you vacuuming?" he asked, pulling a Houston Texans cap off her head to see how her hair tumbled to her shoulders. "I have a housekeeper."

She smiled up at him. "I know but I wanted to stay busy. I'm not a television person."

He pulled her into his arms thinking it had to be hard for her to spend her days with nothing to do. They had both agreed that the less she went out, the better. "Well, I have a surprise for you."

Her eyes lit up. "What?"

"As you know I met with Connor Stewart today, and he was gracious enough to offer me the use of his beach house in California for the weekend."

She eyed him skeptically before asking, "I know how

busy you are with the investigation. Will you have time to get away?"

He smiled. "I'll make time as long as you come with me, and as long as we're back by Monday. I have another meeting with the Braddocks then." She clapped her hands, and her excitement, he thought, was infectious.

"Okay, I can guarantee those two things," she said happily.

He chuckled as he wrapped his arms around her. "Then let's start packing."

Chapter 17

Monday morning Drey eased out of bed and glanced over his shoulder at Charlene, who was sound asleep. They had returned to Houston late last night after having spent a wonderful weekend in Malibu. It had been a lazy weekend where they talked, made love, ate, made love and then repeated the process all over again.

He would be the first to say it was a weekend they both needed. During their talks they found out a lot about each other, and their walks on the beach had been extra, extra special. He stepped into the shower thinking of the meeting he was scheduled to have that day with the Braddocks. He really hadn't discovered anything new since their last meeting. The only good thing he would report was that his former partner with the police department had returned from vacation and was to report in today. He had left a message on his cell phone asking that they meet later today for a private conversation. If any of the cops on the force were dirty, he knew without a doubt that his former partner, Lavender Sessions, was clean.

Drey turned the water on full blast. He would surprise Charlene and prepare her breakfast in bed. She deserved it. He wasn't aware of just how vigorous a sexual appetite he had until he'd met her. The more he made love to her, the more he wanted her. All it took was a look, a touch and he was ready. She brought that out in him, a need he couldn't deny even if he tried. Because of her, he looked forward to his days and especially his nights. What he didn't look forward to was the day she would pack to leave, once he had solved the case and brought Harmon's and Dennis's killer to justice.

Charlene had gotten up to use the bathroom and through the shower glass door saw Drey amidst the steam. She could only stare at the body that had given her so much pleasure over the past week.

Every time she saw his nakedness, a buzz of desire would run through her. And whenever he looked at her through his slanted eyes, it was always in a way that no man had looked at her before. It was as if she were the only woman on this earth. The only woman he wanted.

She suddenly felt a throbbing sensation between her legs and could not understand, especially after their weekend and last night, how she could want him again so soon and with such intensity. She inhaled deeply, deciding not to try and understand it, just accept it as the way things were with them. They were two highly stimulated sexual beings who enjoyed making love to each other.

She shimmied the robe off her shoulders and began walking naked toward the shower. He hadn't seen her yet, but she knew pretty soon he would. He seemed to have a radar system that homed in on her no matter where she was. And she had no complaints.

Drey rubbed a wet hand down his face the moment he heard the shower door open. He reached out and pulled Charlene to him.

"Couldn't sleep?" he asked her in a deep, sexy voice.

She shook her head. "I woke up and you were gone. I missed having you inside me."

It had become the norm when they made love for the final time at night, he would pull her close and go to sleep still inside her. He had the uncanny ability to keep his erection hard while in her. For some reason he needed the connection of their bodies intimately entwined that way and it seemed that she did as well.

He reached out and pushed her hair away from her face to keep most of it from getting wet. "Do you know how beautiful you are?" he asked huskily.

"No," she said, smiling. "Are you going to tell me?"

"Yes. You're beautiful here," he said, lightly touching her lips. "And here," he said, tracing a hand down her chin and neck to fondle her breasts tenderly.

Charlene inhaled sharply from his touch. There was perfection in his fingers, she thought as her eyes gazed deeply into his. And then he leaned down and captured her mouth with his.

The moment their lips touched and their tongues tangled, she released a deep moan as a mirage of stimulating sensations invaded her. He took his time kissing her, as he usually did, stroking his tongue over hers while his hands continued to fondle her breasts, skimming over the hardened tips and making her moan even more.

And then she felt his hand move between her legs and he began touching her there, stirring sensations that begged for release.

She felt herself being lifted and knew the exact moment he had pressed her back against the shower wall, all without breaking their kiss. And when he wrapped her legs around his waist and then used his knee to spread those same legs apart, she knew what was coming.

She moaned deep into his mouth the moment he entered her, his engorged shaft invading her the very way she wanted, and the way she needed. When he began thrusting in and out of her with rapid precision, her moans became whimpers. Moments later, she quickly pulled her mouth away from his when she couldn't take any more.

"Drey!"

Screaming his name seemed to reach something primitive inside Drey. He threw his head back at the same time he thrust deeper inside her, hitting the very spot inside her he wanted to activate—her erogenous zone—and making her scream again. She screamed a third time when she felt the essence of his hot release flooding her, and then he was kissing her again with a hunger that always astounded her.

And that always made her love him even more.

She owed Drey a shirt, Charlene thought as she walked into the store at the mall. After their shower he had gotten dressed for his meeting with the Braddocks and she had gone back to bed. When he was ready to leave and had come into the room to kiss her goodbye, in a playful moment she had tried pulling him down in bed with her, only to rip a few buttons off his shirt. They had ended up making love again before he had gone into his closet to find another shirt to put on. He had teased her about owing him a shirt and she wanted to surprise him with it when he came home later.

She knew what store she wanted to make the purchase from and figured she would be in and out in no time. She felt wonderfully giddy at the thought of buying an item of clothing for him. Other than her father, she had never purchased clothes for a man before.

Charlene had selected a shirt she thought he would like and with the shirt in her hand, she was proceeding toward the cashier station when she heard a loud voice. Some man was arguing with a store clerk. She stopped dead in her tracks, her heart racing and the hairs on the back of her neck standing up. She recognized that voice. It was the same one that had argued with Nate that day in his office. The day before the autopsy report had gotten changed.

She looked around to see where the voice was coming from and whom it belonged to. She spotted him and recognized him immediately as a politician whose picture she'd seen numerous times in the newspapers.

Something made her move in that direction and she got close enough to see he was still giving the store clerk a hard time about a purchase he was trying to exchange. His voice continued to get louder.

She glanced down at his hand. He was holding his key ring, probably the one to his car. But what caught her attention was one of the keys on the ring. It was *that* key. The same one that had been on the autopsy table next to Joe Dennis's body. No wonder neither she nor Drey had been able to find it that night they had gotten into the coroner's office.

Realizing the smart thing to do was to leave before he got a chance to see her, she started to back up. At the same moment the man looked up and caught her staring. Her breath got logged in her throat, but she tried to appear normal. How could he possibly know who she was since their paths had never crossed? However, deciding she would not give him the chance to react one way or the other, she placed the shirt back on the stack and quickly walked out of the store. By the time she got to the parking lot she had begun running to her car.

She needed to contact Drey immediately.

Drey and his former partner, Lavender Sessions, who was now a detective with the Houston Police Department, met in private at Lavender's home.

"You know if I find out anything I'll let you know, Drey. And just so you'll know, I wasn't on vacation for the past couple of weeks like everyone assumes. I was in D.C.," Lavender was saying. "There is reason to believe some of the guys are on the take and the entire police corruption is centered on one man. We're working with the FBI to exposed his identity. It has spread into more areas than the police department and we want to stop it before it spreads any further."

Drey nodded. He then studied his friend, concerned for his safety. "Are you sure that you're safe and they don't suspect you of anything?"

Lavender smiled. "It's too soon for them to suspect anything. Just before I left for two weeks, I was approached to consider making extra money on the side.

I knew then I was being asked to be a part of the bad guys. I'm supposed to give them my answer this week. I'll be the mole the FBI needs to bring things to an end."

Lavender continued. "And you're probably correct in thinking Congressman Braddock was murdered. He had contacted the FBI indicating he had some items to turn over. He never made it back to Washington."

Before Drey could respond, his cell phone rang. "Excuse me." He pulled it out of his jacket pocket and quickly flipped it open once he saw it was Charlene. "Yes, sweetheart?"

"I saw him, Drey," she said in a panicked tone. "I saw the man who was arguing with Nate that day. I recognized his voice. And he has the key. I saw the key that was taken out of Joe Dennis's stomach on his key ring."

Drey was out of his seat immediately. "Where are you?"

"The mall."

"The mall! But I thought we agreed that—"

"I know. I know," she said, cutting him off. "You can spank me later."

Any other time he would have found her statement amusing, but not now. Drey glanced over at Lavender. He knew his friend had been following most of the conversation. Drey turned on the speaker to his cell phone and then placed it on the table between them. He wanted Lavender to hear everything. "Listen, Charlene. Can you tell if you're being followed?"

She paused and he figured she was looking out of her rearview mirror. "No. I ran out of the store and left immediately. I doubt he had time to follow me."

Drey nodded, relieved. "And you recognized the man?"

"Yes, Drey, you won't believe who he is."

Drey glanced over at Lavender. "Okay, who is he?"

Charlene let out a disgusted sigh before saying, "Judge Bruce Hanlon."

Drey instructed Charlene to meet him at home. When she got there he had arrived already with another man. He introduced her to Lavender.

"I need to alert the Braddocks," Drey said. "They consider Hanlon a family friend." Anger ripped through him when he remembered meeting with the judge last week. The man had pretended to be so concerned about how the investigation was going. Now Drey knew why.

"I've already contacted Washington," Lavender added. "They've notified FBI headquarters here. It appears things are going down sooner than we expected. It all makes sense now. The judge is the ringleader who's been working with a local crime family and taking kickbacks. Warrants are being prepared for everyone involved as we speak."

"Good," Drey said, pulling Charlene into his arms, not caring that Lavender was watching. He needed to hold her to make sure she was fine.

After a few moments she pulled back. "We need to go tell the Braddocks," she said. "Weren't you supposed to meet with them today?"

Drey nodded. "I did, earlier. They mentioned they would all be together at the family home this evening. They were joining their mother for dinner." He glanced at his watch. "Come on. They should be arriving now."

Drey and Charlene arrived in record time and were led by the housekeeper to the family room where the

Braddocks and their significant others were sitting around talking. Everyone looked up, surprised to see them.

"Sorry to interrupt," Drey said, "but there has been a major development that I think all of you need to be made aware of immediately."

"What?" Malcolm said, coming to his feet, as the others gave Drey their undivided attention.

Drey glanced around. "Where's Evelyn?" he asked.

"She's taking a stroll in the flower garden," Shondra said. "Drey, what is it? What have you found out?"

Drey sighed, thinking maybe it was for the best that Evelyn wasn't present for this part. He knew how much she thought of Judge Hanlon as a friend. "We discovered the person responsible for both your father's and Joe Dennis's deaths."

"Who?" they all asked simultaneously.

"Judge Hanlon."

The room got completely quiet and then it was Shondra who spoke. "There must be some mistake, Drey. The judge is like a godfather to all of us. He and Dad were good friends. He would never hurt Dad."

"He did, Shondra, and a warrant is already in the works for his arrest."

Tyson was out of his seat in a flash. "Damn, I hope you're wrong because what we didn't say earlier is that Hanlon is here, with Mom in the flower garden. He's joining us for dinner."

Everyone turned toward the French doors, ready to run, when a smiling Evelyn appeared with the judge by her side. Her smile widened when she saw Drey. "Drey, how are you? Glad you could visit. You know Judge Hanlon, don't you?"

The room got silent. Drey narrowed his gaze. "Yes, I know him."

Drey followed the judge's eyes. He was staring at Charlene, probably remembering her from the store at the mall earlier and was probably wondering why she was there. Drey decided to make introductions. "And this is a friend of mine, Charlene Anderson."

Forever the gracious hostess, Evelyn smiled and said, "Welcome to our home, Charlene."

"Thank you."

With all the niceties out of the way, Drey turned his attention back to the judge. "This is a coincidence, Judge Hanlon. You're just the person I want to see. I believe you have something that belongs to the coroner's office."

The man's smile didn't quite reach his eyes when he said, "You must be mistaken."

Drey's smile was likewise. "I don't think so. Charlene works for the coroner's office and it just so happens that a key she saw on your key ring today is one that turned up missing from the coroner's office."

The judge chuckled. "That's not possible."

"It is," Drey said, getting tired of this cat-and-mouse game the judge was playing. "It's the same key that was taken out of Joe Dennis's stomach during an autopsy."

Judge Hanlon looked around to find all eyes on him. "Come on, Drey, do you expect Evelyn and the others to believe that? They've known me for years. Why would a key taken out of someone's stomach interest me?" He turned to Evelyn. "He has insulted me. Either he leaves or I will."

Evelyn looked confused. She glanced from the judge to Drey, then over to Charlene. "Drey, I don't understand, what's going on? How can you accuse the judge of something like that?"

Drey took a deep breath and then said, "Easily, Evelyn, because that's not the least of his deeds. He is also responsible for Harmon's death."

Evelyn let out a startled gasp and clutched her stomach. Then an angry look appeared on her face. "Drey, that is absurd. How dare you accuse Bruce of something like that? I'm going to have to ask you to leave right now."

"No, let him stay," Malcolm said, taking a step forward and keeping his eyes on the judge the entire time.

"Ty, Shondra and I hired Drey to uncover the truth about Dad's death," Malcolm told his mother. Then he turned to the judge. "I don't like the fact that he's accused you any more than you do. But I think we need to hear him out."

Judge Hanlon stiffened and anger exploded in his face. "What! You would take the word of your father's bastard over me?"

Startled gasps went through the room, and seeing that everyone was now staring at Drey, a smirk appeared on the judge's face. "Yes, that's right, Drey. You thought I didn't know, didn't you? Well, I found out the truth. When were you going to tell these good people that you are Harmon Braddock's bastard child and that your mother is Daiyu Longwei, a woman he had an affair with thirty-three years ago?"

Evelyn held her hand over her heart as she continued to look at Drey. She then asked in a low and shocked voice, "It is true, Drey? Are you Daiyu's son? Was Harmon your biological father?"

Drey looked around the room at all the shocked

faces. He then glanced back at Evelyn, seeing the hurt in her eyes. "Yes, Daiyu Longwei is my mother and Harmon Braddock was my biological father."

Charlene's heart went out to Drey at the same time red-hot anger exploded inside her. She knew this was not the way he had wanted his siblings to find out about him, and now this murderer, of all people, was trying to make him look like the bad guy.

Charlene crossed the room and said to the judge, "You ass!" She was angry beyond reason. "It all makes sense now."

The judge looked at her as if she were demented. "I have no idea what you're talking about."

"Well, let me enlighten you. I just figured out the reason Congressman Braddock was trying so hard to reach Drey's mother before he was killed. It was to warn her about you. You were going to blackmail him, weren't you? You were going to expose the truth about Drey if the congressman didn't cooperate. You knew the congressman was going to turn you in and you wanted to blackmail him, the same way you blackmailed my boss into cooperating with you by falsifying documents. Joe Dennis did not die of a heart attack. He was murdered. I saw the original autopsy report myself."

"Lady, you are crazy."

"And, Judge, you are a murderer, two times over. If you're so innocent, then let us see your key ring."

"Yes, Judge, why don't you let us see your key ring?" Connor Stewart said. He moved closer to Shondra's side.

"Fine!" the judge said, fumbling into his pocket. "I'll show everyone my key ring just to prove you're crazy."

He pulled out his key ring and held it up. Charlene recognized the key immediately and pointed to it. "That's it! It's *that* one."

The judge rolled his eyes. "That's the key to my locker at the gym."

Something about the key caught Evelyn's attention. "May I see it for a minute, Bruce?"

He blinked at her request, and trying to keep his cool, he said, "Certainly, Evelyn. But like I said it's the key to my locker at the gym." He removed the key from the ring and handed it to her.

She gazed down at it. Turned it over in her hand. Studied the numbers engraved on the back. When she lifted her head and gazed at Judge Hanlon, she wore a shocked look on her face. "Where did you get this key from, Bruce?"

He shrugged. "Like I said, it's my locker key that—"

"No," she interrupted him. "It's not a locker key. It's a key that's been in the Braddock family for years and it goes to a safe hidden on the mansion grounds where Harmon kept his important papers. What are you doing with this key?"

Before anyone could blink, in a calculated move, Hanlon reached out and grabbed Charlene and held her in front of him as a shield. "Stay back or I'll kill her!"

It was then that everyone noticed the small revolver he had pulled from his jacket. He was holding it close to Charlene's head. "You think you're so smart," he said, his angry words directed at Drey. "I knew Harmon would want to protect you at all costs. The last thing he wanted was for you to know that he was your father. It would have been real simple for him to be a part of everything. But no, he wanted to play Mr. Good Guy and threaten to turn me in unless I got out of it. Hell,

I didn't want to get out of it. The money was good. I liked the power. The corruption suited me just fine."

"Bruce, surely you didn't—"

"Shut up, Evelyn," Hanlon said angrily. "Yes, I had him killed. He was going to the Feds with evidence. I tried blackmailing him and it didn't work. He was going to get to Daiyu before I did. So I had to have him eliminated. Joe Dennis helped. And then he got greedy so I had to eliminate him as well."

"You killed our father?" Shondra asked, coming out of her shock. "How could you?"

He sneered. "The same way I plan to kill all of you, without batting an eye, starting with this crazy one first," he said of Charlene. "She messed things up by snooping around. There's going to be a fire and all of you will perish. The Braddock mansion will burn to the ground and no one will ask any questions because I have several firemen on the take too. Their report will reflect whatever I want it to say."

"You're the one crazy if you think we're going to stand here and let you kill us too," Malcolm said.

Hanlon smiled. "You won't have a choice. I've already called for backup. A few of Houston's finest who happen to be on my payroll," he bragged.

Sirens could be heard in the distance. "I think I hear them coming now," Hanlon said, grinning from ear to ear.

Knowing the cops that were arriving were the good cops Lavender had dispatched and not the bad ones the judge was referring to, Drey figured that he had to get Charlene out of Hanlon's clutches. He gave Malcolm a nod and as if his brother understood what he wanted him to do, Malcolm kept the man talking. Confident the ball was in his court, the judge bragged about all his illegal activities and how Harmon wanted to ruin things for him.

Too late, Hanlon noticed how close Drey had gotten to him, and when he made a move to aim the gun straight at Drey, Charlene elbowed him in the side. It was just the opportunity Drey needed, and within seconds, with one jab to the judge's midsection and several quick karate kicks, the man fell flat on his face. The men in the room rushed forward and used a cord from a nearby curtain to quickly tie his hands and feet.

Lavender stormed in with several police officers on his heels, as well as a couple of FBI agents. Drey stood back to let them do their job while he pulled Charlene into his arms, wanting just to hold her and make sure she was all right. He had never felt such fear as he had when Hanlon had placed the gun to her head.

He felt several pats to his back and glanced over his shoulder to see a smiling Malcolm and Tyson. "You're going to have to teach us some of those quick moves, brother," Malcolm said, grinning.

Brother. Drey inhaled sharply and then returned their smiles. In their own way they were letting him know he was accepted as one of them. "Yes, I will have to do that."

Although later than they had planned, the Braddocks finally settled down to dinner. Drey and Charlene had been asked to stay and join them. After the last platter had been placed on the table and before it was time to say grace, Evelyn stood at the head of the table with a smile on her face to speak to everyone.

"I think all of us can say that today has been full of

surprises. More than anything I am glad that the man responsible for taking Harmon from us will be dealt with. There is no doubt in my mind that justice will be served."

She then centered her gaze on Drey. "And I want to welcome a new addition to our family. At this point in my life, I don't want to let secrets from the past be allowed to shadow the present. Drey, Harmon was your father and as such, you are a Braddock. I want you to know you are welcome here any time you want. You are one of us."

Cheers went up around the table and Charlene had to fight back the tears that threatened to fall. Only a gracious woman such as Evelyn could accept what had happened thirty-three years ago, not hold it against Drey and move on. And she knew in her heart that although Drey had tried convincing her otherwise, he had wanted to belong.

Shondra stood up and said, "And while the family is all gathered together, I have a surprise of my own." She smiled brightly and then reached her hand out to Connor. He took it, kissed it and then stood beside her.

"I want all of you to be the first to know that Connor and I eloped last weekend to Vegas and got married."

Everyone was out of their seats to rush over to the happy couple and give them words of congratulations and best wishes.

When it seemed as though everyone had finally settled down, it was Tyson who got up next. He looked over at his wife, Felicia, before saying to everyone, "And Felicia and I have some wonderful news to share. We found out today that we're having a son and we plan to name him Harmon Braddock."

Charlene saw the tears glistening in Evelyn's eyes. She was getting more and more good news about her family.

Malcolm stood and chuckled. "Gloria and I don't have anything to add since all of you know about our Christmas wedding. But as we head into the final week of the campaign, we're counting on all of you, our family, to help get me into office."

More claps and cheers erupted around the table and then a few minutes later everyone finally settled down for dinner. And by the time it was over, Charlene couldn't help but think it had been one glorious affair.

It was almost eleven o'clock that night when Drey and Charlene entered his home. As soon as the door closed behind them, Drey pulled Charlene close to him and reached out and took her face in his hands. "Do you have any idea how I felt when I saw Hanlon put that gun to your head?" he asked softly.

"No, tell me," she whispered softly. She had stared into his eyes the entire time the incident had been going on and had seen the stark fear evident there. But what had touched her most was something else she could have sworn she'd seen. But she refused to jump to conclusions. She wanted him to tell her if her assumptions were correct.

"I felt like I was about to lose you," he said, breaking into her thoughts. "I was going to lose you without telling you how I feel."

She swallowed deeply. "And how do you feel, Drey?"

For a moment he didn't say anything, he just stood there and tenderly stroked her cheek while gazing into her eyes. Then he spoke. "I love you, Charlene. I didn't realize how much until today. I've been fighting it and denying it. But I can't do so any longer. I know we moved quickly in our relationship, and I'm willing to slow down for us to have a long engagement if that's what you want. But I want to marry you, Charlene. I want you to be a part of my life forever. I want to sleep every night with my body connected to yours. And more importantly, I want for you to one day love me as much as I love you."

Charlene smiled through her tears. "That day is now because I do love you, Drey. I've loved you for some time, but I was afraid to let you know it. You told me in the beginning you didn't want a wife, you wanted a bed partner."

He chuckled. "Now I want both. Will you marry me, Charlene?"

"Yes, I'll marry you," she said past the constriction in her throat.

And then Drey pulled her into his arms and kissed her again. She was simply ecstatic. This man would be her husband, the father of her babies and her best friend. He had made her the object of his protection and now she would make him the object of her love. Totally. Completely. Forever.

Epilogue

Charlene tried not to look any place but straight ahead while her feet moved toward the altar at her father's side. Drey, handsome as ever in his black tux, was standing there waiting for her.

The past six months had been a flurry of events. Malcolm had won his congressional seat, Tyson and Felicia had their baby and Charlene had returned to work. Because she had testified in his behalf, Nate had been given a lighter sentence after his defense attorney had proven that Judge Hanlon had blackmailed him into falsifying documents by threatening to expose an extramarital affair he'd had a few years ago. Charlene had met Daiyu and cherished their growing friendship. And then there were the Braddocks, who had welcomed her and Drey into their clan with open arms.

Charlene had wanted to keep the wedding ceremony small, but Nina would not hear of it. She wanted to go all out for her daughter and she had. Over five hundred guests attended the lavish wedding, but the only person who captured Charlene's attention was Drey.

As soon as she reached where he stood, he took her hand and gently squeezed it, his way of letting her know everything would be all right. Less than a half hour later he was proven right when the minister pronounced them man and wife and gave Drey permission to kiss his bride.

Drey turned her in his arms and not waiting for one of her bridesmaids to do the honor, he brushed her veil aside and eagerly went for her lips. The moment their mouths touched, she felt, as always, a deep connection to him. Today was the first day of their lives together and she looked forward to the many years to come.

When he released her mouth, the smile he gave her brightened her entire world, and when the minister presented them to everyone as Mr. and Mrs. Drey St. John, she knew that would be a name she would wear proudly.

She suddenly felt herself swept off her feet into big, strong, muscular arms. Where they were going on their honeymoon was a secret Drey was keeping from her. All he had said was to pack light…or not pack anything at all since he enjoyed seeing her naked.

When they reached the limo that awaited them at the front of the church he managed to get them inside beneath a shower of rice and pulled her into his lap. Then he was kissing her again and she knew there was no other place she'd rather be than in his arms.

* * * * *

We hope you enjoyed reading

Against the Night
by *New York Times* bestselling author
KAT MARTIN

&

The Object of His Protection
by *New York Times* bestselling author
BRENDA JACKSON

Both were originally MIRA® and
Harlequin® Kimani™ stories!

**Soulful and sensual romance featuring
multicultural characters.**

From passionate, suspenseful and dramatic
love stories to inspirational or historical,
Harlequin offers different lines to satisfy
every romance reader.

New books available every month.

BACIHALO0818

SPECIAL EXCERPT FROM

HQN™

If you like sexy and steamy stories with strong heroines and irresistible heroes, you'll fall for
Love in Catalina Cove *by New York Times bestselling author Brenda Jackson.*

Read on for a sneak peek…

Sawyer took them around back to show the view of the bayou and how he'd be able to stand on his porch every night to see the setting sun. He took hold of Vashti's hand, no longer able to ignore the flagrant heat of that carnal attraction between them. He leaned down and whispered close to her ear, "Come with me." His brain nearly faltered when her scent enveloped him.

Without asking where he intended to take her, she went with him. He placed his arms around her shoulders as they moved farther away from the group and toward the secluded beach. "I hope you're aware there are alligators that come out at night," she said, smiling up at him.

He chuckled. "I can protect you." Moments later, when he stopped, she turned to him and their gazes connected. He took in her features illuminated in the moonlight. Even after all she'd eaten, the cherry-red lipstick still shaded her lips, making her mouth that much more delectable.

She glanced around. "What's so special about this spot?" she asked him.

His mouth curved into a smile. "You're here."

She chuckled. "Yes, I am. I guess I should ask you why," she said as an "I already know" look appeared in her eyes.

"Earlier tonight you asked me a bold question."

"I did?"

"Yes. You wanted to know just what was going on with us."

"You got an answer for me, Sawyer?"

"Not really, but I hope this is the first step in trying to find out." Then he lowered his mouth to slant it across hers.

* * *

HARLEQUIN® *Desire*

Family sagas…scandalous secrets…burning desires.

Save **$1.00**

on the purchase of ANY

Harlequin® Desire book.

Available wherever books are sold, including most bookstores, supermarkets, drugstores and discount stores.

Save $1.00

on the purchase of any Harlequin® Desire book.

Coupon valid until November 30, 2018.
Redeemable at participating outlets in the U.S. and Canada only.
Not redeemable at Barnes & Noble stores. Limit one coupon per customer.

52615955

5 65373 00076 2   (8100)0 12385

Canadian Retailers: Harlequin Enterprises Limited will pay the face value of this coupon plus 10.25¢ if submitted by customer for this product only. Any other use constitutes fraud. Coupon is nonassignable. Void if taxed, prohibited or restricted by law. Consumer must pay any government taxes. Void if copied. Inmar Promotional Services ("IPS") customers submit coupons and proof of sales to Harlequin Enterprises Limited, P.O. Box 31000, Scarborough, ON M1R 0E7, Canada. Non-IPS retailer—for reimbursement submit coupons and proof of sales directly to Harlequin Enterprises Limited, Retail Marketing Department, Bay Adelaide Centre, East Tower, 22 Adelaide Street West, 40th Floor, Toronto, Ontario M5H 4E3, Canada.

U.S. Retailers: Harlequin Enterprises Limited will pay the face value of this coupon plus 8¢ if submitted by customer for this product only. Any other use constitutes fraud. Coupon is nonassignable. Void if taxed, prohibited or restricted by law. Consumer must pay any government taxes. Void if copied. For reimbursement submit coupons and proof of sales directly to Harlequin Enterprises, Ltd 482, NCH Marketing Services, P.O. Box 880001, El Paso, TX 88588-0001, U.S.A. Cash value 1/100 cents.

® and ™ are trademarks owned and used by the trademark owner and/or its licensee.

© 2018 Harlequin Enterprises Limited

BACCOUP0818

Get 4 FREE REWARDS!

We'll send you 2 FREE Books plus 2 FREE Mystery Gifts.

FREE Value Over **$20**

Both the **Romance** and **Suspense** collections feature compelling novels written by many of today's best-selling authors.

YES! Please send me 2 FREE novels from the Essential Romance or Essential Suspense Collection and my 2 FREE gifts (gifts are worth about $10 retail). After receiving them, if I don't wish to receive any more books, I can return the shipping statement marked "cancel." If I don't cancel, I will receive 4 brand-new novels every month and be billed just $6.74 each in the U.S. or $7.24 each in Canada. That's a savings of at least 16% off the cover price. It's quite a bargain! Shipping and handling is just 50¢ per book in the U.S. and 75¢ per book in Canada*. I understand that accepting the 2 free books and gifts places me under no obligation to buy anything. I can always return a shipment and cancel at any time. The free books and gifts are mine to keep no matter what I decide.

Choose one: ☐ **Essential Romance**   ☐ **Essential Suspense**
                    (194/394 MDN GMY7)   (191/391 MDN GMY7)

Name (please print)

Address   Apt. #

City   State/Province   Zip/Postal Code

Mail to the **Reader Service:**
IN U.S.A.: P.O. Box 1341, Buffalo, NY 14240-8531
IN CANADA: P.O. Box 603, Fort Erie, Ontario L2A 5X3

Want to try two free books from another series? Call 1-800-873-8635 or visit www.ReaderService.com.

*Terms and prices subject to change without notice. Prices do not include applicable taxes. Sales tax applicable in NY. Canadian residents will be charged applicable taxes. Offer not valid in Quebec. This offer is limited to one order per household. Books received may not be as shown. Not valid for current subscribers to the Essential Romance or Essential Suspense Collection. All orders subject to approval. Credit or debit balances in a customer's account(s) may be offset by any other outstanding balance owed by or to the customer. Please allow 4 to 6 weeks for delivery. Offer available while quantities last.

Your Privacy—The Reader Service is committed to protecting your privacy. Our Privacy Policy is available online at www.ReaderService.com or upon request from the Reader Service. We make a portion of our mailing list available to reputable third parties that offer products we believe may interest you. If you prefer that we not exchange your name with third parties, or if you wish to clarify or modify your communication preferences, please visit us at www.ReaderService.com/consumerschoice or write to us at Reader Service Preference Service, P.O. Box 9062, Buffalo, NY 14240-9062. Include your complete name and address.

STRS18